CAMPBELL'S KINGDOM

The success of *The White South* in 1949 enabled
Hammond Innes to embark on the first of his four
long journeys into the wilds of Canada. Oil had
just been discovered in the foothills of the Rockies.
Calgary and Edmonton were seething with Texan
drillers and the excitement of the Red River strike.
The result was *Campbell's Kingdom*.

This is the story of a young man with only a few
months to live, who goes out into a raw new world
to seek the mountain kingdom he has inherited.
Time is against him—the time to live, the time to
prove old Campbell's obsession about oil, the time
to save the land before a new dam floods it. And
instead of death, he finds disaster.

HAMMOND INNES

Campbell's Kingdom

FONTANA/Collins

First published 1952
First issued in Fontana Books 1956
Sixteenth Impression June 1974

Printed in Great Britain
Collins Clear-Type Press London and Glasgow

To

Friends in Canada

I was three months getting the background material for this book and from the cities to the ranchlands and up into the high Rockies I received nothing but kindness and much help.

Of the companies that were so willing to give me every facility I would like to thank, in particular, Trans-Canada Airlines and Canadian Pacific for making it possible for me to travel at will regardless of currency difficulties, and Imperial Oil for giving me the freedom of the big new oilfields of Alberta and going to endless trouble in taking me round their rigs and introducing me to the whole process of drilling.

Two friends I would like to mention by name. One was Bruce Bohane, a ranch hand, who for three weeks was my guide and mentor as we rode trail in the Rockies. The other was Bob Douglas, leader of a Government survey party, who made me welcome at his camp near the United States border and gave me a hard week of it among the peaks of the Rockies.

For the rest I would like to say this: If in this story I have managed to pass on something of the atmosphere of energy and friendliness of this great new country it is very largely due to the people I met there.

Contents

Part One

COME LUCKY

I

I HESITATED as I crossed the road and paused to gaze up at the familiar face of Number Thirty-two. There was a coping stone missing from the roof and one of the dirt-blackened panes of the fanlight was cracked. A light on in one of the upper rooms gave it a lop-sided look. For years I had been coming home from the office to this rather drab old Georgian-fronted house on the edge of Mecklenburgh Square, yet now I seemed to be looking at it for the first time. I had to remind myself that those windows on the first floor just to the right of the front door were my windows, that behind them were all my clothes and papers and books, all the things that made up my home.

But there was no reality about it now. It was as though I were living in a dream. I suppose I was still dazed by the news.

I wondered what they'd say at the office—or should I go on as though nothing had happened? I thought of all the years I'd been leaving this house at eight-thirty-five in the morning and returning to it shortly after six at night; lonely, wasted years. Men who had served with me during the war were now in good executive positions. But for me the Army had been the big chance. Once out of it I had drifted without the drive of an objective, without the competitive urge of a close-knit masculine world. I stared with sudden loathing at the lifeless facade of Thirty-two as though it symbolised all those wasted years.

A car hooted and I shook myself, conscious of the dreadful feeling of weariness that possessed my body; conscious, too, of a sudden urgency. I needed to make some sense out of my life, and I needed to do it quickly. As I crossed to the pavement, automatically getting out my keys, I suddenly decided I wasn't going to tell the office anything. I wasn't going to tell anybody. I'd just say I was taking a holiday and quietly disappear.

I went in and closed the door. Footsteps sounded in the darkness of the unlighted hall.

"Is that you, Mr. Wetheral?"

It was my landlady, a large, cheerful and very loquacious Scots lady who with their Lords of the Admiralty managed to support a drunken husband who had never done a stroke of work since his leg was blown off in the First World War.

"Yes, Mrs. Baird."

"Ye're home early. Did they give ye the afternoon off?"

"Yes," I said.

"Och now, fancy that. Would it be some Sassenach holiday or was there nobody wishing to insure themselves against all those things, like arson and accident and annuity that you were talking about the other day?"

I smiled to myself, wondering what she would say if I told her the truth. As I started up the stairs she stopped me. "There's two letters for you in your room—bills by the look of them. And I put some flowers there seeing that ye'd no been verra well lately."

"That's very kind of you, Mrs. Baird."

"Och, I nearly forgot. There was a gentleman to see you. He ha'na been gone for more than ten minutes. He said it was very important, so I told him to come back again at six. He said that was fine for he'd to go to the Law Courts about anither matter."

"The Law Courts?" I stopped and stared down at her. "Did he look like a lawyer?"

"Aye, he did that. He'd a black hat and a brief case and a rolled umbrella. Ye've no got yersel' into any trouble, Mr. Wetheral, have ye noo?"

"Of course not," I answered, puzzled. "You're sure he was a lawyer?"

"Aye, he was a lawyer all right. Shall I bring him straight up when he comes? I told him you'd be back at six. If ye're no in any trouble, perhaps it's some good news—one o' your relatives dead maybe?"

"I'm making my will," I said and laughed as I went on up to my rooms.

The last red flicker of the sunset showed through the trees of the square. I switched on the light. The trees stood out in bare silhouette against the lurid sky. But across the street it was already getting dark. My reflection stared back at me from the long french windows leading to the balcony—a ghostly transfer of myself against the brick facade of the houses.

I pulled the curtains quickly and turned back into the room. I suddenly felt desperately alone, more alone than I had felt in all my life.

For a while I paced back and forth, wondering what the devil a lawyer could want with me. Then I turned abruptly and went through into the bedroom. God! I was tired. I took off my coat and lay down on my bed and closed my eyes. And as I lay there sweating with fear and nervous exhaustion my life passed before my mind's eye, mocking me with its emptiness. Thirty-six years, and what had I done with them —what had I achieved!

I must have dropped off to sleep for I woke with a start to hear Mrs. Baird's voice calling me from the sitting-room. "Here's the lawyer man to see ye again, Mr. Wetheral."

I got up, feeling dazed and chilled, and went through into the other room. He was a lawyer all right; no mistaking the neat blue suit, the white collar, the dry, dusty air of authority. "Mr Wetheral?" His hand was white and soft and the skin of his long, sad face looked as though it had been starched and ironed.

"What do you want?" The rudeness of my tone was un-intentional.

"My name is Fothergill," he replied carefully. "Of Anstey, Fothergill and Anstey, solicitors of Lincoln's Inn Fields. Before I state my business it will be necessary for me to ask you a few personal questions. A matter of identity, that is all. May I sit down?"

"Of course," I murmured. "A cigarette?"

"I don't smoke, thank you."

I lit one and saw that my hand was shaking. I had had too many professional interviews in the last few days.

He waited until I was settled in an easy-chair and then he said, "Your christian names please, Mr. Wetheral?"

"Bruce Campbell."

"Date of birth?"

"July 20th, 1916."

"Parents alive?"

"No. Both dead."

"Your father's christian names please."

"Look," I said, a trifle irritably. "Where's all this leading to?"

"Please," he murmured. "Just bear with me a moment longer." His voice was dry and disinterested. "Your father's christian names?"

"John Henry."

"An engineer?"

I nodded. "He died on the Somme the year I was born."

"What were your mother's names?"

"Eleanor Rebecca."

"And her maiden name?"

"Campbell."

"Did you know any of the Campbells, Mr. Wetheral?"

"Only my grandfather; I met him once."

"Do you remember his names?"

"No, I don't think I ever knew them. He called my mother Ella, if that's any help."

"Where did you meet him?"

"Coming out of prison."

He stared at me, an expression of faint distaste on his face as though I had been guilty of some shocking joke.

"He did five years in prison," I explained quickly. "He was a thief and a swindler. My mother and I met him when he came out. I was about nine at the time. We drove in a taxi straight from the prison to a boat train." After all these years I could not keep the bitterness out of my voice. I stubbed out my cigarette. Damn it, why did he have to come asking questions on this day of all days. "Why do you want to know all this?" I demanded irritably.

"Just one more question." He seemed unperturbed by my impatience. "You were in the Army during the war. In France?"

"No, the Desert and then Sicily and Italy. I was in the R.A.C."

"Were you wounded at all?"

"Yes."

"Where?"

"By God!" I cried, jumping to my feet. "This is too much." My fingers had gone automatically to the scar above my heart. "You come here poking and prying into my affairs, asking me a lot of damn-fool questions, without even having the courtesy——"

"Please." He, too, had risen to his feet and he looked quite scared. "Calm yourself, Mr. Wetheral. I am only carrying out my instructions. I am quite satisfied now. I was instructed to locate a Bruce Campbell Wetheral and I was given certain information, including the fact that he was a Captain in the Royal Armoured Corps during the war and that he was wounded shortly after Alamein. I am now quite satisfied that you are the man I have been looking for."

"Well, now you've found me, what do you want?"

"If you'll be seated again for a moment——"

I dropped back into my chair and lit a cigarette from the stub of the one I had half crushed out. "Well?"

He picked up his brief case and fumbled nervously at the straps as he perched himself on the edge of the chair opposite me. "We are acting for the firm of Donald McCrae and Acheson of Calgary in this matter. They are the solicitors appointed under your grandfather's will. Since you only met him once it will possibly be of no great concern to you that he is dead. What does concern you, however, is that you are the sole legatee under his will." He placed a document on the table between us. "That is a copy of the will, together with a sealed letter written by your grandfather and addressed to you. The original of the will is held by the solicitors in Calgary. They also hold all the documents, share certificates and so on relating to the Campbell Oil Exploration Company, together with contracts, leases, agreements, etcetera, and all the books of the company. You now control this company, but it is virtually moribund. However, it owns territory in the Rocky Mountains and Donald McCrae and Acheson advise disposal of this asset and the winding up of the company." He burrowed in his brief case again and came up with another document. "Now, here is a deed of sale for the territory referred to. . . ."

I stared at him, hearing his voice droning and remembering only how I had hated my grandfather, how all my childhood had been made miserable by that big, raw-boned Scot with the violent blue eyes and close-cropped grey hair who had sat beside my mother in that taxi and whom I had only seen that once.

"You're sure my grandfather went back to Canada?" I asked incredulously.

"Yes, yes, quite sure. He formed this company there in 1926."

That was the year after he came out of prison. "This company," I said. "Was a man called Paul Morton involved in it with him?"

The solicitor paused in what he was saying, an expression of mild irritation on his face. He glanced through the sheaf of documents on the table. "No," he said. "The other two directors were Roger Fergus and Luke Trevedian. Fergus was one of the big men in the Turner Valley field and Trevedian owned a gold mine. Now, as I was saying, the shares in this company are worthless. The only working capital it seems to have had was advanced by Fergus and the only work it has carried out appears to have been financed by him, the money being advanced on mortgage. This included a survey——"

"Do you mean my grandfather was broke when he returned to Canada?"

"It would seem so." Fothergill peered at the documents and then nodded. "Yes, I should say that was definitely the case."

I leaned back, staring at the lamp, trying to adjust myself to a sudden and entirely new conception of my grandfather. "How did he die?" I asked.

"How?" Again the solicitor glanced through the papers on the table. "It says here that he died of cold."

"Of cold?"

"Yes. He was living alone high up in the Rockies. Now, as regards the company; it does not seem likely that the shares are marketable and——"

"He must have been a very old man." I was thinking that my mother had been thirty-two when she had died in 1927.

"He was seventy-nine. Now this land that is owned by the company. Your representatives in Calgary inform me that they have been fortunate enough to find a purchaser. In fact, they have an offer——" He stopped and the polished skin of his forehead puckered in an impatient frown. "You're not listening to me, Mr. Wetheral."

"I'm sorry," I said. "I was just wondering what an old

man of seventy-nine was doing living alone in the Rocky Mountains."

"Yes, yes, of course. Very natural. Let me see now. It's all in Mr. Acheson's letter. Ah, here we are—apparently he became a little queer as he grew old. His belief that there was oil up in this territory in the mountains had become an obsession with him. From 1930 onwards he lived up there in a log cabin by himself, hardly ever coming down into the towns. It was there that he was found by a late hunting party. That was on the 22nd of November, last year." He placed the letter on the table beside me. "I will leave that with you and you can read it at your leisure. There is also a cutting from a local paper. Now, about this land. There is apparently some scheme for damming the valley and utilising the waters for a hydro-electric project. One of the mining companies . . ."

I sat back and closed my eyes. So he had gone back. That was the thing that stuck in my mind. He had really believed there was oil there.

"Please, Mr. Wetheral, I must ask for your attention. This is important. Most important."

"I'm sorry," I murmured. I was trying to remember every detail of that one meeting, but it was blurred. I could remember the prison gates, the battered leather suitcase he had carried, the brass headlamps of the taxi—but not a word of the conversation between him and my mother. I looked across at the little lawyer. "You were saying something about a hydro-electric scheme."

"We must have your signature to this document at once. The matter is most urgent. The company concerned apparently has alternative sources of power which if we delay much longer may render your property valueless. As I say, your solicitors in Calgary regard the terms as generous and advise immediate acceptance. When all debts have been paid and the company wound up they estimate that the estate will be worth some nine or ten thousand dollars."

"How long will all this take?" I asked.

"Donald McCrae and Acheson are very business-like people. We have had dealings with them on several occasions." He pursed his lips. "I think we can expect to prove probate in say about six months' time if this deal goes through as smoothly as they anticipate."

"Six months!" I laughed. "That's just six months too long, Mr. Fothergill."

"How do you mean? I assure you we will do everything possible to expedite proceedings and you can rest assured——"

"Yes, of course," I said, "but in six months——" I stopped. Why should I bother to explain?

I leaned back and closed my eyes, trying to think it out clearly. The money wasn't any use to me. I'd nobody to leave it to. "I'm not sure that I want to sell," I said, almost unconsciously voicing my thoughts.

I opened my eyes and saw that he was looking at me with astonishment. "I don't think you quite understand, Mr. Wetheral. The executors inform us that the land itself is quite worthless. As I've already told you, it lies at over 7,000 feet in a most inaccessible area of the Rockies. The greater part of the year it is buried in snow. . . ."

"Can I see that newspaper cutting?" I asked him.

He handed it across to me. It was from the *Calgary Tribune* and datelined—*Jasper, 4th December: All those who made the pilgrimage up Thunder Creek to Campbell's Kingdom will mourn the loss of a friend. Stuart Campbell, one of the old-timers of Turner Valley and the man who coined the phrase "There's oil in the Rocky Mountains," is dead. His body was found by a late hunting party headed by the Jasper packer, Johnnie Carstairs. It was lying stretched out on the floor of his log cabin, the eyrie he built for himself 7,000 feet up in the Rockies just east of the famous Cariboo area.*

Campbell was a great character. He will be remembered affectionately by the hunters, miners and loggers, as well as the tourists, who visited him in his mountain kingdom and listened to his stories of the oilfields and heard him make the surrounding peaks ring with the skirl of his pipes. Even those who lost money in his ill-starred Rocky Mountain Oil Exploration Company and declared him a swindler and worse cannot but render the homage of admiration to a man who was so convinced he was right that he dedicated the last twenty-six years of his life to trying to prove it. . . .

I started to read the paragraph through again, but the type blurred, merging into a picture of a man standing in the dock at the Old Bailey accused of swindling the public by floating a company to drill for oil that didn't exist and then absconding with the capital. He had been arrested boarding the *Majestic* at Southampton. The other director, Paul Morton, had got clean away. The bulk of the company's funds had vanished. That was the story as I knew it. And then I thought of myself as a kid at that wretched school, jeered at because I had no football boots and my clothes were threadbare and because my grandfather was a thief. I had never thought of sticking up for him. I had accepted his guilt as I had accepted our utter poverty. They were part of the conditions of my life. And now . . . I stared down at the cutting, trying to adjust my mind to a new conception of him. He had gone back. That was the incredible thing. He had gone back as though he were convinced. . . . I looked up at the lawyer. " He really believed there was oil up there," I said.

" Just a will-o'-the-wisp." Fothergill gave me a dry smile. " The matter is covered by Mr. Acheson in his letter. I think you can be satisfied that Mr. Campbell's beliefs were entirely erroneous and that the executors' opinion that the property in itself has no value is a true statement of the situation. Now, here is the deed of sale. You will see that at the moment details as to price and date of take-over have not been inserted. These are still matters for negotiation, but if you will sign both copies. . . ."

" I don't think I'll sell," I said. I needed time to think this out, to adjust myself to this new view of my grandfather.

" But, Mr. Wetheral. Really—in a matter of this sort we must be guided by the people on the spot. If Mr. Acheson advises——"

" I can't make a decision now," I said. " You must give me time to consider."

" You cannot expect this company to wait indefinitely for your answer. Mr. Acheson was most pressing. That is why I undertook to locate you myself. Every day's delay——"

" There's already been a delay of four months," I said. " Another few days shouldn't make much difference."

" Perhaps not. I must remind you, however," he went on in a patient voice, " that it is only the fact that the largest creditor was Mr. Campbell's friend that has saved the company from bankruptcy long ago. It is your duty as Mr. Campbell's heir to consider this gentleman."

" I won't be stampeded," I said irritably.

He glanced round the room in a bewildered manner. I think he found it difficult to reconcile my reluctance to sell with the drabness of my surroundings. He got to his feet. " I will leave these documents with you, Mr. Wetheral. I think when you have had time to consider them——" He snapped the lock of his empty brief case. " Here is my card. I shall be in my office between nine and ten in the morning. Perhaps you will telephone me then, or better still come in and see me."

" I'll let you know what I decide," I said and took him down to the front door.

Then I hurried eagerly back to my room. I wanted to read the personal letter attached to the will. It was addressed in a bold, upright, rather childish hand. I slit the envelope. Inside was a single sheet: it was very direct and simple. No words were wasted. It was the letter of a man who had lived a lot of his life alone out in the wilds.

For my grandson   *"Campbell's Kingdom,"*
To be attached to my will   *Come Lucky, B.C.*
                                     15th March, 1947

Dear Bruce,

It is possible you may recall our one meeting, since the circumstances were peculiar. With your mother's death I became entirely cut off from you, but in the last few weeks I have been able to obtain some information concerning your progress and your military record in the recent conflict. This leads me to believe that there is enough of the Campbell in you for me to hand on to you the aims, hopes and obligations that through age and misfortune I have been unable to fulfil.

I imagine that you are fully informed of the circumstances of my imprisonment. However, in any case you should have attributed your mother's belief in my innocence to filial loyalty, here is the testimony of a man who, when you receive this letter, will be dead:

I, Stuart Macaulay Campbell, swear before God and on His Holy Book that everything I did and said in connection with the flotation of an oil company in London known as the Rocky Mountain Oil Exploration Company was done and said in all good faith and that every word of that section of the prospectus dealing with the oil possibilities in the territory now commonly known as " Campbell's King-

dom" was true to the best of my knowledge and belief, based on more than twelve years in the Turner Valley Field and neighbouring territories. And may the Lord condemn me to everlasting fires of Hell if this testimony be false.

Signed: *Stuart Macaulay Campbell.*

After my release I returned to Canada to prove what I knew to be true. With the help of kind friends I formed the Campbell Oil Exploration Company. All my shares in this I leave to you, together with the territory in which my bones will rest. If you are the man I hope you are, you will accept this challenge, so that I may rest in peace and my life be justified in the end. May the Good Lord guide you and keep you in this task and may success, denied to me by the frailty of old age, attend your efforts.

Your Humbled and Grateful Grandfather
Stuart Macaulay Campbell

P.S. The diary of my efforts to
prove the existence of oil up here
you will find with my Bible. S.M.C.

I put the letter down and sat staring at the wall, picturing this strange, God-fearing man alone in that log cabin high in the Rocky Mountains, isolated by winter snow, carefully penning this letter to his unknown grandson. I could see him sitting alone at some rudely-made table, his Bible beside him, wrestling with the unaccustomed task of putting thoughts into words.

I read it through again, more slowly. Every word carried weight—and his honesty and simplicity shone through it like a clean wind out of the high mountains.

I had a feeling of guilt at having accepted so readily the verdict of the courts, at never having troubled to discover what he had done on leaving prison. And suddenly I found myself kneeling on the floor, swearing before a God whom I had scarcely troubled to get to know in the whole of my thirty-six years that whatever remained to me of life I would dedicate to the legacy my grandfather had left me.

As I rose to my feet I realised that I was no longer afraid, no longer alone. I had a purpose and an urgency.

The other papers which Fothergill had left me seemed prosaic and dull after reading what my grandfather had written. There was the will, couched in legal terms and signed " this Fifteenth day of March, Nineteen hundred and forty-seven." It bequeathed " to my grandson, Bruce Campbell Wetheral, sometime Captain in the Royal Armoured Corps, all my property and effects, together with such debts, obligations and hopes as I shall have at the time of my death " and it appointed Messrs. Donald McCrae and Acheson, solicitors, as executors. There was a letter from them explaining the hydro-electric project and attached to it was a deed of sale for my signature. " There is no question of obtaining a better offer. Indeed, you must agree that we have been fortunate in promoting the company's interest in the particular area included in your legacy and we feel sure that you will appreciate the urgency of your signature to the attached deed of sale if your legacy is to have any value and if the debts and obligations referred to in your grandfather's will are to be met. Please deliver the signed deed to Mr. Fothergill, of Anstey, Fothergill and Anstey, who represent us in London."

Every line of their letter took it for granted that I should agree to sell. I tossed it back on the table and as I did so, I caught sight of the newspaper cutting lying on the floor where I had dropped it. I picked it up and continued reading where I had left off:

". . . Only those whose values are entirely material will belittle his efforts because time has proved him wrong. He was a man of boundless energy and he squandered it recklessly in pursuit of the will-o'-the-wisp of black gold. But people who know him best like Johnnie Carstairs and Jean Lucas, the young Englishwoman who for the last few years has housekept for him during the summer months, declare that it was not the pursuit of riches that drove him in his later years, but the desire to prove himself right and to recover the losses suffered by so many people who invested in his early ventures.

Like so many of the old-timers, he was a God-fearing man and a great character. His phrase—There's oil in the Rocky Mountains—has become a part of the oil man's vocabulary, denoting an area not worth surveying: but who knows? When

*told of the discovery of the Leduc field Campbell is reported
to have said: "Sure there's oil down there. And there's oil
up here, too. The Rockies are young mountains, thrust up
out of the same area of inland seas." The result of a single
survey would not have altered his convictions. He always
believed that there was one way to prove an area and that
was to drill it.*

*Some day perhaps he'll be proved right. In the meantime
local people, headed by Mr. Will Polder, are organising a
fund to raise a monument to the memory of "King"
Campbell. It will be erected about a mile from his cabin on
the site of the original drilling in 1913. Johnnie Carstairs
hopes to pack it up to the Kingdom as soon as the snows
melt. It will carry the design of a cable-tool rig and the
epitaph "There's oil in the Rocky Mountains."*

I put the cutting down and sat staring at the wall, seeing
nothing of the faded picture of Nelson dying at Trafalgar,
only the little log cabin high up in the Rockies and the old
man whose hopes had died so hard. *There's oil in the Rocky
Mountains.* The phrase rang in my head. I twisted it round
and said it the way the oil men were using it, contemptuously.
But still it had a ring about it. I could see the words etched
deep on a marble monument and imagine tourists in later
years coming there to mock and eat their oranges. It would
be something to prove the phrase true, to wipe out the stigma
that had haunted me all my early life, to prove him innocent.
Why shouldn't there be oil in the Rocky Mountains? Maybe
I was a fool. I knew nothing about geology or the Rockies.
But I had something to bite on now—an objective, a purpose.
And somehow it lessened the shock of Maclean-Harvey's
pronouncement.

And as I sat there thinking about Campbell's Kingdom high
up in the mountains, trying to picture the place in my mind,
I was suddenly possessed with an urge to see it, to discover for
myself something of the faith, the indomitable hope, that had
sent my grandfather back there after conviction and imprisonment. It couldn't have been an easy decision for him. The
newspaper cutting had hinted that many people out there had
lost heavily through backing him. It must have been hell for
him. And yet he had gone back.

I got up and began to pace back and forth. Failure and

twenty-two years of utter loneliness had not destroyed his faith. His letter proved that. If I could take up where he had left off. . . .

I realised with a shock that I had bridged the gap of 6,000 miles that separated me from Campbell's Kingdom and was imagining myself already up there. It was absurd. I'd no knowledge of oil, no money. And yet. . . . The alternative was to sign the deed of sale. I went over to the table and picked it up. If I signed it Fothergill had said I might get $10,000 out it in six months' time. It would pay for my funeral, that was about all the good it would be to me. To sign it was unthinkable. And then it gradually came to me that what had at first seemed absurd was the most reasonable thing for me to do, the only thing. To remain in London, an insurance clerk in the same monotonous rut to the end, was impossible with this prospect, this hope of achievement dangling in front of my eyes. I tore the deed of sale across and flung the pieces on to the floor. I would go to Canada. I would try to carry out the provisions of my grandfather's will.

II

IT TOOK me just a week to get to Calgary. Taking into account that this included a night's flying across the Atlantic and two and a half days by train across Canada I think I did pretty well. It did not take me long to clear up my own affairs, but the major obstacle was foreign exchange. I got over this by emigrating and here I had two slices of luck: Maclean-Harvey knew the High Commissioner and the Canadian Government were subsidising immigrant travel by air via Trans-Canada so that the quickest route as far as Montreal became also the cheapest. I think, too, that my sense of urgency communicated itself to those responsible for clearing my papers.

Throughout the journey I had that queer feeling of detachment that comes to anyone suddenly jerked out of the rut of life and thrust upon a new country. I remember feeling very tired, but physical exhaustion was overlaid by mental excitement. I felt like a pioneer. There was even a touch of the knight errant in the picture I built of myself, tearing across the globe to tilt at the Rocky Mountains and make an old man's dream come true. It was all a little unreal.

This sense of unreality allowed me to sit back and relax, content to absorb the vastness of Canada from a carriage-window. The only piece of organisation, apart from getting myself on the 'plane as an immigrant, was to arrange for a friend to look up the newspaper reports of my grandfather's trial and send a resumé of it on to me when I could give him an address. The rest I had left to chance.

The night before we reached Calgary, just after we had left Moose Jaw, the coloured attendant brought a telegram to my sleeper. It was from Donald McCrae and Acheson:

For Bruce Campbell Wetheral, Canadian Pacific Railways,
Coach BII, The Dominion, No. 7.
IMPORTANT YOU COME TO OUR OFFICES IMMEDIATELY ON ARRIVAL. PURCHASERS HAVE GIVEN US TILL TO-MORROW NIGHT TO COMPLETE DEAL. THIS IS YOUR LAST CHANCE TO DISPOSE OF PROPERTY. SIGNED—ACHESON.

I lay back and stared at the message, thinking of all the cabling that must have gone on before they were able to locate me on a train halfway across Canada. They were certainly a very thorough and determined firm. They'd have me sell whether I wanted to or not. I crumpled the form up and dropped it on the floor. Like Fothergill they found it impossible to accept my attitude.

We arrived at Calgary at 8.30 a.m. Mountain Time and I went straight to the Palliser Hotel. It was a palatial palace, railway-owned like so many of the Canadian hotels, a symbol of the way the country had been opened up. I had breakfast and then rang Acheson's office and made an appointment for eleven o'clock. That gave me time to have a look round. Calgary is a cow town, the ranching capital of Alberta, but there was little evidence of this in the streets which were cold and dusty. There were good, solid stone buildings in the centre of the town—stores like the Hudson's Bay Company Store and offices such as those which housed the Calgary Herald—but they dwindled rapidly as the streets ran out into the flat grey of the sky. It was strangely without atmosphere, a quiet, provincial town going about its business.

The firm of Donald McCrae and Acheson had their offices

in an old brick building amongst a litter of oil companies. Blown-up photographs of oil derricks and of the Turner Valley field decorated the stairs and from wooden-partitioned offices on the second floor came the clatter of typewriters and the more staccato clacking of a tape machine. By comparison the third floor was quiet, almost reserved. Mahogany doors surrounded a landing that boasted a carpet, a big black leather settee and a pedestal ash tray, the base of which was formed by the bit of a drill. I sat down for a moment on the settee to get my breath. The names of the various firms who had offices on this floor were painted in black on the frosted glass panels of the doors that faced me. There were four doors, the one on my immediate right being that of Donald McCrae and Acheson. But it was the name on the door to my left that caught my eye, for it was the name of the man who had backed my grandfather. At the top was The Roger Fergus Oil Development Company Ltd., and underneath—operating companies: Fergus Leases Ltd., T. R. F. Concessions Ltd., and T. Stokowski-Fergus Oil Company Ltd. The other two doors were occupied by Louis Winnick, Oil Consultant and Surveyor, and Henry Fergus, Stockbroker. Under the latter and newly painted-in was the name—The Larsen Mining and Development Company Ltd.

I glanced at my watch. It was just eleven. I found myself strangely nervous. The atmosphere of the place was one of business and money. Sentiment seemed out of place. I pulled myself to my feet and went through the door marked Donald McCrae and Acheson, Solicitors. A girl secretary asked me my business and showed me into a small waiting room. The place smelt faintly of leather and cigars. The furnishings were Edwardian. But through the open door I saw a young man seated in his shirt sleeves dictating into a dictaphone.

A few minutes later the secretary returned and showed me through into Acheson's office. He was a big man, rather florid, with smooth cheeks that shone slightly as though they had been rubbed with pumice stone. He had a high, domed forehead and round blue eyes. "Mr. Wetheral?" He rose to greet me and his hand was soft and plump. "Glad to see you." He waved me to a chair and sat down. "Cigar?"

I shook my head. Behind him was a portrait of himself in cowboy garb riding a big chestnut. Round the walls were photographs of oil rigs. "Pity you didn't write me before you came out," he said. "I could have saved you the journey. However, now you're here maybe I can clear up any points that are worrying you." He flicked a switch on the house phone box. "Ellen. Bring in the Campbell file, will you? Now then . . ." He sat back and clipped the end of a cigar. "Fothergill writes that for some reason best known to yourself you don't want to sell."

"No," I said. "Not till I've seen the place, anyway."

He gave a grunt. "There's been too much delay already." The door opened behind me and the secretary placed a file on his desk. He opened it and flipped through the documents, the tips of his fingers smoothing his cheeks along the line of the jaw. Then he sat back and lit his cigar. "I quite appreciate your wanting to see the property before disposing of it, but in this case it's just not possible. Did Fothergill give you all the details?"

"Yes," I said. "But I wasn't able to get the position regarding mineral rights clear and——"

"Mineral rights!" He laughed. "I wouldn't worry about the mineral rights, if I were you." He leaned back and stared at me out of small, clear blue eyes. "It's oil you're thinking of, is it? I warned Fothergill to make it perfectly clear to you that there wasn't any oil. Did he give you my letter?"

"Yes," I said.

"And you're not satisfied? All right. Well, let me tell you that Roger Fergus had a geophysical outfit up in the Kingdom last summer and Louis Winnick's report on that survey finally damns Campbell's ideas about oil up there as a lot of moonshine." He reached forward and pulled a document from the file. "Here's a copy of that report." He tossed it on to the desk in front of me. "Take it away and read it at your leisure. In any case, the mineral rights don't belong to you. They belong to Roger Fergus."

"But I thought I had a controlling interest in the Campbell Oil Exploration Company?"

"Certainly you do. But the mineral rights were mortgaged as security for the cash Fergus advanced the company. Of course," he added, with a shrug of his shoulders, "that was just a matter of form. They weren't worth anything. Roger Fergus knew that. He was just being kind to the old fellow and we fixed it that way so that Campbell wouldn't think it was charity."

He paused, evidently to let this piece of information sink in. His manner was vastly different to Fothergill's—to any solicitor I had ever met, for that matter. It was more the manner of a business man, hard and factual. He was like a battering ram and I could feel him trying to steamroller me into selling. To gain time and sort out my impressions I glanced down at the report and my attention was caught by the final paragraph: *". . . Therefore I have no hesitation in saying there is absolutely no possibility whatever of oil being discovered on this property.—Signed—Louis Winnick, Oil Consultant."*

"Is a survey of this nature conclusive?" I asked him.

"Not entirely. It won't prove the presence of oil. But it's pretty well a hundred per cent in indicating that a territory is not oil-bearing. In this case, when you read the report through, you'll find that the strata under the surface is far too broken up to contain any oil traps."

"I see."

So that was that. My grandfather's vision of a great new oilfield in the Rockies was scientifically destroyed. I suddenly felt tired and dispirited. I had come a long way, buoyed up with the feeling that I had a mission to accomplish. "I'd like to see the place," I murmured.

He leaned back and drew slowly on his cigar. I think he was giving me time to adjust myself. "Ever seen a big mountain range?"

"I've ski-ed in the Alps."

He nodded. "Well, the Rockies are just about as high. The difference is that they extend north and south the length of the North American continent and they're about 500 miles through. Travel gets to be pretty difficult at this time of the year. It's still winter in the mountains and most of the roads are blocked. The Kingdom is a goodish way from any railroad. You might not get through for a month, maybe more. Meantime, the company that's interested in the property has got to get organised so that work on the dam begins as soon as they can get up there. The season is a short one." He leaned forward and searched among the papers on his desk. "Here you are." He pushed a document across to me. "All you have to do is sign that. I'll look after the rest. You'll see the figure they agree to pay is $50,000. It's a damn sight more than the property is worth. But they're willing to pay that figure to avoid a court action on compensation. They already have the authority of the Provincial Parliament to go ahead with the construction, so whether you sign or not they are in a position to take over the property and flood it, subject to payment of compensation."

I didn't say anything and there was an awkward silence. I was thinking that the dam had still to be built. For a few months the Kingdom could be mine. Even if there wasn't any oil it was a patch of land that belonged to me. I'd never owned any property before. I'd never really owned anything.

" I must warn you," Acheson said, " that the purchasers' original plan was to take power from one of the existing companies. This hydro-electric scheme is subsidiary to their main business which is the opening up of some low grade lead mines. If you don't sign now the odds are they'll abandon the project."

So the Kingdom could still be saved. I lit a cigarette, thinking it over.

" Well?"

I stared down at the deed of sale. " I notice you've not inserted the name of the purchasing company."

" No." He seemed to hesitate. " A subsidiary will be formed to operate the power scheme. If you'll sign the deed, I'll insert the name of the company as soon as it's formed. Then there'll be just the deeds and the land registration to be settled. I'll look after all that." His eyes fastened on mine, waiting.

" You seem very anxious for me to sell," I murmured.

" It's in your interests." He took the cigar out of his mouth and leaned forward, his eyes narrowed. " I don't understand you," he said. His tone was one of exasperation. " In the letter I sent you via Fothergill I made it perfectly clear to you that my advice was to sell. Instead you come all the way out here, wasting time and delaying the whole project." He got suddenly to his feet. " I should tell you, Wetheral, that it's largely as a result of my efforts that these people have become interested in the Kingdom at all. As I told you, their original plan . . ." He turned and crossed the room towards me. " For two pins I'd tell you to get somebody else to handle your affairs. I've had nothing but trouble acting for Stuart Campbell and not a nickel for it. If it weren't for the interests of another client . . ." He was standing over me. " I act for old Roger Fergus. He's sunk nearly $40,000 in Campbell's

company. Now that Campbell's dead I consider it my duty
to see that the company is wound up and that debt paid off."
He leaned down, tapping my shoulder with a large, podgy
hand. " I'd go further. I'd say that you have a moral obligation to see that Roger Fergus is repaid." He turned slowly
away and resumed his seat at his desk. " You've got till this
evening," he said. " Where are you staying?"

" The Palliser."

"Well, you go back to your room and think it over." He
got to his feet. " Take the report with you. Read it. If there's
anything you want to know give me a ring."

He paused and then said, " I would only add one other
thing. Roger Fergus met the cost of that survey out of his
own pocket. You owe him nothing on that score, but . . ."
He shrugged his shoulders. " I think you will agree that it's
in everyone's interests that the deal goes through." He pressed
the bell-push on his desk. " Come and see me about five."

The secretary showed me out. As I made for the stairs I
checked at the sight of the door oposite me. The Roger
Fergus Oil Development Company. On a sudden impulse I
opened the door and went in. There was a counter and beyond the counter a rather stuffy office with one typewriter and
the walls massed with files. There was an electric fire and
some unwashed cups on a dusty desk. A door led off it with
the name Roger Fergus on it. The door was open and I got
a view of a bare desk and a table on which stood nothing but
a telephone. The door of the neighbouring office slammed
and a girl's voice behind me said, " Can I help you?"

" I'm looking for Mr. Fergus," I explained.

" Old Mr. Fergus?" She shook her head. " He hasn't been
coming to the office for a long time now. He's been ill."

" Oh." I hesitated.

" Is your business urgent? Because his son, Mr. Henry
Fergus——"

" No," I said. " It wasn't really business—more a social call.
He was a great friend of my grandfather, Stuart Campbell."

Her eyes lit up in her rather pale face. " I met Mr. Campbell once." She smiled. " He was a wonderful old man—quite
a character. There was an awful lot about him in the papers
when he died." She hesitated and then said, " I'll ring Mr.
Fergus's home. I'm sure he'd like to see you if he's well

enough. He had a stroke, you know. He's paralysed all down one side and he tires very easily."

But apparently it was all right. He would see me if I went straight over. "But the nurse says you're not to stay more than five minutes. The Fergus Farm is a little way out of town on the far side of the Bow River. The cab drivers all know it."

I thanked her and went down the stairs, past the photographs of oil wells and the clatter of the ticker tape and the typewriters on the second floor. The notice board at the entrance, listing the companies occupying the building, caught my eye. The second floor was occupied by Henry Fergus, Stockbrokers. I wondered vaguely how the Calgary stock exchange was able to support a business that appeared to be as large as most London stockbroker's offices.

The Fergus home was a low, sprawling ranch-house building. As we swung up past the stables I saw several fine blacks being taken out for exercise, their blankets marked with the monogram RF. What appeared to be a small covered wagon stood in the yard, its canopy bearing the name The RF Ranch. "That's the old man's chuck wagon," my driver said. "Always enters a team for the chuck wagon races at the Stampede. He's got a big ranch down in the Porcupine Hills. He started in when the Turney Valley field was opening up. Been making dough ever since." The corners of his mouth turned down and he grinned. "Still, we all come to the same end, I guess. They say he won't last much longer."

It was a manservant who let me in and I was taken through into a great lounge hall full of trophies, prizes taken by cattle and horses at shows up and down the country. A nurse took charge of me and I was shown into a sombre study with the temperature of a hot house. There were a few books. The walls were lined with photographs—photographs of oil rigs, drilling crews, oil fires, a panorama of snow-covered mountains, horses, cattle, cowhands, chuck wagon races, cattle shows. And there were drilling bits, odd pieces of metal, trophies of a dozen different money-making discoveries. All these I took in at a glance and then my gaze came to rest on the man seated in a wheel chair. He was a big man, broad shouldered with massive, gnarled hands and a great shock of white hair. He had a fine face with bushy, tufty eyebrows and a way of craning his neck forward like a bird. His skin had been tanned and wrinkled by weather, but now transparency was evident in the tan and the effect was of dry, wrinkled parchment. "So you're Stuart's grandson." He spoke out of one corner of his mouth; the other twisted by paralysis. "Sit down. He often spoke of you. Had great hopes that one day you'd be managing an oilfield for him. Damned old fool." His voice was surprisingly gentle.

"Five minutes, that's all," the nurse said and went out.

"Like a drink?" He reached down with his long arm to a cupboard under the nearest pedestal of the desk. "She doesn't know I've got it," he said, nodding towards the door through which the nurse had passed. "Not supposed to have it. Henry smuggles it in for me. That's my son. Hopes it'll kill me off," he added with a malicious twinkle. He poured out two Scotches neat. "Your health, young feller."

"And yours, sir," I said.

"I haven't got any." He waved his left hand vaguely. "They're all hanging around waiting for me to die. That's what happens when you've made a fortune." He craned forward, peering at me from under his eyebrows. "You're from the Old Country, aren't you? What brought you out to Canada? Think you're going to drill a discovery well up in the Kingdom?"

"There doesn't seem much chance of that," I said. "Acheson just showed me the report on that survey."

"Ah, yes. A pity. And Bladen was so enthusiastic. Good boy, Bladen. Fine pilot. Half Indian, you know. Seems he's not so good as a surveyor." His voice had dropped almost to a mutter. But he rallied himself and said, "Well now, what's the purpose of this visit?"

"You were a friend of my grandfather's," I said. "I wanted to meet you."

"Fine." He peered at me. "Any financial propositions up your sleeve?"

"No," I said. "It never occured to me——"

"That's okay." He gave me a twisted smile. "When you're old and rich you get kinda suspicious about people's motives. Now then, tell me about yourself."

I started to tell him about Fothergill's visit to my digs in London, and then suddenly I was telling him the whole story, about Maclean-Harvey's verdict and my decision to emigrate.

When I had finished his eyes, which had been closed, flicked open. " Fine pair we are," he said and he managed a contorted grin that somehow made me realise that he was still something of a boy at heart. " So now they're going to drown the Kingdom and you're here to attend to obsequies. Well, maybe it's for the best. It brought Stuart nothing but trouble." He gave a little sigh and closed his eyes.

I liked him and because of that I felt I had to get the financial obligations settled. " I've seen Acheson," I said. " He'll settle up with you for the amount you advanced to the company. But I'm afraid the purchase price they're prepared to pay won't cover the survey."

He fixed his grey eyes on me. " I thought this wasn't a business visit," he barked. " To hell with the money. You don't have to worry about that. You're under no obligation as far as I'm concerned. Do you understand? If you want to throw good money after bad and drill a well, you can go ahead."

I laughed. " I'm not in a position to drill a well," I said. " In any case, you're the only person who could do that. You own the mineral rights."

" Yes. I'd forgotten that." He took my glass and returned it with the bottle and his own glass to the cupboard. Then he leaned back and closed his eyes. " The mineral rights." His voice was a barely audible murmur. " I wonder why Bladen was so keen ; as keen as Stuart." His left shoulder twitched in the slightest of shrugs. " I'd like to have seen one more discovery well brought in before I died. I'd like to have been able to thumb my nose just one more at all the know-alls in the big companies. There's oil in the Rocky Mountains." He gave a tired laugh. " Well, there it is. Winnick is a straight guy. He wouldn't pull anything on me. You'd best go home, young feller. You want friends around you when you die. It's a lonely business anyway."

The nurse came in and said my time was up. I got to my feet. He held out his left hand to me. " Good luck," he said. " I'm glad you came. If your doctor feller's right, we'll maybe meet again soon. We'll have a good chat then with all eternity ahead of us." His eyes were smiling ; his lips were tired and twisted.

I went out to my taxi and drove back to the hotel, the memory of that fine old shell of a man lingering with me.

I went up to my room and sat staring at Winnick's report and thinking of the old man who had been my grandfather's friend. I could understand him wanting that one final justification of his existence, wanting to prove the experts wrong. I needed the same thing. I needed it desperately. But there was the report and he himself had said Winnick was straight. I think I had already made up my mind to sign the deed of sale. I might have done it there and then and in that event I should not now be writing this story with the snowcapped peaks all around me and winter closing in. Probably I should have been quietly buried away under the frozen sods of Canada. But I was hungry and I pushed the papers into my suitcase and went down to get some lunch. Instead of pocketing the key I handed it in automatically at the desk. By such a trivial act can one's whole future be changed, for when I came out of the dining-room I had to go to the desk to get it and at the desk was a short, stockily-built man in an airman's jacket with a friendly face under a sweat-stained stetson. He was checking out and as I stood behind him, waiting, he said to the clerk, " If a feller by the name of Jack Harbin asks for me, tell him I've gone back to Jasper. He can ring me at my home."

" Okay, Jeff," the clerk said. " I'll tell him."

Jasper! Jasper was in the Yellowhead Pass, the Canadian National's gateway into the Rockies and the Fraser River valley. The Kingdom was barely fifty miles from Jasper as the crow flies. " Excuse me. Are you going by car?" The words were out before I had time to think it over.

" Yeah." He looked me over and then his face crinkled into a friendly smile. " Want a ride?"

" Have you got room for me?"

" Sure. You can have the front seat and the whole of the back. You're from the Old Country, I guess." He held out his hand. " I'm Jeff Hart."

" My name's Wetheral," I said as I gripped his hand. " Bruce Wetheral."

" Okay, Bruce. Make it snappy then. I got to be in Edmonton by tea time."

It was all done on the spur of the moment. I didn't have time to think of Acheson until I was in the big station wagon trundling north out of Calgary, and then I didn't care. I was moving one step nearer the Kingdom and I was content to let it go at that. The sound of the wheels was lost in the drift of powdery snow that whirled past the windshield and ahead of me the ranchlands rolled away to the horizon. I lay back and relaxed in the warmth of the heater and the steady drone of the engine, listening to Jeff Hart's gentle, lazy voice giving me a verbal introduction to the province of Alberta.

We reached Edmonton just before six and got a room at the Macdonald. I had moved into another world. Where Calgary was static, an established, respectable town, Edmonton was on the move. The place bustled with life, an exciting, exotic life that had washed up from as far away as Texas and down from the Yukon and the North West Territories. It flooded through the lobbies of the hotels and out into the streets and cafés—oil men, trappers, prospectors, bush fliers, lumber men, scientists and surveyors. This was the jumping-off place for the Arctic, the first outpost of civilisation on the Alaskan Highway. It had atmosphere, the atmosphere of a frontier town on which an oil boom had been superimposed.

We left after lunch next day and just about four that afternoon we topped a rise on the Jasper road and I got my first glimpse of the Rockies, a solid wall of snow and ice and cold, grey rock, extending north and south as far as eye could see. The sun was shining bleakly and in the bitter cold the crystal wall glittered and sparked frostily. And over the top of that first rampart rose peaks of ice and black, wind-torn rock.

" Quite a sight, eh?" Jeff yawned. " You're seeing them at the right time. They get to look kinda dusty by end of summer."

We ran down to the stone-strewn bed of the Athabaska and passed the check point that marked the entrance to Jasper National Park. The mountains closed in on us, bleak, wind-torn peaks that poked snouts of grey rock and white snow above the dark timber that covered the lower slopes. Below us the river ran cold and milky from the glaciers. There was tarnished snow on the road now and a nip in the air. Though the sun still shone in a blue sky its warmth seemed unable to penetrate this glacial valley.

But though the place looked gloomy with its dark timbers and grey rock and the dead white of the snow, I felt the excitement of having reached a milestone on the long road I had come. I could see the railway now, twin black lines ruled

C.K.   B through the snow climbing in great banking curves to the Yellowhead Pass. This way my grandfather had come, riding with a caravan of ox carts because he was too poor to travel on the newly-opened railroad.

"Do you know a man called Johnnie Carstairs?" I asked my companion.

"Sure. He wrangles a bunch of horses and acts as packer for the visitors in the summer."

Jeff Hart dropped me at the hotel. I couldn't face any food and went straight up to my room. I felt tired and short of breath. Looking in the mirror I was shocked to see how gaunt my face was, the skin white and transparent so that the veins showed through it. The stubble of my beard, by contrast, appeared a metallic blue. I lay down on the bed, lit a cigarette and pulled from my pocket the only map I had so far been able to acquire—the Esso road map for Alberta and British Columbia. It was already creased and torn for I had acquired it at Canada House in London and all the way over I had been constantly referring to it.

I knew it almost by heart. Through the double glass of the window I could just see the peak of Mount Edith Cavell, a solitary pinnacle of ice and snow. Like a cold finger it pointed into the chill blue of the sky, a warning that my legacy was no soft one. Campbell's Kingdom was little more than 60 miles due west as the crow flies. Lying there, feeling the utter exhaustion of my body, I wondered whether I should ever get there.

I must have dropped off into a sort of coma, for I woke up to find Jeff Hart bending over me, shaking me by the shoulders. "Christ! You gave me a turn," he said. "Thought you'd never come round. You all right?"

"Yes," I murmured and forced myself to swing my feet off the bed. I sat there for a minute, panting and feeling the blood hammering in my ears.

"Would you like me to fetch a doctor?"

"No," I said. "I'm all right."

"Well, you don't look it. You look like death."

"I'm all right," I gasped, fighting for breath. "How high up are we here?"

"About three thousand five hundred." He was bending over me, peering at me. "You look real bad, Bruce."

"I tell you I'm all right," I whispered peevishly.

"Sure, sure. Here, take a look at yourself."

I lifted my head from my hands. He had taken the mirror from the wall and was holding it in front of me. I stared at myself. My jaw seemed to have got bluer in my sleep, the veins of my forehead were more deeply etched, my lips were bloodless and my mouth open, gasping for breath. I struck out at the mirror, knocking it out of his hands. It shivered into a thousand splinters on the floor.

"That'll cost you two bucks," he said with an attempt at a laugh.

"I'm sorry," I murmured, staring rather foolishly at the broken glass.

"That's all right. I'll go over and fetch the doctor."

I got to my feet then and caught him by the arm. "No. There's nothing he can do about it."

"But goldarn it, man, you're ill."

"I know." I crossed to the window and stared at the peak of Edith Cavell, now a white marble monument against the darkening shadows of night. "I've anæmia. Something to do with the blood. I don't get enough oxygen."

"Then you'd better go to sleep again, I guess."

"No, I'll be all right," I said. "Just wait while I wash and then we'll go down to the bar."

As we went down a party of skiers came in. They were Americans and their gaily coloured wind-cheaters made a bright splash of colour in the drab entrance to the hotel. We went through into the saloon. It was a bare, rather utilitarian place full of small, marble-topped tables and uncomfortable chairs. It was about half full, workers from the railway yards mostly, their war surplus jackets predominating over the brighter pattern of lumber jackets and ski clothes. There were no women.

"I sent word for Johnnie to meet us here," Jeff Hart said. He glanced at his watch. "He'll be here any minute now." The bartender came up. "Four beers."

"No," I said. "This is on me. And I want a brandy. What about you—will you have a short?"

Jeff laughed. "Anybody can see he comes from the Old Country," he said to the barman. "Let me put you wise on the drinking habits of Canadians out West. This is a beer parlour. No women are allowed, you may not drink standing up and you may not order more than a pint at a time. If you want hard liquor, you buy it at a Government liquor store and drink it in your room." His gaze swung to the door. "Here's Johnnie now. Make it six beers, will you, George. Johnnie. This is Bruce Wetheral!"

I found myself looking at a slim-hipped man in a sheepskin jacket and a battered stetson. He had a kindly face, tanned by wind and sun, and his eyes had a faraway look as though they were constantly searching for a distant peak. His eyelids appeared devoid of lashes and were slightly puffed as though he had been peering into snow and wind since birth. "Understand you bin asking for me, Bruce?" He smiled and perched himself on a chair with the light ease of a man who sits a horse most of his time. "Guess I ain't used to comin' to lowdown places such as this."

"Don't pay any attention to him," Jeff said. "The old coyote is here every night."

"What is it you're wanting—horses?" He had a soft, lazy smile that crinkled the corners of his mouth and eyes.

"I'm not here on business," I said. "I just wanted to meet you."

"That's real nice of you." He smiled and waited.

"You knew an old man called Stuart Campbell, didn't you?"

"King Campbell? Sure. But he's dead now."

"I know. You were one of the party that found his body."

"That's so, I guess."

"Would you tell me about it?"

"Sure." His eyes narrowed slightly and he frowned. "You a newspaper guy or somethin'?"

"No," I said. "I'm Campbell's grandson."

His eyes opened wide. "His grandson!" He suddenly smiled. He had the softest, gentlest smile I've ever seen on a man's face. "Well, well—King Campbell's grandson." He leaned across the table and gripped my hand. And Jeff Hart clapped me on the shoulder. "Why in hell didn't you say who you were? I'd never have let you stop off at the hotel if I'd known."

The barman came with six half-pint glasses of beer. "Make it the same again, George," the packer said as he distributed the beers.

"You know the regulations, Johnnie."

"Sure I do, but we're celebrating. Know who this is, George? King Campbell's grandson."

"You don't say." The barman wiped his hand on his apron and held it out to me. "Glad to know you. Why I mind the time old Campbell stopped off at Jasper—remember, Johnnie? There was a bad fall up beyond the Yellowhead. He had to stop over the Sunday and they got him to read the lesson."

"Sure, I remember. Reckon it was the only time they got me inside the place."

"Yeah, me too. An' about the only time they had to put the House Full notices up outside the door."

"That's for sure." Johnnie Carstairs laughed. "Now bring those beers, George. We'll be finished by the time you're back." He turned to me. "What's brought you up here? You his heir or somethin'?"

I nodded.

He smiled that lazy smile of his. "Reckon he didn't leave you much. What happens to the Kingdom? Do you own that now?"

"Yes."

"Well, well." The smile broadened into a puckish grin. "You got all the oil in the Rocky Mountains, Bruce."

"You were going to tell me how you found his body," I reminded him.

"Yeah." He sat back, sprinkled salt into one of his glasses of beer and drank it. "Queer thing that," he said, wiping his mouth with the back of his hand. "He was fine and dandy when we got up there. An' a week later he was dead."

"What happened?" I asked.

"Well, it was this away. I'd bin totin' a couple of Americans round for the best part of two months. They were climbers and they did stuff for magazines back in the States." He produced a little white cotton bag of tobacco and rolled himself a cigarette. "Well, we coralled our horses at Campbell's place and went south over The Gillie. We were away about a week and when we came down into the Kingdom again it was snowing hard. I figured somethin' was wrong as soon as I heard the horses. Besides, there weren't no smoke coming from any of the chimneys and no tracks in the snow outside either. The whole place had a dead look. The old man was lying face down on the floor just inside the door, like as though he was struggling to get outside and bring in some logs. Judging by the state of the stable I guess he'd been dead about three days."

"What do you think caused his death?" I asked.

He shrugged his shoulders. "Old age, I guess. Or maybe he had a stroke and died of cold. I hope when it comes to my turn I'll go like that. No fuss, no illness—and no regrets. Right to the end he believed there was oil up there."

He relit the stub of his cigarette and leaned back, his eyes half-closed. "Ever hear him playin' the pipes, Bruce?"

I shook my head. "I only met him once. That was in England, and he'd just come out of prison."

His sandy eyebrows lifted slightly. "So the prison stuff was true, eh? That was the only story I ever heard him tell more than once—that and about the oil. Mebbe they're both true and you're the richest man this side of the 49th Parallel." He laughed. "*There's oil in the Rocky Mountains*. Be a joke, Jeff, if it were true, wouldn't it now?" He leaned across to me. "That's how the nights always ended up—the old man poundin' the table with his fist and glaring at his visitors through the mat of his white hair and roaring *There's oil in the Rocky Mountains* fit to bust." He laughed and shook his head. "But he could play the pipes."

He leaned back again and rubbed his hand over his eyes. "I mind one evening some years ago ; it was very still and he came out of the ranch-house as the sun was setting and began to march up and down playing the pipes. The sound was clear and thin and yet it came back from the mountains as though all the Highlanders who ever lived were assembled there on the peaks and all of them a' blowin' to beat hell out of their pipes. And when he played *The Campbells are Coming* a million Campbells seemed to answer him. I guess it was about the weirdest thing I ever heard." He leaned forward and picked up his glass. "Your health!"

I raised my glass, thinking of the picture he was giving me of my grandfather and the Kingdom. "How do I get there?" I asked.

"Up to the Kingdom?" Johnnie shook his head. "You won't get up there yet awhiles—not until the snow melts."

"When will that be?"

"Oh, in about a month, I guess."

"I can't wait that long," I said.

Johnnie's eyes narrowed as he peered across at me. "You seem in a goldarned hurry."

"I am," I said.

"Well, Max Trevedian might take you up. He acts as packer and guide around Come Lucky. But it'd be a tough trip, an' he's an ornery sort of crittur anyway. Me, I wouldn't look at it, not till the snows melt. But then I ain't much use without a pony. Had the devil's job getting down last fall."

I brought the dog-eared map out of my pocket and spread it on the table. "Well, how do I get to Come Lucky anyway?" I asked.

Johnnie peered at it and shook his head. "Maps ain't much in my line," he said. "I go by the look of the country."

It was Jeff who gave me the information I wanted.

"You'll have to take the Continental down as far as Ashcroft. From then on it's a car ride up through 150 Mile House, Hydraulic, Likely and Keithley Creek. Do you reckon the roads will be open, Johnnie?"

Johnnie Carstairs shrugged his shoulders. "Depends on the chinook. If it's blowing then you might find somebody to take you through."

I thanked him and folded the map up.

He looked across at me and his hand closed over my arm. "You're a sick man, Bruce. Take my advice. Wait a month. It's too early for travelling through the mountains except by rail. Don't you agree, Johnnie?"

"Sure, sure. Leastaways I wouldn't try it."

"I can't wait that long," I murmured.

"Be sensible," Jeff pleaded. "Johnnie and I have lived up in this country a long time."

"I must get up there," I insisted.

"Well then, wait a month."

"I can't."

"Why in hell not?"

"Because——" I stopped then. I couldn't just tell them I hadn't much time.

"Let him find out for himself, Jeff." Johnnie's voice was gruff with anger. "Some people are just cussed. They got to learn the hard way."

"It's not that," I said quickly.

"All right, then—what is it? What's the goldarned hurry?"

"It isn't any of your business." I hesitated and then added, "I've only two months to live."

They stared at me. Johnnie's eyes searched my face and then dropped awkwardly. He brought out his tobacco and concentrated on rolling a cigarette. "I'm sorry, Bruce," he said gently. Accustomed to dealing with animals I think he'd read the truth of Maclean-Harvey's opinion in my features. But Jeff was a mechanic. "How do you know?" he asked. "You can't know a thing like that."

"You can if you've got cancer of the stomach." My voice sounded harsh. "I had the best man in London. He gave me six months at the outside. The anæmia is secondary," I added. I got to my feet. My lips were trembling uncontrollably. "Good night," I said. "And thanks for your help." I didn't want them to see that I was scared.

III

I LAY AWAKE for hours that night, fighting for breath and looking out at the frozen moonlight glinting on the white needle of Edith Cavell. I can admit it now—I was scared. The idea that I could do in a few months what my grandfather had failed to do in thirty-odd years had carried me over the first hurdle of shock and across 5,000 miles of the earth's surface. Now that that idea was finally shattered the ground seemed to have been cut away from under my feet. But the more sick at heart I felt the more determined I became to reach Campbell's Kingdom. Like a dog I wanted to crawl into some safe retreat to die, away from the prying eyes of my fellow creatures.

Next day Jeff Hart and Johnnie Carstairs both came down after lunch to see me off. They didn't ask me how I was and they studiously avoided looking at me. They insisted on carrying my two handgrips and walked one on either side of me as though they were afraid I'd die on them right there. "Damn it," Jeff growled, "if it had been a month later I'd have driven you over myself." A cold wind flung puffs of powdered snow in our faces.

They saw me into my carriage and left cigarettes and magazines the way visitors leave flowers in a sick room. As the train pulled out Johnnie called to me: "Any time you need help, Bruce, there's a couple of pals right here in Jasper you might call on."

"We'll be up to see you some time," Jeff added.

I waved acknowledgment and as I watched the black outline of the station fade in the wind-driven snow I felt a lump in my throat. The sense of loneliness had closed in on me again and I went back to my seat.

The train puffed laboriously into a world of virgin white. Our only contact with the outside world was the twin black threads of the line reaching back towards the prairies. The mountains closed in around us, monstrous white shapes scarred here and there by black outcrops of wind-torn rock.

The train threaded its way inexorably southwards, through Thunder River, Redsand, Blue River and Angushorn. At Cottonwood Flats it began to rain and as dusk fell we drew in to Birch Island and I saw for the first time a stretch of road clear of snow.

We reached Ashcroft just before midnight. It was still raining. The darkness was full of the sound of water and great heaps of dirty snow filled the yard with gurgling rivulets. When I asked at the hotel about the roads they told me they had been open for the last two days. I felt my luck was in then and nothing could stop me. Next morning I bought a pair of good water-proof boots and tramped the round of the local garages. My luck held. At one of them I found a mud-bespattered Ford filling up with gas, a logger bound for Prince George. He gave me a ride as far as 150 Mile House. The country poured water from its every crevice, the creeks were roaring torrents and we ground our way through falls of rock and minor avalanches. It took us most of the day to do the 100-odd miles to 150 Mile House.

I spent the night there and in the morning got a lift as far as Hydraulic. By then the rain had turned to a wet snow. I was getting back into the high mountains. After a wait of two or three hours and some lunch, a farm truck took me on to Keithley Creek. It was dark when I arrived. The country was deep in snow and it was freezing hard. I crawled into bed feeling dead to the world and for the first time in months slept like a log.

I slept right through to eleven o'clock and was woken with the news that the packer was in from Come Lucky and would be leaving after lunch. It was blowing half a gale and snowing hard. They served me a steak and two fried eggs and when I'd packed and paid my bill I was taken out and introduced to a great ox of a man who was loading groceries into an ex-army fifteen hundredweight.

We pulled out of Keithley just after two, the rattle of the chains deadened by the soft snow. Visibility was very poor, the snow driving up behind us and flying past the windows as we ground slowly along the uneven track. I glanced at my companion. He was wrapped in a huge bearskin coat and he had a fur cap with ear flaps and big skin gloves. His face was the colour of mahogany. He had thick, loose lips and he kept licking at a trickle of saliva that ran out of the corners of his mouth. His nose was broad and flat and his little eyes peered into the murk from below a wide forehead that receded quickly to the protection of his Russian-looking cap. His huge hands gripped the steering wheel as though he had to fight the truck every yard of the way. " Do you live at Come Lucky?" I asked him.

He grunted without shifting his eyes from the track.

"I suppose there's a hotel there?"

A nod accompanied the grunt this time. I let it go at that and relaxed drowsily in the engine-heated noise of the cab.

For a long time we ran through a world of virgin white, between heaped-up banks of snow where the road had been cleared of drifts, only the occasional black line of a stream to relieve the monotony. Then we were climbing and gradually the timber closed in around us. The snow no longer drove past the cab windows. The trees were still and black. I wondered vaguely why the trail to Come Lucky had been cleared of snow, but I was too drowsy to question the driver. It was open and that was all I cared about. I was on the last stage of my journey.

I tried to imagine what it had been like up here less than a hundred years ago when the Cariboo gold rush had been on and these creek beds had been crowded with men from all parts of the world. But it didn't seem possible. It was just a wilderness of snow and mountain and timber.

After half an hour the snow eased off. We were climbing steadily beside the black waters of the Little River. Timbered mountain slopes rose steeply above me and I got a momentary glimpse of a shaggy head of rock high above us and half veiled in cloud. I glanced at my companion and suddenly it occurred to me that this might be the packer that Johnnie Carstairs had talked about. " Is your name Max Trevedian?" I asked him.

He turned his head slowly and looked at me. " *Ja*, that is my name." He seemed to consider for a moment how I knew it and then he turned his attention back to the track.

So this was the man who could take me up to Campbell's Kingdom before the snow melted. " Do you know Campbell's Kingdom?" I asked him.

" Campbell's Kingdom!" His voice had a sudden violence of interest. " Why do you ask about Campbell's Kingdom?"

" I want to go up there."

" Why?"

For some reason I didn't wish to tell him why. I stared out of my side window. We were running along the shores of a small lake now. It was all frozen over and the flat surface of the ice was covered with a dusting of snow.

" Why do you wish to go there?" he asked again.

" I've heard about it, that's all," I replied vaguely, wondering why the mention of Campbell's Kingdom should so suddenly rouse him from his tactiturn silence.

" Why do you go to Come Lucky, huh? It is too soon for visitors. Are you an oil man?"

" No," I said.

" Then why do you come?"

" That's my business," I answered, annoyed by his childlike persistence.

He grunted.

" What made you ask if I was an oil man?"

" Oil men come here last year. There is an old devil lived up in the mountains who thought there was oil there." He suddenly began to laugh, a great, deep-throated sound. " Damned old fool! All they found were rocks. I could have told them there was no oil."

" How do you know?"

" How did I know?" He stared at me angrily.

" What made you so certain?"

" Because he is a swindler," he growled. " A dirty, lying, bastard old man who swindle everyone." His voice has risen suddenly to a high pitch and his little eyes glared at me hotly. " You ask my brother."

His words swept me back to my childhood, to the taunts

and jeers I had suffered. " You're referring to Campbell, are you?"

" Ar. Campbell." There was an incredible vibrance of hatred in the way he spoke the name. " King Campbell! Is that why you come here—to see Campbell?" He laughed " Because if you have, you will waste your time. He is dead."

" I know that."

" Then why do you come, huh?"

I was beginning to understand what Johnnie Carstairs had meant when he had said the man was an ornery crittur. I didn't answer him and I didn't ask any more questions. It was like travelling with an animal you're not quite sure of and we drove on in silence.

As dusk began to fall we came out on the shores of a narrow lake. Come Lucky was at the head of it. My first sight of the place was as we slid out of the timber on to the lake shore. The town was half-buried in snow, a dark huddle of shacks clinging to the bare, snow-covered slopes of a mountain and leaning out towards the lake as though in the act of being swept into it by an avalanche. Beyond it a narrow gulch cut back into the mountains and lost itself in a grey veil of cloud. The road appeared to continue along the shore of the lake and into the gulch. We turned right, however, up to Come Lucky and stopped at a long, low shack, the log timbers of which had been patched with yellow boards of untreated pine. There was a notice on one of the doors— *Trevedian Transport Company: Office.* This was as far as the track into Come Lucky had been cleared. A drift of smoke streamed out from an iron chimney. A door slammed and a fat Chinaman waddled out to meet us. He and Max Trevedian disappeared into the back of the truck and began off-loading the stores. I stood around waiting and presently my two grips were dropped into the snow at my feet. The Chinaman poked his head out of the back of the truck. " You stay here?" he asked.

" Is this the hotel?"

" No. This is bunkhouse for men working on road up Thunder Creek."

" Where's the hotel?" I asked.

" You mean Mr. Mac's place—The Golden Calf?" He pointed up the snow-blocked street. " You find up there on the right side."

I thanked him and trudged through the snow into the town of Come Lucky. It was a single street bounded on either side by weather-boarded shacks. Dotted amongst them were log cabins of stripped jack pine. The place seemed deserted. There wasn't a soul about and only in two instances did I see smoke coming from the ugly clatter of tin chimneys. The roofs of many of the shacks had fallen in. Some had their windows ripped out, frames and all. Doors stood rotting on their hinges. The untreated boards were grey with age and soggy with moisture. Scraps of paper hung forlornly to hoardings and the faint lettering above the empty shops and saloons proclaimed the purpose for which the crumbling bundle of wood had originally been assembled. The King Harry Bar still carried the weathered portrait of an English King and next door there was a doctor's brass plate, now a green rectangle of decomposing metal. The wooden sidewalks stood up above the level of the snow, a crazy switch-back affair of haphazard design and doubtful safety. It seemed to be constructed on stilts. In fact the whole place was built on stilts and it leaned down the slope to the lake as though the thrust of the coast wind had pushed it outwards like a flimsy erection of cards. Here and there a shack was held together by pieces of packing cases and rough-cut planks; evidence of human existence. But in the main Come Lucky was a rotten clutter of empty shacks.

It was my first sight of a ghost town.

The Golden Calf was about the biggest building in the place. Faded gilt lettering proclaimed its name and underneath I could just make out the words: *If it's the Gaiety of the City for You, This is the Best Spot in the whole of Cariboo.* And there was the picture of a calf, now grey with age. The sidewalk was solid here and roofed over to form a sort of street-side verandah.

The door of the hotel opened straight into an enormous bar room. The bar itself ran all along one side and behind it were empty shelves backed by blotchy mirrors. There were faded pictures of nude and near-nude women and yellowing bills advertising local events of years gone by. The few marble-topped tables and rickety chairs, the iron-framed piano and the drum stove which roared against the opposite wall took up little of the dirt-ingrained floor area. The room was warm, but it had a barrack-room emptiness about it that was only heightened by the marks of its one-time Edwardian elegance.

Two old men playing cards at a table near the stove turned to stare at me. Above them was the picture of a voluptuous young beauty of the can-can period. Pencil shading had been added in appropriate places and she had been given a moustache. The crudity of it, however, produced only speculation as to the circumstances in which the trimmings had been added. I put my bags down and drew up a chair to the stove. The warmth of the room was already melting the snow on my windbreaker. My trousers steamed. I took off my outer clothes and sat back, letting the warmth seep into my body. I felt deathly tired.

The two old men continued to stare at me. They looked sad and surprised. Their moustaches drooped. " Is the hotel open?" I asked them.

The shock of being asked a question was apparently too much for them. One of them blinked uncertainly, the other coughed. As though they understood each other's thoughts, they turned without a word and continued their game.

Beyond the stove there was a door and beside it a bell push. I pulled myself to my feet and rang. A buzzer sounded in the recesses of the building and slippers shuffled on the wooden floor of a corridor. The door opened slowly and an elderly Chinaman entered. He stopped in front of me and stared up at me impassively with a fixed smile that showed the brown of decaying teeth. He was a little wizened man with a monkey face. His clothes hung on him like a bundle of rags and he wore a shapeless cloth cap. On his feet were a pair of tattered carpet slippers. " You want something?"

" Yes," I said. " I'd like a room for the night."

" I fetch Mr. Mac." He shuffled off and I sat down again.

After a time the door was opened by a dour-faced man whose long body was stooped at the shoulders. He was bald except for a fringe of iron-grey hair. His eyelids and the corners of his mouth drooped. He had the appearance of a rather elderly heron and he looked me over with the disinterest of one who has seen many travellers and is surprised at nothing.

" Are you Mr. Mac?" I asked him.

He seemed to consider the question. " Me name's Mc-Clellan," he said. " But most folk around here call me Mac. Ye're wanting a room Slippers tells me." He sighed. " Och weel, I daresay we'll manage it. Ye're from the Old Country by the sound of your voice."

"Yes," I said. "My name's Bruce Wetheral. I've just arrived from England."

"Weel, it's a wee bit airly in the season for us, Mr. Wetheral. We don't generally reckon on visitors till the fishermen come up from the Coast around the end of June. But we've an engineer staying already, so one mair'll make little difference. Ye'll no mind feeding in the kitchen wi' the family?"

"Of course not."

The room he took me to was bare except for the essentials: an iron-framed bed, a wash basin, a chest of drawers and a chair. A text—*Stay me with flagons, comfort me with apples; for I am sick of love*—was the only adornment on the flaking paint of the wood-partitioned walls. But the room was clean and the bed looked comfortable.

They kept farmhouse hours at the hotel and I barely had time to wash and unpack my things before the old Chinaman called me for tea. By the time I got down the McClellan family was all assembled in the kitchen, a huge room designed to feed the seething population of Come Lucky in its hey-day. Besides the old man and his sister, Florence McClellan, there was his son, James, and his family—his wife, Pauline, and their two children, Jackie aged nine and Kitty aged six and a half. James McClellan was a small, wiry man. Keen blue eyes peered out from under his father's drooping lids and his nose was as sharply chiselled as the beak of a hawk. His expression was moody, almost sour, and when he spoke, which was seldom, there was the abruptness of a hot, violent-tempered man. Pauline was half French, raven-haired and buxom with an attractive accent and a wide mouth. She laughed a little too often, showing big, white teeth.

There was one other person at the big, scrubbed deal table, a thick-set man of about forty with tough, leathery features and sandy hair which stood up from his scalp and from the backs of his big hands. His name was Ben Creasy and he was introduced to me as the engineer who was building the road up Thunder Creek. The meal was cooked and served by the old Chinaman. He had drifted into the gold mines from Vancouver's Chinatown during the First World War and had been at the hotel ever since.

Nobody spoke during the meal, not even the children. Eating was a serious business. We had clam chowder and steaks and there was a jug of milk for those who wanted to drink.

"You do not eat much, Mr. Wetheral," Pauline McClellan said. "The meat, is it tough? I get you another steak if you like."

"No," I said. "No, I'm just not hungry."

The whole table stared at me as though I were some queer freak. An apple pie followed with cream from a great bowl on the table. Coffee was served with the pie. After the meal the men drifted over to the furnace-hot range and sat and smoked whilst the women cleared up.

Old Mac and his son were talking cattle and I sat back, my eyes half-closed, succumbing to the warmth. I gathered James McClellan ran a garage in Keithley Creek and farmed a piece of land the other side of the lake.

"And what brings ye up to Come Lucky at this time of the year, Mr. Wetheral?" the old man asked me suddenly.

The question jerked me out of my reverie. He was looking across at me, his drooped lids almost concealing his eyes, his wrinkled face half hidden in the smoke from his short-stemmed briar. "Do you know a place near here called Campbell's Kingdom?" I asked him.

"Aye." He nodded, waiting for me to go on.

"I came to have a look at it," I said.

They eyed me curiously and in silence.

"How do I get up there?" I asked.

"Better ask Ben." The old man turney to Creasy. "Do ye ken what the snow's like at the head o' the creek, Ben?"

"Sure. It's pretty deep. Anyway, he couldn't get past the fall till it's cleared."

"Why do you want to go up to the Kingdom?" the younger McClellan asked.

There was something about the manner in which he put the question that made me hesitate. "I just wanted to have a look at it," I said. I turned to Creasy. "Does this road you're building go towards the Kingdom?"

"Yeh."

"What's it for?"

"It ain't for the convenience of tourists anyway."

Old Mac cleared his throat. "Ye were telling me, Mr

Wetheral, that ye'd come straight out from England?" I
nodded. "Then how is it ye've got the name Campbell's
Kingdom so pat on your tongue?"

"I'm Campbell's grandson," I said.

They stared at me in astonishment. "His grandson, did ye
say?" The old man was leaning forward, staring at me, and
his tone was one of incredulity.

"Yes."

"Ye're no exactly like him in appearance. He was a big
man—broad across the shoulders and tough." He shook his
head slowly. "Och, weel, a man's no' entirely responsible for
his kith and kin, I guess. So ye've come to see the Kingdom?"

I nodded.

James McClellan darted his head forward. "Why?" There
was sudden violence in the way he put the question.

"Why?" I stared at him, wondering at the tenseness of his
expression. "Because it belongs to me."

"Belongs to you!" He stared at me unbelievingly. "But
the place is sold. They sold it to pay old Campbell's debts."
He glanced at his father and then back at me. "It was sold
to the Larsen Mining and Development Company."

"The Larsen Mining and Development Company?" It was
the name that had been newly painted on the frosted door of
Henry Fergus's office. "I had an offer from a company," I
said. "But I turned it down."

"You turned it down!" McClellan kicked his chair out
from under him as he jerked to his feet. "But——" He
stopped and looked slowly across at Creasy. "We'd better go
and have a word with Peter." The other nodded and got to
his feet. "You're sure you really are Campbell's heir?" he
asked me.

"Is that anything to do with you?" I was a little uncertain,
disturbed by the violence of his reaction. He looked scared.

"By God it is," he said. "If——" He seemed to take hold
of himself. "You're still the legal owner of the property,
are you?"

I nodded.

"Can you prove it?"

"How do you mean?"

"Have you got anything on you to show that you really
do own the place?"

He seemed so darned worried I got out my pocket book and

showed him the wire I had received from Acheson on the train. He almost snatched it from my hand and I could see his lips moving as he read it. "Did you see Acheson?" His hands shook slightly and his face was grey as he looked down at me.

"Yes."

"What did you decide?"

"I said I'd think about it and came on up here. Why?"

"Christ Almighty!" he breathed. "That means——" He stopped and his eyes went to the window as though there was something out there he wanted to look at. But the panes were dark squares reflecting the interior of the kitchen.

"May I see it?" Creasy held out his hand and McClellan gave him the wire. He read it through and then he said, "Yeh, we'd better see Peter right away." He handed the slip back to McClellan who asked me if he could have the loan of it.

"You can keep it, if you like," I said. "But what's the trouble?"

"Nothing," he answered quickly. "Nothing at all. We just thought the place was sold, that's all." And he hurried out of the room, followed by Creasy.

I turned and stared after them in astonishment. "What was all that about?" I asked the old man. He was still sitting there thumbing tobacco into his pipe.

He didn't say anything for a moment and as he lit his pipe he stared at me over the flame of the match. "So you're Campbell's heir and the legal owner of the Kingdom," he murmured. "What brought ye all the way out from the Old Country?"

"I wanted to see the place."

"You'll not be as daft as the old man, surely?"

"How do you mean?"

"Campbell had oil fever the way some folk have malaria. If he'd struck lucky he might have been a great figure. As it was . . ." He shrugged his shoulders.

"Did you know him well?" I asked.

"Aye, about as well as any man in this town. But he wasna a very easy man to get to know. A solitary sort of crittur wi' a quick temper. He spoke verra fast and violent and he'd a persuasive tongue, damn him." He sighed and shook his head. "The river of oil was just a dream, I guess." He looked

across at me and then asked abruptly, " What would ye be
planning to do with the Kingdom now you've come out
here?"

" I thought I might live up there," I said.

" Live up there!"

" My grandfather lived there," I reminded him.

" Aye. For nigh on twenty years old Campbell lived there."
His voice was bitter and he spat out a piece of tobacco.
" Dinna be a fool, laddie," he said. " The Kingdom's no place
for ye. And if it's oil you're looking for ye won't find it as
many of us in this town have learnt to our cost. There's no oil
in these mountains. Bladen's survey proved that once and for
all. The place isn't worth two nickels. Och, there's a bit of
ranching to be done up there. The alfalfa's good and if the
chinook blows there's little need for hauling feed. But it
doesna always blow." He got to his feet and came and stood
over me. " This is no your sort of country," he said, reaching
out a bony hand and gripping my shoulder. " It's a hard
country, and it doesna take easily to strangers."

I stared at him. " It's supposed to be very lovely in
summer," I murmured. " A lot of visitors——"

" Oh, aye, the visitors. But ye're no a visitor. Ye're
Campbell's heir." He stared down at me. " Take my advice ;
sell out and gang home where you belong."

His hard, grey eyes were staring down at me unwinkingly.
It was as though his words were meant as a warning. " I'll
think about it," I muttered, feeling strangely ill-at-ease under
his scrutiny.

" Aye, ye think about it." He hesitated, as though about to
say something further. But he shook his head. His lids
drooped down over his eyes and he turned away with a little
shrug and shuffled out of the room.

I leaned back slackly in my chair. Everything was so
different from what I had expected—the place, the people, the
way they regarded my grandfather. I felt suddenly very tired.
I was at the end of my journey now and I went to bed
wondering what to-morrow would bring.

When I got down to breakfast next morning there was only
a single place laid at the long deal table. It was eight-thirty,
but already the others had finished. The Chinaman served me
bacon and eggs and coffee and after I had fed I got my coat
and went out to have a look at Come Lucky. The snow had

stopped. It was a grey, windless morning. The place seemed utterly deserted. I walked the length of the street along the rickety boards of the sidewalk and saw only one shack with glass in the windows and curtains. The town was the most derelict place I'd ever seen, worse than the bombed villages of Italy during the war. It reminded me faintly of Pompeii— a place where people had lived long, long ago.

I turned down through the snow towards the bunkhouse. There was a heavy American truck with a bulldozer loaded in the back drawn up outside the office of the Trevedian Transport Company. The driver came out just as I reached it. " Miss the bus this morning?" he asked with a grin. He was a big, cheerful man in an old buckskin jacket and olive-green trousers.

" How do you mean?" I asked.

" Aren't you working on the road?"

" No."

" You mean you live here. Christ. I didn't know anyone under sixty lived in this dump."

" No, I'm just a visitor. Are you taking that bulldozer up Thunder Creek?"

" Yeh. Want to ride along and see how the work's progressing?"

There seemed no point in hanging around Come Lucky. Now I was here I had all the time in the world. " Yes," I said. " I only got in last night. I haven't had a chance yet to see much of the country." I climbed up into the cab beside him and he swung the big truck down the snow-packed grade to the lake-shore road. There we turned right and rumbled along the ice-bound edge of the lake towards the dark cleft of Thunder Creek. " Where's this road going to lead to when it's finished?" I asked him.

He stared at me in surprise. " Shouldn't have thought you could stay a night in Come Lucky and not know the answer to that one. It's going up to the cable hoist at the foot of Solomon's Judgment. Pity about the cloud. On a fine day there's quite a view of the mountains from here. You know this part at all?"

" No," I said. " I've never been in the Rockies before."

" Well, I guess you haven't missed much. Winter lasts just about the whole year round up here." He peered through the windshield. " Seems like the clouds are lifting. Maybe you'll get a glimpse of Solomon's Judgment after all. Quite a sight where the big slide occurred. Happened around the same time as the Come Lucky slide." He nodded through his side window. " Doesn't look much from here when it's covered in snow like it is now. But you see those two big rocks up there? That's just about where the entrance to the old Come Lucky mine was. They reckon there's three or four hundred feet of mountainside over that entrance right now."

The line of the timber loomed ahead. Soon it had closed round us, the trees silent and black, their upper branches sagging under the weight of the snow. The road was furrowed by wheel tracks and here and there the broad tracks of a bulldozer showed through the carpet of snow. Wherever there were drifts the snow had been shovelled aside in great banks and the edges of the road were piled with the debris that had been torn out to make it ; small trees, chunks of ice and hard-packed snow, gravel and dirt and stones and the rocks of minor falls.

The road was about twelve feet wide with passing points almost every mile. Where streams came down, which was often, the gullies had been packed with timber to form a bridge and damp patches had been surfaced with logs placed corduroy-fashion.

We were climbing steeply now, reaching back into a tributary of Thunder Creek to gain height. The road twisted and turned, sometimes running across bare, smooth rock ledges, sometimes under overhanging cliffs.

We topped a shoulder of rock, bare of trees, and I caught a brief glimpse of two snow-covered peaks towering above the dark, timbered slopes and of a sheer wall of rock that fell like a black curtain across the end of the valley, its gloom emphasised by a tracery of snow-packed crevices and occasional patches of ice. " That's the slide I was telling you about," the driver shouted. " And that's Solomon's Judgment, those twin peaks." He revved the big diesel engine and changed gear.

" Do you know Campbell's Kingdom?" I asked him.

"Heard of it," he said, keeping his eyes on the road, which was running sharply down to the bed of a ravine. " Can't say I've ever been there."

" Do you know where it is?"

" Sure." He eased the big truck over the logs that bridged the stream bed and nursed it up the further side. As the lorry's snout lifted above the slope the twin peaks rose to meet us above the trees until they filled the whole sky ahead. " Campbell's Kingdom is up there," he said, pointing to the peaks.

My heart sank. It looked a hell of a climb. " How far does the road go?" I asked.

" The road? Well, it doesn't go up to the Kingdom." He laughed. " There's two thousand feet of cliff there."

He swung the truck round a bend and there, straight ahead of us, two bulldozers and a gang of men were working on a section of the track that had been completely obliterated. There was a closed three-tonner parked at the end of the road and we drew in behind it and stopped.

We were standing on the lip of an almost sheer drop of several hundred feet. Somehow the pines managed to cling to the slope and I found myself looking down over their snow-laden tops to the creek below. Now that the engine was stopped I could hear the roar of the water. Ahead of us, where the construction gang was working, the road swung round under an overhang. Part of the cliff had gone, taking the road with it. The place looked as though it had been blasted by shell fire. All the trees had been swept clean away on a broad front, swept down into the valley bottom with millions of tons of snow. " An avalanche did that by the looks of it," the driver said. The snow had completely engulfed the waters of Thunder Creek which flowed out from a black arch underneath it. " Heh, Ben! I got your other bulldozer for you."

Creasy was coming back up the road towards us. He was dressed in a fleece-lined jacket and ski cap. " About time," he said. " This is a fair cow, this one." He looked across at me. " You haven't wasted much time getting out here." He turned to the driver who was already in the back of the truck loosening the securing tackle of the bulldozer. " Okay, George. There's a good snow bank over there. I'll get some men on to it right away, then you back up and we'll run her off same as we did the others."

I left them to it and went down the road to where the bulldozers were working. They had blasted back into the cliff face and the big D7s were hefting the rocks out with their broad blades and shovelling them over the edge, steadily building outwards. I stood on the lip of the road and stared up at the twin peaks of Solomon's Judgment. From their summits powdery snow streamed lazily upward like smoke. Separating the two peaks was a narrow cleft, a dark gash in the mountain face, and across the upper end of it was wedged a shelf of rock like a wall. Something about that wall caught and held my gaze. Though it was breached in the centre it was too regular to be natural and it was of a lighter shade than the rock walls of the cleft.

"Like to have a look through these?" The driver was standing beside me and he was offering me a pair of binoculars. I focused them on the cleft and instantly the lighter coloured rock resolved itself into a wall of concrete. I was looking at a dam, completed except for the centre section.

"When was that built?" I asked the driver.

"It was begun in the summer of 1939," he replied, "when the Government reckoned they'd need to open up the Larsen mines for the rearmament drive. They stopped work when the States came into the war. It became cheaper to get out ore from across the border, I guess. Now, of course, with the price of lead at the level it is to-day——"

"They're going to complete the dam—is that it? That's what this road is for?"

He nodded. "You can just see the cable of the hoist if you look carefully. It runs up to a pylon at the top."

I searched the cliff face and gradually made out the slender thread of the cable rising to a concrete pylon on the cliff top and snaking back to a squat housing to the left of the dam and a little above it."

I lowered the glasses, the truth slowly dawning on me. "Where exactly is Campbell's Kingdom?" I asked him.

"Up there." He nodded towards the dam. "Just through the cleft."

"Where's the boundary of the property?"

"I wouldn't know exactly."

I turned as a bulldozer thrust a great pile of blast-shattered rock towards the lip of the road. They'd been so damned sure I'd sell that they'd started the work without even waiting for me to sign the deeds.

I looked round. Creasy was standing a little way up the road. I got the impression he had been watching me. No wonder they'd been worried last night. Anger boiled up inside me. If they'd given me the details, if they'd explained that there was a dam three-quarters built already. . . . I went over to him. "Who ordered you to build this road?" I demanded.

"That any of your business?" His tone was sullen.

"This road is being built to bring material up to complete the dam, isn't it?" I asked. "And if the dam is on my property——"

"It isn't on your property."

"Well, where's the Campbell land start?"

"Just the other side of the dam." He turned away and moved towards the face of the overhang. "Looks like we got to do some more blasting," he said to his foreman. I followed him over and listened to him giving instructions to the driller. The compressed air unit started up with a roar and the drills began to eat into the rock. Above the din I shouted, "You still haven't told me who you're building this road for?"

He turned on me angrily. "Suppose you leave me to get on with it. I'm paid to build the damned thing, not to answer a lot of questions. You may own old Campbell's Kingdom, but this is Trevedian land and what happens down here is nothing to do with you."

"I think it is."

"All right. Then go and talk to Peter Trevedian and stop worrying me. Blasting this stuff isn't as easy as it looks." He turned his back on me and shouted instructions to his drillers. Somebody yelled at me to get out of the way and a bulldozer started towards the lip of the road, thrusting about five tons of rubble in front of its blade.

I walked back up the road a bit and stood looking up to the cleft in the mountain they called Solomon's Judgment. The sound of the bulldozers eating their way relentlessly towards the Kingdom echoed in my ears. I hadn't expected anything like this. I might just as well have signed the deeds of sale, borrowed on the result and spent a few, pleasant carefree months travelling.

The driver shouted to me that he was leaving and I went slowly back up the road and climbed into the cab beside him. Back in Come Lucky I dropped off at the office of the Trevedian Transport Company, but it was locked and I went on to the hotel. There were several old men in the bar drinking beer. They turned as I entered and stared at me curiously. "Do you know where I'll find a man called Peter Trevedian?" I asked one of them.

"Sure. Over to Keithley Creek. He and Jamie McClellan went in early this morning."

I sat down at one of the marble-topped tables and got the Chinaman to bring me a beer. I didn't know what to do for the best. It seemed absurd to try and stop the completion of a dam that was two-thirds built for the sake of a dead man's whims. And yet. . . . I found myself thinking back to that one meeting I had had with my grandfather. There must have been something in it surely for a man to come back here and spend the rest of his life up in that mountain fastness. As I sat drinking my beer it occurred to me it was about time I had a word with Acheson. I got up and went across to where old Mac sat with several of his cronies. "Can I use your phone?"

He looked up at me. "Aye, ye can use it," he said. "But ye'll no' contact anybody. The line's been down for a week past." He smiled dourly. "Ye see, there's only two subscribers in Come Lucky now—meself and Trevedian. The company dinna worry over much about us."

I went back to my seat and ordered another beer. I had a sudden sense of being cut off. A bell rang in the depths of the hotel and the Chinaman came to tell me dinner was ready. As I got to my feet a man pushed open the street door and came in. He was short and dark, with black hair and a smooth, coppery skin. There was something arresting in the way he threw open the door and stood there, looking round the room. But it was the scar that made me look at him more closely. It ran all across the right side of his face, from the corner of his lip to his ear, half of which was missing. It didn't exactly disfigure his face, but it gave a queer twist to features that were almost classic in their cleanness of line, the jaw hard and square, the forehead broad and the nose sharply chiselled and quite straight. "Hiya, Mac." He came forward into the bar, a pleasant, cheerful smile on his face that disclosed the even line of very white teeth. He carried a leather grip and the backs of his hands were marked with the dark purple of burns.

Old Mac got to his feet and shook his hand. "It's grand to see you, Boy." There was real pleasure in the old man's voice. "Jean was only saying the other day it was time you came back for your trucks."

"She's still here then?"

" Aye."

" Are they through to the hoist yet?"

" Not quite. But they'll no' be long now. Creasy's working through the fall right this minute." Mac shook his head. " It was bad luck that fall. How did you make out this winter?"

The other grinned. " Oh, not too bad. Went wildcatting with a bunch of hoodlums up in the Little Smoky country. Have you got a room for me? I guess I'll stay up here now until the hoist's working and I can get my trucks down."

" Aye, there's a room for ye. And ye're just in time for dinner."

" Well, thanks, but I thought I'd go and scrounge a meal off Jean."

" Ye think the lass had been pining for ye, eh?" The old man poked him in the ribs.

" I wouldn't know about that," the other grinned. " But I've been pining for her."

Their laughter followed me as I went through into the kitchen. When Mac came in I asked him who the newcomer was. " That was Boy Bladen," he said.

" Bladen?"

" Aye. He's the laddie who did the survey up in the Kingdom last summer."

Bladen! ". . . Bladen was keen, as keen as Stuart." I could hear of Roger Fergus's words still. It seemed that providence had delivered Bladen into my hands for the sole purpose of discovering the truth about that survey.

". . . and he had to abandon all his equipment, leave it up in the Kingdom all winter," old Mac was saying. " You saw that fall they were clearing when you went up the road to-day?" I nodded. " Well, that happened just before he was due to come down." He shook his head sadly. " That's tough on a boy, all his capital locked up in a place like that. Never had anything but trouble from the Kingdom," he growled.

" About that survey," I said. " Did my grandfather know the result of it?"

" No. He went and died while the letter containing the report was waiting for him down here in my office. It would just about have killed him anyway."

After the meal I went up to my room and lay on the bed and smoked and tried to think the thing out.

It was shortly after four that I heard James McClellan shouting for his father. If he was back, presumably Trevedian was too. I got up, put on my coat and went down through the hard-packed snow to the bunkhouse. The door of the transport company's office was ajar and as I climbed the wooden steps I heard the sound of voices. I hesitated, my hand on the knob of the door. " . . . you should have thought of that before you took your trucks up there." The man's tone was easy, almost cheerful. " If I weren't clearing that fall and rebuilding the road you'd never get them out. I've got a lot of dough tied up in——"

I was just turning away when another voice cut in, harsher and less controlled. "You may own the valley, but you've only a half share in the hoist. McClellan's got some say in——"

" McClellan will do what I tell him," the other replied. "You do as I say and you'll get your trucks down."

"God damn you, Trevedian!" The door flung open and Bladen came out, pushing past me and walking angrily up the slope towards Come Lucky.

I knocked and went in. The office was small and bare and dusty. An old-fashioned telephone stood on a desk littered with papers and cigarette ash and behind the desk sat a stocky man of about forty-five. The bone of his skull showed through the close-cropped, grizzled hair and, since it was a round, solid head jammed close in to the shoulders on a short neck, it bore a remarkable resemblance to those concrete balls that adorn the gate pillars of Victorian houses. But though the head was round, the position of cheek bones and jaw gave the features length, so that with the long nose and rather pursed lips under the clipped grey moustache the features seemed to lose some of the strength of the head. The eyes were black and they had little pouches of loose flesh under them. He was like a fine Rugby scrum-half gone to seed, and yet the heaviness of his body wasn't fat, for, apart from the greyness of his skin, he looked fit. " Mr Peter Trevedian?" I asked.

He rose to greet me. " You must be Bruce Wetheral." His hand was hard and rough, the smile of welcome rubber-stamped on his leathery features. " Sit down. James told me you'd arrived. Cigarette?" He produced a silver cigarette case from the pocket of his jacket and held it out to me. " You're

Campbell's heir, I understand." He flicked his lighter for me and his small, black eyes were fastened on my face.

I nodded.

" Well, I think I can guess why you've come to see me." He smiled and sat back in his chair with a grunt. " Fact is I was just coming up to have a talk with you." He lit his cigarette and blew out a cloud of smoke. " I'll be quite frank with you, Wetheral, your refusal to sell the Kingdom has put me in a bit of a spot. As you probably know, through my holding in the Larsen mines, I've got the contract for supplying all materials for the completion of the Solomon's Judgment dam. But the contract is a tricky one. The dam has to be completed this summer. To get all the materials up on the one hoist I had to be in a position to begin packing the stuff in the moment the construction people were ready to start work on the dam. To do that I had to have the road cleared ready. I couldn't wait for the okay from Fergus. So I took a chance on it."

" A bit risky, wasn't it?" I said.

He shrugged his shoulders. " If you want to make money out here you've got to take risks. If I'd waited for Fergus's okay, I'd have been too late to pack all the stuff in on the one hoist. I'd have had to build a second hoist and believe me that would have cost a lot at current prices." He leaned back. " Well now, what are you holding out for—more dough?" The unwinking stare of his black little eyes was disconcerting.

" No," I said. " It's not that."

" What is it then? Mac said something about your planning to live up there."

" Yes."

" What the hell for? It's pretty God-damn lonely up there and in the winter——"

" My grandfather lived up there," I said. " If he could do it——"

" Campbell didn't live there because he liked it," he cut in sharply. " He lived there because he had to; because he didn't dare live down here amongst the folk he'd swindled."

" Are you suggesting he was a crook?" I demanded angrily.

He leaned forward and stubbed his cigarette out in a big quartz ash-tray. " See here, Wetheral. You know Campbell's history as well as I do. He was committed to trial and

sentenced by an English jury for fraud. If I remember right
he got five years. To that jury it was just a Stock Exchange
ramp. But out here it was the last gamble of men trying to
recoup themselves for the loss of the Come Lucky mine. They
believed in Campbell. Maybe I'm a bit bitter. Perhaps you'll
understand my attitude better if I tell you that my father,
Luke Trevedian, backed Campbell when he decided to drill up
beyond the cleft of Solomon's Judgment. Most of the old-
timers were with him in that venture. Well, it failed. The
rock was hard, it cost more than they budgeted to get equipment up there. When they found they'd bitten off more than
they could chew Campbell went to England to raise capital.
My father put every last penny he possessed into the Rocky
Mountain Exploration Company and when he got the news
that Morton, the director brought in by your grandfather as
financial adviser, had disappeared with all the capital, he got
on his horse and rode out into the snow of a winter's night.
We never saw him again."

"I'm sorry," I said.

He laughed. "No need to be sorry. It was his own fault
for being such a sucker. I'm telling you this so you'll understand why old Campbell lived up in the Kingdom. You don't
want to take too much notice of the newspaper stories. That's
just tourist stuff and I'll admit he put on a good act for them.
But the truth lies here in Come Lucky. This derelict bunch
of shacks is his doings. There was a lot of wealth here in this
town when the big slide sealed the mine." He lit another
cigarette and snapped his lighter shut by closing his fist on it
as though he meant to crush it. "And it isn't only the town
that's derelict," he added. "Take a look at the old men
around here. They're all old-timers, men who put their money
into Campbell's oil companies and now eke out a pittance
doing a bit of farming on the flats around Beaver Dam lake.
They just about fill their bellies and that's all."

There was nothing I could say. He was giving me the other
side of the picture and the violence in his voice emphasised
that it was the truth he was telling me. It explained so much,
but it didn't make my problem any easier.

"Well," he said, "what are you going to do? If you sell
the Kingdom, then Henry Fergus will go ahead with the
hydro-electric scheme and Come Lucky will become a
flourishing little town again."

" And if I don't?" I asked.

He hesitated. " I don't know. It just depends." He got up and walked over to the window. For a time he stood there, staring up the straggling length of Come Lucky's main street. Then he turned suddenly to me. " This place is what they call a ghost town. You've got a chance to bring it back to life."

" My grandfather's will imposed certain obligations on me," I said. " You see, he still believed——"

" Obligations, hell!" he snapped. He came and stood over me. " Suppose you go and think this thing over." He was looking down at me, his eyes slightly narrowed, the nerves at the corners quivering slightly. " I phoned Henry Fergus this morning when I was in Keithley. I tried to get him to increase his offer to you."

" It's not the money," I said.

" Well, maybe." He smiled sourly. " But money's a useful commodity all the same. He's coming up to see the progress they're making at Larsen. I suggested he came on up here and had a talk with you. He said he would." His hand dropped to my shoulder. " Think it over very carefully, will you. It means a lot to the people here."

I nodded and got to my feet. " Very well," I said. " I'll think it over."

" Yes. Do that."

When I got back to the hotel it was tea-time. There was an extra place laid at the big deal table and just after we'd sat down Bladen came in. Several times in the course of the meal I noticed James McClellan looking at me out of the corners of his eyes. He didn't eat much and as soon as the meal was over he hurried out, presumably down to Trevedian to discover the result of our interview. I went over to Bladen. " Can I have a word with you?" I asked him.

He hesitated. " Sure." His voice sounded reluctant. We drew our chairs a little apart from the others. " Well?" he said. " I suppose it's about the Kingdom?" His voice sounded nervous.

" I believe you did some sort of a survey up there last summer?"

He nodded. " A seismographic survey." His voice was very quiet, a gentle, musical sound. The scar was white across the smooth, gypsy skin. His eyes were fixed on his hand as he pressed back the cuticles of the nails. The nails were pale against the dark skin. " If you want the results of that survey an account was published in the *Edmonton Journal* of 3rd December."

" The results were unfavourable?"

" Yes."

" How reliable is a seismographic survey?"

He raised his head and looked at me then. " It won't tell you definitely where there's oil, if that's what you mean. But it gives a fairly accurate picture of the strata and from that the geophysicist can decide whether it's a likely spot to drill."

" I see." That was what Acheson had said. " Oil is trapped in the rock formations, isn't it?" I asked.

" Yeh, like in an anticline where you have a dome formation and the oil is trapped under the top of the dome."

" So the sort of survey you did in Campbell's Kingdom last year is pretty well a hundred per cent in showing where there's no likelihood of oil?"

He nodded.

" In your opinion did that survey make it clear that there could be no oil in the Kingdom?"

" I think you'll find the report makes that quite clear."

" I'm not interested in the report. I want your opinion."

His eyes dropped to his hands again. " I don't think you quite understand the way this thing works. My equipment records the time taken by a shock wave to be reflected back from the various strata to half a dozen detectors. It's the same principle as the echo-sounding device used by ships at sea. All I do is the field work. I get the figures and from these the computers map the strata under the surface."

" But you must have some idea how the survey is working out," I insisted.

" All I do is get the figures." He got to his feet. " You'd better go and talk to Winnick in Calgary if you want to query the results. He charted the area."

I caught him as he turned towards the door. " I'm only asking for your opinion," I said. " I haven't time to go to Calgary again."

" I have no opinion," he replied, his eyes looking towards the door as though he wanted to escape from my questions.

" All I want to know," I said, " is whether there is any chance of oil existing under the surface of the Kingdom."

"The report says No," he replied. "Why don't you write Winnick for a copy and read it?"

Something about his insistence on the report made me wonder. "Do you agree with the report?" I asked him.

"Look, I'm in a hurry. I've already told you——"

"I'm asking you a very simple question," I said. "Do you or do you not agree with the report?"

He seemed to hesitate. "Yes," he said, and pushed quickly by me to the door.

I stood there for a moment, staring at the still open doorway, wondering why he had been so reluctant to commit himself. I went back to the stove and sat there for a while, smoking a cigarette and thinking. I went over again my conversation with Roger Fergus. He had given me to understand that Bladen had been as enthusiastic as my grandfather. And yet now, when I had asked Bladen. . . .

I looked round the room. It was quite empty, but through the door to the scullery I could see Pauline busy at the sink. I went across to her. "Could you tell me whether there's a girl called Jean Lucas still living here?" I asked. Her little girl clung to her apron and stared up at me with big round eyes, sucking a dirty thumb. "She's English and she used to go up——"

"Yes, she's still here," she replied. "She lives with Miss Garret and her sister." She looked at me out of slanting brown eyes as she stretched up to put a plate on the rack. She had a fine, firm figure. "If you like I'll take you over there when I've put Kitty to bed."

I thanked her and went back to the stove.

IV

It was about seven-thirty when we left The Golden Calf. We went out by the way of the bar. A little huddle of men were bunched around the stove. Their talk ceased abruptly as we entered and they stared at me dumbly, curiously. James McClellan and Creasy were there and the man with the fur cap and the two who had been playing cards when I first arrived. There were others I had never seen before and a little removed from them was the loutish figure of Max

Trevedian staring stupidly into the red glow of the stove. At a table by himself Bladen sat over a glass of beer, the scar more noticeable than ever, his dark eyes fixed on my face.

"I'm just taking Mr. Wetheral down to see Jean," Pauline told her husband.

I saw Bladen start and realised suddenly that this was the same Jean he had been so anxious to see when he arrived. James McClellan grunted. The others watched us in silence as we crossed to the door.

Outside it was pitch dark. Not a light showed anywhere. It was warmer than it had been during the afternoon and there was a light wind from the West. We stopped outside the door and in the stillness of the night the only sound was the gentle murmur of water seeping down to the lake. From behind the closed door I heard the murmur of conversation starting up again. "I suppose they're talking about me?" I said.

"But of course." My companion laughed. "What else would they talk about? We have little enough to talk about in the wintertime. They will talk of nothing else for weeks."

"They don't seem to have liked my grandfather very much," I said.

"Oh, they are bitter, that is all. All the time he was living up there in the Kingdom they had something to hope for. Now he is dead and they have nothing to stand between them and the reality of their lives here. Look at the place." She shone her torch out across the snow to the crumbling shape of the shacks on the other side of the street. They looked forlorn and wretched in the brightness of the beam. "Do you wonder they are bitter? Come on." She took my arm. "I will guide you because it is dangerous. This sidewalk has many boards missing. There is no money to repair them, you see. If anything becomes rotten in this town it stays rotten. If you are here till the spring you will see how dreadful this place is. The main street is axle-deep in mud and the whole mountainside seems to be slipping beneath the houses. More and more houses collapse each year when the mud comes. You will see."

"Tell me," I said, "is Max Trevedian the brother of the man who runs the transport company?"

"Oui. You would never believe to look at them, would you?" She gave a little gurgle of laughter. "Half brothers,

C.K.   C

I think. But do not tell them so. That is just gossip, you know. Jimmy says Peter takes after his father and is a real Cornishman, while the younger one, Max, is very German like his mother." Her hand tightened on my arm. " Be careful here. It is very bad." A single rotten plank spanned a gap in the sidewalk. " Do you know what my children call Max?" she added as we stumbled through softening snow to the next safe stretch of the sidewalk. " They call him the Moose Man. Have you ever seen a moose?"

" No," I said. " Only in pictures."

" You will see plenty here if you go into the timber, then you will understand how very amusing the name is." She flicked her torch towards the pale glimmer of a lighted window ahead. " That is where the Miss Garrets live. They are terrible gossips and very old-fashioned. But I like them."

" And Jean Lucas—what's she like?" I asked.

" Oh, you will like her. She is very *intéressante*, I think." She gave my arm a squeeze. " She and I are great friends. We talk in French together."

" She speaks French?" Somehow the idea of an English girl out here in the wilds speaking French seemed absurd.

" But of course. She is English, but she has some French blood."

" What is she doing in Come Lucky?" I asked. " Has she relatives here?"

" No. I also think it is queer." I felt her shrug her shoulders. " I do not know. I think perhaps it is because she is not happy. She worked in France during the war. Here we are now." She knocked and pushed open the door. " Miss Garret," she called. " It is Pauline. May we come in?"

A door opened and the soft glow of lamplight flooded the small entrance hall. " Sure. Come on in." Miss Garret was small and dainty, like a piece of Dresden china. She wore a long black velvet dress with a little lace collar and a band of velvet round her neck from which hung a large cameo. To my astonishment she quizzed me through a gold lorgnette as I entered the room. " Oh, how nice of you, Pauline," she cooed. " You've brought Mr. Wetheral to see us."

" You know my name?" I said.

" Of course." She turned to the other occupant of the room. " Sarah. Pauline's brought Mr. Wetheral to see us." She spoke loudly and her sister darted a rapid, bird-like glance in my direction and looked away again. "My sister's a little deaf. It makes her shy. Now take off your coat, Mr. Wetheral, and come and tell us all about your legacy."

"Well, actually," I said, "I came here to see Miss Lucas."

"There's plenty of time." She gave me a tight-lipped, primly coquettish smile. "That is one thing about Come Lucky; there is always plenty of time. Right now Jean's in her room; reading I expect. She reads a great deal, you know. She's very well educated. But I do think she should get out more in the winter, don't you, Pauline? I'm always telling her education is all very well, but what's the use of it here in Come Lucky. Just put your coat over there, Mr. Wetheral. No, not on that chair—on the stool. Sarah. Mr. Wetheral has come to see Jean."

The other old lady darted me another quick glance and then got up. "I'll go and fetch her, Ruth." She escaped to the door with a quick patter of feet. In appearance she was the image of her sister. But her face was softer, plumper and there was no lorgnette. I gazed round the room. It was fantastic. I was in a little copy of a Victorian drawing-room. An upright piano stood against the wall, the chairs had cross-stitch seats and the back of the armchairs were covered with lace antimacassars. There was even an aspidistra. The whole place, including the occupants with their over-refined speech, was a little period piece in the Canadian wilds.

"Now, Mr. Wetheral, will you sit over there. And you, Pauline—you come and sit by me." She had placed me so that she could sit and watch me. "So you are Mr. Campbell's grandson."

"Yes," I said.

She raised her lorgnette and stared at me. "You don't look very strong, Mr. Wetheral. Have you been ill?"

"I'm convalescing."

"Oh, and your doctors have said the high mountain air will do you good." She nodded as though agreeing with their verdict. "I'm so glad to hear that you are not allowing this little backwater of ours to become an industrial centre again. Do you know, Mr. Wetheral, they even had the Japanese working up here during the war when they were building the dam. I am sure if you were to permit them to complete it they would now have Chinese labour. It is quite terrible to think what might happen. Opium, you know, and now that they are all communists——"

"But wouldn't it be a good thing for Come Lucky?" I said. "It would mean new homes here and a road."

"That is what Peter Trevedian says. But my sister and I remember what it was like here at the beginning of the war. The homes are all very much in the future. Meanwhile we have to put up with the labour gangs. You have no idea what it was like here when they began working on the dam. We hardly dared to go outside the house. They had cabins built for the men up the valley of course, but the old King Harry saloon was converted into a hospital for them and some of the Japanese were actually billeted in the town. Such horrible little men! They shouldn't have been allowed outside their camp, but then Peter Trevedian owns most of Come Lucky and he was collecting rent as well as making money out of the sale of land and the operation of the cable hoist. I am so glad, Mr. Wetheral, you are not a mercenary man. Everybody here——"

"I'm surprised my grandfather agreed to the building of a dam," I said.

"Oh, it wasn't Mr. Campbell. It was Peter Trevedian. It's on his property, you know. I'm sure Luke wouldn't have done it, not when it meant making a lake of Mr. Campbell's property." She gave a little sigh. "I'm afraid Peter is a much harder man than his father." She leaned forward and tapped me playfully on the arm with her lorgnette. "But you are a civilised person, Mr. Wetheral, I can see that. You will stand between us and the factories and things they are planning. My sister and I remember when the mines were working here. You have no idea the sort of men who are attracted by gold. They were most uncouth, weren't they?" She had turned to Pauline. "Oh, of course, you don't remember, child. Do you know, Mr. Wetheral, I remember the days when the street outside was a seething mass of brawling miners. Every other building was a saloon in those days. Really, a girl wasn't safe. We were never allowed out at night and even in the seclusion of our room we were kept awake by the noise they made."

Footsteps sounded in the hall and then Jean Lucas entered

the room. "Mr. Wetheral?" She held out her hand. "I've been expecting for some time."

Her manner was direct, her grip firm. She had the assurance of good breeding. In her well-cut tweed suit she brought a breath of the English countryside into the room. I stared down at her, wondering what on earth she was doing buried up here in this Godforsaken town. Her eyes met mine—grey, intelligent eyes. I think she must have guessed what I was thinking for they had an expression of defiance in them.

"You knew I'd come?" I asked.

She nodded slowly. "I knew your war record. I didn't think you'd let him down."

The room seemed suddenly silent. I could hear the ticking of the clock in its glass case. There seemed nobody there but the two of us. I didn't say anything more. I stood there, staring down at her face. Her skin was pale and there was a tired droop to her mouth which, because the lips were rather full, gave it a sulky look. There were lines on her forehead and lines of strain at the corners of her eyes. The left cheek and jaw were criss-crossed with scars that showed faintly through the skin. The cast of her features seemed to be a reflection of her real self and as I stared at her I suddenly felt I had to know her.

"We'll go into my room, shall we?" she said.

I was dimly aware of Miss Ruth Garret's disapproval. Then I was in a room with a log fire blazing on the hearth and bookshelves crowding the walls. It was furnished as a bed-sitting-room and though most of the furniture belonged to the house, it had a friendly air. White narcissi bloomed in the light of the oil lamp and filled the room with their scent and on the table beside them was a large photograph of an elderly man in Army uniform.

"My father," she said and by the tone of her voice I knew he was dead. A big brown collie lay like a hearthrug before the fire. He thumped his tail and eyed me without stirring. "That's Moses," she said. "He belonged to your grandfather. He found him as a pup in the beaver swamps the other side of the lake. Hence the name." She glanced at me quickly and then bent to pat the dog. "What do you think of my two old ladies?"

"Are they relatives of yours?" I asked.

" No."

" Then why do you live up here?"

" That's my business." Her voice had suddenly become frozen. " There are some cigarettes in the box beside you. Will you pass me one please?"

" Try an English one for a change," I said, producing a packet from my pocket. " I'm sorry," I said. " I shouldn't have tried to——"

" There's no need to apologise." Her eyes met mine over the flame of my lighter. " It's just that I know it's odd and I'm sensitive about it. I imagine you think it was odd of me to live up in the Kingdom with your grandfather during the summer months?"

" Now that I've seen you—yes."

She gave a quick little laugh. " What were you expecting? Something out of Dickens?"

" Perhaps."

She turned away and poked at the fire. " I believe there are still people in the town who are convinced I'm Stuart's illegitimate daughter." She looked up suddenly and smiled. " We call this decrepit bundle of shacks a town, by the way. Would you care for a drink? I've got some Scotch here. Only don't tell my two old dears or I'd get thrown out on to the streets. Naturally they don't approve of liquor—at least Ruth doesn't."

We sat for a while over our drinks without saying anything. It wasn't an uneasy silence though. It seemed natural at the time as though we both needed a moment to sort out our impressions of each other. At length she looked across at me with a faintly inquiring expression. The firelight was glowing on her right cheek and, with the scars not visible, I realised with surprise that she looked quite pretty. " What did you do after the war?" She smiled. " That's a very rude question, but you see Stuart was very anxious to know what had happened to you." She hesitated and then said, " You see, after your mother died he lost touch with home. It was only when I came out here——" She looked away into the fire. " I wrote to friends of mine and I think they got in touch with the War Office. At any rate, they reported that you'd been working in the City before the war and that you'd been a Captain in the R.A.C. out in the Middle East. They couldn't discover what had happened to you after you were invalided out."

"You were very fond of him, weren't you?" I asked.

She nodded. "Enough to hear his voice again in yours. You've something of his manner, too, though not his build. He was a very powerful man." She suddenly looked across at me. "Why did you never write to him or come out and see him? Were you ashamed of him—because he had been to prison?"

"I didn't know his address," I murmured.

"You could have found it out."

"I—I just didn't think about him," I said. "I only met him once. That was all. When I was nine years old."

"When he'd just come out of prison."

"Yes."

"And so you decided you'd forget all about him. Because he'd done five years for—for something he didn't do."

"How was I to know he didn't do it?" I cried, jolted by her attitude out of any pretence that he'd meant nothing in my life. "If you want to know I hated him."

Her eyes widened. "But why?"

"Because of what he did to my life."

"What he did?"

"Oh, he didn't mean to hurt us. Listen. My father died when I was only a few months old. After the war my mother got a job as a nurse. She worked at several hospitals in London and then, when I was nine, we moved to Croydon and she became matron at a boarding school. That was for my benefit so that I could get a good education. Then my grandfather came out of prison. I think there was a paragraph in one of the papers about our meeting him. At any rate, the headmaster learned that my mother was his daughter and he fired her. He let me remain on at the school out of charity. My mother's health broke down then. Nursing became too much for her and she went to work in a clothing factory in the East End of London."

"And what about you?"

"I stayed on at the school until——" I lit another cigarette. I'd never told anybody about this before. "There was some money missing. The boys didn't like me—I didn't wear the right sort of clothes or have the right sort of background.

They believed that I'd taken it and they concocted evidence to fit their beliefs. There was a case. The headmaster produced the information that my grandfather had been to prison. I think he was anxious to get rid of me. I was sent to a reform school. A few months later my mother died. So you see, I hadn't much affection for my grandfather."

She looked at me sadly. "It never occurred to you that he also might have been wrongly convicted?"

"No, it never occurred to me."

She sighed. "It's strange, because you meant a lot to him. You were his only relative. He was an old man when he died, old and tired. Oh, he kept up a front when Johnnie and people brought visitors. But deep down he was tired. He'd lost heart and he needed help."

"Then why didn't he write to me?"

"Pride, I guess. He wasn't the type to cry for help when he was in a spot." She stared at me, frowning slightly. "Would you have come if he'd written to you, if you'd known he was innocent?"

"I—I don't know," I said.

"But you came when you heard he was dead. Why? Because you thought there might be oil here?"

The trace of bitterness in her voice brought me to my feet. "Why I came is my own business," I said harshly. "If you want to know my plan was to live up there."

"Live there." She stared at me. "All the year round?"

"Yes."

"Whatever for?"

I turned and stared angrily at her. "I've my own reasons, the same as you have for living in this dump."

She shifted her gaze to the fire. "Touchée," she said softly. "I only wanted to know——" She hesitated and then got to her feet. "I've some things here that belong to you." She went over to an ottoman and brought out a cardboard box tied with ribbon. "I couldn't bring any more, but these things I know he wanted you to have." She placed the box on a table near me. As she straightened up she said, "There's a question you still haven't answered. What did you do after the war?"

"Just drifted," I said.

"Did you go back to the City?"

"Yes." I was thinking of the grimy brick building in Queen

Victoria Street, of the long room with the typists and adding machines and the little frosted-glass cubicles that had served as offices. She made it sound so damned important.

She hesitated, her hand still on the box. "You said your plan was to live up in the Kingdom?"

I nodded. "Yes, but that was before I came to Come Lucky."

"You've changed your mind then?"

"I didn't know there was a half-completed dam up there."

"I see. So now you're going to sell out and go back to England?"

I laughed. The sound was harsh in that pleasant little room, but it gave vent to my feelings. "It's not as easy as that. I've rather burned my boats. You see, I've emigrated."

"You've——" She stared at me, the thin line of her eyebrows arched in surprise. "You're a queer person," she said slowly. "There's something about you I don't quite understand." She spoke more to herself than to me. I watched her as she went back to her seat by the fire and sat there, gazing into the flames. At length her eyes came round to my face. "What's made you change your mind?"

"How do you mean?"

"When you came here you'd already turned down Henry Fergus's offer for the Kingdom."

"How did you know that?" I asked.

"Gossip." She laughed a trifle nervously. "You can't keep anything secret in this place." She turned and faced me squarely. "Why have you changed your mind?"

"I haven't yet," I told her.

"No, but you're going to." She waited for a moment and when I didn't say anything she said, "I suppose Peter has been getting at you. And the old men. . . ." There was anger and contempt in her voice. "I suppose they've tried to tell you that you're under an obligation to make good some of their losses?"

She seemed to expect some sort of reply so I said, "Well, I suppose from their point of view I am being a little unreasonable."

"Unreasonable! Was it Stuart's fault they went oil-crazy and bought up half the mountain peaks around here regardless of the geological possibilities just because he reported a big oil seep at the head of Thunder Creek." She leaned suddenly forward. "Do you think they helped him when things went wrong? When he was on trial in England for fraud they swore affidavits that he was a liar and a cheat. And when he came back here they hounded him up into the Kingdom so that all the last years of his life were spent in solitude and hardship. When Luke Trevedian died Stuart hadn't a friend in Come Lucky. You owe the people here nothing. Nothing." She paused for breath. The fierceness of her tone had had something personal in it and I found myself unconsiously toying with the idea that she might after all be the old man's natural child. "Now you're here," she added in a quieter tone, "don't believe everything people tell you. Please. Check everything for yourself."

She spoke as though I had all the time in the world. I passed my hand wearily across my eyes. "Am I to take it that you believe my grandfather was right?"

She nodded slowly. "Yes. It was impossible to live with him for any length of time and not believe him. He had tremendous faith—in himself and in other people, and in God. He wouldn't understand that some people——" She stopped, her mouth suddenly a tight, hard line. "I met many fine men—during the war. But he was one of the finest. . . ." Her voice died and she stared into the flames. "I want him to be proved right." Her hand had tightened on her jaw. "I want desperately for the world to know that he wasn't a crank, that he believed everything he said and that it was the truth."

"But what about this survey?" I said. "I understand it proved conclusively that there was no oil in the Kingdom."

"Of course it did. Do you think Henry Fergus would have agreed to postpone his plans for a whole season without ensuring that the results proved what he wanted them to prove? I tried to warn Stuart. But he was getting old. He couldn't believe he wouldn't get a straight deal from his old friend Roger Fergus. He couldn't understand that Roger Fergus was an old man, too—that it was his son, Henry, who really controlled his affairs. And Henry has all the meanness of a man who has taken over wealth that someone else has made for him." She looked across at me. "Before you do anything, go and talk to Boy Bladen. He's here in Come Lucky now. Ask him what he thinks of that report."

"But——" I stared at her. "I've already spoken to Bladen. He agrees with it."

"He does not." Her eyes were wide. "Ever since he saw the results of the first charge he's been as enthusiastic as your grandfather. It just isn't true that he agrees with the report."

"Well, that's what he told me, and scarcely two hours ago."

"I'll talk to him," she said. "He's coming to see me this evening. There's something behind this. I'll send him straight over to see you when he leaves here."

I was suddenly remembering the expression of violent anger on Bladen's face as he had pushed past me on the steps of Trevedian's office. "Yes," I said. "Perhaps if you have a talk with him——"

There was a knock at the door and Miss Ruth Garret entered with a tray. "I've brought you some tea, dear." Her sharp, inquisitive eyes seemed to miss nothing.

"That's very kind of you." Jean Lucas got up and took the tray. "Is Pauline still here?"

"Yes, she's waiting for Mr. Wetheral."

"We won't be long."

Miss Garret stood there uncertainly for a moment, her eyes fixed on the box on the table beside me. Then she turned reluctantly and left us. "Poor old thing," Jean said. "She just loves to know everything. Once they went as far as Prince George and saw the river steamers and the trains. That was thirty years ago and I don't think they've been out of Come Lucky since." She glanced at the box beside me. "You'd better have a look at the things I brought down for you. It may help you to learn something about your grandfather.

I took the box on my knees, slipped the ribbon off and lifted the lid. Inside everything had been carefully wrapped in tissue paper. There were faded photographs and medals from the first war. A little silver tobacco jar carried the outline of an oil rig on the lid and inside the inscription: *To Stuart Campbell from the Management of the Excelsior Oil Company of Turner Valley on his leaving to form his own company—April 8, 1912. Good luck, Stuart!* The first of the signatures was Roger Fergus. There were several other personal oddments, including a mining diploma.

As I laid them out on the table beside me, I said, "When

did he give you these?" I was thinking he must have known he was going to die.

" He didn't give them to me. I brought them down myself. I knew what he wanted you to have. I suppose I should have sent them on to you, but I didn't know your address and somehow I was convinced you'd come here yourself."

" You went up after his death?" I asked.

" Yes."

" By the hoist?"

" No, the hoist wasn't working then."

" But——" I was trying to reconcile this quiet rather tense girl with the journey up those mountain slopes to the cleft of Solomon's Judgment. " Do you mean to say you went up there on your own?"

" Of course." She smiled. " There's an old Indian trail. It's only a day's journey each way. I just wanted to be sure that everything was all right."

" But when I saw Johnnie Carstairs in Jasper he said the snows had started and he had great difficulty in getting his party down."

" Yes, I know. But afterwards the chinook started blowing and when the snows had gone I decided to go up. I'm afraid I could only bring some of the lighter things. But you'll find a lot of rock specimens at the bottom. He was very anxious always that you should have those. They were evidence in support of his case."

" Is his Bible here by any chance?" I asked, starting to remove the specimens which were also wrapped in tissue paper.

" Yes. Why do you ask?"

" He said there would be some papers with it." I pulled it out and removed the tissue paper. It was about a quarter the size of an old-fashioned family Bible, bound in leather and held by a leather tab and a gilt hasp. " Have you got the key?" I asked her.

" No. He carried it on a little silver chain round his neck." She was staring into the fire again. " There was a signet ring and a gold watch and chain you should have had, too. But they buried him just as he was." She got up slowly and brought me a pair of scissors. " You'll have to cut it."

I slit the leather above the hasp and opened the book. It seemed in a way sacrilegious, for I was opening it to find papers whereas the owner had always been opening it in order to read. But there were no papers. I riffled through the pages. A single sheet of notepaper fell out. I stared at it, wondering where the progress report had got to. And then the contents of the note riveted my attention:

> *The Kingdom,*
> *20th November,*

Dear Bruce,

When you read this the Kingdom will be yours. I shall not last the winter. And I have no longer the energy or the will to fight for my beliefs.

This day I have received the results of Bladen's survey. The chart shows a quite unbelievable jumble of rock strata below the surface. I have it before me as I write together with the consultant's report. . . .

I stared at the paragraph and read it through again. Then I looked across at Jean.

"What is it?" she asked.

"I thought he died without knowing the results of that survey?" I said.

She nodded. "Yes. I was so glad. I don't think he understood what a seismographic survey was exactly, but he knew the oil companies could be convinced if the survey were successful and in view of Boy's reaction he was very optimistic that at last——"

"He knew the result," I said.

"But that's impossible. Johnnie was the last person up there—except for me."

"Well, listen to this," I said. "*This day I have received the results of Bladen's survey.*"

"But——" She was staring at me, her eyes wide. "When was it written?" She held out her hand. "Let me see."

"It was written on the 20th November," I said. "Johnnie Carstairs found him on the 22nd." I passed her the sheet of paper.

She stared at it unbelievingly. "*It is clear, therefore——*" her voice trembled as she read—"*that in the upheaval which raised these mountains, as might be expected, such disturbance of the rock strata occurred as to make the possibility of oil-traps, either stratigraphical or in the form of anticlines, quite out of the question."* Her voice died away and she stared at the paper which trembled violently in her hands. "Oh, my God!" she breathed. Her hands clenched suddenly. "How could they be so cruel?" She turned on me, her face suddenly older and stronger in the violence of her feeling. "What an incredible, beastly way to kill a man—to kill him through his hopes. If they'd stuck a knife into him——" She turned away struggling to get control of herself. "Here." She thrust the letter out to me. "Read the rest of it, will you. I can't."

I took the crumpled sheet and spread it out:

. . . so finally I have to face the fact that I can do no more. You may regard this as the obstinacy of a cranky old man set in his beliefs. I only ask you to remember that I have been studying rock strata all my life and I absolutely refuse to believe that the very broken nature of the strata below the Kingdom as shown by this survey can be correct. You have only to look at the fault at the head of Thunder Creek to know this to be true. Further, though I cannot vouch for there being oil, I do know there was oil here in 1911 when the big slide occurred. The trap that held that oil must have shown on the chart if this survey were accurate. I fear there are things moving that I do not understand living alone here in my kingdom.

My final and urgent request to you is that you somehow find the money to test my beliefs by drilling, which is the only sure method. Do this before they complete the dam and drown the Kingdom for ever.

I pray God you will accept the mantle of my beliefs and wear it to the damnation of my enemies. God keep you, and if I am wrong know that I shall be suffering the torments of the Damned for I shall have wasted half of the life God gave me.

Affectionately and with Great Hopes of You
Stuart Campbell.

My hands dropped to my knees and I sat staring at the fire, seeing in my mind the old man writing that last pitful plea, knowing that there were people down in the valley who hated him enough to climb through a snow storm to give him the bad news before winter closed in on him. "I'd like to get my hands on the man that took that report up to him." My voice grated harshly on the silence of the room.

"If they'd killed him with their own hands," Jean whispered, "they couldn't have done it more cruelly."

"Who hated him that much?"

"Oh, George Riley, the Trevedians, the McClellans, Daniel Smith, the Hutterite, Ed Schiffer—everybody who'd lost money." She turned to me suddenly. "You've got to prove him right. He had such faith in you."

I leaned back and stared at the fire. That was all very well, but it meant drilling. It meant time and money, and I hadn't much of either. "I'll see what Bladen has to say."

She nodded and then rose slowly to her feet. "You must go now. He'll be here shortly and I don't want him to meet you before I've talked to him. Besides——" She hesitated. "He has fits of moodiness that I don't think you'd understand, and I want you to like him."

I had also got to my feet and I wondered what was coming. She was staring down at her nails, her fingers interlocked. Suddenly she raised her head. "I think perhaps I'd better tell you something about him, just in case other people start talking to you first. Boy is the only son of the Canadian actor, Basil Bladen. His mother was a full-blooded Iroquois. The Iroquois, by the way are one of the few Indian tribes that have been absorbed into the white man's world without ill effects. But it still didn't work out. This was some time ago, mind you. I think it would be different now. They were idyllically happy, but Basil Bladen began to find parts difficult to get, particularly in the States where he had been very well known. It was the usual story: he took to drink. He became a dipsomaniac. His resting periods became longer and longer and eventually he couldn't even get parts in Canada. When they were flat broke he shot his wife and then himself." She paused. "Boy was thirteen at the time."

"Who brought him up," I asked.

She shrugged her shoulders. "Life, I guess. He's been everything—gold prospector, trapper, Hudson's Bay Company trader. Then he took to flying. He became one of the best bush fliers in the North Western Territories. Maybe that was the Indian in him. He could find his way anywhere. Then the war came and he was shot down in flames over Germany.

That's where he got the scar and the burned hands. He had a year in a prison camp and when he came back to Canada he found he couldn't fly any more. His eyesight was bad and he'd lost his nerve." She looked up at me and added, " I wanted you to know about him so that——" She shrugged her shoulders. " He's a queer mixture of daring, poetry and utter, wretched silence. He's full of childish enthusiasm one minute and then suddenly it's gone and he's silent and moody and goes off on his own." She gave a quick laugh. " I'm afraid I've made him sound very odd indeed. But he's one of the nicest men. . . ." She turned towards the door. " Pauline will be getting tired of waiting."

She took me back to the Victorian drawing-room and the two old ladies. A few minutes later I was walking through wet snow in the dark, dismal street of Come Lucky.

V

WALKING back to the hotel my mind unconsciously dwelt on the hatred these people had for my grandfather and thinking about this had a queer effect on the way I saw Come Lucky. The place was no longer just an ordinary shack town that was gradually falling into ruin. The desolation seemed suddenly to have a menace of its own. It had become something alive and positive. The hardness of the mountains seemed to have moved in among the dark shapes crouched against the glimmer of the snow and as I negotiated the crumbling sidewalk, clutching the cardboard box under my arm, I felt fear creeping up my spine and prickling my scalp.

I think something of this communicated itself to Pauline for she suddenly said, " How long will you be staying here?"

" I don't know," I answered.

Her hand tightened on my arm. " Do not forget the winters are long here."

" How do you mean?"

We had reached The Golden Calf. Lights showed through the window and there was a murmur of voices. She paused with her hand on the door. " Things that are small to you become big to us here at this time of the year."

I remembered the Victorian drawing-room and the sharp

grey eyes of Miss Garret avid for gossip, the sudden violence of Max Trevedian and the sullenness of James McClellan. The wind blew up the valley with the damp chill of the sea. The water gurgled under the snow.

"We will go in through the bar," Pauline said. "The snow is too soft now for us to go round the back. It is always like this when the chinook is blowing." She pressed the latch of the door and pushed it open. The murmur of voices died as we entered. There were fully a dozen men clustered round the fire now and they stared at us with the dumb, curious gaze of cattle scenting a stranger. "Here he is now," one of them hissed. "Give him the telegram, Hut." I saw Peter Trevedian watching me. He was sitting with his brother at one of the tables. Bladen was there, too, talking to Mac.

An old man with long, sad moustaches rose slowly and came towards me. He was dressed all in black with a shapeless, wide-brimmed hat on his head and he was as slim-hipped as a boy. "You Bruce Wetheral?" His voice was mild and gentle.

"Yes," I said.

"Then this'll be for you, I guess." He held out a telegraph form. "I brought'n in from Keithley this evenin'."

The paper was creased and much thumbed. I opened it out and took it to the lamp, wondering who could possibly know I was here. *Bruce Wetheral, Come Lucky, B.C.* The message read: *Have persuaded Larsen Company to increase offer. Urgent I see you. Hope arrive Come Lucky Tuesday, bringing Henry Fergus, chairman Larsen Mines. Please await our arrival. Vital we finally come to terms re purchase of Kingdom or alternative plan will definitely be adopted. Signed— Acheson.* I glanced at the head of the form. It had been handed in at Calgary at 4.10 p.m.

The silence in the room was intense as I stuffed it into my pocket. The men's eyes fixed hungrily on my face and it was obvious that they knew the contents of that wire. The beast that had crouched out there in the darkness of the tattered town seemed to have moved into the huge, empty bar-room. I turned quickly and started for the door, intent upon escaping to my room.

But the old man who had given me the wire barred my way. "We'd take it as a favour if you'd spare us a moment of your time," he said.

"What is it?" I asked him.

He tugged awkwardly at his moustache. "We-ell. It's like this, I guess, Mr. Wetheral. What we want to know is—are you going to sell or not?"

"I don't see that it concerns you." I tried to keep my voice natural, but it sounded abrupt against the tension in that room.

He stared at me. "You wouldn't understand, I guess. You're a stranger here. But the completion of the Solomon's Judgment dam means a lot to us. You've seen what Come Lucky is—they call it a ghost town." He suddenly raised a gnarled fist and declaimed. "The wrath of the Lord descended upon it and upon us, its inhabitants. Fire and brimstone was sent to destroy the cities of Sodom and Gomorrah. Here for our sins the Lord has sent age and decay." His eyes gleamed like bright stones as he got into his stride. "We came from far places, from decent communities of honest, hard-working people, lured by the riches of gold and oil. We worshipped Mammon and we were abased. We worshipped the golden calf and the Lord sent avalanches to destroy our mines. Oil sprang from the rocks and we took it for a sign." He flung wide his arms like some fantastic scarecrow. "I tell you it was the Devil who——"

"It was old man Campbell, Hut," somebody cut in.

"Campbell was the instrument—the means of our temptation," the old man cried. "We were tempted. We forgot the forty days in the wilderness. We forgot the words of the Holy Book. We were tempted and we fell, and for our sins the Lord decreed that our sons should leave us and our town decay, that we should waste our lives in fruitless hopes and finally perish and be sentenced to everlasting Hell fire."

"Come to the point, Hut." It was the man with the fur cap.

The old man glared at the interruption. "Peace, George Riley. *The way of the wicked is as darkness.* We have been tempted and have fallen into evil ways, but the day of our redemption is nigh." And then, reverting to his ordinary voice with startling abruptness, he added, "You, sir, hold the power to redeem us."

"What he means is that if they complete the dam Come Lucky will have a new lease of life." This from James

McClellan. He turned to his wife. "You clear off, Pauline. You shouldn't be in here." His eyes slipped back to me, hard and anxious. "You may not realise it, but your grandfather is largely responsible for the way things are in this town. This damned story of oil flowing out of the rocks below the Kingdom was believed by my father and most of the men in this room now. Campbell talked them into putting——"

"He was the Devil himself," the old Hutterite cried. "The Devil himself come to tempt us. He offered us riches and we sold our families into slavery and brought ruin to our town. Wretched is he——"

"Campbell was a swindler." The cry piped shrilly from Max Trevedian's huge bulk. "A bloodsucking——"

"Shut up, Max." Peter Trevedian's quiet voice silenced his brother instantly.

"Max is right," McClellan said. "Your grandfather got the people of this town to put their money into his oil companies and they lost everything. The place gradually fell into decay and when their sons and daughters grew up they left home and went——"

"The sins of the fathers——" the old man cried.

"Oh, for God's sake, Hut." McClellan half shrugged his shoulders and then he came slowly across the room towards me. "See here, Wetheral. Your grandfather was an obstinate old man. He thought more of his damned Kingdom than he did of the people he'd ruined." There was a growl of agreement. "This scheme has been talked about for more than a year now. But he wouldn't sell and he swore he wouldn't leave. They didn't dare drown the old——" He left the sentence unfinished and his hand clenched tight. "The damned visitors who came up here regarded him as a character. They went up there and filled him full of rye and listened to his stories. Newspaper men, too. They wrote columns about him and they'd have fought the company if they'd tried to flood him out. Well, he's dead now. And nobody ain't going to fight for you, Wetheral. You're a stranger here." He looked round the men at the tables. "We want to be sure that you're not going to stand in the way of the townsfolk here the way the old man did."

The others nodded. "We want to be certain sure you're going to sell to the company," the bundle of old rags with the fur cap said in a reedy voice. "If you do that then there'll be money in Come Lucky again, I guess. I can open up my store. Ain't bin open since 1941."

"George is right," exclaimed another. "There'll be money, and work for those that want it. Peter'll have the cable going again, won't you, Peter? There'll be all the machinery to haul up and the materials to complete the dam. It'll be like old times here in Come Lucky."

"It sure will."

"Well?" McClellan asked. "What are you going to do? Let's have it right here and now so that we know where we stand."

"Ar. Let's hear now."

I stared at them, all eyeing me, all silent now, waiting. McClellan's eyes were fixed on me greedily. And suddenly all of them seemed to have the hunger of greed in their eyes, as though the old boom days were just around the corner. They were like a bunch of shiftless curs eyeing a bone.

"Well?" The old Hutterite's voice was hard with eagerness.

"I'm not selling," I said.

Peter Trevedian's chair flung back against the wall with a crash as he got to his feet. "You said you were going to think it over."

"I've done so," I said. "And I've made up my mind. I'm not selling."

He swung round on the others. "I told you what it would be. We're going to have the same damned nonsense all over again." He got control of himself then and came towards me. "Look, the townsfolk here want this scheme to go through. It's important to them." His tone was considered and reasonable, but his eyes were hard and angry as they stared at me. "You owe it to the people your grandfather ruined."

"And suppose he was right?" I said.

"What—about the oil?"

There was a hoot of laughter.

"Then show us the river of oil," somebody called out. And another shouted, "Aye. You drown Come Lucky with oil. We'll drown the Kingdom with water. See who's flooded out first." A shout of laughter followed this.

Under cover of it Trevedian said quietly, "Take my advice, sell the place and get out."

I turned to Bladen. "Tell me the truth about that survey," I said.

"Oh, to hell with the survey," Trevedian snapped. "Why don't you think about the people here for a change?"

"Why should I?" I cried. "What did they ever do for my grandfather except try and cash in on his discovery and then blame him when they lost their money. I might have been willing to sell out——" I looked round at the group facing me. The watery eyes of the old men glistened in the lamplight. They looked as ghostly as the town and their eyes had the fever-brightness of men about to jump a claim. "But I've just discovered that my grandfather knew the results of that survey. Somebody took a copy of the report up to him just before winter set in."

"What's that got to do with it?" James McClellan demanded.

"Just this." My voice trembled. "In my opinion the man who did that was responsible for my grandfather's death. Because of that the welfare of this town is no longer a consideration as far as I'm concerned. And if I knew who'd done it——"

"If you knew, what would you do, huh?" Max Trevedian had thrust his massive body to its feet. "I took that report up. I gave it to Campbell." He lurched forward, hot hate in his eyes. "It killed him, did it? That is good."

I stared at the foolish grin on his thick lips. "You're mad," I heard myself say.

"How was my brother to know that the report showed there was no possibility of oil up there?" Peter Trevedian said . "We naturally thought the old man would want to know the result."

I turned to him, staring at him. "You sent your brother up with that report," I said.

He nodded. "Yes. I sent him."

"And how did you get hold of a second copy?" He didn't say anything, but just stood smiling at me. "Did this man Henry Fergus send it to you?"

He moved a step closer and his hand gripped my arm. "What do you think we are—a bunch of cattle to be sucked dry without any feelings about it? There's forty years of hatred stored up in this town, hatred of Campbell and everything he did to us." He dropped my arm and turned away.

I looked round at the others. What I had seen in his eyes was reflected in theirs. It was then I noticed that Bladen had left. Feeling suddenly sick at heart I crossed to the door and went up to the seclusion of my room. It was bare and cold and very quiet. I put the cardboard box gently down on the chest of drawers. I had been clutching it very tightly as though it were the old man's ashes and my fingers were stiff. My face looked grey and haggard in the blotched mirror. I poured myself a stiff whisky, but the liquor didn't warm me and I was still shaking as I slumped down on to the bed. The stillness seemed to close round me, the embodiment of the utter loneliness I felt. The scene in the bar-room had given me a foretaste of the struggle that lay ahead. All I had wanted to do was to crawl away to the seclusion of my grandfather's kingdom and forget the outside world. I heard myself laugh. I hadn't known the place was dominated by a half-completed dam. That dam was growing in my imagination to nightmare proportions. It seemed to hang over me.

I must have fallen asleep for I was suddenly startled by a knock on the door. "Come in," I murmured. It was Pauline McClellan. She stood looking at me nervously. "Are you all right?"

"Yes," I said, pushing myself up on to my elbow. "What is it?"

"Boy Bladen is down below. He wants to talk to you. Shall I tell him to come up?"

"Yes."

She hesitated. "Is there anything I can get you?"

"No thanks."

"Goodnight then." She smiled and closed the door. I sat up and lit a cigarette. A moment later I heard Bladen's feet on the stairs. He knocked and pushed open the door. "Mind if I come in?" His voice was quiet, but his dark eyes had a peculiar brightness. He shut the door and stood there, hesitantly. "I've just been talking to Jean."

He didn't seem to know how to go on so I said, "Pull up a chair."

I don't think he heard me for he turned away towards the window. "When you spoke to me after tea this evening I didn't know you'd emigrated to Canada, prepared to live up in the Kingdom and start out where Stuart had left off."

He turned suddenly round on his heels, a quick, lithe movement. "Why didn't you tell me that?"

"I didn't see any necessity," I murmured.

"No, of course not." He lit a cigarette with quick, nervous movements. I had the feeling of something boiling up inside him. "You were outside Trevedian's office this afternoon. How much did you hear of what we were saying?"

"Enough I think to understand why you agreed with the report on your survey."

"You knew all the time I wasn't being honest with you?"

"No," I said. "It was only when Jean Lucas confirmed that you'd been enthusiastic about the prospects of finding oil in the Kingdom that I began to put two and two together."

"I see." He turned away again towards the window. "I'm sorry," he said, still with his back to me. "I thought you were just out to get the best price you could for the property. I thought. . . . Hell!" he said, turning sharply and facing me. "I was scared of losing my trucks. I've a lot of dough tied up in that equipment and if Trevedian had refused to bring them down the hoist——" He shrugged his shoulders. "All I've made in years of flying and in prospecting since the war is invested in that outfit."

He suddenly pulled up a chair and sat down astride it, his hands gripping the back. "Now then, about the survey I did: I don't know what the hell Winnick has been playing at, but I formed the impression I was surveying a perfect anticline. I can't be sure. I'd need to plot the figures I got on a seismogram. But that was certainly my impression. It ran just about east and west across the Kingdom. Whether the nature of the rock strata was likely to be oil bearing I wouldn't know. You have to be an expert geologist to determine that. But I do know this—the report Winnick made on the figures I sent him is a lot of hooey. I was never more surprised in my life than when I saw that article in the *Edmonton Journal*. I came across it quite by chance in a bar in Peace River. I was in town for a couple of days' rest from the wildcat I was working on. I wrote to Louis right away, but all he said in reply was that if I cared to come and check the figures against the seismograms his office had prepared I'd find them accurate." He paused and blew out a streamer of smoke. "Maybe I slipped up. I'm not an expert and I've only been in the game three years. But I took time out to get a working knowledge of how the results of a seismographic survey were worked out and I can't believe that the figures I sent him could have given the results he reported."

" Have you seen him?" I asked.

" No. I haven't had a chance. I've only just come off this wildcat. But I will."

" You know him, do you?"

" Oh, sure. I know him all right."

" Is he straight?"

" Louis Winnick? Straight as a die. He wouldn't be old Roger Fergus's consultant if he weren't. Why. What's on your mind?"

" I was just wondering how he could have produced a report that differs so violently from your impression."

" Well, maybe I was wrong. But Jean asked me to come and tell you what I really thought."

" Have you checked your figures with the ones Winnick worked from?"

" I tell you, I haven't seen him. But as soon as I get back to Calgary——" He stopped. " What are you getting at?"

" Did you take the results of your survey down to Winnick yourself?"

" Of course not. I was working up in the Kingdom all the time. We sent them to him in batches."

" How?"

" We had them mailed from Keithley."

" Yes, but how did you get them down to Keithley?"

" By the hoist. Max Trevedian was running supplies up to us and each week——" He stopped then. " Of course. All they had to do was substitute the figures of some unsuccessful survey." He jumped up to his feet and began pacing violently up and down the room. " No wonder Trevedian needed to be sure I kept my mouth shut." He stopped by the window and stood there, silent for a long time, drawing on his cigarette. " There's something about the Kingdom," he said slowly. " It clings to the memory like a woman who wants to bear children and is looking for a man to father them. Last year, when I left, I had a feeling I should be coming back. There is a destiny about places. For each man there is a piece of territory that calls to him, that appeals to something deep inside him. I've travelled half the world. I know the northern territories and the Arctic regions of Canada like my own hand. But nothing ever called to me with the fatal insistence of the Kingdom. All this winter it has been in my mind, and I have been afraid of it." He turned slowly and faced me, eyes alight as though he had seen a vision. " I just wanted to get my trucks and go. But now. . . ." He half-shrugged his shoulders and came towards me. " Jean said you wanted to prove Stuart right." His voice was suddenly practical. " She said you'd got guts and you'd do it if you had someone in with you to handle the technical side."

" She's right about the first part," I said. " But it means drilling."

" Sure it means drilling. But——" He hesitated. " How much is a drilling operation worth to you?"

I laughed then. " All I've got is a few hundred dollars."

" I don't mean that." He resumed his seat astride the chair facing me. " Look. If I find the capital and the equipment, will you split fifty-fifty? By that I mean fifty-fifty of all profits resulting from drilling operations in the Kingdom."

" Aren't you anticipating a bit?" I said. " Even supposing your survey did show an anticline, you admit yourself it doesn't necessarily mean there's oil there."

He nodded slowly. " You're too damn level-headed," he said, grinning. " All right. Let's take it step by step. To-morrow I'll leave for Calgary. I'll have a talk with Louis and look over the figures from which he prepared that report. Meantime, you get up to the Kingdom just as soon as they get the road through and the hoist working. You'll find my trucks in one of the barns there. Somewhere in the instrument truck there are the results of the final surveys I did. In the worry of not being able to get my trucks out I forgot all about them. Bring them down with you and mail them direct to Louis. While you're doing that I'll go and see old Roger Fergus. He's always been very good to me. I used to pilot for him quite a lot in the old days. He's a pretty sick man now, but if I could get him interested he might put up the dough." He got to his feet, a gleam of excitement in his dark eyes. " Ever since I started in on this business I've dreamed of bringing in a well, of seeing the thing through right from the survey to the completion of drilling, knowing I had a stake in the result. If I can make Roger Fergus a proposition——" He paused and lit another cigarette. "Would you split fifty-fifty for the chance of proving Stuart right?"

"Of course," I said. "But——"

He held up his hand. "Leave it to me. Roger Fergus is an old man and he's a gambler. That's why he put up the dough for the survey. I don't think he believed in Stuart, but he'd lost a lot of money in his ventures and he was willing to take a chance."

"The only person you could do it with is Fergus," I said. "Otherwise we'd be up against his son's company. Besides, he owns the mineral rights. Of course," I added, " if you could get one of the big companies interested——"

He laughed. "There's oil in the Rocky Mountains! You try and sell them that one. They've been caught for a million dollars on one wildcat in the Rockies and it brought in a dry well. No, if we're going to bring in a well, it will have to be without the help of the companies." He turned towards the door. "You leave it to me. So long as I have your assurance that you're perpared to split fifty-fifty?"

"Of course," I said.

"Okay then. You let Louis have those figures just as soon as you can get them. His office is on Eighth Avenue. I forget the number——"

"I've got his address," I said. "His office is right next door to Henry Fergus and the Larsen Company."

He glanced at me quickly. "You don't think—— Look, Bruce, Winnick is okay. There's nothing crooked about him. That I'm certain of. I'll talk to him and then I'll see the old man. I'll wire you as soon as I've any news."

"And what about your trucks"?

"Oh, to hell with the trucks," he grinned. "Anyway, we'll maybe need them to check on the anticline." He took hold of the handle of the door. "I'll leave you now. Jean said you were pretty tired. It's the altitude. You'll soon get used to it. Goodnight."

"Goodnight," I said. "And thanks for your help."

He smiled. "Time enough to thank me when we bring in a well."

The door closed and I was alone again. I lit another cigarette and lay back on the bed. The thing seemed suddenly to have moved beyond me. I didn't feel I had the energy to cope with it.

During the next few days I saw quite a lot of Jean Lucas. She found me an old pair of skis and with the dog we trekked as far as the timber and across the lake to a little torrent where trout could be seen swimming in the dark pool among the rocks. She was a queer, quiet girl. She never talked for the sake of talking, only when she had something factual to say. She seemed a little afraid of words and mostly we trekked in silence. When we did talk she always kept the conversation away from herself. I found these expeditions very exhausting physically, but I didn't tell her that because I enjoyed them. And they had one advantage, they made me sleep better than I had done in years.

Meantime, Creasy and his construction gang broke through the fall where the avalanche had carried the old road away and the talk after the evening meal was all of opening up the camp at the head of the creek and getting the hoist working.

When I got in on the Saturday Mac handed me a slip of paper. "Telegram for ye," he said. It was from Bladen. "*Convinced figures not mine. Send Winnick those from Kingdom soonest possible. Roger Fergus died two days ago. Leaving for Peace River. Signed—Bladen.*" I looked across at the old man. "How did this come?" I asked.

"The telephone line has been repaired," he said. "They phoned it through to me from Keithley."

I thanked him and went up to my room. So Roger Fergus was dead and that was that. I was sorry. There'd been something about him, a touch of the pioneer, and he had been my grandfather's friend. And then I remembered how he'd talked of our meeting again soon and I shivered.

When Creasy got in that night he announced that they were through to the camp. "We're wondering about the hoist," he said to James McClellan.

"You don't have to," McClellan answered. "It'll work all right—I built it to last."

"Aye, ye did that," his father said and there was a sneer in the old man's voice.

Hot, sudden anger flared in the younger man's eyes. "Lucky I did," he said. "Ain't anything more useless than a hoist that don't work, I guess; unless it's a gold mine that's covered by a hundred feet of slide—or the mineral rights in a country that ain't got any oil."

Father and son glared at each other sullenly. Then the older man shrugged his shoulders. " Aye, ye may be right, Jamie."

The son thrust his chair back and got to his feet. " You'll get your money back," he said sullenly.

When I went down to see Jean that evening it was raining hard and blowing half a gale from the west. Miss Sarah Garret opened the door to me. " Come in, Mr. Wetheral, come in." She shut the door. " My sister and I were so sorry to hear about the death of Roger Fergus."

I stared at her. "How did you know he was dead?"

" But you received a telegram from Boy to-day saying so."

I wondered whether Trevedian, too, knew the contents of that wire yet and if so what he was going to do about it. I wished now I had told Bladen to write.

". . . such a distinguished-looking man. He came here several times. That was when he was interested in Mr. Campbell's oil company. You're very like Mr. Campbell, you know." She cocked a bird-like glance at me. " Not in appearance, of course. But in—in some indefinable way. Things always happened in Come Lucky when Mr. Campbell was around. And I do like things happening, don't you?" She smiled at me and here eyes twinkled. " So sensible of you to get Boy to do the organising of your venture."

" Why?" I asked.

" Why?" She tapped me with her fingers. " Go on with you. Think I don't know why? I was young once, you know, and I understand only too well how lonely it can be for a girl up here in Come Lucky."

" But——" I didn't know what to say as she stood there twinkling at me. " I didn't send Boy to Calgary," I said.

" Of course not. You just let his enthusiasm run away with him." She gave a little tinkling laugh and then turned quickly at the sound of footsteps. " Ah, here she is," she said as Jean entered the room.

" I gather you know about the wire I got from Boy," I said.

She nodded. " Miss McClellan was here two hours ago with the details of it. The news will be all over Come Lucky by now." She took me through into her own room. "You look tired," she said.

"I feel it," I answered. "Fergus's death——" I hesitated. I think it was only then that the full implication of it dawned on me. I suddenly found myself laughing. It was so damned ironical.

"Please," she cried. She had hold of my arm and was shaking me. "What is it?"

"Nothing," I said, controlling myself. "Only that Henry Fergus will now inherit the mineral rights of the Kingdom."

She turned and stared at the fire. "I hadn't thought of that." She reached for my arm. "But it'll work out. You see." Her eyes were suddenly bright. "You've got a good partner in Boy. He'll get the backing you need."

She had spoken with unusual warmth. "Are you in love with him?" I asked.

She stared at me in sudden shocked surprise and then turned away. "We'll talk about the Kingdom, not me if you don't mind," she said in a voice that trembled slightly. She sat down slowly by the fire and stared for a moment into the flames, lost in her own thoughts.

"Why has Boy gone to Peace River, do you know?" I asked her.

She stared slightly. "Has he? I didn't know." Her voice was flat. She turned her head and looked at me. "He was working there during the winter."

For some reason she had withdrawn into herself. I left shortly after that and returned to the hotel. I was tired anyway. The rain streamed down, steel rods against the lamplit windows of the bar, drilling holes in the greying snow. Jean had lent me several books; rare things in Come Lucky—the hotel only had American magazines and a few glossy paper backs with lurid jackets. I planned to laze and read myself quietly to sleep. As I was starting upstairs Pauline came out of the kitchen. "Going to bed already, Bruce?"

"Can you suggest anything better for me to do in Come Lucky?" I asked her.

She smiled a trifle uncertainly. "I am sorry," she murmured. "It is very dull here." She hesitated. "And I am afraid we have not been very 'ospitable." And then quickly, as though she wanted to say it before she forgot. "Jimmy is going up to the dam to-morrow."

"Do you mean up to the top, to the Kingdom?" I asked. She nodded.

"When?"

"They leave to-morrow after breakfast—he is going with Ben."

"Why do you tell me this?"

"He ask me to tell you."

"Why?"

She hesitated. "Perhaps he thinks that if you see the dam for yourself you will understand what it means to him and to the others." She leaned forward and touched my arm. "You will go with him, won't you, Bruce? He wants so badly for you to understand why it is we do not want this scheme to fall through. If you could see the hoist that he built. . . ." She stopped awkwardly. "He is not unfriendly really, you know. It is only that he is worried. The farm is not doing well and this hotel——" She shrugged her shoulders. "The visitors are not enough to keep a barn like this running."

"Tell him I'd like to come with him, provided he'll take me to the top if the hoist is working."

"Yes, I will tell him that." She flashed me a smile. "Goodnight, Bruce."

"Goodnight, Pauline."

I went up to my room, suddenly too excited to think of reading. At last I was going to get a glimpse of the Kingdom.

I awoke to find daylight creeping into the room. The wind still howled and a sheet of corrugated iron clanked dismally. But the rain had ceased. The clouds had lifted, ragged wisps sailing above cold, white peaks. Footsteps sounded on the bare boards below and a door banged. Then silence again; silence except for the relentless sound of the wind and the gurgle of water seeking its natural level, starting on its long journey to the Pacific.

I was called at seven. The old Chinaman shuffled across the room to the wash basin with a steaming jug of water. "You sleep well, Mister?" His wrinkled face smiled at me disinterestedly as he gave me the same greeting he had given me every morning I had been there. "Snow all gone. Plenty water. Plenty mud. You get to the dam okay to-day."

By the time I had finished breakfast James McClellan was waiting for me. He took me down to the bunkhouse through a sea of mud. There was a truck there and Max Trevedian was loading drums of diesel fuel into the back of it.

"All set?" I turned to find Peter Trevedian slithering down through the mud towards us. He wore an old flying jacket, the fur collar turned up, and a shaggy, bearskin cap.

"Just about," McClellan said.

Max Trevedian paused with one of the drums on his shoulders. "You are going to Campbell's Kingdom to-day." He had a foolish expectant look on his face, and his eyes were excited.

"We're going to the dam," his brother replied, glancing at me.

"The dam—the Kingdom, same thing," Max growled. "We go together, huh?"

"No."

"But——" His thick, loose lips trembled. I thought how like the lips of a horse they were. "But I must go up. You tell me he do not rest. You tell me——"

"Shut up!" His brother's voice was violent and the poor fool cringled away from him. "Get to work and finish loading the truck."

Max hesitated, half turning. But then he reached out a long arm and gripped his brother's elbow. "Maybe the old devil still alive, eh? Maybe if we——" His brother struck him across the mouth then and seized him by his jacket and shook him. "Will you shut up," he shouted. And then as Max gaped at him, a lost, bewildered expression on his ugly features, Trevedian put his arms affectionately round his shoulders and drew him aside out of earshot. He talked to him for a moment and then Max nodded. "*Ja, ja.* I do that." He stumbled back to the truck, mumbling to himself, picked up a drum and hurled it into the back.

"Well, what do you want here, Wetheral?" I turned to find Peter Trevedian coming towards me.

"McClellan offered to take me up to have a look at the dam," I said.

"He did, did he?" He called to McClellan and took him on one side. "It can't do any harm," I heard McClellan say. They were both looking at me as they talked. Finally Trevedian said in a voice that was loud enough for me to hear: "Well, he's not coming up in one of my trucks. If he

wants to go up there, he can find his own damn way up."
McClellan said something, but Trevedian turned with a shrug
and climbed into the cab of the truck.

McClellan hesitated, glancing at me. Then he came over.
" I'm sorry, Wetheral," he said. " Trevedian says there isn't
room for all of us. I'm afraid we'll have to leave you behind.
There's a lot of fuel to take up, you see," he added lamely.

" You mean he refuses to let me go up?"

" That's about it, I guess."

" And you take orders from him?"

He glanced at me quickly, a hard, angry look in his eyes.
Then he turned away without another word, his shoulders
hunched. He and Creasy climbed into the cab. The engine
roared and I stood there watching the truck as it slithered
through the mud to the lake-shore road and turned up towards Thunder Creek. My eyes lifted to the peaks of
Solomon's Judgment, half-veiled in twin caps of cloud. The
Kingdom seemed as far away as ever. As I turned angrily
away I saw Max standing just where his brother had left him,
his long arms hanging loose, his eyes watching the truck. His
mouth was open and there was a queer air of suppressed
excitement about him. Suddenly he turned with the quickness
of a bear and went up into the shacks of Come Lucky at a
shambling trot.

I went slowly back to the hotel. Mac was in the bar when
I entered. " Are ye not going up to the hoist wi' Jamie?"

" Trevedian refused to take me," I said.

He growled something under his breath. " Well, I've a
message for you. Two friends of yours are down at 150
Mile House. 'Phoned up to find out whether you were still
here."

" Two friends?" I stared at him. " Who were they?"

" Johnnie Carstairs and a fellow called Jeff Hart. Said
they'd be up here this afternoon to see you if the road wasn't
washed out."

I turned away towards the window. Johnnie Carstairs and
Jeff Hart. It was the best news I had had in a week. And
then my eyes focused on a figure on horseback slithering
down the track from the bunkhouse. He reached the lake-
shore road, turned right and went into a long, easy canter.
No need to ask myself who it was. The size of the man told

me that. But he was no longer an ungainly lout. The horse was a big, raw-boned animal and the two of them merged to form a pattern of movement that was beautiful to watch.

"Why is Max Trevedian so eager to go up to the Kingdom?" I asked as I lost sight of him behind the shacks opposite.

Old Mac turned away. "Och, the man's just simple. Ye dinna want to worry about him. He's been crazy for a long time. All he understands is horses." And he shuffled out to the kitchen.

It was around tea-time that Johnnie and Jeff rolled into Come Lucky in a station wagon plastered with mud. I met them down at the bunkhouse and walked with them up to the hotel. And it wasn't long before I knew what had brought them. Jeff had met Boy Bladen down at Edmonton. "He said something about that survey being phoney," Johnny said. "He said Trevedian fixed it and then sent his brother up to the Kingdom with the report." His eyes were hard and narrowed under their puffy lids. "He said you could give us the whole story. The road's just open so we came over. I was kinda fond of the old man," he added.

I took them up to my room and gave them a drink and then I told them what had happened. When I had finished Johnnie was on his feet, pacing angrily up and down. "So they got at him through the survey. The bastards! I don't care what they think of him here, Campbell was a fine old man."

"Did you know they hated him?" Jeff asked.

"Sure, sure. But I didn't think they'd stoop to a trick as mean as this." He turned to Jeff. "You never went up to the Kingdom, did you? Then you wouldn't understand how I feel about this. You had to see the man in the place he'd made his own. By God. . . ." His long, bony hands were clenched and his eyes were hot with anger in the pallid tan of his face. "When a man's as lonely as Campbell was he talks. Night after night I've sat up with him. . . . I know him as well as I know myself. He was a fine man—it was just that the luck ran against him, I guess." He suddenly turned to the window, staring through it towards the peaks of Solomon's Judgment, looking towards the Kingdom.

He turned abruptly, facing me. "Where's Trevedian?"

"Up at the hoist," I said. And then, because I was shocked by the tenseness of his features, I added, "There's nothing you can do about it, Johnnie."

"No?" He suddenly smiled gently. "I'm madder'n hell. And when I'm that way the meanest crittur on four legs won't get the better of Johnnie Carstairs—nor on two legs neither." He turned abruptly to the door. "C'm on. Let's go an' feed."

Johnnie was one of those men whose values are real. I had thought of him as a quiet, rather withdrawn man. And yet the violence of his reaction wasn't unexpected. His code was the code of Nature, physically hard but with no twists. The unnatural was something that struck deep at his roots. I watched him as he sat eating, quiet and easy and friendly, exchanging banter with old Mac. Only his eyes reflected the mood that was still boiling inside him.

McClellan and Creasy were late getting back and we had nearly finished our meal by the time they arrived. "Was it all right, Jamie?" Mac asked.

"Of course it was." For the first time since I had known him James McClellan was smiling. It gave a queer twist to his features for it was not their accustomed expression. "The motor was all right and so was the cable. There was a lot of ice on it up at the top, but underneath there were still traces of the grease packing I put on last year." He nodded perfunctorily to Johnnie as he sat down and got straight on with his meal. "What brings you here?" he asked. "Bit early in the season for visitors, isn't it?"

"This is Jeff Hart, from Jasper," Johnnie said. "We came over to see friend Bruce here. Understand you wouldn't take him up to the Kingdom this morning."

"Peter Trevedian runs the transport here," McClellan replied sullenly.

"Sure, sure. Peter Trevedian runs you and the whole goldarned town from what I hear. Did you know about him sending his brother up to old Campbell with the report on that survey?" Johnnie was rolling himself a cigarette. "Pity I didn't know what had happened. I had a couple of newspaper boys along who would have been interested."

Nobody said anything. The table had become suddenly silent. Anger underlay the mildness of Johnnie's tone, and it showed in his eyes.

"You'd better go and talk to Peter Trevedian," McClellan said awkwardly.

"Sure I will, but at the moment I'm talking to you. Jeff here saw Boy Bladen in Edmonton the other day."

"Well?"

"Boy seemed kinda mad about something. You wouldn't know what that something was, would you now?"

"No."

Johnnie was lighting his cigarette, and his eyes were on McClellan through the smoke. "I thought you were Trevedian's partner?"

"Only on the hoist."

"I see. Not when it comes to substituting phoney survey figures and driving an old man to his death."

McClellan pushed back his chair and got to his feet. "What the hell are you getting at?"

"Nothing that you can't figure out for yourself." Johnnie had turned away. "My advice to you, McClellan, is—watch your step," he said over his shoulder. "You're riding in bad company, boy." He turned suddenly. "Now, where will I find Trevedian?"

McClellan didn't answer. He just turned on his heel and walked out. Johnnie gave a slight shrug. "Know where Trevedian is, Mac?" he asked.

I don't think the old man heard the question. He seemed lost in thought. It was Creasy who answered. "You'll find him down at the bunkhouse. If he's not in his office, he'll most likely be in his quarters round at the back."

"Okay. Thanks." Johnnie had turned to the door. Jeff and I got up and followed him. "You boys stay here," he said. "You can order me a beer. I'll be thirstier'n hell by the time I get through with Trevedian."

We sat and waited for him by the stove in the bar. He was gone the better part of an hour and by the time he got back men from Creasy's construction gang were filtering in in ones and twos. They were a mixed bunch, their hands hard and calloused; Poles, Ukrainians, Italians, a negro and two Chinamen. They wore war surplus clothing relieved by bright scarves and gaily coloured shirts. They were the same crowd that I had seen in the bar each evening. "Well?" Jeff asked as Johnnie slid into the vacant chair at our table.

"Trevedian wasn't there," he said and called to the China-man to bring more beer. "I went along and saw Jean in-stead." His eyes crinkled as he looked across at me. "Least-aways you got yourself one friend in Come Lucky. She's a real dandy, that girl. If I were a few years younger ..." He smiled gently to himself and drank his beer.

"If you were a few years younger, you'd still be a bachelor," Jeff said.

"Sure, I know." He nodded slowly. "A girl's all very well, but when it comes to living with her ..." He stopped suddenly, his gaze fixed over my shoulder.

I turned in my chair. Peter Tervedian was standing in the doorway, looking round the bar. He went over to Creasy and asked him a question. Creasy shook his head. "No. Ain't seen him." Trevedian straightened up, facing the room. "Just a minute, boys." His solid, throaty voice silenced the murmur of conversation. "Anybody here seen my brother to-day?"

"Wasn't he loading a truck outside the bunkhouse when we left this morning?" a voice said.

"Sure he was ... I seen him myself." There was a chorus of assent all round the room.

"I know that," Trevedian answered. "We left him at the bunkhouse when we went up to the hoist. I want to know what's happened to him since then."

"Maybe he went out for a walk and lost hisself." It was the driver of one of the bulldozers.

"Max doesn't lose himself," Trevedian said harshly.

"Maybe he lose his memory, eh?"

There was a laugh and somebody added, "Per'aps he for-got where he is going."

Trevedian's eyes narrowed. "Another crack like that and I'll send the man who makes it back where he came from. Just confine yourselves to statements of fact. Has anybody seen Max since this morning?"

"Yeah. I seen him." It was one of the old men, the one they called Ed Schieffer. "I seen him right after you left. Saddled his horse an' rode off. I seen him from the window of me shack."

"Where was he headed for?"

"He followed you. Up Thunder Creek."

Trevedian growled a curse and turned towards the door.

It was then that Johnnie slid to his feet. I grabbed hold of him by the arm. But he threw me off. "Just a minute, Trevedian."

Something in the quietness of his voice silenced the murmur of talk that had started in the bar. Trevedian turned, his hand on the door. "Why, if it isn't Johnnie Carstairs." He crossed the room, his hand outstretched. "What brings you up here this early in the year?" His tone was affable, but his head was sunk into his shoulders and his eyes were watchful under the shaggy eyebrows.

Johnnie was in the middle of the room now. He ignored the other's hand. He was rocking gently on his high-heeled boots, anger building up inside him like steam in a boiler. "I came on account of what I heard from Bladen."

"Well?" Trevedian had stopped. His hand had fallen to his side. "What did you hear from Bladen?"

"Did you have to play a dirty trick like that on an old man who never did you——"

"What are you talking about?"

"You know damn well what I'm talking about. I'm talking about Stuart Campbell. You killed him." Johnnie's voice vibrated through the silence of the room. "Why the hell did you have to do it like that, striking him through his——"

"Oh, stop talking nonsense. I didn't touch the old man and you know it." Trevedian's eyes glanced round the room, seeing it silent and listening. "We'd better go down to my office. We can talk there." He turned towards the door.

"There's nothing private in what I got to say." Johnnie had not moved, but his hands had shifted to the leather belt round his waist. "What were you afraid of—that he'd talk to some newspaper feller, that he'd tell them what he knew about the dam?"

"What do you mean?" The other had swung round.

"Campbell wasn't a fool. Why do you think he let them go on with the construction of the dam at the start of the war without making any demand for compensation?"

"He'd have put in a claim only Pearl Harbour brought the Yanks into the——"

"It wasn't Pearl Harbour. It was because he knew the dam wouldn't stand the weight of the water."

"I don't know what the hell you're talking——"

"Sure you do. I'm talking about the *Marie Bell* and her

cargo of cement. I took a Vancouver shipowner up to the Kingdom in 1940 and he told us the whole thing."

"The construction of the dam is nothing to do with me—never has been. I just pack the materials in." Trevedian's voice had risen slightly. He moved a step nearer. It was like seeing a bull about to charge a matador.

Johnnie laughed softly. It reacted on Trevedian like a slap in the face. His head came down and his fists clenched. A tingle of expectation ran through the room. "Think I don't know what packing rates are?" Johnnie said. "You didn't make enough out of transporting the stuff to start a transport and construction company in Alaska."

"The Government was responsible for building the dam," Trevedian snapped. "They had inspectors."

"Sure they had inspectors. But how were they to know you were packing in cement that had lain for a year on the rocks of the Queen Charlotte Islands."

"That's a lie." Trevedian's face was livid. "All the cement I delivered was from an American company down in Seattle."

"Sure. They were shipping cement up to Alaska for military installations. One of their ships——"

Trevedian suddenly straightened up. He had got control of himself and his big laugh boomed through the room. "So I'm supposed to have killed Campbell because he knew I'd supplied dud cement for the dam." He slapped his thigh with amusement. "That's damn funny. In the first place I didn't kill Campbell, and every God-damned person in this room knows it. In the second place, that dud cement you talk about seems to be standing up to it pretty well since the dam's still there and there isn't a crack in the whole structure. You want to get your facts right before you come storming up here making a lot of wild accusations." And still laughing he turned on his heel and went out into the night, leaving Johnnie standing there in the middle of the floor.

Johnnie didn't move. He stood there, staring at the closed door and for a moment I thought he was going to follow Trevedian. But instead he came back to our table and knocked back the rest of his beer. "What's all this about the dam?" Jeff asked.

"To hell with the dam." Johnnie's eyes were angry. "But if that bastard——" He suddenly laughed. "Well, maybe Stuart was right. If he was willing to let things take their course, I guess I should be, too." He put down his glass. "I'm going down to have a talk with Jean." He turned then and went out of the room. And as the door closed behind him a buzz of conversation filled the smoke-laden atmosphere.

"What did he mean—about the dam?" I asked Jeff.

"I don't know. Never heard him mention it before."

We discussed it for a while and then Jeff said, "You know, I'd like to see this dam there's all the fuss about. Have you seen it?"

"Yes," I said. "I saw it the other day from Thunder Creek. What I want to do is get up there. I want to see the Kingdom."

"Thunder Creek's where they're building the road, isn't it?"

"That's right."

He suddenly laughed. "Well, what are we waiting for? It's a fine night and there's a moon. Let's go right on up there."

I stared at him. "Now?"

"Sure. Why not?"

But some instinct of caution made me hesitate. "It would be better to go up by daylight," I said. "Could we go up to-morrow? Then you'd get a good view of the dam and I might be able to persuade——"

"To-morrow's no good," he said. "We're leaving to-morrow." He got to his feet. "Come on," he said. "We'll go up there now."

"What about Johnnie?"

"Johnnie?" He laughed. "Johnnie wouldn't come anyway. He just hates automobiles. We'll leave a message for him. How far do we have to go up Thunder Creek?"

"I think it's about ten or eleven miles," I said.

"And the road has only just been made. Hell! We can be there and back in an hour and a half. Come on. You don't need a coat. We got some in the station wagon and it's got a heater, too."

Part Two

THE KINGDOM

I

THE ROAD up Thunder Creek was like the bed of a stream. Water poured across it. The groundgrips of the big car were either slithering and spinning in a morass of yellowish mud or bumping over stones and small boulders washed down from above. Some of the log bridges were unable to dispose of the volume of water coming down the gullies they spanned. It banked up above them and poured across, a foot deep in places, so that they looked like small weirs. But Jeff never once suggested turning back. A car to him was an expendable item, a thing to fight nature with and he sang softly to himself as he wrestled with the wheel.

Above us, through the trees, the moon sailed fast among ragged wisps of cloud, a full circle of luminous yellow that lit the winding trail in a macabre light, half drowning the brilliance of the headlights. Thunder Creek, below us to the left, was a dark canyon of shadow out of which came the steady, relentless roar of water. And as we climbed, the black shadow of the fault capped by the snow-white peaks shouldered its way up the sky till it blotted out the moon and seemed to tower right over us.

It was here, in the dark shadows, that we suddenly emerged from the timber into a clearing where roofless log huts sprawled amongst the sapling growth. We had reached the camp built in 1939 when work on the dam had begun. The trial, blazed by the piles of slash on either side, ran straight across it and into the timber again. Gradually the trees thinned out. The surface of the road under its frozen powdering of snow became hard and bumpy. Then the timber finally fell back behind us and the headlights blazed on the most colossal rock fall I have ever seen. Great blocks of stone the size of houses were piled one on top of the other, balanced precariously and hung like the playthings of the

Cornish giants against the moon-tipped edges of the racing cloud wisps. And above the slide—high, high above it— towered the black shadow of the cliff face, a gleam of white at the top where the moon caught the snowcaps, a gleam of white that wavered and moved as mare's tails of wind-driven snow streamed from the crests.

The headlights swung across the fantastic, gargantuan jumble of the slide as the track turned away into the wind that funnelled up the dark cleft of the valley. The track here had been hammered out of the edge of the slide itself and the wheels bounced and jolted over the uneven surface of stones. We dropped steeply several hundred feet and fetched up at a square, concrete building that looked like an enormous pill-box. On the side facing us was a timbered staging on which rested a heavy wooden cage suspended by wires to a great cable the thickness of a man's arm. Jeff stopped the car and switched his spotlight on to the cable, following it up the slope of the slide. It gleamed dully in the light like the thick thread of a spider, running in a long loop away up the slide until it faded into nothing, reaching beyond the range of the spotlight. Below it two subsidiary cables followed the pattern of the loop.

"Well, that's it, I guess," Jeff said. "Quite a place, isn't it?"

I didn't say anything. I was staring along the threadlike line of the cable, following it in my imagination up the dark face of the cliff, up into the narrow V between the peaks of Solomon's Judgment. The slender thread was the link bridging the dark gap that separated me from the Kingdom. If I could travel that cable. . . . A queer mood of excitement was taking hold of me. I pushed open the door. "Let's have a look in the enginehouse," I said.

"Sure."

The door flung to behind me, slammed by the wind. Inside the car we had had the heater going full blast and had been protected from the wind. Outside I found I could hardly stand. The wind tore up the valley. It was not a cold wind, but it had no power to dispel the frozen bite of the air trapped in the circle of the valley head. It was a gripping cold that thrust through one's clothing and ate into one's guts.

Jeff flung me a duffle coat from the back of the car and then we pushed down through the wind to the engine housing.

Though McClellan had only left the place a few hours ago snow was piled up against the pinewood door and we had to scoop it away before we could open it. Inside we were out of the wind, but the cold was bitter. A powdery drift of snow carpeted the floor and the draught of air that whistled in through the horizontal slit window that faced the slide could not dispel the dank smell of the concrete and the less unpleasant smell of oil and combustion fumes.

The interior of the engine housing was about the size of a large room. One wall was taken up entirely by a huge iron wheel round which the driving cable of the hoist ran. This was connected by a shaft to a big diesel engine that stood against the other wall, covered by a tarpaulin lashed down with rope through the eyeholes. Shovel marks showed on the floor where the party which had come up that morning had cleared out the winter's accumulation of snow. A control panel was fixed to the concrete below the slit and there was an ex-service field telephone on a wooden bracket. Back of the main engine house was a store room and in it I saw the drums of fuel oil that had been brought up from Come Lucky.

I stood there for a moment, absorbing it all, while Jeff peered under the tarpaulin at the engine. I turned slowly, drawn by an irresistible impulse. I went over to the slit and, leaning my arms on the sill, peered up to the snow-lipped top of the cliff face. The moon was just lifting above the left-hand peak of the mountain. I watched the shreds of cloud tearing across the face of it, saw the shadows of the mountain receding, watched till all the whole slide was bathed in the white light of it. The thick thread of the cable was plainly visible now, a shallow loop running from the engine housing in which I stood up to a great concrete pillar that stood on a huge slab of rock that marked the highest point of the slide. From there the cable rose steeply, climbing the black face of the cliff and disappearing into the shadows. My eyes followed the invisible line of it, lifting to the top of the cliff and there, etched against the bright luminosity of the sky, was another pillar, no bigger than a needle, standing like an ancient cromlech on the lip of the cliff.

The thing that had been in my mind ever since I had seen the slender thread of that cable suddenly crystallised and I turned to Jeff. "They had that engine going to-day, didn't they?"

He nodded, straightening up and facing me, a frown on his friendly, open features. "What's on your mind?"

I hesitated, strangely unwilling to put my idea into words for fear it should be impracticable. "You're a mechanic, aren't you?" I said.

"I run a garage, if that's what you mean."

"Can you start that engine?"

"Sure, but——" He stopped and then he stepped forward and caught hold of my arm. "Don't be crazy, Bruce. You can't go up there on your own. Suppose the thing jammed or the motor broke down?"

The thought had already occurred to me. "There must be some sort of safety device," I said.

He nodded reluctantly. "There'll be something like that, I guess. If the driving cable were disconnected gravity ought to bring it down." He took me outside and we climbed on to the cage. It was a big contraption, bigger than anything I had seen in the Swiss Alps. He flashed the beam of his torch on to the cradle where the two flanged wheels ran on the cable. "There you are," he said. It was a very simple device. The driving cable was fixed to the cradle by a pinion on a hinged arm. If the motor failed all one had to do was knock the pinion out. The driving cable then fell on to a roller and a breaking wheel automatically came into action. It was then possible to let the cage slide down on the brake. "See if you can get the motor started," I said.

Jeff hesitated, his gaze held by the shadowed void of the cliff face with its sugar-icing of snow at the top. Then he turned with a slight shrug of his shoulders. "Okay," he said, "But it'll be cold up there."

There was a pilot engine for starting the big diesel. It was a petrol engine with battery starter. It started at a touch of the button. Jeff pulled the tarpaulin clear of the diesel, turned on the oil and a moment later the concrete housing shook to the roar of the powerful motor. I went to the car and got another coat and a rug. Jeff met me at the entrance to the housing. "Better let me go up," he said. "Tell me where that recording tape is that Boy wants and I'll get it."

"No," I said. "I'm not a mechanic and I couldn't run the engine. Besides, I want to see the place."

He hesitated. "I don't like it," he said. "These aren't English mountains. You don't want to go fooling around with them."

"I'll be all right," I said.

He looked at me, frowning slightly. "Okay," he said. "Better take this." He handed me his torch. "They've rigged a phone up by the look of it. The wire probably runs through the main cable. Ring me from the top." He glanced at his watch. "If there's anything wrong with the phone, I'll bring the cage down at nine o'clock, giving one false start to warn you. If you don't come down then I'll run it up again and bring it down every half-hour. Okay?"

I nodded and checked my watch with his. Then I climbed on to the wooden platform of the cage. He shouted "Good luck" to me and disappeared into the concrete housing. A moment later the note of the diesel deepened as it took up the slack of the driving cable. I watched the loop of the cable level out and become taut. The cage shook gently and then lifted from its staging. The wheels of the cradle began to turn, creaking slightly. The cage swung gently to and fro. I watched the engine housing slowly grow smaller and then I turned and faced the black rampart of the cliff.

It was an odd journey, alone there, slung in space in the moon-filled night. The rock jumble of the slide fell away steeply below me, a chequer-board of black and white. But ahead all was deep in shadow. A great concrete pillar moved towards me and slid past in the night, a vague shape as the cage ran from moonlight into shadow. For a moment the sound of the cradle wheels changed as they ran on the solid fixing of the cable. Then the whole cradle began to tilt sharply and the rate of progress slowed as it began to climb the vertical cliff face. I could just make it out now, a wall of bare rock criss-crossed with a pattern of white where snow and ice had lodged in crevices and on ledges. Looking back, the moon-white valley seemed miles away. I could barely see the tiny square of the engine housing. There was no sound except for the creaking of the wheels. The wind whistled up through the cracks in the floor timbers. It was bitterly cold. I seemed hung in space, like a balloonist caught in an up-draught of air and slowly rising. I had no sense of vertigo. Only a great sense of loneliness.

It could only have been a few minutes, but it seemed an

age that the cage was climbing the bare rock face of the fault. Then we lipped the top and I was in moonlight again and the world around was visible and white. The concrete pylon passed me so close I could have touched it. The cradle toppled down to an almost horizontal position. There was the sound of water in the shadowed bottom of the cleft and I glimpsed the slender veil of a fall wavering as it plunged the full length of the fault. Ahead of me now I could see the dam, a gigantic concrete wall, unfinished at the top and crumbling away in the centre where the stream ran through. The cage climbed the northern slope of the cleft until I was looking down on the top of the dam. Then it slowed and moved gently into a wooden staging that finished abruptly at a concrete housing similar to the one at the bottom. The cage stopped with a slight jerk that set the cables swaying.

I climbed stiffly out and looked about me. The dam was below me, looking like some pre-historic rampart built by ancient inhabitants to defend the pass. In places the concrete had crumbled away to spill out the great boulders that formed its core. The unfinished centre section, where the water frothed white over a small fall, gave it the appearance of having been breached in some early raid.

The top of the dam was partially covered by snow, but it was still possible to see the nature of its construction ; two outer walls of concrete and the space between filled with rock and sealed with concrete.

My gaze swung to the Kingdom itself. It was a natural bowl in the mountains some five to ten miles long ; it was impossible to judge the distance in that queer light. I couldn't tell the width because a buttress of rock, part of the shoulder of the mountain, blocked my view. The place was completely bare, a white expanse of snow through which ran the black thread of the stream, branching here and there like the spine of a leaf into tributaries that faded rapidly beneath the snow. There was no sign of habitation.

I went into the concrete housing. There was no motor here, of course. It contained nothing but the big iron wheel round which the driving cable ran and some cans of grease. There was a field telephone on a wooden bracket. I lifted the receiver and wound the handle. Faint in my ear came the sound of Jeff's voice. " You all right, Bruce?"

" Yes. I'm fine." It was odd to think of him still down

there in the valley with the car outside and the road snaking back to Come Lucky. I seemed to have moved into another world. " I can't see Campbell's shack from here," I told him. " It's probably on the north side of the Kingdom and that's hidden from me by a buttress of rock. I'll ring you when I'm ready to come down."

" Okay. But don't be too long. And see you don't slip or anything."

" I'll be all right," I said. " It'll probably take about an hour if I'm to have a look round and get those figures."

" Okay."

I hung up and went outside. I stood there for a moment, gazing beyond the buttress to the Kingdom. It was a crystal bowl surrounded by peaks and it wasn't difficult to imagine how my grandfather had felt when he had first seen it. Spring would come late here, but when it came it would be splendid, and solitary. The light died out of the whiteness of the plateau until it was no more than a distant glimmer. The moon had blacked out behind a veil of cloud. The mountains closed in on either side, dark, hulking shapes. I glanced back across the lip of the fault towards the valley now deep in shadow. Far away beyond Come Lucky the moon showed white on snowy mountain slopes. I watched as the light sailed up the valley, until the dam and the rock around me were picked out in ghostly brilliance again. The moon sailed clear of the cloud veil. The stars shone in the pallid purple of space and way, way to the west a dark shadow climbed the sky. The clouds were thickening up. I turned and climbed the rock-strewn slope to the buttress.

It didn't take me long to reach it and from the summit the whole Kingdom lay before me. And there, huddled against the lower slopes of the mountain away to my left was a low range of buildings half-buried in snow. There was nothing of the shack about them and they appeared to be constructed of logs after the fashion of Norwegian saeters. A belt of timber fringed the slopes above them.

It shouldn't have taken me long to reach them, for it was not more than a mile, but the going was very slippery, the snow frozen into a hard crust and glazed over so that it was like ice. The altitude was also affecting me and I had to stop repeatedly to get my breath. The solitude was frightening.

I felt curiously as though I were entering a dead man's world. Everything was so white and so frozen still.

I was sheltered from the wind by the mountain, but from the slopes above me a whirl of snow came hurtling, curling and curving towards the moon like a scimitar blade. The huddle of buildings seemed crouched low against the on-slaught, attempting to hide beneath their mounds of snow. The whirling snow devil swept over them and flung itself on me, a howling rush of wind and ice powder small as ground glass. It stung my face and swept on and all was still again.

I glanced back, panting with the shortness of my breath. The line of my footprints showed faintly in the powdery top layer of snow leading back to the buttress and the dark shadow of the cleft. I could no longer see the valley of Thunder Creek. I was ringed with rock and snow and the dam was again a puny man-made wall against the vast bulk of the southern peak of Solomon's Judgment.

Behind the crystal white of the peak a heavy cloud obscured the sky like a back-drop of deepest black erected to offset the cold remoteness of the mountain. It was a monster of a cloud, great billows piled up and up into the night. Even as I watched I saw the hard edge of it reach out and clutch at the moon.

The shadow of it raced towards me across the snow. I glanced at the buildings, now less than five hundred yards away. The light was queer, distorted and refracted by the snow. It seemed to me a figure, stood there, watching me from the corner of the nearest of the buildings. I thought I saw it move. But then the shadow of the cloud was upon me and I had to adjust the focus of my eyes. And in that second the shadow had passed on and engulfed the buildings and I could see nothing but the snow gleaming white in the moon-light on the further side of the Kingdom. And then the peaks vanished, too, as though blotted out by a giant hand.

All was sudden and impenetrable blackness, and from high up on the peaks above came a dry rustling, a murmur like leaves or the soft escape of steam.

I hesitated, uncertain what to do; whether to go on to the homestead or turn back to the dam. Then all hell broke loose. There was a steady roaring on the mountain slopes above me.

The wind came with a drift of powdery snow whipped up from frozen ground and behind the wind came snow, heavy, driving flakes that were cold and clinging, that blinded my eyes and blanketed the whole world that only a moment before had been so bright and clear in the moonlight.

There was no question now of fighting my way back to the top of the hoist. I knew the direction in which the homestead lay and I made for it, head down against the bliding fury of the blizzard and counting my steps so that I should not overshoot it in the impenetrable dark. I switched on the torch Jeff had given me, but it was worse than useless. It converted absolute blackness to a dazzling white world of driving flakes.

I walked straight on with the wind over my left shoulder for seven hundred counted yards and then stopped. I could see nothing. Absolutely nothing. I put the wind on my back and walked two hundred yards, turned right and walked another two hundred; faced into the wind and completed the square, eyes and nostrils almost blocked by the icy, clinging particles of the blizzard. I walked into it for another two hundred paces and again made a square. But I couldn't see anything and I couldn't even tell whether I was walking on the flat or not. For all I knew I might have stumbled right over the top of the buildings, half-hidden as they were under drifts. Only if I walked bang up against a wall of the homestead had I any chance of locating it.

I stood still for a moment and considered, knowing that I mustn't panic, that I must keep calm. Carefully, with the wind as my one fixed point, I searched the ground, patterning it in squares. But I might have been stumbling through an empty plain. I began to doubt whether I had seen any buildings at all. And that figure standing in the snow. . . . There wasn't a soul up in the Kingdom besides myself. If I could have imagined one thing I could have imagined the others. I stopped and wiped the snow from my frozen face. God, it was cold! I glanced at the luminous dial of my watch. Nine-fifteen. Nearly nine hours to go before dawn began to break. Those buildings had to be real—they had to be!

I started off again and then stopped, trying to remember what square in my pattern I had completed last, trying to get some spark of sense out of my numbed brain. It was then that I saw a faint glow though the snow, an aura of warmth as though a weak sun were trying to rise and penetrate the murk of the blizzard. It was away to my left and I stared at it, wondering whether it was a trick of my imagination or whether it was real. I blinked and rubbed at my snow-encrusted eyes. But the glow remained, a soft radiation that lit the driving snow like the deeper tints of a rainbow. It was unnatural, a queer emanation of colour that warmed the frozen solitude of the Kingdom.

I turned towards it automatically, drawn like a moth to a candle flame in the dark. With every step the colours deepened—orange and red and yellow flamed in the blackness, spreading rosy tints into the flakes of driven snow. And then suddenly the veil of the blizzard seemed to fall back and I saw flames licking skywards and against their lurid light was etched the rough-hewn corner of a log building. A few steps more and I was in the shelter of a group of buildings low, log-built barns stretching out like two arms from a central ranch-house that had doors and windows. It was one of the barns that was on fire.

The warmth of the flames came licking out of the storm and I ran towards them, drawn by the heat, absorbing it with a feeling of sudden lassitude and wonderful, weary gratefulness. And as the warmth closed round me, melting the snow from my clothes, there was a slow creaking, a crackling of timbers, a movement, a sagging in the heart of the flames. Then with a great roar the roof collapsed. A shower of sparks shot upwards to be caught and extinguished instantly by the storm. The whole centre of the fire seemed to collapse inwards and as it collapsed half-melted snow rolled into the gap from the drift at the back. Steam rose with a roar, a great cloud that was momentarily lit by the glow of the fire. Then the fire was gone. Black darkness closed in and all that was left was a few glowing embers and the soft sizzling of snow melting in contact with red-hot ash.

I stood for a moment quite still. I think I was bewildered. It had all happened so suddenly. But it had lighted me in like a beacon. It was as though God had set forth His hand to guide me. And yet there had been no lightning. There had been nothing to cause the fire. A sudden sense of awe descended on me.

I shivered as the cold gripped me again. Whatever the

cause of it the fire had shown me the place I was seeking. I felt my way through pools of melted snow to the main building, felt my way along the warm wood of the log face until I found the door. It yielded to my touch and I stumbled inside, closing it after me.

The place was cold, cold with the griping chill of a room that has had no heat in it for a long time. I fumbled for the torch again and in its beam I saw a big, ghostly room full of shadows. The walls were of log, ceiling and floor-boards of split pine planks and there was the gaping hole of a huge stone chimney. On a table stood a lamp. It still had oil in it and I removed the glass chimney and lit the wick. When I set the chimney back the warm lamplight flooded the place. I stood back and stared at a room that might have been constructed by one of the pioneers who had moved into the Fraser River country a hundred years ago.

The place was dominated by the huge stone chimney which broadened out just below the rafters to a big open fireplace. It was built of rocks mortared together and on either side were baking ovens. The grate still held some half-burnt pine logs and a great heap of ash. The beams and rafters that supported the roof were rough-hewn, the marks of my grand-father's axe plainly visible. Most of the furniture was hand-made, but there were a few small pieces that had been im-ported. A door to the right led into a kitchen. A small range backed into the rough stone of the chimney and in one corner was a hot-water tank and an old galvanised tin bath. Near it was a lavatory and against the window a sink. A door led through into the undamaged barn, a long, low building full of shadow which the lamp could not penetrate. On the other side of the living-room was a bedroom. There was an old drum stove in one corner with an iron pipe running up through the roof. The bed was unmade. Clothes were strewn around—heavy ski boots, an old pair of jeans, a buckskin jacket beauti-fully worked with beads, an old and battered stetson, high-heeled cowboy boots of a fancy pattern, a gaily coloured plaid shirt, faded and sweat-stained under the armpits.

I felt as though I were an intruder in a private house, not the sole legatee of a man four months dead come to look over his property. Everywhere I turned there was evidence of my grandfather. It seemed inconceivable that the man himself wouldn't come in through the front door at any moment.

A pool of water was forming at my feet. There were logs piled in a bin beside the fireplace, logs brought in by Johnnie and his party when they had returned. There was a box of axe chippings and sawdust. In a few minutes I had a fire blazing in the hearth and had stripped off my clothes. I went through into the bedroom and got some things of my grandfather's—a pair of jeans, a plaid shirt and a big fur-lined jacket. They were old and had been patched with great care. I stood close against the fire as I put them on. The flames roared, sucked up by the wind that drove across the top of the chimney. The heat of it slowly penetrated to my bones, warming the cold core of my body. The uncurtained windows showed the snow thick in the lamplight. But the only sound was the crackle of the flames in the hearth. The storm was muffled by the snow. It did not penetrate this warm, well-built ranch-house.

I lit a cigarette and went over to the desk. The drawers were full of an indescribable litter of correspondence, bills, receipts, copies of oil magazines, notes on crops, odd pieces of rock, cheque book stubs, some deeds, a few photographs, old keys, part of a broken bit. Some of the letters dated from the early thirties.

It was in the bottom of the empty Bible box lying on the floor beside the desk, that I found what I was looking for ; rolled sheets of cartographic paper and a black, leather-bound book. The seismograms were quite incomprehensible to me. I rolled them up and put them back in the drawer. Then I opened the book.

This was what I had hoped to find. On the first page was written: *An Account of the Efforts of one, Stuart Campbell, to Establish the Truth that there is Oil in the Rocky Mountains.* The report was written in ink. It had faded a little with age and the paper had yellowed and become brittle. All the entries were dated. It began with the 3rd March, 1911, and went straight through to the entry made on the 20th November of the preceding year, the same day that he had written me that letter, the day of his death. The writing throughout was clearly recognisable as his own, but it gradually changed, the boldness blurring into the shakiness of age, and different inks had been used.

I turned back to the beginning and read with fascination the account of his discovery of oil in the valley of Thunder Creek.

"*This day, whilst on a visit to my old friend, Luke Trevedian, I was involved in the terrible disaster that overtook the goldmining community of Come Lucky. It had been snowing heavily for a week and the chinook beginning to blow there began at half-past eight in the morning a series of avalanches high up on the peak of the Overlander. These avalanches developed rapidly into a great slide that engulfed all the mine workings and spread for a whole mile across the flats of Thunder Creek, some of the rocks being of the size of large houses. For the next week everyone laboured for the release of miners trapped in the workings. But it was hopeless. In all forty-seven men and eleven boys missing in the mine and thirty-five people, including eight women and ten children, buried utterly, their dwellings standing in the course of the slide.*"

There followed more details and then this passage:

"*. . . 11th March, I was able to push up the valley of Thunder Creek, the snows having largely melted. Geologically a most interesting journey since I was skirting the edge of the slide and could examine rocks that only a little time before had been deep below the surface of the mountain. . . . Turning a bastion of Forked Lightning Mountain I got my first view of the falls. Imagine my astonishment on finding that the whole head of Thunder Valley had broken away. Instead of a series of falls from the hidden punch bowl Luke had shown me on my previous visit there was now a sheer cliff of new rock. The whole course of the creek had broken away and spilled forward. . . . The awe-inspiring sight of a new cliff-face, unmarked by vegetation and standing stark and sheer for hundreds of feet, was most instructive regarding the strata of the country. . . . In going down to slake my thirst I saw a black slime on the rocks at the edge of the swollen creek. These rocks were newly broken off and should have had no mark of vegetation. The waters of the creek were running dark and thick with a curious viscosity, and though they were swirling and thundering among the rocks, they did so smoothly. . . . It was a river of oil. What proportion was oil and what was water I could not tell, but the deposit on the rocks was undoubtedly crude oil. It was the biggest seep I*" *had ever seen. I made great efforts to climb up the slide to the source of the seepage, but shortly after midday it began to snow. Further falls of rock occurred and I had the greatest difficulty in getting safely down.*

13th March: It snowed all day yesterday and I waited with the greatest impatience to take Luke and others up to the oil seep. To-day we managed to get through, but alas, fresh falls had occurred and there was no evidence that we could find of any seep, nor could I discover any trace of the original seep though I searched the course of the creek wherever possible. I had great difficulty in convincing my companions that what I had seen two days ago. . . ."

A draught of cold air touched my cheek and I looked up. The door to the bedroom was open. I turned with a start as something moved in the room behind me. The figure of a man was walking slowly towards the fire, his feet dragging, his long arms swinging loose. His huge body was white with snow and he had his hand to the side of his face and it was blackened as though charred by fire. He stopped in front of the grate, staring at the flames. There was something frightening in his stillness, in his complete absorption in the fire. His shadow flickered on the log walls and pools of water formed at his feet.

I got to my feet and at the scrape of my chair he jerked round. His eyes widened at the sight of me and his lips opened, but no sound came. It was Max Trevedian and naked fear showed in his blackened face. He mumbled something incoherently. His gaze darted past me to the door and he ran blindly towards it, the whites of his eyes showing in the blackened mask of his face. His big hands fumbled clumsily at the latch; then he had lifted it and the wind tore the door from his grasp and flung it wide. A blast of bitter air swept into the room. I had a momentary glimpse of him struggling in a blinding whirl of snow and then the lamp blew out and the flames of the fire flickered redly on the drift that was rapidly powdering the floor.

For a moment he disappeared into the black void of the doorway. But it was only for a moment. He couldn't stand against the freak force of wind and snow and he staggered in again, bent low, his arms almost touching the ground, a monstrous, shapeless figure shrouded in snow. I flung myself against the door and forced it to. As I turned, panting from the effort, I found him standing facing me, a dark silhouette against the firelight. He was trembling and his teeth were chattering. I can still remember the sound they made, a queer, rodent sound against the roar of the wind. Then he seemed to crumple up, falling on his knees, his lips emitting a gibbering that was only half intelligible:

". . . only a letter. I never hurt you. Never touched you. Max never mean to hurt anyone . . . like I do with Alf Robens. Not like that. Never hurt you. . . . Please God believe. . . ." His voice died away in incoherent mumblings. And then quite clearly: "You ask Peter. Peter knows."

I moved a step towards him, peering down at him, trying to see his face, to understand what it was that was scaring him, but he scrambled away from me on his knees like a horribly human land-crab. "Go away. Go away." He screamed the words out. "Dear God believe me. I do you no harm."

"Did Peter send you here?" I asked. My voice sounded hoarse and unnatural.

"Ja, ja. Peter send me. He tell me you will not rest till all is burned. You kill my father, so I come here to burn this place. I love my father. I do it for him. I swear it. I do it for him."

"Who was Alf Robens?" I asked.

"Alf Robens!" I had moved so that I was between him and the fire. A log fell and in the sudden blaze I saw his face. The eyes were wide like two brown glass marbles, his lower lip hung down. It is the only time I have seen a man petrified with fear. His muscles seemed rigid. The sweat glistened on his face and seamed the charred blackness of his skin. Then his mouth began to work and at last a sound came: "He was a boy. Older than I was. A lot older. But I didn't mean to kill him. They used to tie me on to the broncs—for sport. Then they tie me to a bull. And when I am free I get Alf Robens by the throat and beat his head against a stone. But I mean nothing by it. Like it was with Lucie. She make sport with me and when I am roused she is frightened. I do not hurt her, but they "—he swallowed and licked his dry lips—"they try to hang me. I do not want to hurt anyone. I do not hurt you. Please leave me. Please." This last on a choking sob of fear.

I stood there for a moment, staring at this childish hulk

of a man who was scared of something that was in his mind and feeling a strange sense of pity for him. At length I put my hand out and touched his shoulder. " It's all right, Max. I'm not Stuart Campbell.' I went over to the desk then and relit the lamp. As I set the chimney back and the light brightened Max got slowly to his feet. His jaw was still slack and his eyes wide. He was breathing heavily. But his expression was changing from fear to anger.

Deep down within me I felt fear growing. Once I showed it I knew I should be lost. The man had colossal strength. The secret I knew was to treat him like an animal—to show no fear and to treat him with kindness and authority. " Sit down, Max," I said, not looking at him, concentrating on adjusting the wick of the lamp. My voice trembled slightly, but maybe my ears were over-sensitive. " You're tired. So am I." I picked up the lamp and walked towards the kitchen, forcing myself to go slowly and easily, not looking at him. " I'm going to make some tea."

I don't think he moved all the time I was crossing the room. Then at last I was through to the kitchen. I left the door open and went to the store cupboard. There was tea in a round tin. I found cups and a big kettle. There was a movement by the door. I looked round. Max was standing there, staring at me, a puzzled frown on his face.

" Do you know where my grandfather kept the sugar?" I asked him.

He shook his head. He had the bewildered look of a small boy. " All right," I said. " I'll find it. You take this kettle and fill it with snow." I held the kettle out to him and he came slowly forward and took it. " Ram the snow in tight," I said. And then as he stood there, hesitating, I added, " You like tea, don't you?"

He nodded his big head slowly. " *Ja.*" And then suddenly he smiled. It almost transformed his heavy, rather brutish face. " We make some good tea, eh?" And he shambled out.

I wiped the sweat from my forehead and stood there for a moment thinking about Max, thinking of the hell his childhood must have been—with no mother, the boys of Come Lucky making fun of him and tying him on to broncs and bulls, having their own cruel stampede, and then the boy killed and a girl crying Rape and the town trying to lynch him. I wondered how his brother had maintained his domination over him during years of absence. His childhood memories must have remained very vivid.

I found some biscuits and some canned meat. We ate them in front of the fire waiting for the snow to melt in the kettle and the water to boil. The wind moaned in the big chimney and Max sat there, wrapped in a blanket, silent and withdrawn. The kettle boiled and I made the tea. But as we sat drinking it I suddenly felt the silence becoming tense. I looked up and Max was staring at me. " Why do you come here?" His voice was a growl. " Peter say you are not to come—you are like Campbell."

I began to talk then, telling him about my grandfather as he appeared to me, how I had come all the way from England, how I was a sick man and not expected to live. And all the time the storm beat against the house. And when silence fell between us again and I sensed the tension growing because his interest was no longer held, I searched around in my mind for something to talk to him about and suddenly I remembered the *Jungle Books* and I began to tell him the story of Mowgli. And by the time I had told him of the first visit of Shere Khan I knew I needn't worry any more. He sat enraptured. Maybe it was the first time anybody had ever taken any trouble with him. Certainly I am convinced he had never been told a story before. He listened spell-bound, the expression of his face reacting to every mood of the story. And whenever I paused he muttered fiercely, " Go on. Go on."

When at length I came to the end the tears were streaming down his face. " It is very—beautiful. *Ja*, very beautiful." He nodded his head slowly.

" Better get some rest now, Max," I said. He didn't seem to hear me, but when I repeated it, he shook his head and a worried frown puckered his forehead. " I must go to Come Lucky." He clambered to his feet. " Peter will be angry with me."

" You can't go down till the storm is over," I said.

He crossed to the door. A howl of wind and snow entered the room as he opened it. He stood there for a moment, his body a hulking shadow against the lamplit white of the driven snow. Then he shut the door again and came slowly back to the fire, shaking his head. " No good," he said.

" Do you think it'll last long?"

"Two hours. Two days." He shrugged his shoulders. He was accustomed to the waywardness of the mountains.

"How did you come up here?"

"By the old pony trail."

"Did you ride up then?"

"*Ja, ja.* I ride."

"Where's your horse?"

"In the stable. He is all right. There is good hay there."

"Well, you'd better come down with me on the hoist when it clears," I said. "I don't think you'd get far on a pony trail by the time this is over."

"We will see," he said and wrapped himself in his blanket and lay down in front of the fire. I went into the bedroom and got some blankets and stretched myself out near him. I felt desperately tired. I was worried, too, about Jeff down there alone at the bottom of the hoist.

I don't remember much about that night. Once I got up and put more logs on the fire. Mostly I slept in a coma of exhaustion. And then suddenly I was awake. It was bitterly cold, the fire was a dead heap of white ash and a pale glimmer of daylight crept in through the snow-bordered windows. Max was not in the room.

I pulled myself to my feet and stumbled across to the door. It had stopped snowing and I looked out on to a world of white under a grey sky. Footprints led to an open door at the far end of the half-burnt barn. They did not return. "Max!" My voice seemed to lose itself in the infinite stillness. "Max!" I followed the footsteps through deep drifts of new snow to the stable door. The place was empty. The snow was trampled here and the tracks of a horse went out into the driven white of the Kingdom, headed for the cleft.

I went back into the house, rebuilt the fire and got myself some breakfast. The warmth and the food revived me and as soon as I had finished I carried out a quick inspection of the premises. The place was built facing south, the barns spreading out from either side of the house like two arms. Fortunately Bladen's trucks were in the undamaged barn and it didn't take me long to find the spools containing the recordings of his final survey. I slipped the containers into my pocket and then I set out along the trail Max had blazed. The snow was deep in places and it took me the better part of an hour to reach the buttress of rock. From the top of it I could see the hoist. The cage was not in its staging. The thought that it might have broken down flashed into my mind. The place was so damnably still. A frozen silence seemed to have gripped the world. There were no mare's tails on the peaks of Solomon's Judgment. Not a breath of air stirred.

From the buttress Max had led his horse. Only a powdery drift of snow covered the shelving rock. It was slippery like ice. The black line of the water showed through the gap in the dam; it was the only thing that moved. To my left were the rusted remains of some machinery and part of a timbered scaffolding.

I was very tired by the time I staggered into the concrete housing of the hoist. I went straight over to the telephone, lifted the receiver and wound the handle. There was no answer. A feeling of panic crept up from my stomach. It was entirely unreasoned for I could always return to the ranch-house. I tried again and again, and then suddenly a voice was crackling in my ears. "Hallo! Hallo! Is that you, Bruce?" It was Jeff Hart. A sense of relief hit me and I leaned against the ice-cold concrete of the wall. "Yes," I said. "Bruce here. Is the hoist working——"

"Thank God you're okay." His voice sounded thin and far away. "I was scared stiff you'd got lost. And then that fool, Max Trevedian, came down and galloped off before I could ask him whether you were all right. Were you okay up at Campbell's place?"

"Yes," I said. And I told him how I'd found it.

"You were pretty damned lucky. I'll get them to send the hoist up for you. Johnnie's here. He'll come up with it. I'm just about all in. What a hell of a night. Okay. She's on her way up now."

I put the phone down. The big cable wheel was clanking monotonously as it turned. I went over to the slit, watching the lip of the cliff. All the valley was white and frozen.

Ten minutes later the cage dropped into its housing with a solid thud and Johnnie was there, gripping my hand as though I'd returned from the Arctic. "You goldarned crazy fool!" That was all he said and then he went over to the phone and rang for them to take us down. He didn't talk as we dropped through space to the slide and the concrete housing at the foot of it. I think he realised that I was just about at the end of my tether.

As we dropped into the housing at the bottom I noticed that Jeff's car had gone. In its place was one of the transport company's trucks. Johnnie had to help me over the side of the cage. Now that I was out of the Kingdom my body seemed weak and limp. The engine of the hoist died away and a man came out of the housing towards us. My vision was blurred and I didn't recognise him. And then suddenly I was looking into the angry, black eyes of Peter Trevedian. "Seems we got to lock our property up out here now," he said in a hard voice. "Next time, let me know when you want to play around and we'll see you get a nursemaid."

"Cut it out, Trevedian. Can't you see he's dead beat?" Johnnie's voice sounded remote, like the surgeon's voice in an operating theatre just before you go under.

I don't remember much about that drive, just the blessed heat of the engine and the trees coming at us in an endless line of white. Then we were at the bunkhouse and Jean was there and several others and they half-carried me up to the hotel. The next thing I knew I was up in my room and my body was sinking into warm oblivion, surrounded by hot-water bottles.

It was getting dark when I woke. Johnnie was sitting by the window reading a magazine. He looked up as I stirred. "Feeling better?"

I nodded and sat up. "I feel fine," I said. There was a note of surprise in my voice. I hadn't felt so good for a long time. And I was hungry, too.

He rolled a cigarette, lit it for me and put it in my mouth. "Boy got in to-day. Wants to see you as soon as you feel okay."

"Boy Bladen?"

"Yeh. He's got an Irishman with him—a drilling contractor, name of Garry Keogh. And your lawyer feller, Acheson, rang through. He's coming up here to see you to-morrow. That's about all the news, I guess. Except that Trevedian's madder'n hell about your going up to the Kingdom."

"Because I used his hoist?"

"Mebbe."

"Did McClellan object?"

"Oh, Jimmy's okay. He was just scared you'd gone and killed yourself. Oh, I nearly forgot." He reached into his pocket and pulled out an envelope. " Mac asked me to give you this." He tossed it on to the bed.

It was a long envelope and bulky. It was sealed with wax. I turned it over and saw it was postmarked Calgary. " That'll be Acheson," I said. " Another copy of the deed of sale for the Kingdom. He just doesn't seem able to take No for an answer." I put it on the table beside me. " Johnnie."

" Yeh?"

" I'm hungry. Do you think you could get them to produce something for me to eat?"

" Sure. What would you like?"

" I wouldn't mind a steak. A big, juicy steak."

He cocked his head on one side, peering at me as though he were examining a horse. " Seems the Kingdom agrees with you. I was only saying to Jeff just now that you looked a hell of a lot better than when we saw you at Jasper." He turned towards the door. " Okay. I'll tell Pauline to cook you up something real big in the way of a T-bone steak. All right for Boy and Keogh to come up?"

I nodded. " What's the time?"

" A little after seven."

I had slept for over twelve hours. I got up and had a wash. I was still towelling myself when footsteps sounded on the stairs. It was Boy Bladen and there was something about the way he erupted into the room that took me back to my school days. He was like a kid bursting with news. The man with him was big and heavy and solid with a battered face and broken teeth. His clothes, like himself, were crumpled and shapeless. And in that shapelessness as well as in the loose hang of his arms, the relaxed state of his muscles, there was something really tough. He looked like a man whom the world had tossed from one end to the other and battered all the way.

" Bruce. This is Garry Keogh." I found my hand engulfed in the rasping grip of a fist that seemed like a chunk of rock. Garry Keogh took off his hat and tossed it on to the chair. His grizzled hair was cut short and he was partly bald. He looked like an all-in wrestler, but his eyes were those of a dreamer with a twinkle of humour in them that softened his face to something friendly. " I've almost talked him into doing the drilling for us," Boy added. " It was Garry's rig I was wildcatting on during the winter."

I stared at the big rig operator. "You think there's oil up there?"

"Sure and there maybe." He was Irish, but he spoke slowly, as though words were an unaccustomed commodity. It gave emphasis to everything he said. "Boy's impetuous, but he's no fool. I never met Campbell. I heard he was a crazy bird. But then the story of every strike is the story of men who were thought crazy till they were proved to have staked a mine." He grinned, showing the gaps in his teeth. "My father went to the Yukon in '98. That's where I was born."

"But I don't own the mineral rights of the Kingdom," I said. "Didn't Boy tell you? They were mortgaged to Roger Fergus by my grandfather's company and now that he's dead they'll pass to his son."

Garry Keogh turned to Boy. "Why the hell didn't you tell me that?"

"But——" Boy was staring at me. "Louis Winnick told me the old man had given you back the mineral rights. The day after you saw Roger Fergus he sent for Louis. He said he'd left him a legacy under his will. He told him about your visit and instructed him that he was to give you all the help you needed—free of any charge. He said it was a condition of the legacy. He wouldn't have done that unless he'd known you were free to go ahead and drill in the Kingdom if you wanted to. You haven't heard from the old man?"

I shook my head.

"You've had no communication from him at all, or from his lawyers?"

"Nothing," I said. "The only mail I've had——" I stopped then and turned to the table beside the bed. I picked up the envelope and split the seal. Inside was a package of documents. The letter attached to them wasn't from Acheson. It was on Bank of Canada notepaper and it read: *On the instructions of our client, Mr. Roger Fergus, we are enclosing documents relating to certain mineral rights mortgaged to our client by the Campbell Oil Exploration Company. Cancellation of the mortgage is effective as from the date of this letter and we are instructed to inform you that our client wishes you to know that from henceforth neither he nor his estate will have any claim to these rights and further that any debts outstanding with the company referred to above, for which these*

*documents were held as security, are cancelled. You are re-
quested to sign the enclosed receipt and forward it. . . ."* I
opened out these documents. They were in respect of "The
mineral rights in the territory known generally as Campbell's
Kingdom." There followed the necessary map references. I
passed the papers across to Boy. "You were quite right," I
said.

Boy seized hold of them. "I knew I was. If Roger Fergus
said he'd do a thing, he always did it. Louis said he was
pretty taken with you. Thought you'd got a lot of guts and
hopes for Stuart's sake you'd win out."

I thought of the old man, half paralysed in that wheel-chair.
I could remember his words—*"A fine pair we are."* And
then: *"I'd like to have seen one more discovery well brought
in before I die."* There was a lump in my throat as I remembered those words. *"I'm glad you came. If your doctor
fellow's right, we'll maybe meet again soon."* It would be nice
to tell him I'd brought in a well. But I wished he were in the
thing with me. It would have been much easier. I needed
somebody experienced. I looked across at Keogh and then at
Boy, the two of them so dissimilar, but neither of them
capable of fighting a big company backed by the solid weight
of unlimited finance and with lawyers to make legal rings
round our efforts. Boy didn't understand what we were up
against.

Keogh looked up from the documents Boy had passed him.
He must have seen the doubt in my face for he said, "What
do you plan to do, Wetheral—go ahead and drill?"

I hesitated. But my mind slid away from the difficulties.
I could see only that old man sitting in the wheel-chair and
behind him the more shadowy figure of my grandfather.
Both of them had believed in me. "Yes," I said. "If Winnick reports favourably, I'll go ahead—provided I can get
the capital."

Keogh fingered his lower lip, his eyes fixed on me. They
were narrowed and sharp—not cunning, but speculating.
"You'd find it a lot easier to raise capital if you'd brought
in a well," he murmured.

"I know that."

"Boy mentioned something about your being willing to
split fifty-fifty on all profits with those who do the development work."

"Yes," I said. "That's about it."

He nodded abstractedly, stroking his chin. His fingers made a rasping sound against the stubble of his beard. Then suddenly he looked up. "I've been in the oil business over twenty years now and I've never had a proposition like this made to me. It's the sort of thing a drilling contractor dreams of." His broken teeth showed in a grin. "It'd be flying in the face of providence to refuse it." He turned to Boy. "If Winnick's report on that recording tape is optimistic then you'll go up to the Kingdom and do another survey. Okay?" Boy nodded. "If the proposition still looks good, then I'll come up here again and look over the ground." He hesitated, staring down at me. "I'll be frank with you, Wetheral. This is a hell of a gamble. I've made a bit on the last two wildcats I drilled. Otherwise I wouldn't be interested. But I'm still only good for about a couple of months operating on my own. To be any use to me, there's got to be water handy and the depth mustn't be more than a few thousand feet, dependent on the nature of the country we have to drill through. But if all that's okay, then it's a deal."

"Fine," I said.

He was staring down at his hands. "I started as a roustabout," he said slowly. "I worked fifteen years as roughneck, driller and finally tool-pusher before I got together enough dough to get my own rig. I was another five years paying for it. Now I'm in the clear and making dough." He smiled gently to himself. "Funny thing about human nature. Somehow it don't seem able to stop. You own a rig and you think that's fine and before you know where you are you're wanting an interest in an oil well." His smile spread to a deep laugh. "I guess when a man's finished expanding, he's finished living." He turned abruptly to the door. "Come on, Boy. Time we had a drink. You care to join us, Wetheral?"

"Thank you," I said. "But I've got some food coming up."

"Okay. Be seeing you before I leave."

He went out. Boy hesitated. "It was the best I could do, Bruce. Garry's straight and he's a fighter. Once he gets his teeth into a thing he doesn't let up easily. But I'm sorry about Roger Fergus."

"So am I," I said.

He had taken the spools containing the recording tape out of his pocket and was joggling them up and down on the palm of his hand. "Funny to think that these little containers may be the start of a new oilfield." He stared at them, lost in his own thoughts. And then he said an odd thing: "It's like holding Destiny in the palm of one's hands. If this proves Louis' first report wrong. . . ." He slipped them into his pocket. "Jeff lent me his station wagon. I'll get over to Keithley to-night so that they'll catch the mail out first thing in the morning. We should get Louis' report within three days." He had moved over to the door and he stood there for a moment, his hand on the knob. "You know, somehow that makes me scared." He seemed about to say something further, but instead he just said, "Goodnight," and went out.

I lit a cigarette and lay back on my bed. Things were beginning to move and, like Boy, I felt scared. I wondered whether I'd have the energy to handle it all. Acheson would be arriving to-morrow. Probably he'd have Henry Fergus with him. Once they knew my intention. . . .

There was a knock at the door and Jean came in. "How's the invalid?" She had a tray of food and she put it down on the table beside me. "Pauline was out, so I did the best I could. Johnnie said you were hungry."

"I could eat a horse."

"Well, this isn't horse." She smiled, but it was only a movement of her lips. She seemed tensed up about something. "Boy and that big Irishman are down in the bar drinking."

"Well?" The steak was good. I didn't want to talk.

She was over by the window, standing there, staring at me. "It's all over the town that you're going to drill a well up in the Kingdom."

"That's what you wanted, wasn't it?"

"Yes, but——" She hesitated. "Bruce. You should have made your plans without anybody here knowing what you were up to."

I looked up from my plate. Her face was pale in the lamplight, the scars on her jaw more noticeable than usual. "I haven't any capital," I said. "And when you haven't any capital you can't plan things in advance."

"If Henry Fergus decides to proceed with the dam you're headed for trouble."

"I know that."

"And if he doesn't then the people here will be sore and

they'll get at you somehow. Johnnie wasn't exactly clever in making an enemy of Peter."

" Appeasement is not in his line."

" No, but——" She gave a quick, exasperated sigh and sat down in the chair. " Can I have a cigarette, please?"

I tossed her a packet and a box of matches. " You don't seem to realise what you're up against, any of you. Boy I can understand, and Johnnie. But you're English. You've fought in the war. You know what happens when people get whipped up emotionally. You're not a fool." She blew out a streamer of smoke. " It's as though you didn't care—about yourself, I mean."

" You think I may get hurt?" I was staring at her, wondering what was behind her concern.

" You're putting yourself in a position where a lot of people would be glad if an accident happened to you."

" And you think it might?"

" After last night anything could happen." She was leaning forward. " What made you do such a crazy thing? You're now branded as a fool where mountains are concerned."

" What are you trying to tell me?"

" That you're going about this business so clumsily that I'm afraid. . . ." She stopped short, and then in a sudden rush of words: " How do you think you're going to get a drilling rig up to the Kingdom? From now on Trevedian will have a guard on the hoist. He won't even allow your rig to move on the new road. It's on his property and he's every right to stop you from trespassing. Even supposing you did get the rig up there, do you think they'd let it rest at that?" She got to her feet with a quick movement of anger. " You can't fight a man as big as Henry Fergus, and you know it."

" I can try," I said.

She swung round on me. " This isn't the City of London, Bruce. This is the Canadian West. A hundred years ago there was nothing here—no railways, no roads; the Fraser River was only just being opened up. This isn't a lawless country but it's been opened up by big companies and they've bulldozed their way through small interests. They've had to. Now you come out here from England and start throwing down the gauntlet to a man like Henry Fergus. Henry isn't his father. He isn't a pioneer. There's nothing lovable about him. He's a financier and as cold as six inches of steel." She turned away to the window. "You're starting something that'll end on a mountain slope somewhere out there." She nodded through the black panes of the window. "I know this sort of business. I was two years in France with the Maquis till they got me. I know every trick. I know how to make murder look like an accident." She dropped her cigarette on to the floor and ground it out with the heel of her shoe. "You've made it so easy for them. You have an accident. The police come up here to investigate. Whatever I may say and perhaps others, they'll hear about last night and they'll shrug their shoulders and say that you were bound to get hurt sooner or later."

I had finished my steak and I lit a cigarette. "What do you suggest I do then?"

She pushed her hand through her hair. "Sell out and go back home." Her voice had dropped suddenly to little more than a whisper.

"That wasn't what you wanted me to do when I first came to see you. You wanted me to fight."

"You were a stranger then."

"What difference does that make?"

"Oh, I don't know." She came and stood over me. Her face had a peculiar sadness. "This happened to me once before," she said in a tired voice. "I don't want it to happen again." She suddenly held out her hand. "Good-bye, Bruce." She had control of her voice now and it was natural, impersonal. "I'll be gone in the morning. I'm taking a trip down to the Coast. It's time I had a change. I've been in Come Lucky too long."

I looked up at her face. It was suddenly older and there was a withdrawn set to her mouth. "You're running out on me," I said.

"No." The word came out with a violence that was unexpected. "I never ran out on anybody in my life—or anything." Her voice trembled. "It's just that I'm tired. I can't——" She stopped there and shrugged her shoulders. "If you come out to Vancouver——" She hesitated and then said, "I'll leave my address with the Garrets."

"Would you really like me more if I threw in my hand because the going looked tough?"

Her hands fluttered uncertainly. "It isn't a question of

liking. It's just that I can't stand——" She got hold of herself with a quick intake of breath. "Good-bye, Bruce." Her fingers touched mine. She half-bent towards me, a sudden tenderness in her eyes. But then she straightened up and turned quickly to the door. She didn't look round as she went out and I was left with the remains of my meal and a feeling of emptiness.

I went round to see her in the morning, but she had already left, travelling to Keithley with Max Trevedian and Garry Keogh in the supply truck. "Did she leave any message?" I asked Miss Garret.

"No. Only her address." She handed me a sheet of paper and her sharp, beady eyes quizzed me through her lorgnette. "Do you know why she left so suddenly, Mr. Wetheral?"

"No," I said. "I don't."

"Most extraordinary. So unlike her to do anything suddenly like that. My sister and I are very worried."

"Didn't she give you any explanation?" I asked.

"No. She just said she needed a change and was leaving."

"Did she say when she'd be coming back?"

"No. She hardly spoke at all. She seemed upset."

"Ruth," her sister's voice called from the other side of the room. "Don't forget the little box she left for Mr. Wetheral."

"Of course not," Ruth Garret answered a trifle sharply. "It's in my room. I'll get it for you."

As she went through the door her sister scurried across the room to me. Her thin, transparent hand caught hold of my arm. "You silly boy," she said. "Why did you let her go?"

"Why?" I was a little taken aback. "What could I do to stop here?"

"I wouldn't know what men do to stop a girl running away from them. I'm an old maid." The blue eyes twinkled up at me. And then suddenly they were full of tears. "It's so quiet here without her. I wish she hadn't gone. She was so warm and—comforting to have around." She dabbed at her eyes with a lace handkerchief. "When you have lived shut away for so long, it is nice to have somebody young in the house. It was so restful."

"You're fond of her, aren't you?" I asked.

"Yes, very. It was—like having a daughter here. And now she's gone and I don't know when she'll be coming back." She began to sob. "Youth is very cruel—to old people."

I took hold of her by the shoulders, feeling the thin frailty of her bones. "Stop crying, Miss Sarah. Please. Tell me why she went away. You know why she went, don't you?" I shook her gently.

"She ran away," she sobbed. "She was afraid of life—like Ruth and me. She didn't want to be hurt any more."

"Do you know anything about her, before she came to Come Lucky?"

"A little—not much. She was in France, a British agent working with the Resistance. She operated a radio for them. She was with her father and then when he was killed she worked with another man and——" She hesitated and then said, "I think she fell in love——" Her voice trailed off on a note of sadness.

"Was he killed, this fellow she was in love with?"

She nodded. "Yes, I think so. But she wouldn't talk about it. I think she used up a whole lifetime in those few years. She is a little afraid of life now."

"I see." Footsteps sounded on the stairs and I let go of her shoulders.

"Here you are." Ruth Garret held out a small mahogany box to me. "I almost forgot about it. She gave it to me last night."

"Did she say anything when she handed it to you?"

"No. Only that it was for you. The key is in the lock." I looked at her and knew by the way her eyes avoided mine that she had opened it and knew what was inside. She hadn't intended to give it to me.

"Is there any message inside?" I asked.

She stiffened angrily. "No." She turned away and walked out of the room, holding herself very erect. Her sister suddenly giggled. "Ruth doesn't like to be found out. I shall have to be very deaf for at least a week now." Her eyes twinkled at me through her tears. And then with a sudden disconcerting change of mood: "Please go to Vancouver and bring her back. I shall miss her terribly."

"I'm sorry," I said. "I shan't be going to Vancouver."

The corner of her mouth turned down petulantly and her lips trembled. "Will you let pride——"

"It isn't pride," I said. "It's common sense." On a sudden impulse I bent down and kissed her forehead. "Thank you for telling me a little about her. And if she does come back, tell her to stay away from the Kingdom. Tell her to go back to Vancouver till it's all over."

" Till—it's all over?"

" Yes. Till it's all over." I went out on to the boarded sidewalk then and walked slowly back to the hotel, the little mahogany box clutched under my arm. Johnnie Carstairs and Jeff were just leaving. I left the box in my room and walked with them down to their car. I hadn't seen Boy that morning and I asked about him. " He's gone off into the mountains," Johnnie answered. " He's like that. As long as Keogh was here he was full of optimism. But now—he's like a broody hen." His fingers dug into my flesh as he held my arm. " Bruce. You know what you're doing, do you?"

" I think so," I said.

He nodded slowly, looking me straight in the eyes. " Yes, I guess you do. You don't care do you?"

" How do you mean?"

" About life—and death. It doesn't scare you the way it does most people." He bit on the end of the matchstick clamped between his teeth and spat the chewed end of it out. " If you want me, phone Jeff. If I'm in Jasper I'll come. Understand?" His hand gripped mine.

" That's good of you, Johnnie," I said.

He climbed into the station wagon and a moment later they were slithering down through the mud to the lakeside.

I walked slowly back to the hotel. The big bar-room was empty, the whole place strangely silent and deserted. My friends had gone. I had nothing to do now but wait for the arrival of Acheson. I climbed wearily up to my room. The mahogany box lay on the bed where I had tossed it. I picked it up and went over to the window, weighing it in my hands, speculating about its contents and oddly reluctant to open it. The twin peaks of Solomon's Judgment gleamed white against the grey of the sky. I could see her face in the panes of the window sill. The scars of her jaw were more marked in my mental picture of her than they were in reality. A mood of sadness enveloped me, a bitter sense of frustration. If only . .

With a quick movement of my fingers I turned the key in the lock and opened the lid. Inside the box there was some thing wrapped up in a silk scarf. I took it out, still wrapped, and held it in my hand, feeling the hardness of the metal, the old familiar shape of it. I had stripped one of these from the dead body of an officer of the 21st Panzer Division and I'd carried it in my holster over two thousand miles of desert warfare.

I unwound the silk scarf and the Luger fell into the palm of my hand as naturally as that other had done all those years back. My finger curled automatically to the trigger. The black butt of it was notched as mine had been. I counted seven notches. And above the notches was scratched a name —Paul Morton.

I sat down on the bed, staring at the thing. Paul Morton! Paul Morton was the name of a man who had been my grandfather's partner in the flotation of the Rocky Mountain Oil Exploration Company, the man who had run out on him with all the capital of the company. Could it be the same Morton? I searched quickly in the box, but there was no message, nothing but four spare magazines, all loaded. I wondered how Morton had come to possess a Luger. And I wondered also how Jean Lucas had become the owner of Morton's gun.

There was a knock on the door. I slipped the ugly-looking weapon under my pillow. " Come in."

It was Pauline. " There are two men here asking for you, Bruce."

Acheson! " Tell them I'm coming down right away." I locked the box in one of my grips and slipped the Luger into my hip-pocket. The action was quite automatic and I found myself smiling at it as I went downstairs. Jean was being a little over-melodramatic. They might play it rough, but not that rough. And yet the odd thing is that I'm certain the presence of that gun in my pocket gave me confidence. Not a gunman's confidence. I don't mean that. But it was as though the years between the end of the war and that moment were wiped away and I was back, in command, with men under me and a life to be lived for the day only with no thought of the future except how you could destroy the enemy. It was a good feeling. I liked it. It seemed to give me buoyancy and energy. And when I found myself face to face with Acheson and Henry Fergus I almost laughed, thinking of how they'd have made out at Knightsbridge with only a couple of tanks left and the whole ring of dunes spitting flame. "Let's go into the bar," I said. "We can talk there."

Henry Fergus was a tall, spare man with a slight stoop to his shoulders. He had a thin, unemotional face and even out here he managed to retain something of the man of money about him. He came straight to the point. "How much do you want, Wetheral?"

"I'm not selling," I said.

"What was this drilling contractor doing out here?" Acheson asked.

"Is that any business of yours?" I demanded. I was thinking how Fergus had indirectly been responsible for Campbell's death. Acheson had been in on it, too, I had no doubt. "I suppose you've been talking to Trevedian?"

Acheson nodded. "We've just been up to the dam. That's why we came out here. If you're thinking of drilling up in the Kingdom I have to remind you that you don't own the mineral rights. They were mortgaged to Mr. Fergus's father. Now that he is dead——"

"Just who are you acting for, Acheson," I said. "Me or Fergus?"

His eyes widened slightly at my tone and the florid colouring of his smoothly polished cheeks deepened. "For both of you," he said sharply. "And it lucky for you that I am, otherwise Mr. Fergus here would never have considered the idea——"

"That's a lie," I said. "Fergus was considering completing the dam over a year ago. It was only because his father insisted on a survey first that construction was postponed until this year."

He stared at me, his mouth slightly open. "You're not acting for me, Acheson," I said. "You never have been. You're acting for Fergus here. As for the mineral rights, I suppose you didn't bother to check with the Bank of Canada who has them now?"

"What are you getting at?" Fergus demanded.

For answer I pulled out my wallet and handed him the covering letter I had received with the documents. He read it through slowly. Not a muscle of his face moved. Then he passed it across to Acheson. I watched the solicitor's face. He wasn't a poker player like Fergus. "How did you get these?" he demanded angrily. "What yarn did you spin the old man?" He turned to Fergus, "I think we could challenge this. It might be a question of false pretences."

I leaned back. "Now I know where I am," I said. "When you get back to Calgary, Acheson, will you kindly lodge all the documents relating to Stuart Campbell with the Bank of Canada together with a statement of any actions you have taken regarding his affairs without my knowledge. And I warn you, I'll have the whole thing checked through by a competent and honest lawyer." And then, before he could recover himself, I added, "Now perhaps you'll leave us to discuss this business privately since it no longer concerns you."

He sat staring at me for a moment, his mouth open, quite speechless. Then he turned to Fergus, who had lit a cigarette and was watching the scene with the detachment of a spectator. "I think," Fergus said, "Wetheral and I will get on better on our own."

Acheson hesitated. He wanted to say something. I could see him struggling to get it out, but he didn't know what to say. In the end he pulled himself to his feet and left us without a word.

Fergus watched him go and then leaned towards me. "It seems you're a good deal cleverer than Acheson gave you credit for. Suppose we put the cards on the table. In the first place, I have no alternative source of power. The Larsen Mines are low grade ore. It's all right taking power from one of the existing companies now when lead prices are high. But I'm operating on the long view. I want cheap power permanently in the hands of the company. Therefore, you can take it as quite definite that whatever your attitude I shall go ahead with the completion of the Solomon's Judgment dam and in due course—about five months from now—the Kingdom will be a lake. I have full powers to do this under the legislation passed by the Provincial Parliament in February, 1939. You can either accept my offer, which is $60,000, or we can go to arbitration."

"Then we go to arbitration," I said. "And if there's oil up there——"

"There's only one way for you to prove that there's oil up there," he said, "and that is to drill a well."

I nodded. "That's exactly what I intend to do."

He smiled. "Then you'll have to drill it with a bit and brace for you won't get a rig up there. I'll see to that. Better face it, Wetheral. The courts won't grant you anything like $60,000 in compensation."

"We'll see," I said. "You've already monkeyed about with a survey and caused the death of an old man. That won't look too good if it comes out in court."

But he just smiled. "You think it over." He got to his feet. "$60,000 is a lot of money for a young man like you. It would be a pity to lose it all trying to drill a well. And don't do anything foolish. Remember, Campbell was a crook and his record wouldn't help you any if you got yourself into the criminal courts." He nodded to me, still with that thin-lipped smile on his face, and turned to the door. "Acheson! Acheson!" His voice gradually faded away as I sat there, rigid, my hands gripping the edge of the table, my whole body cold with anger. My grandfather's record hadn't been thrown in my face like that since I was a kid.

At length I got to my feet and went slowly up to my room. From the window I watched the two of them leave and walk down to Trevedian's office. I looked down and saw I was holding the gun in my hand. I threw it quickly on to the bed. I couldn't trust myself to have it in my hand.

I was still standing there, staring up to the twin peaks of Solomon's Judgment, when old Mac came in. His face was sour and his burr more pronounced than ever as he told me I could no longer stay at the hotel. I didn't argue with him. From the window I could see Trevedian's thick-set figure walking back to the bunkhouse and down the lake-shore a big American car was ploughing through the slush in the direction of Keithley.

The gloves were off and I began to pack my things.

II

Two days later I was in Calgary and Boy and I heard from Winnick's own lips his report on that last recording we had mailed to him. He was guardedly optimistic. The pulses recorded by the geophones were not clearly defined, but at least there was no evidence of the broken strata referred to in his original report. "All I can say is that it looks like an anticline. Before I can tell you anything definite I'll need to have the results of a dozen or so more shots from different points over the same ground."

It wasn't much to go on, but it was enough to confirm our suspicions that there had been substitution of the original recordings. Boy wired Garry Keogh the result and left for Edmonton at once to pick up the rest of his team. He planned to go up to the Kingdom by the pony trail just as soon as he could get through. He would bring the results of the survey out himself. He reckoned it would take about a month. I asked him how he was fixed for money, but he just shrugged his shoulders. "We'll make out, I guess. There's gas up in the Kingdom and cans of food. We won't have to pack anything up there, just ourselves. As for wages, I'll look after that."

I stayed on in Calgary. I had a lot to see to. Acheson's office handed over all the documents relating to my grandfather's affairs and by the time I had unravelled the affairs of the Campbell Oil Exploration Company and had got somebody to act for me a week had passed. At the same time I did everything I could to make myself familiar with the operation of a drilling rig. Winnicks, a little man with pale eyes and spectacles and a rather sad-looking face, took Roger Fergus's instructions very literally. He gave me every possible assistance. He lent me books. He took me out to dinner at the Petroleum Club, introduced me to oil men, and sent me to have a look over the Turner Valley field. At the end of that week I really felt that I was beginning to know something about oil.

And at the end of that week the jaded mechanism of my body ran down and I hadn't the strength to crawl out of bed. Winnick came round to see me and sent at once for his doctor. I knew it wasn't any use and I told him so. But he insisted. He seemed to feel personally responsible. I think at the back of his mind was the sense of having let old Roger Fergus down over that survey. He was a kind-hearted little man, fussy over details and with an immense regard for the infallibility of his own judgment.

The doctor, of course, wanted me to go straight into hospital. But I refused. I was afraid once I got inside a hospital I'd never get out. I'd been better in the cold, crisp air of the Rockies. I wanted to get back there. I felt that time was running out and if I were going to die I wanted to

die up in the Kingdom. As I lay in my bed in the Palliser
Hotel, in a half coma of inertia, this became almost an
obsession with me. I think it was this that pulled me through.
I just refused to die down there in Calgary with the level
ground of the ranchlands spreading out round me and the
dust blowing through the streets.

A few days later, very weak and exhausted, I staggered
down to Winnick's car and we headed north for Edmonton
and Jasper. We spent the night at Jasper and Johnnie Carstairs and Jeff Hart came to see me in my room. I remember
something that Johnnie said to me then. Winnick had told
him I'd been ill and he knew what the cause of it was. He
said, " Take my advice, Bruce. Stay in the Rockies. The
mountains suit you."

" You may be right," I said. " I was damn glad to see them
again."

He nodded. " Climate is the same as food. What you want
is what you're deficient of. And no damned quack blethering
a lot of scientific nonsense will convince me otherwise. You
stay up in the mountains, Bruce."

" I intend to," I said. " I'm going up to the Kingdom."

He nodded. " Well, if they try and smoke you out, send
for me."

Next day we made Keithley Creek and the following morning we ploughed through the mud of the newly-graded road
to Come Lucky. Now that I was in the mountains again I
felt better. My heart was racing madly, but the air was cool
and clear and I was suddenly quite confident that I should get
my strength back. The sight of the peaks of Solomon's
Judgment against the clear blue of the sky gave me the same
feeling that the cliffs of Dover had done when I came back
at the end of the war ; this was home to me now.

We didn't turn up to the bunkhouse, but continued straight
along the lake-shore road to the dark, timbered mouth of
Thunder Creek. I had warned Winnick that we might not be
allowed to go up by the hoist, but he wasn't convinced. He
was Henry Fergus's oil consultant and he'd known him since
they were kids together. He thought that would be enough.

But it didn't work out that way. About a mile up the creek
where the road cut back into the mountainside to bridge a
torrent we were stopped by a heavy timber gate supported
by a tall post like the corral gates around Calgary. There

was a log hut with an iron chimney that sent a drift of wood through the trees. A man came out of it as we drew up and threw the open doorway I saw a rifle propped against a wooden bench. " Can I see your pass?" The man was short and stocky and he was chewing gum.

I certainly hadn't expected precautions as elaborate as this and my companion was equally surprised. " My name's Winnick," he said. " I'm a friend of Henry Fergus."

" I don't know any Henry Fergus," the man replied. " I take my orders from Trevedian and he says you got to have a pass if you want to go on up to the camp."

" Who's in charge up at the camp?"

" Fellow named Butler, but that won't help you, mister. You got to have a pass signed by Trevedian an' Trevedian's down at Come Lucky. You'll find him at the company's office." The last words were almost drowned by the sound of a horn. " Pull over, will you. There's a truck coming through." I turned round. Coming up the grade behind us was a big American truck, heavily loaded and grinding up in low gear.

We pulled into a turning section that had been bulldozed out of the hillside and watched the truck grind past, through the wide-swung gate. It was loaded with bags of cement roped down under a tarpaulin. " For two pins I'd crash through behind it," Winnick said.

" You'd only get your tyres shot up." I nodded to the open doorway of the hut.

He didn't say anything for a moment, but sat staring first at the rifle inside the hut and then at the man who was leaning on the gate watching us. At length he put the car in gear, turned her and headed back down the valley. " Seems you were right after all. We'll have to find Trevedian."

" You won't get a pass out of him," I said.

" Of course I will," he said.

We were running out of the timber and the lake lay blue in the sunshine and the whole hillside above it glistened with water from the melted snow so that the shacks of Come Lucky were like dilapidated houseboats plunging down the glittering cascade of a fall. He swung the car towards Come Lucky and stopped at Trevedian's office. " You wait here," he said.

He was gone about ten minutes and when he came out his

mouth was set in a tight line. "We'll have to ride up," he said. "Do you know where we can get horses and a guide?"

"No," I said. "Unless . . ." I paused, looking up to the line of shacks that marked the single street of Come Lucky. Then I climbed out of the car. "Let's walk up to the hotel and have a drink. There's just one person who might help us."

"Who's that?"

I didn't answer. It was such a slender chance. But if we didn't get the horses here it would mean going back to Keithley and starting out from there. As we walked up along the rotten boarding of the sidewalk to the Golden Calf Winnick said, "Maybe you were right about that survey."

"How do you mean?"

"About Henry arranging for the recording tapes to be switched. When Trevedian refused to give us a pass to go up the creek, I got through to Calgary. Henry told me I'd no business to be here. He warned me that if I continued to act for you he'd see to it that I got no more business from his companies or from any of his friends. I knew he was a cold-blooded devil, but I never thought he'd try to pull a thing like that."

"What are you going to do?"

"Go up to the Kingdom with you."

We had reached the Golden Calf. As we pushed open the door old Mac came to meet us. "Ah'm sorry, Wetheral,'" he said sourly, "but ye ken verra well Ah canna have ye here."

"Trevedian phoned you we were coming up, did he?" I said.

He shrugged his shoulders awkwardly. "Ah canna help it, man."

I said, "Well, don't worry, we're not here for the night. We just want a drink, that's all."

Mac hesitated and then he said angrily, "Och, o' course ye can have a drink." He looked at me and his face softened slightly, "If ye'd care to come into ma office there's a wee drap o' Scotch ye could have."

We went through into a small room with a roll-top desk and a grandfather clock. I introduced Winnick. The old man stood looking at him for a moment and then he went over to the desk and brought out a bottle and glasses from the cupboard underneath. "So ye're the oil consultant from

Calgary." He passed the bottle across to Winnick. "And what brings ye to Come Lucky, Mr. Winnick?"

"We want to get up to the Kingdom," I said. "But there's a guard at the entrance to Thunder Creek."

He nodded. "Aye. And there's anither at the hoist. Ye'll no' get to the Kingdom that way, laddie, not unless ye get Trevedian's permission, and I dinna think ye'll get that."

"He's already refused," I said.

"Aye." He nodded. "An' he's within his rights. Thunder Creek's all Trevedian land right up the fault to the dam."

"Where's the pony trail start?" I asked.

"The pony trail?" He rubbed the stubble of his chin with his bony fingers. "You cross Thunder Creek by a ford a few hundred yards above the lake and it runs up through the timber below Forked Lightning Mountain and then over the Saddle below the northern peak of Solomon's Judgment." He shook his head. "It's a hard trail to follow. Ye'd never make it on your own."

"I was afraid of that," I said. "Is Max around to-day or has he gone to Keithley for supplies?"

"Max Trevedian? Aye, he'll be doon at his place. But Max'll no' take ye up."

"Where's his shack?"

The old man stared at me for a moment and then took me to the window and pointed it out to me, a dilapidated huddle of buildings standing on their own a few hundred yards above and beyond the bunkhouse. "It's Luke Trevedian's old place." He shook his head sadly. "One time it was a fine farmhouse with flowers and all the people from miles around coming to parties there. He had some of the finest horses in the country and a big ranch over in the Kootenay. Och, the times I've had up there."

"You wait here," I said to Winnick. "I won't be long."

Mac stopped me at the door. "Take care," he said. "Max is an uncertain sort of crittur. He doesna realise his own strength."

"I know," I said.

As I walked down the street I saw Trevedian come out of his office and get into the truck parked by the bunkhouse. He drove down to the lake shore and turned up towards Thunder Creek. I couldn't help smiling. Trevedian was making certain of his guards, and all because I had arrived in Come

Lucky. A wisp of smoke came from the stone chimney of the old Trevedian home. Even now, though it was falling into ruins, it had an air of solidity about it. The stables and barns were of split pine, but the house itself was built of stone and there was the remains of a carriage driveway. A big saddle horse stood tethered to the railing of the verandah and it pricked its ears at me as I knocked on the patched wood-work of the front door. Nothing stirred inside the house and I knocked again. Below me Beaver Dam Lake lay like a sheet of glass mirroring the blue of the sky and the sharp-etched white of the mountains beyond. Boots sounded on bare boards. Then the door was flung open and Max Treve-dian stood there, staring at me, his fool mouth agape. His eyes slid towards the shape of the bunkhouse.

"It's all right," I said. "Your brother's gone up Thunder Creek. Can I come in?"

"Ja, ja. Come in." He closed the door after me and stood there, watching me. But for a moment I was too astonished to say anything. I was in a big lounge hall of tawdry mag-nificence, looking at the faded grandeur of Luke Trevedian, mine-owner and collector. He had apparently had a taste for old furniture, but it was entirely indiscriminate. Exquisite little Queen Anne pieces were mixed up with suits of armour, Chippendale and Adam mahogany and ornate Italian furni-ture. There was a superb Jacobean refectory table surrounded by Hepplewhite chairs. And everywhere there was dust and an air of decay.

"Why do you come here?" Max's voice, hard and teutonic, growled round the rotting tapestry hangings of the walls.

I turned and faced him, trying to measure his mood. He hadn't moved from the door. His small eyes were narrowed, his body hunched forward with the arms hanging loose. His expression was one of resentment at my intrusion. He glanced furtively round and then, with a sudden smile that was like a gleam of wintry sunshine in his rugged face, he said, "We go into my father's room. This——" His big hands indicated the room. "This is hers."

He took me down a short passage and into a small, very simple room. It was furnished almost entirely with Colonial pieces from the loyalist houses of the East. The furniture here gleamed with the care that had been lavished on it. I had a sudden feeling of warmth towards Max. He was clumsy and loutish and yet he'd kept this corner as a shrine to his father's memory with the delicate care of a woman. " It's a beautiful room," I said.

" It is my father's room." There was pride and love and longing in his voice.

" Thank you for letting me see it." I hesitated. " Will you take me up to the Kingdom, Max?"

He stared at me and shook his head slowly. " Peter does not wish you to go to the Kingdom. I must not go there again."

I went over and sat at the desk, fitting my mood to the atmosphere of the room, to the man who had once occupied it. I looked at Max Trevedian, trying to visualise the little boy who must have stood here before his father after he had killed another boy. " Max," I said gently. " You didn't have a very happy childhood, did you?"

" Childhood?" He stared at me and then shook his head. " No. Not happy. Boys made fun of me and did cruel things. Little girls. . . ." He swung his head from side to side in that bear-like way he had. " They laugh at Max."

" Boys made fun of me, too." I said.

" You?"

I nodded. " I was poor and half-starved and my grand-father was in prison. And later, something was missing—some money—and they ganged up on me and said I'd stolen it. And because my grandfather had been to prison and my mother was poor they sent me to a reform school." God, it seemed only yesterday. It was all so vivid in my mind still. " You loved your father, didn't you?"

He nodded. " *Ja.* I love my father, but always there is my stepmother. She hated me. She made me live in the stables after . . ." His voice trailed away, but I knew that what he had been going to say was *after I killed Alf Robens.*

" It was different with me," I said. " I had no father. He was killed in the first war. I loved my mother very dearly. She always believed my grandfather innocent. She brought me up to believe it, too. But when I was sent to the reform school and she died I began to hate my grandfather." I went slowly across to him and put my hand on his arm. " Max, I now know I did him a great wrong. I know he is innocent. I'm going to prove him innocent. And you're going to help me because then Campbell and your father will once again be remembered as friends. He didn't ruin your father. He was convinced there was oil up in the Kingdom. And so am I, Max. That is why you're going to take me up to the Kingdom."

He shook his head slowly, unwillingly. " Peter would be angry."

I wanted to say Damn Peter, but instead I said, " You know I've been to Calgary?"

He nodded.

" I was very ill there. I nearly died. I haven't much time, Max. And it's important. It's important for both of us. Suppose there is oil up there—then you've done Campbell a great injustice. You remember when you took that report to him up in the Kingdom? That killed him as surely as if you'd battered his head against a stone." I saw him wince. " You had hate in your heart, that was why you went up, wasn't it—that's why you did what Peter asked you? But you had no cause to hate him and you must give me the chance to prove it." I saw his childish mind struggling to grasp what I had been saying and knew I must put it in a way that was positive. " Campbell will never rest," I said, " until I have proved there is oil up there."

I saw his mouth open, but I didn't give him the chance to speak. I turned to the door. " Meet us at the entrance to Thunder Valley in half an hour," I said. " I'll need two saddle horses. I've an oil man with me. You needn't worry about your brother. He's gone up to the dam." I paused, my hand on the door. " If you don't do this for me, Max, may the dead ghost of Stuart Campbell haunt you to your dying day."

I left him then. Outside the sunlight seemed to breathe an air of spring. I paused when I reached the Golden Calf and looked back to the old house. Max was making his way slowly towards the stables. I knew then that we'd get up to the Kingdom. I turned and went into the hotel, feeling a sense of pity, almost of affection for that great, friendless hulk of a man.

Quarter of an hour later Winnick parked his car in a clearing at the entrance to the valley of Thunder Creek. It was screened from the road and we waited there for Max. Half an hour passed and I began to fear that I had failed. But then the clip-clop of hooves sounded on the packed, rutted surface of the road and a moment later he came into sight leading three horses, two saddle and one pack. He dismounted and helped us into the saddle, adjusting our stirrup leathers, tightening the cinches. "You ride good?" he asked Winnick.

"I'll be okay."

Max turned to me then, his eyes keen and intelligent. "But you do not ride, huh?"

"Not for a long time," I said. "And not on a Western saddle." It was a big, curved saddle shaped like a bucket seat with a roping horn in front. It was elaborately decorated and there were thongs of leather to tie things on to it.

He stared at me critically. In all else he might be a child, but he was a man when it came to horses. He was in his own element now and his stature increased immeasurably. He was the leader and he behaved like a leader. "It is different from the English saddle, huh? Now you ride with long stirrups and a long rein. Relax yourself and get down in the saddle. We have some bad places to cross. Let the pony have her head." He turned and swung himself on to his big black in a single, easy movement.

We moved off then, Max leading the pack-horse, myself following and Winnick bringing up the rear. We went down through thick brush and black pools damned by beavers to the rushing noise of Thunder Creek. We crossed the swirling ice-cold waters, the horses swimming, their heads high, their feet stumbling on the bottom. Then we were in timber again and climbing steadily.

Now and then we paused to rest the horses. At the stops nobody talked, but I saw Winnick watching me, speculating whether I'd make it or not. When I had returned to the Golden Calf with the news that I'd got horses and a guide, he'd tried to dissuade me. I think his scientific mind was convinced that a man who only a few days ago had been ordered into hospital by a doctor could not possibly stand up to a gruelling trek in the mountains. I think it was this as much as anything else that made me determined to reach the Kingdom. It was as though I'd been given a challenge. My heart hammered as it pumped thin blood through my system to give me oxygen, my ankles were swollen and the tips of my fingers ached. But as my muscles became exhausted my body sank lower and more relaxed into the saddle until the movement of the horse became easy and natural, as though it were a part of me and I a part of it.

Shortly after noon we came out above the timber line. The black gash of Thunder Creek cleaved the mountains below us and all round white peaks glimmered in the azure sky. Little rock plants, saxifrages mostly, thrust up among the stones and there was a warm, invigorating smell about the mountain-side. Ahead the peaks of Solomon's Judgment stood guard over the gateway to the Kingdom and gradually, as we moved along the mountainside, climbing steadily, the position of these peaks changed until one was almost screened by the other and ahead of us rose the rock-strewn slopes of the Saddle that swept up to the northern peak.

The sun was low in the sky as we crossed the Saddle and saw the bowl of the Kingdom at our feet. There was little snow now. It was green ; a lovely, fresh emerald green, and through it water ran in silver threads. I could see Campbell's ranch-house away to the right, and towards the dam, two trucks stood motionless, connected to the ranch-house by the tracks their tyres had made through the new grasses. I was tired and exhausted, but a great peace seemed to have des-scended upon me. I was back in the Kingdom, clear of cities and the threat of a hospital. I was back in God's own air, in the cool beauty of the mountains. I turned to Max. "We can find our way down from here," I said. I held out my hand to him. "Thank you for bringing us."

He didn't move. He sat motionless, staring down into the bowl of the Kingdom. "You rebuild the house," he said.

I nodded.

He looked at the peak rising above us. "Perhaps they are together—my father and Campbell." He turned to me. "You think there is some place we go when we die?"

"Of course," I said.

"Heaven and hell, huh?" He gave a derisive laugh. "The world is full of devils, and so is the other place. How then can there be a God? There is only this." He waved his hand towards the mountains and the sky.

"Somebody made it, Max."

"Ja, somebody make it. He make animals, too. Then somebody else make men. Tell Campbell I have done what you ask." He clapped his heels to his horse's flanks and turned back the way he had come.

"What about the horses?" I called to him.

"Keep them till you return to Come Lucky," he shouted back. "The grass is good for them now."

"Queer fellow," Winnick said. "What did he mean about *tell Campbell I have done what you ask?*"

I shrugged my shoulders and started my horse down the slope. I couldn't tell him Max was a soul in torment, that he was a mixture of Celt and Teuton and that circumstances and the mixture of his blood had torn him apart from the day he was born.

The mountain crests were flushed with the sunset as we rode into Campbell's Kingdom and from the end of the wheel tracks where the trucks were parked came the sharp crack of an explosion as Boy fired another shot and recorded the sound waves on his geophones. The echo of that shot ran like a salvo of welcome through the mountains as we slid from our saddles by the door of the partly-burned barn. I stood there, hanging on to the leather of my stirrup, staring out across the new grass of the Kingdom. Early crocuses were springing up in the carpet of green. The air was still and clear and cold, and the shadow of the mountains crept across us as the sun went down. I was too weak with exhaustion to stand on my own and yet I was strangely content. Winnick helped me into the house and I sank down on to the bed that my grandfather had used for so many years. Lying there, staring at the rafters that he had hewn from the timbered slopes above us, the world of men and cities seemed remote and rather unreal. And as I slid into a half-coma of sleep I knew that I wouldn't be going back, that this was my kingdom now.

I slept right through to the following morning and awoke to sunshine and the clatter of tin plates. They were having breakfast as I went out into the living-room of the ranch-house. Sleeping bags lay in a half circle round the ember glow of the wood ash in the grate and the place was littered with kit and equipment. Boy jumped to his feet and gripped hold of my hand. He was seething with excitement like a volcano about to erupt. "Are you all right, Bruce? Did you have a good night?" He didn't wait to reply. "Louis has been up all night, computing the results. We've all been up most of the night. He wouldn't let us wake you. I knew it was an anticline. I did my own computing and allowing for weathering I was certain we were all right. And I'm right,

Bruce. That shot we fired just as you got in was the last of five on the cross traverse. It's a perfect formation. Ask Louis. It's a honey. We're straddled right across the dome of it. Now all we've got to prove is that it extends across the Kingdom and beyond."

I looked across at Winnick. "Is this definite?"

He nodded. "It's an anticline all right. But it doesn't prove there's oil up here. You realise that?" The precise, meticulous tone of his voice brought an air of reality to the thing.

"Then how did Campbell see an oil seep at the foot of the slope if it isn't oil bearing?" Boy demanded.

Winnick shrugged his shoulders. "Campbell may have been mistaken. Anyway, I'll ride over the ground to-day and do a quick check on the rock strata. It may tell me something."

But however matter-of-fact Winnick might be there was no damping the air of excitement that hung over the breakfast table. It wasn't only Boy. His two companions seemed just as thrilled. They were both of them youngsters. Bill Mannion was a university graduate from McGill who had recently abandoned Government survey work to become a geophysicist. He was the observer. Don Leggert, a younger man, was from Edmonton. He was the driller. These two men, with Boy, were mucking in and doing the work of a full seismographical team of ten or twelve men. I didn't need their chatter of technicalities to tell me they were keen.

I stood in the sunshine and watched them walk out to the instrument truck. They walked with purpose and the loose spring of men who were physically fit. I envied them that as I watched them go. Winnick came out and joined me. He had a rucksack on his back and a geologist's hammer tucked into his belt. "Well," he said. "What are you going to do now you know you're on an anticline?"

"Sit in the sun here and think," I said.

He nodded, his eyes peering up at me from behind his thick-lensed glasses. "Why not let me try and interest one of the big companies in this property?"

"You honestly think you could persuade them to risk a wildcat right up here in the Rockies?"

"I could try," he answered evasively.

I laughed. "There's oil in the Rocky Mountains?" His eyes

avoided mine. "No," I said, staring out towards the ring of the mountains. "There isn't a chance, and you know it. If it's to be done at all, I'll have to do it myself."

"Maybe you're right," he said. "But think it over. Now Roger Fergus is dead, his son controls a lot of finance. You're a one-man show up against a big outfit. You'll be running neck and neck with the construction of the dam and every dollar that's sunk in that project will make it that much more vital to Fergus that you don't bring in a well up here."

"How far do you think he'll go to stop me?" I asked.

He shrugged his shoulders. "I wouldn't know. But that dam is going to cost money. Henry Fergus will go a long way to see that his money isn't thrown away." His hand gripped my arm. "Don't rush into this. Think it over. At best your contractor may lose his rig. At worst somebody may get hurt."

"I see."

There was nothing new in this. He was only saying what Jean had said, what I knew in my heart was inevitable. And yet hearing it from him, coldly and clearly stated, forced me to face up to the situation. I watched him ride out across the Kingdom and then I brought a chair out into the sunshine and most of the day I lay there, relaxed in the warmth, trying to work it out.

That night I wrote to Keogh telling him the result of the survey to date and instructing him to talk to no one and to come up on his own in three days' time. *Drive through from 150 Mile House without stopping, arriving at the entrance to Thunder Creek at 2 a.m. on the morning of Tuesday. We'll meet you there with horses.* I underlined this and gave Winnick the letter to take down with him.

Winnick left next day. I was feeling so much better that I rode with him up to the top of the Saddle. High up above the Kingdom I said good-bye to him and thanked him for all he'd done.

I sat there watching his small figure jogging slowly down the mountain slope till it was lost to view behind an outcrop. Then I turned my horse and slithered down through the snow back into the bowl of the Kingdom. As I came out below the timber I saw the drilling truck like a small rectangular box away to the right close beside the stream that was the source of Thunder Creek. They were drilling a new shot hole as I rode up, the three of them working on the drill which was turning with a steady rattle as it drove into the rock below. Boy pointed towards the dam. "They've started," he shouted to me above the din.

I turned and looked back at the dam. Men were moving about the concrete housing of the hoist and there were more men at the base of the dam, stacking cement bags that were being lowered to them from the cable that stretched across the top of the structure. My eye was caught by a solitary figure standing on the buttress of rock above the cable terminal. There was a glint of glass in the sunlight, a flicker like two small heliographs. "Have you got a pair of binoculars?" I shouted to Boy.

He nodded and got them from the cab of the drilling truck. Through them every detail became clear. There was no doubt about the solitary figure on the buttress. It was Trevedian and he was watching us through glasses of his own. "Did you have to start at this end of the Kingdom?" I shouted to Boy.

He turned down the corners of his mouth. "Got to start somewhere," he said. "They were bound to find out what we were up to."

That was true enough. I swung the glasses towards the dam. The cage was just coming in with another load, two tip trucks this time and a pile of rails. More cement was being slung along the top of the dam. And then in the foreground, halfway between us and the dam I noticed a big rusty cog wheel and some rotten baulks of timber bolted together in an upright position. There was the remains of an old boiler and a shapeless mass of machinery. I called to Boy. "What's that pile of junk there?" I asked him.

"Don't you know?" He seemed surprised. "That's Campbell Number One."

"How far did they get down?"

"Don't know. Something over four thousand, I guess."

I rode over and had a look at it. The metal was rotten with age. The teeth of the big cog wheel disintegrated into a brown powder at the touch of my fingers. The wooden baulks that had formed the base of the rig were so rotten I could put my fist through them. There was the remains of a hole with a dirty scum of water in it. I called to Boy. "Where's the top of the anticline?"

"We're on it now," he shouted back.

I stared at the rusty monument to my grandfather's one and only attempt to drill and wondered how he'd felt when they'd had to give up. A whole lifetime lost for the sake of a thousand odd feet of drilling. I turned and rode slowly back to the ranch-house.

After that first day I took over the commissariat and the cooking, so relieving the survey team to some extent. The weather became unsettled. Sometimes it snowed, sometimes it blew. The change from sunshine to almost blizzard conditions could be astonishingly rapid.

Shortly after midday on the Monday Boy left Bill and Don drilling the second shot hole in the longitudinal traverse and we saddled our horses and started out for the Saddle and the pony trail down to Thunder Creek. It was blowing half a gale and mare's tails of snow were streaming in a white drift from the crests of the mountains. It had snowed during the night and part of the morning and the Kingdom lay under a white drift. The two trucks were black specks about a mile from the ranch-house. We could see the drill working, but the sound of it was lost in the wind.

As we neared the crest of the Saddle wind-blown drifts of snow stung our faces. The going became treacherous and we had to lead the horses, Boy leading the spare as well as his own. On the crest we met the full force of the wind. It stung the eyes and drove the breath down into our throats. "Sure you're okay?" Boy shouted. "I can manage if you feel——"

"I'm fine," I shouted back.

He looked at me for a moment, his eyes slitted against the thrust of wind and powdered snow. Then he nodded and we went on down the other side on a long diagonal for the line of the timber.

As we dropped down from the crests the snow worried us less. Through blurred eyes I got occasional glimpses of the road snaking up the valley from the lake. Sometimes there was movement on the road, a truck grinding up towards the hoist. And as we neared the shelter of the timber the great fault opened out to the left and we could see the slide and men moving around the little square box that was the concrete housing of the hoist.

The going was easier once we reached the timber though we were hampered by soft drifts of deep snow. I tried to memorise the trail, but it was almost impossible coming into it from above for the timber was pretty open and the pattern of drifts swirling round solitary firs or groups of firs repeated itself over and over again, all seemingly alike. We came across the track of a moose; big, splay-footed tracks that seemed to be able to cross the softest drift without sinking very deep.

Gradually the timber became denser and the trail clearer. Sheer slopes patterned by gnarled roots and deadfalls gave place to lightly timbered glades, criss-crossed with game tracks, and at one point we ploughed through almost half a mile of beaver dams. The lower we went the more game we encountered; mule-deer, moose, porcupines and an occasional coyote.

I asked Boy about bears, but he said they were still in hibernation and wouldn't be out for another month at least. He was full of information about the wild life of the mountains. It was part of his heritage, and when I was getting tired his stories of his encounters with animals kept me going.

It was dark when we swam the ford of Thunder Creek and dismounted close by the road in the glade where Winnick had parked his car. We had some food sitting on a fallen tree. Once in a while headlights cut a swathe through the night and a truck went rumbling up the road to the hoist. We had a cigarette and then rolled ourselves in our blankets on a groundsheet. The horses were hobbled and I could hear their rhythmic munching and the queer jerking sound they made as they reared both front legs together to move forward. It was bitterly cold, but I must have slept for suddenly Boy was shaking me. " It's nearly two," he said.

We went out then to the edge of the road, standing in the screen of a little plantation of cottonwood. Headlights blazed and we heard the roar of a diesel. The heavy truck lumbered past, lighting the curving line of the road. We watched the timber close behind its red tail-light. Darkness closed in round us again and we listened as the sound of the truck's engine slowly died away up the valley. Then all was still, only the murmur of the wind in the trees and the unchanging sound of water pouring over rocks. Somewhere far above us the cry of a coyote split the night like a bloodcurdling scream. An owl flapped from a tree.

It was nearly 3 a.m. when the darkness began to glow with light and we heard the sound of a car. Boy pushed forward to the edge of the road. The headlights brightened until the whole pattern of the brush around us stood in stark silhouette against two enormous eyes of light. It was a car all right and we flagged it down with our arms. It stopped and Garry Keogh got out, his thick body bulkier than ever in a sheepskin jacket. " Sorry I'm late. Had a flat. What in hell are we playing at, meeting like this in the middle of the night?"

Boy held up his hand, his head on one side. A faint murmur sounded above the noise of creek. " Is there a truck behind you?" Boy asked.

" Yeah. Passed it about six miles back."

" Quick then." Boy jumped into the car with him and guided him off the road to the glade where our horses were. We sat in the car with the lights off watching the heavy truck trundle by.

" What's all the secrecy about?" Garry asked.

I tried to explain, but I don't think I really convinced him. If Trevedian had been in charge of a rival drilling outfit I think he'd have understood. But he just couldn't take the construction of a dam seriously. " You boys are jittery, that's all. Why don't you do a deal with this guy Trevedian. You've got to use the hoist anyway to get a drilling rig up there. You're not planning to take it up by pack pony, are you?"

And his great laugh went echoing around the silence of the glade.

I told him the whole story then, sitting there in the car with the engine ticking over and the heater switched on. When I had finished he asked a few questions and then he was silent for a time. At length he said, " Well how do we get the rig up there?"

I said, " We'll talk about that later, shall we—when you've had a look at the place and decided whether you're willing to take a chance on it."

The lateness of the hour and the warmth of the heater was making us all drowsy. We settled down in the seats then and slept till the first grey light of day filtered through the glade. Then we covered the car with brushwood and started back up the trail to the Kingdom.

It was midday before we reached the top of the Saddle. It

was snowing steadily and the wind was from the east. My heart was pumping erratically and I was so tired I found it difficult to stay in the saddle. When we got to the ranch-house I went straight to bed and stayed there till the following morning. Next morning my buttocks were sore and the muscles of my legs stiff with riding, but once I was up I felt fine. My heart seemed steadier and slower and I had recovered my energy. Garry Keogh spent the day out with Boy riding over the territory, planning his drilling site, working out in his own mind the chances of success. In the evening, after supper, we got down to business.

We had a roaring log fire going and hot coffee. Garry sat with his notes in his hand and a cigar clamped between his teeth, the bald dome of his head furrowed by a frown. " You think we'll run into a sill of basalt at about four thousand?" He looked across at Boy.

" I think so," Boy answered. " That or something like it stopped Campbell Number One in 1913. They were drilling by cable-tool and they just couldn't make any impression. With a rotary drill——"

" It's still a snag," Garry cut in. He turned to me. " I think I told you, Bruce, I could stand two months operating on my own, no more. Well, that's about the size of it. Boy here says if we're going to hit oil, we'll hit it at around five, six thousand. That's okay, but this isn't Leduc. We aren't down in the plains here. There's this sill he talks about, and down to that it'll be metamorphic rocks all the way. It'll be tough going. And on top of that we may drill crooked and have to fool around with a whipstock. Anything could happen in this sort of country. And we're working on a financial shoe-string with no facilities. We can't take a core sample. We've no geologist. We'll just have to log on the cuttings—by guess and by God. We've no certainty that we're on top of country that is oil bearing. We've no knowledge whatever of the nature of the strata at five thousand feet. We're working entirely in the dark with minimum crew, no financial backing and against time." He sat back, sucking at his cigar. " The only clue to what's under the surface is this story of Campbell's that thirty years ago he saw some oil on the waters of Thunder Creek." He shook his head. " It's a hell of a risk."

" Campbell knew a lot about oil," Boy murmured.

" So you tell me."

" Bruce showed you the old man's progress report. It's obvious from that that he's a sound geologist."

" Sure. I've seen what he's written, but how do I know that it bears any relation to the ground itself? All I know about Campbell is that he was reckoned to be crazy."

" I can confirm a good deal of it from my own observations," Boy said.

" Yeah, the straightforward stuff. But what about the conclusions he draws? Can you confirm them?"

" There's nothing particularly revolutionary about them," Boy answered. " We all know that the oil deposits in the North American continent derive from the marine life deposited on the floor of the central sea area that ran from Hudson's Bay to the Caribbean. These mountains here are a fairly recent formation. I know most geologists take the view that this is not a likely area. Yet the fact remains that many of the first wells were drilled at points of seepage on the eastern escarpment. Because those wells were not successful it doesn't necessarily mean that there wasn't any oil there. They were drilled early in the century and their equipment wasn't good enough to reach down to any great depth."

" In two months I won't be able to drill much deeper than five thousand, not in this sort of country." Garry relit his cigar. " There's water here, there's all the ingredients for making mud of about the right consistency, the weather shouldn't be too bad from now on and Winnick has a sound reputation, but . . ." He shook his head gloomily.

" If Louis' original report had been based on the results we're now giving him—in other words if those recording tapes hadn't been switched—Roger Fergus would have drilled a well up here by now."

" Sure and he would. But I'm not Roger Fergus. He could afford to lose any amount of dough. I can't. I'm just in the clear and I mean to stay that way." He rubbed his fingers along the line of his jaw. " The only thing that makes me go on considering the idea is this fifty-fifty proposition of yours, Bruce." He stared at me with a sort of puzzled frown. " I keep telling myself I'm a fool, but still I keep considering it. Perhaps if I were younger . . ." He shook his head slowly from side to side like a dog trying to remove a buzzing from its ears. " You know if this location were just beside a good highway I guess I'd be crazy enough to fall for your proposition, but how the hell am I to get my rig up here?"

"By the hoist," I said.

He stared at me. "But you've told me about this fellow Trevedian. He owns the valley of Thunder Creek. He owns the road and he owns the hoist and he doesn't aim to have any drilling done up here. Because of him I have to come up here. All this tom-foolery because he's got guards on the valley route and now you tell me you're going to bring my rig up by the hoist."

"I think it can be done," I said. "Once."

"I see." His leathery face cracked in a grin. "You're going to play it rough, eh? Well, I don't know that I blame you, considering what you've told me. But I've got my equipment to think of."

"It's insured, isn't it?"

"Yeah, but I don't know how the insurance company would view my acting outside the law, busting through two guard points and then slinging my equipment up through a mile of space to a mountain eyrie. How do I get it down anyway?"

"I don't think there'll be any difficulty about that," I said. "If you bring in a well here, you won't need to get it down. And if you don't then I think you'll find Trevedian only too happy to give you a free passage out of the area."

"Yeah." He nodded slowly. "That's reasonable, I guess. What about the cable? Will it take my equipment?"

"I don't know what the breaking point is," I said. "But I've been up it and from what I've seen it'll take about three or four times the tonnage that can be got on to the cage." I turned to Boy. "You brought your trucks up by it last year. What's your view? Will it take Garry's rig?"

"I don't think you need worry about that, Garry," he said. "It's like Bruce says. The thing is built to carry a heavy tonnage."

He nodded slowly. "And how do you propose we get the use of this hoist? As I understand it, there's a guard at the entrance to Thunder Creek, another at the hoist terminal and near the terminal there's a camp. I'll have five, possibly six trucks——" He hesitated. "Yes, it will be at least six trucks if we're to haul in everything we need for the whole operation, including fuel and pipe." He shook his head. "It's a heck of an operation, you know. We'll need two tankers for a start and two truck-loads of pipe. Then there's the rig, draw works, all equipment, tools, spares, everything. And casing." He hesitated and looked at Boy. "We'd have to take a chance on that. In this sort of country it might be all right. Well, say seven trucks. That'll mean a minimum of four to five hours at the hoist. Now how the hell do you think you're going to fix that?"

"I don't know," I said. "At least, I think I know, but I've not worked out all the details yet. Anyway, that's my problem. If you're game to try I'll give you an undertaking to get your equipment up here. If I fail I'll undertake to make good any loss you have sustained. How's that?"

"Very generous," he said. "Except that I understood you only possess a few hundred dollars."

"I'd sell the Kingdom," I said, "to meet the obligataion."

"To Fergus? But——" He stopped and looked down at his hands. "Knowing how you feel about this place . . ." He hesitated, sucking on his cigar. Then he lumbered to his feet. "Okay, Bruce," he said, gripping my hand. "You get my stuff up here and I'll accept your proposition and drill you a well." He hesitated. "That is, providing Winnick gives me a written report on the two traverses when they're completed and that report is good."

We settled down then to work out the details. Everything that would be required from the time Garry spudded in to the time he brought in a well, presuming that he did, would have to be trucked in on the one operation. It meant buying or hiring trucks and tankers. It worked out at seven vehicles. Seven seperate trips on the hoist with difficult loadings between each trip. Boy was a help here for he was able to give us some idea of the time he had taken to load his trucks and off-load them at the other end. It meant allowing forty minutes minimum for each truck, to cover loading, the trip up to the dam, off-loading and the running down of the empty cage. We went through all the stores we should require—tools, spares, pipe, casing, food, cigarettes, bedding, oils, mud chemicals suitable for all types of strata ; an endless list. Bill and Don agreed to stay on and become roughnecks, so that additional personnel was reduced to six, which allowed two teams of four and the rest of us available to cook, hunt, stand in for anyone sick and generally organise the operation.

We finished just after two in the morning and went to bed, but for ages I couldn't get to sleep as my mind went over and over the lists we had made out. Several times I switched on my torch and made a note of something that had occurred to me. Under the agreement that I was making with Boy and Garry the drilling was their responsibility, but I was convinced that neither of them fully appreciated what the situation would be once we had got the rig and equipment up to the Kingdom. There would be no going down for things we had forgotten. We should be isolated up here in the mountains. Trevedian would see to that. Anything we had ommitted from our lists we would have to do without. I had explained this to them, but Garry had shrugged his shoulders and said, " Sure, but there's always the pony trail." I had left it at that. I saw no reason to scare him by explaining to him the lengths to which I should have to go to carry out my side of the bargain and get the rig up the hoist.

Boy took Garry down the next day. " If everything goes well I'll be seeing you in about three weeks," Garry said as he shook my hand. And then he added, " You're sure you can get us up the hoist?"

" If I don't I've got to sell up to pay your expenses," I said. " Isn't that enough of a guarantee?"

" Sure and it is, but I'd like to know just how you're going to fix it. A bit of bribery and corruption, eh?" He laughed and slapped me on the shoulder.

If he liked to think it could be done by bribery. . . . I smiled and said nothing.

" Well, see you let me have details before I bring my convoy up."

" I will," I said. " I'll mail you full instructions in advance."

" Okay." He nodded and hauled himself up on to his horse. " Be seeing you, Bruce." He waved his hand and started up towards the Saddle.

When Boy got in that night he was packing the haunches of a deer on the back of his saddle. Stocks of canned food were running low and fresh meat was a welcome sight. All we lacked was flour to bake bread.

In the days that followed Boy and the rest of his team worked from first light till darkness to complete the longitudinal traverse. All the time the geophysical work was going on we were very conscious of the growing activity at the dam. Each day when the weather was good I rode up to an outcrop above the buttress and had a look at what they were doing. Once when it was fine I climbed a shoulder of the northern peak of Solomon's Judgment. From this eyrie I could see the camp. It was now clear of all sapling growth with paths beginning to be worn between the quarters and the dining hall and the cookhouse and the latrines. It seemed filling up with men. Trucks were coming into the hoist regularly. As soon as they were off-loaded a grab crane filled them up with hard core from the slide and they went out loaded with stone. Farther down the valley I caught glimpses through my glasses of road gangs working, spreading hard core on sections where the surface was breaking up.

Two days later the peace of the Kingdom was shattered by an explosion that ran a thundering echo round the mountains. I didn't need to ride out to my rock outcrop to know what it was. They were blasting at the quarries on either side of the dam. The construction work had begun. When I did get up to my vantage point I saw the whole area of the dam crawling with workers. Rails were laid out and tip wagons were trundling back and forth. Giant cement mixers were rattling away and loads of rock were being slung across by cable to the centre of the dam.

The race was on and we hadn't even got our rig up.

"How long do you reckon they'll take?" Boy asked when he got in that night. His dark face was sullen and moody.

"We've plenty of time," I said.

But it had a depressing effect on all of us. After supper we all walked as far as the buttress. There was a young moon and we wanted to see what the new construction looked like. My one fear was that they'd work at night. But I suppose it was too cold that early in the season to work shifts round the clock. As it was they had to use large quantities of straw to protect the new concrete from frost. We went down as far as the hoist. In the queer light everything looked flat and white, a dead world from which man seemed suddenly to have vanished leaving the orderly evidence of their industry behind them.

"*I think I never saw such starved ignoble nature*," Boy quoted. And then he added, " It seems the ultimate in futlity —all this effort to build a hundred-foot high rampart and all around Nature has raised great peaks to seven and eight thousand feet."

" Isn't that the measure of our greatness?" Don said. " We go on, whatever the odds."

"Ants," Bill said. " It's all comparative. Compare these peaks with the stars, with the limitlessness of space."

" Is it worth it—the efforts we make?" Boy asked.

Bill looked across at me. " What do you say, Bruce?"

I shrugged my shoulders. " What is anything but an idea?" I turned away, climbing the slope of the mountain. I didn't like Boy's mood. There was a note of fatalism in it.

From higher up the mountain we looked down on the deep shadows of Thunder Creek. Lights twinkled below us, marking the camp, and an up-draught of air brought the sound of a radio to us and the lilt of a dance band, mingled with the murmur of a diesel engine. A battery of arc lights surrounded the hoist terminal where loaded trucks were parked, waiting for the morning, and far down the valley the headlights of a vehicle weaved their tortuous way up through the timbered slopes of Thunder Creek.

" We're wasting our time, fooling around on a survey up here," Boy murmured moodily.

" What makes you say that?" I asked him.

" There must be nearly a hundred men down in that camp now. You haven't a hope in hell of getting one truck, let alone seven, up that hoist."

" The number of men doesn't make much difference," I said.

" Are you crazy? Well, if the number of men doesn't make any difference, what about those arc lights?"

" We'll need them to load by."

He gripped my arm. " Just what are you planning to do?"

I hesitated but I decided not to tell him what was in my mind. The less anybody knew about it the better. " All in good time," I said. " Let's go back and get some sleep."

But he didn't move. " You can't take on that outfit. It's too big, and you know it. The whole thing is too organised."

" Then we'll have to disorganise it."

He stared at me, his mouth falling open. " You're not planning to——" He checked himself and passed his hand wearily across his face. " No, I guess you wouldn't be that crazy, but——" His hand gripped my arm. " I wish I could

C.K.   F see into your mind, Bruce. Sometimes I feel I'm on the edge of a precipice and you're a stranger. There's something inside of you that brushes things aside, that isn't quite of this world. You know you're licked and yet you get people like me and Louis and even a tough character like Garry Keogh to string along. What's driving you?"

"I thought you were as keen about this thing as I was," I said, keeping my voice low.

"Sure I am, but——" He waved his hand towards the lights in the valley. "I know when it's time to back down. You don't." He caught hold of my arm as though he were about to say something further. Then he let it drop. "Come on," he said. "It's time we got back."

He was very silent the next few days. Often I'd catch him looking at me and I got the impression he was a little afraid of me. Like most Canadians, he was a very law-abiding person. Conflicts such as we had been involved in during the war were alien—a gun was for use against the wild, equipment was man's tools to tame Nature, human life was something you travel two, three hundred miles to shake by the hand.

On May 29th, Boy completed the longitudinal traverse and the following morning he left for Calgary with the recordings. Before he left I gave him a letter for Garry Keogh, instructing him to move up with his vehicles to 150 Mile House not later than 5th June. I would contact him there. I enclosed a signed undertaking to reimburse him for all expenses if I failed to get the rig up to the Kingdom and Boy had with him my agreement to split profits fifty-fifty with those involved in the development of the property. I also gave Boy a letter to Winnick in which I asked him to let Keogh have a report signed by him and if that report were optimistic I asked him to drop a hint here and there amongst the oil company scouts. I was preparing the ground for the possibility of ultimately having to fight a legal battle. He had with him also a final list of items we required.

I rode with him part of the way up to the Saddle. It was sleeting and the mountains were grey hulks half hidden by mist. The wind blew through our clothing and the horses hung their heads as they plodded up the mountainside. Halfway up, however, the clouds lifted, the snow on Solomon's

Judgment showed the white sweeps of the cornices and the sleet moved away from us in a leaden curtain towards the east. At the edge of a shelf of rock over which the horses had to be led I turned back. Boy gripped my hand. " I hope it turns out as you want it, Bruce."

" I'm sure it will," I said. " You'll come straight back?" He nodded. " I'll be back inside of a week."

" And you'll cable me the result at the Golden Calf."

" Sure. And don't worry about the rig. If I know Garry he won't be waiting for Louis's final report. He'll be getting team and equipment together right now."

" I hope so," I said. " Every day we delay weakens our chances of bringing in a well before the dam is completed."

" Sure. I know."

" And don't forget that telephone equipment."

He looked up at me, his head on one side. " Would that have something to do with your plans to get the rig up the hoist?"

" Without it we're sunk," I said.

" Okay. I'll remember." He waved his hand and started across the rock shelf. It was wet and it gleamed like armour plate. I watched him for a moment and then turned my horse and began to descend. I hadn't gone far before the sun came out and suddenly it was warm and spring had come to the Kingdom. The emerald green of the grass was splashed with the colours of flowers like a huge meadow. I stopped and stared down at it, absorbing the warmth of the sun, thinking how beautiful it was—the dark band of the timber below me, the silver thread of water in the colours of the bowl and beyond, the mountains, warm and brown till rock merged into the glittering white of the snows. Away to the right I could just see the far end of the dam. Figures were moving there like ants and the stillness of the air was sullied by the rattle of concrete mixers. I wondered how the Kingdom would look when all its beauty was a sheet of water and I went on down through the timber hating the thought of it.

There was nothing much for us to do now the survey was over. There were two rifles at the ranch-house, one belonging to Boy and one to my grandfather, and I encouraged Bill and Don to get out after game whenever they could. For myself I just lazed, gaining in energy every day and spending a good deal of time going over and over my plans to get the rig up the hoist. If everything worked smoothly it would be all right, but I had to plan for every eventuality.

Three days later I took Bill Mannion with me and we rode down to Come Lucky. We carried blankets and rucksacks stuffed with spare clothing and food. In a bag tied to my saddle were several of the charges used by Boy for his survey shots together with detonators, coils of wire and the plunger and batteries for shot firing. The sun was hot as we went down the pony trail to Thunder Creek. The timber had a warm, resinous smell and all about us pulsed the early summer life.

As we rode into Come Lucky I saw a change was coming over the place. New huts were going up; some were rough, split pine affairs, others pre-fabricated constructions trucked in from the sawmills. Some of the old shacks were being patched up and repainted. A new life stirred in the ghost town and for the first time since I had set eyes on the place it was possible to walk up the centre of the main street. The mud and tailings from the old wooden flumes above the town had set hard in the sun and wind to produce a cracked, hard-baked surface like a dried-out mud hole. There were even little drifts of dust blowing about.

It was near midday and several of the old men were in the Golden Calf for a lunch-time beer. They stared at us curiously, but without animosity. The dam was going ahead. Come Lucky was coming to life. They'd nothing to fear from me any more.

Mac was in his office. He was seated at the desk working on some accounts and he stared at me doubtfully over his steel-rimmed glasses. "Getting tired of living up in the Kingdom?" he asked me.

"No," I said. "I just came down to see if there was any mail for me."

"There's a telegram for you. Nothing else." He reached into a pigeon hole of the desk and produced it.

I slit open the envelope. It was from Boy and had been handed in at Calgary the day before, June 1st. *"Results perfect. Have seen G. He will be at House as arranged. Returning immediately arriving Come Lucky Tuesday."* I handed it to Bill. "Where will I find Trevedian?" I asked Mac.

"Maybe in his office, but most of the day he's up at the hoist."

"Does he sleep up at the camp?"

"No. He'll be in town by the evening."

"Fine," I said. "If you see him, tell him I'm looking for him."

The old man stared at me with a puzzled frown. "What would ye be wanting him for?"

"Just tell him I'd like to have a word with him."

As I turned to go he said, "A friend of yours was asking about you."

"Who's that?" I asked him.

"Jean Lucas."

"Jean! Is she back?"

"Aye. Came back two days ago. She came to see me last night. Wanted to know what ye were up to."

"What did you say?"

The corners of his lips twitched slightly and there was a twinkle in his blue eyes as he said, "I told her to go up and find out for herself."

"Well, if she'd taken your advice we'd have met her on the way down," I said.

"Aye, ye would that. Maybe she didna feel like it. Sarah Garret tells me she's no' looking herself despite her holiday."

I was very conscious of the Lugar in the rucksack on my back, of a sudden restlessness compounded of spring and the smell of the woods and a desire to see her again. I went out through the bar into the sunshine, my heart throbbing in my throat.

"Where now?" Bill asked.

"We'll go down and see Trevedian," I said and climbed on to my horse and rode back down the street, lost in my own thoughts and the memory of that last time I'd seen Jean, wrought-up, unhappy and strangely close to me. I remembered the vibrance of her voice, the reflection of her face in the blackness of the window panes as I lay in my bed.

But at the sight of the open door of Trevedian's office I put all thought of her out of my mind. There was no time to start dreaming about a girl.

The office of the Trevedian Transport Company had been enlarged by knocking down the partition at the back. There was another desk, more filing cabinets, a field telephone and

an assistant with sleek black hair who affected high-heeled cowboy boots, blue jeans and a fancy shirt. Trevedian was on the telephone to Keithley as I came in. He was in his shirt sleeves and his big arms, covered with dark hair, were bronzed with sun and wind. He momentarily checked his conversation as he caught sight of me, unable to conceal his surprise. He waved me to a seat, finished his call and then put the receiver back on its rest. "Well, what can I do for you?" he asked.
"I suppose Bladen wants to get his trucks out, is that it?"

"No," I said. "Rather the reverse. I want to get some trucks in."

"How do you mean?" His eyes had narrowed as though the sun's glare was bothering him.

"What do you charge per load on your hoist?" I asked him.

"Depends on the nature of the load," he said guardedly. "What's the trouble? Running short of supplies?"

"No," I said. "I want to know what rate you'll quote me for hoisting a drilling rig up to the Kingdom?"

"A drilling rig!" He stared at me. And then his fist came down on the desk top. "What the hell do you take me for, Wetheral? No drilling rig is going up Thunder Creek."

I turned to Bill. "Take note of that, will you. This, by the way is Bill Mannion," I introduced him. "Now, about this rig. I quite realise that the road up Thunder Creek runs through your property and that the hoist is owned and run by you and James McClellan jointly. Naturally a toll is payable to the two of you for the transport of personnel and equipment up to the Kingdom. Perhaps you'd be good enough to quote me your rates."

"Quote you my rates!" He laughed. "You must be crazy. The road's a private road and the hoist is private, too. It's being operated for the Larsen Mining Company. You know that damn well. And if you think I'm going to transport any damned rig up to the Kingdom——" He hesitated there and leaned forward. "What's the idea of taking a rig up there?"

"I'm drilling a well."

"You're drilling a well." He repeated my words in an offensive imitation of my English accent. Then his eyes slid to Bill Mannion and in a more controlled voice he said, "And what makes you think it's worth drilling up there?"

"Bladen's done a check on his original survey," I said.

"Well?"

"There's ample evidence that the original survey was tampered with. Louis Winnick, the oil consultant, has computed the results. The seismograms show a well defined anticline. The indications are promising enough for me to go ahead and drill."

"And you expect me to get your rig up there for you?"

"I'm merely asking you to quote me a rate."

He laughed. "You're not asking much." He leaned across the desk towards me. "Get this into your thick head, Wetheral. As far as you're concerned there aren't any rates. Your rig isn't going up Thunder Creek. You can pack it up the pony trail." He grinned. "I give you full permission to do that, free of charge, even though it is partly on my land."

"I'm sorry," I said. "I must insist on a quotation for the hoist."

"Insist? Are you trying to be funny?"

"Do I get a quotation or not?"

"Of course you don't."

"I see." I got to my feet. "That's all I wanted." He was staring at me in surprise as Bill and I moved towards the door. I paused in the entrance. "By the way," I said, "you do realise I suppose, that the original road up Thunder Creek, was constructed in 1939 by the Canadian Government. The fact that you have improved it recently does not stop it being a public highway. Are you acting on Fergus's instructions in putting a guard on it and holding up private transport?"

"I'm acting for the Larsen Mining Company."

"Fine," I said. "That means Fergus."

After that I went back up the street to the Golden Calf. Mac was still in his office. "Can I use your phone?" I asked him.

"Aye." He pushed the instrument towards me. "Would it be something private?" He had got to his feet.

"No, it's all right," I said. "There's nothing private about this." I picked up the instrument and got long distance. I gave them the number of the *Calgary Tribune* and made it a personal call to the editor. Half an hour later he was on the line. "Did Louis Winnick let you have his final report on Campbell's Kingdom?" I asked him.

"Yes," he replied. "And a fellow called Bladen was in here with the whole story of the original survey. Who am I talking with?"

" Bruce Wetheral," I said. " Campbell's heir."

" Well, Mr. Wetheral, we ran the story pretty well in full a couple of days back."

I thanked him and then brought him up to date with Trevedian's refusal to allow a rig to proceed to the property. When I had finished he said, " Makes a dandy little story. Private enterprise versus big business, eh? Well, Mr. Wetheral this won't be the first time we've backed the small operator."

" You're going to back us then?"

" Oh, sure. It's in the interests of the country. We've always taken that line. What are you going to do about getting your rig up there?"

" Take the matter into my own hands."

" I see. Well, go easy on that. We don't want to find we're backing people who get outside the law."

" I'm not getting outside the law," I said. " It's Fergus and Trevedian who have got outside the law."

" We-ell——" He hesitated. " So long as nobody gets hurt. . . ."

" Nobody's going to get hurt," I said.

" Fine. Well, good luck. And, Mr. Wetheral—if you do bring in a well be sure and let us have details. Later on I'd like to send one of my staff up to have a look at things if that's all right with you?"

" Any time," I said. " And thanks for your help." I put the receiver back.

" So ye're going to drill?" Mac said.

I nodded. " I suppose your son wouldn't take the responsibility of getting the rig up there?"

" Jamie'll no' do anything to help ye, I'm afraid." He kept his eyes on the pipe he was filling avoiding my gaze.

" No," I said. " I suppose not." I hesitated. " Trevedian will ask you what I'm up to. There's no harm in telling him that I've been on to the *Calgary Tribune*. But I'd be glad if you'd forget that bit about my taking things into my own hands. Will you do that?"

" Aye." He gave me a wintry smile. " I'll no' spoil yer game, whatever it is. But dinna do anything foolish, lad." He peered up at me. " Ye ken the advice I ought to gie ye? It's to forget all aboot the Kingdom—sell oot and gang hame. But it's no' the sort o' advice a young feller would be taking." He shook his head. " Mebbe I'm getting old." He held out his hand. "Good luck to ye. And if I should see Jeannie?" He cocked his head to one side.

I hesitated and then I said, " If she should happen to ask about me, tell her there's a vacancy for cook-general up in the Kingdom—if she wants her old job back?"

He smiled and nodded his head. "Aye. I'll tell her that."

I paid for the call and we left then, riding down the hard-baked gravel of Come Lucky's street, conscious here and there of faces peering at us from the windows of the shacks. Through the open door of his office I caught a glimpse of Trevedian. He was on the phone again, but he looked up as we rode by and stared at us, his heavy forehead puckered in a frown.

The sun was hot as we rode down to the lake shore and there were gophers standing like sentinels on the mounds of their burrows. Their shrill squeaks of warning ran ahead of us as one by one they dropped from sight. Beaver Dam Lake was still and dark, mirroring the green and brown and white of the mountains beyond. A truck ground past us as we turned up towards Thunder Creek, a haze of white dust hovering behind it. And when it was gone and the dust had settled, everything was still again. Summer had come to the Rockies.

"Will you wait down here for Boy?" Bill asked.

I nodded. "We'll camp down by the creek to-night."

We found a suitable spot, well concealed in the cottonwood close to the waters of Thunder Creek, cooked ourselves a meal and slept for a couple of hours in the sun. Then we saddled the horses again and started up the road towards the camp. All I carried was my rucksack. The shadows were lengthening now and as we entered the timber the air was cool and damp. Every now and then Bill glanced at me curiously, but he didn't say anything. He had the patience and tenacity of all geologists. He was content to wait and see what I was up to.

We reached the bend that concealed the round gate and its guard and I struck up into the timber. The timber was not very thick here and as we made the detour we caught glimpses of the guard hut. We came back on to the road about half a mile above it. The surface was much drier than it had been when Jeff and I had made that moonlight run and wherever there was water, hard core had been poured in by the truck load. Even so the surface was heavily rutted and some of the

log culverts showed signs of breaking up. Every now and then
I glanced up at the telephone wires that hung in shallow loops
from the bare jack pine poles. There were just the two lines
and at most points it would be possible to reach them from
the top of a truck. At a point where the road reached down
almost to the floor of the valley we saw beavers working in
the black pools they'd damned and once we caught a glimpse
of two coyotes slinking through the timber. But my mind
was on practical things and not even the sight of a small
herd of mule-deer distracted me from reconnaissance. We
kept to the road all the way, only pushing into the timber
when we heard the sound of a truck.

About a mile above the guard hut I found what I was
looking for. The grade had been getting steadily steeper as
we climbed up from the creek bed and we came face to face
with a shoulder of the valley side. The road swung away to
the right and we could see it zig-zagging in wide hair-pin
sweeps as it gained height to by-pass the obstruction. Ahead
of us a trail rose steeply up the shoulder, a short-cut that
would come out on to the road again. We forced the horses
up the slope and came out on to a rocky platform that looked
straight up the valley to the slide and the sheer cliff of the
fault. It was a most wonderful sight with the white peaks of
Solomon's Judgment crimsoned in the sunset.

About a mile further on we came out on to the road again
where it swung round a big outcrop of rock. It had been
blasted out of the face of the outcrop and above it the rocks
towered more than a hundred feet, covered with lichen and
black where the water seeped from the crevices. We waited
for a truck to pass, going down the valley, and then we rode
out on to the road.

I sat there for a moment looking at the overhang. This was
what I had remembered. This was the place that had been in
my mind when I first conceived my plan. The question was
would I find what I wanted. I rode forward, a tight feeling
in my throat. Everything depended upon this. The rock had
been blasted. There was no question about that as I began
eagerly examining the wall of it.

"What are you looking for, Bruce?" my companion asked.

"I'm wondering if there are any drill holes," I said. I'd
banked on the driller going ahead, drilling ·his shot holes,
regardless of whether they'd blasted sufficiently. Twice we

had to canter off into the timber whilst a truck went by. Each time I came back to the same point in the face of the rock, working steadily along it. And then suddenly I had found what I had hoped for; a round hole—like the entrance to a sandmartin's nest. There was another about ten feet from it and a third. They were about three feet from the ground and when I cut a straight branch from a tree and had whittled it down into a rod I found two of them extended about eight feet into the rock. The third was only about two feet deep. I took off my rucksack then, got out my charges and pushed them in, two to each shot hole. The wires to the detonators I cut to leave only about two inches protruding. Then we rammed wet earth in tight, sealing the holes. I marked the spot with the branch of a tree and we rode on.

About half a mile further on the road dipped again and crossed a patch of swampy ground. Road gangs had been busy here very recently. A lot of hard core had been dumped and rolled in and just beyond the swamp the trees had been cut back to allow trucks to turn. There was good standing here for a dozen or more vehicles. Over a slight rise a bridge of logs spanned a small torrent. Again I slipped my rucksack from my shoulders and got to work with the charges, fixing them to the log supports of the bridge and trailing the wires to a point easily reached from the road. I marked the spot and climbed back on to the road.

" Okay, Bill," I said. " That's the lot."

We turned our horses and started back. There was still some light in the sky, but down in the valley night was closing in.

It was past nine when we rode into our camp. We built a fire and cooked a meal, sitting close by the flames, talking quietly, listening to the sound of the creek rumbling lakewards. I felt tired, but content. So far everything had gone well. But as I lay wrapped in my blankets, going over and over my plans, I wondered whether my luck would hold. I wondered, too, whether I wasn't in danger of creating a situation I couldn't handle. I was planning the thing as a military operation, relying on surprise and confusion to carry me through, banking on being able to present the other side with a *fait accompli*. I wondered chiefly about Garry Keogh. He was Irish and he was tough, but he ran his own rig and he'd got to live. His aproach to the whole thing was entirely different from mine.

The following morning, Tuesday, June 3rd, broke in a grey mist. The sun came through, however, before we had finished breakfast and for three hours it shone from a clear blue sky and insects hovered round us in the heat. But shortly after mid-day, thunder heads began to build up to the west. Boy got in about two. He'd hitched a ride up from Quesnel in one of the cement trucks and had picked up his horse in Come Lucky on the way down to our rendezvous at the entrance to Thunder Creek. He had a copy of the *Calgary Tribune* with him. They had run the story of Campbell's Kingdom as a news item on the front page and there was a long feature article inside. Boy had seen the editor, so had Winnick. They had talked to some of the scouts from the big companies. The legend of oil in the Rocky Mountains had got off to a good start. But his big news was that Garry was already at 150 Mile House. It only needed a phone call from us to get his convoy rolling.

I looked up at the gathering clouds. " What's the weather going to do to-night?" I asked.

" I'd say rain," Bill answered.

Boy didn't say anything, but walked across the clearing to where there was a view up the valley. He stood for some time, staring up towards Solomon's Judgment where small puffs of snow were being driven down the forward slopes. "The weather's breaking."

"Rain?" I asked.

He shook his head. " Snow more likely. The wind's from the east."

" Snow?" It might be even better than rain. " Have you brought that phone testing equipment?"

" It's in my pack." He went over to the two saddle bags he had dropped on to the ground and got out the instruments. " What are you planning to do, Bruce?"

" Get Garry and his trucks up to-night," I said. " How long do you reckon it will take him from 150 Mile House?"

" Six, seven hours." He hesitated, glancing up at the mountains. " If the snow is heavy he may bog down, you know. There's a lot of weight in some of his trucks."

" We'll have to risk that."

We rode down the highway, past the turning up to Come Lucky, until we reached a stretch where it ran through trees.

The telephone wires were close against the branches here. I posted the two of them as guards and climbed a fir tree. There was no difficulty in tapping the wires. I had to wait for a while, listening to Trevedian talking to Keithley Creek. As soon as he got off the line I rang the exchange and got put through to 150 Mile House. I was afraid Garry might not be ready to move, but I needn't have worried. When I asked him how soon he could get started, he said, "Whenever you say. The gear's all stowed, everything's ready. We only got to start the engines."

"Fine," I said. "Can you make the entrance to the creek by eleven-thirty to-night?"

"Sure. Providing everything's okay we could probably make it by ten, mebbe even earlier."

"I don't want you earlier," I replied. "I want you there dead on eleven-thirty. The timing is important. What's your watch say?"

"Two twenty-eight."

"Okay." I adjusted my watch by a couple of minutes. "Now listen carefully, Garry. Keep moving all the time and try not to get involved with any truck coming in with materials for the dam. As you approach the rendezvous only the leading truck is to have any lights. Keep your convoy bunched. We'll meet you where the timber starts. If we're not there, turn around and go back as far as Hydraulic and I'll contact you there to-morrow. It will mean something has gone wrong with our plans. Okay?"

"Sure."

"See you to-night, then."

"Just a minute, Bruce. What are our plans? How do you propose——'

"I haven't time to go into that now," I cut in quickly. "See you at eleven-thirty. Good-bye."

I unclipped my wires and climbed down to the ground. Boy heeled his horse up to me as I packed the instrument away. "Where did you learn to tap telephone wires?" he asked.

"The war," I said. "Taught me quite a lot of things that I didn't imagine would be of any use to me after it was over."

He was very silent as we rode back to our camp and several times I caught him looking at me with a worried frown. As we sat over our food that evening he tried to question me about my plans, but I kept on putting him off and in the end I walked down to the edge of the creek and sat there smoking. Every now and then I glanced at the luminous dial of my watch. And as the hands crept slowly round to zero hour the sense of nervousness increased.

At twenty to eleven I walked back to where the two of them sat smoking round the blackened embers of the fire. The night was very dark. There were no stars. A cold wind drifted down the valley. "What about your snow?" I asked Boy.

"It'll come," he said.

"When?"

Something touched my face—a cold kiss, light as a feather. More followed. "It's here now," Boy said. I shone my torch into the darkness. A flurry of white flakes was drifting across the clearing. "Going to be cold up by the dam, if we get there."

I glanced at my watch again. Ten forty-five. "Bill."

"Yeah?"

"Get on your horse and ride up to the road to the bend just before the gate. Tether your horse in the timber and work your way unobserved to a point where you can watch the guard hut. Now listen carefully. At eleven-fifteen exactly the guard will get a phone call. As a result of that call he should leave immediately, going up the road towards the hoist on foot. If he hasn't left by eleven twenty-five get your horse and come back down the road as fast as you can to let us know."

"And if he does?"

"Wait till he's out of earshot, then open the gate and block it open. Get your horse and follow him up without him knowing. Okay? About a mile up the road there's a trail cutting straight over a rocky bluff. He should take that trail. Wait for us there to let us know whether he took it or kept to the road. I'll also want to know the exact time he started up the trail. When we've passed ride back down here, collect the two remaining horses and get part of the way up the pony trail to the Kingdom before camping. We'll see you up at the Kingdom to-morrow, if all goes well. If by any chance we're not in the Kingdom by the time you get there, then I'm afraid you'll have to come down again with the horses. All right?"

He went through his instructions and then I checked his watch with mine. " Good luck," he said as he mounted his horse. " And see you don't make me come down off the Kingdom again. I kinda want to see a rig operating up there now." He grinned and waved his hand as he walked his horse out of the clearing.

" What now?" Boy asked.

" We wait," I said. I glanced at my watch. Five to eleven. Thirty-five minutes to wait. " Hell!" I muttered.

He caught hold of my arm as I turned away. " Don't I get any instructions?"

" Not yet," I said.

I could just see his eyes staring at me in the darkness. I wondered whether he could see in the dark. His eyes were large and luminous. " I don't like going into something without a briefing."

" There's nothing to brief you on."

For a moment I thought he was going to insist. But then he dropped his hand. " All right. I understand. But just tell me one thing. Is anybody going to get hurt?"

" Nobody's going to get hurt," I said.

" Then why are you carrying a gun?"

" How the——" I stopped. What did it matter? Probably he'd just opened my rucksack by mistake in the dark. I hesitated and then groped my way forward, found my pack and got out the Luger Jean had given me. " Here," I said, handing it to him. " Does that make you happier?"

He took it and stood for a moment, holding it in his hand. I glanced at my watch. Eleven o'clock. " Come on," I said. "Time we were moving."

As we walked up towards the road, lights cleaved the darkness away to our right. We waited, watching them grow nearer, watching the trees become black shapes fringed already with a coating of snow. I put my watch to my ear, listening for the tick of it, afraid for the moment that it had stopped and this was Garry's convoy. Then a single truck swept by giving us a brief glimpse of the road curving upwards through the timber, already whitening under the curtain of snow swirling down through the gap in the trees.

A moment later I was climbing a fir tree that stood close against the telephone wires. I had my testing box slung round my neck. I clipped the wires on and waited, my eyes on my watch. At eleven-fifteen exactly I reached into my pack, pulled out a pair of pliers and cut both wires close by my clips. Then I lifted my receiver and wound the handle in a long single ring. There was no answer. I repeated the ring. Suddenly a voice was crackling in my ears. "Valley guard."

I held the mouthpiece well away from me. "Trevedian here," I bawled, deeping my voice. "I've had a report——"

Another voice chipped in on the line. "Butler, Slide Camp, here. What's the trouble?"

"Get off the line, Butler," I shouted. "I'm talking to the Valley guard. Valley guard?"

"Yes, Mr. Trevedian."

"I've had a report of some falls occurring a couple of miles up from you. Go up and investigate. It's by that first overhang just after the hairpin bends."

"It'd be quicker to send a truck down from the camp. They could send a gang down——"

"I'm not bringing a truck down through this snow on a vague report," I yelled at him. "You're nearest. You get up there and see what it's all about. There's a short-cut——"

"But, Mr. Trevedian. There's a truck just gone up. He'll be able to report at the other——"

"Will you stop making excuses for getting a little snow down your damned neck. Get up there and report back to me. That's an order. And take that short-cut. It'll save you a good fifteen minutes. Now, get moving." I banged the receiver down and stayed there for a moment, clinging to the tree, trembling so much from nervous exhaustion that I was in danger of falling.

"Are you coming down?" Boy called up.

"No," I said. "Not for a moment." I lifted the receiver again and placed it reluctantly to my ears. But the line was dead. Neither the man up at the camp nor the guard had apparently dared to ring back. As the minutes passed I began to feel easier. I glanced at my watch. Eleven twenty-three. The guard should be well up the road by now.

"Got rid of the guard?" Boy asked, as I climbed down.

"I think so," I said. "If Bill isn't here in the next five minutes we'll know for sure."

We waited in silence after that. It was very dark. The snow made a gentle, murmuring sound as it fell and the wind stirred the tops of the firs. From behind us came the sound of water. Every now and then I glanced at my watch and as the minute hand crept slowly to the half-hour my nervousness increased. One of the trucks might have developed engine trouble. Maybe the snow had already drifted down towards Keithley. Or they might have got bogged down.

Suddenly Boy's hand gripped my arm. Above the snow familiar sounds of water, wind and snow I though I heard a steady, distant murmur like the rattle of tanks in a parallel valley. The sound steadily grew and then a beam of light glowed yellow through the curtain of the snow. The light increased steadily till we could see each other's faces and the shape of the trees around us. Two eyes suddenly thrust the black dots of the snow aside and an instant later the hulking shape of a diesel truck showed in the murk and panted to a stop. I glanced at my watch. It was eleven-thirty exactly.

" That you, Garry?" Boy called.

" Sure and it's me. Who d'you think it was?" Garry leaned out of the cab. " What now, Bruce?"

I signalled Boy to clamber on and swung myself up on to the step. " All your trucks behind you?" I asked.

" Yeah. I checked about five miles back. What do we do now? What's the plan, eh?"

" Get going as fast as we can," I said.

The driver leaned forward to thrust in his gear, but Garry stopped him. " Before we go ahead I want to know just what sort of trouble I'm headed for."

" For God's sake," I said.

" I'm not budging till I know your plan, Bruce. There's six vehicles here and a man to each vehicle. I'm responsible for them. I got to know what I'm heading into."

" We'll talk as we go," I said.

" No. Now."

" Don't be a fool," I shouted at him angrily. " The guard is off the gate. Every second you delay——" I took a deep breath and got control of myself. " Get going," I said. " My plan works on split timing over this section." I glanced at my watch. " You're half a minute behind schedule now. If you can't make up that half a minute you might just as well not have run over from 150 Mile House. And if you miss it this time, there won't be another chance. All your effort will have been wasted. I can only do this once."

He hesitated, but I think the earnestness of my voice convinced him as much as my words. He motioned to the driver. The gears crunched, the big motor roared and the trees began to fall away from us on either side as the heavy rig truck gathered speed.

"I see you cut the telephone wires." Garry's voice was barely audible above the roar of the engine.

"That's why I can't do it again," I said. "All we've got to do is rely on confusion. I've been tapping the telephone wires and issuing orders in the name of Trevedian. That enough for you to go on with?"

He hesitated. Then he suddenly nodded and squeezed my arm. "All right," he said. "You got something up your sleeve. I know that. But if the guard is off the gate up here, I'll agree you've been smart and leave it at that for the moment."

All the way up I was watching for Bill, but there was no sign of him and as we rounded the bend where the guard was posted I saw that the gate was swung open and knew that it was all right so far. I caught a glimpse of the deserted guard hut as we passed and then we were climbing. "Can you manage on sidelights?" I shouted to the driver.

For answer he switched off the heads. The night closed in. Snow was beating against the clicking windscreen wipers. He switched on the heads again. "Too dangerous." I leaned out from the running board and looked back. The other trucks had their headlights on now. I counted five. A pity about the heads, but it couldn't be helped. I glanced at my watch. Eleven thirty-six. The guard should be on the short-cut now. Slowly we approached the point where the shoulder of rock rose, blocking the road and forcing it away to the right into the hairpins. A figure loomed suddenly in the headlights— a figure on horseback, ghostly in his mantel of white.

At a gesture from me the driver checked. "Bruce?" Bill called. And then as he saw me leaning out towards him he shouted, "It's okay. He's on the trail now. Started up at eleven thirty-three."

"Fine. See you at the Kingdom."

His "Good luck!" came faintly as the engine roared and we swung to the first of the hairpins.

That first bend had me in a panic. The truck was big,

probably a lot bigger than the ones Trevedian was using. If we got stuck on the hairpins. . . .

But we didn't get stuck. The driver knew his stuff and we scraped round with inches to spare. The second and third bends were easier, but on the fourth we were forced to run back slightly. And then we were over the top and running out to the cliff where the overhang was. " Now listen, Garry," I shouted. " I'm dropping off in a minute. You'll go on till you get to an area of swamp ground where a lot of hard core has been thrown in to make a causeway. Just beyond that you'll find a place where you can turn off to the right into the brush. Get all your vehicles parked in under the trees and all facing outwards, ready to go on up the road at a moment's notice. All lights out. No smoking. No talking. I'll bring the last truck in myself a little later. Okay?"

He nodded. " Another phone call to make?" he said with a grin.

" That's right," I said. The road was a shelf now, running along the cliff face. The headlights showed rock and road, and beyond, nothing but black emptiness. Slowly the big truck rounded the bend under the overhang and then dipped her nose for the long, straight run down to the swamp ground. And as the nose dipped I dropped to the ground.

One by one the trucks passed me—a pair of round eyes beaming into blazing headlights as they pierced the snow and then sudden blackness as the bulk of it ground past me. Three—four—five; and then I was flagging down the last truck, jumping for the running board. " I'm Bruce Wetheral," I shouted to the driver. " Pull up a moment, will you?"

He hesitated, eyeing me uncertainly. " It's all right," I said. " I've just dropped off Garry's truck."

" Okay." The engine died and the big tanker pulled up with a jerk. " What now?"

" We're acting as rear guard," I told him, unslinging my pack. " They'll be waiting for us about a mile further on." I pulled out the box containing batteries and detonating plunger slung the coil of wire over my shoulder and flicked on my torch. " I'll be about five minutes," I said.

The snow was thicker now as I walked back down the road. In places it was drifting. My feet made no sound. Visibility was almost nil—the torch revealed nothing but a world of whirling white. I found the cliff wall and felt my way along it, probing with the torch for the branch with which I had marked the shot holes. The branch was still there, white with snow. I found the wires without difficulty, connected up with them and walked back, trailing the battery wires out behind me. At the limit of the wires I connected to the batteries, checked my connections carefully and then stood back, hesitating for a moment, wondering whether I had fixed the detonators correctly, scarcely believing that a thrust of the plunger could bring down thousands of tons of rock. Then quickly I stooped, grasped the handle and plunged it down.

There was a terrifying roar that went on and on, reverberating through the valley, plunging downwards, scattering debris in the trees, shaking the snow from them, stripping their branches. A chip of rock as big as my head thudded into the ground at my feet. And then quite suddenly there was silence.

I ran forward, probing with my torch, stumbled and almost fell. Piled in front of me was a mountain of debris. The results couldn't have been better. The whole cliff face had fallen outwards, spilling across the road and over the precipice beyond. I tugged at the wires till they came free, coiled them over my arm and went back to the truck. The driver was out on the road. "For Chrissakes," he said. "What was that?"

"Just blocking the road behind us," I said. "Can you pull your truck over so that I can reach those telephone wires?"

It was difficult. The wires were sagging loosely. I got my telephone equipment, clipped on to the wires, and rang and rang. At length a voice answered me. "Butler, Slide Camp, here. What's going on? I been trying to get——"

"Listen, Butler," I shouted, again holding the mouthpiece well away from my face. "There's been an accident. That cliff face. It's fallen. There's——"

"I can't hear you. Speak up please. The line's very bad."

"Probably because it's down," I shouted.

"I been trying to ring you. That truck just got in. The driver says there's no sign of any falls——"

"To hell with the truck. Listen, damn you," I shouted. "Can you hear me?"

"Yes. Is that Mr. Trevedian?"

"Yes. Now listen. There's been a bad fall. The cliff has fallen in and buried one of our trucks. Have you got that?"

"Yes."

" Right. How many men have you got up there?"

" Men? Including everybody?"

" Including every Goddam soul."

" About fifty-three, I guess."

"How many trucks?"

"Four. No, five—counting the one that's just arrived."

" Okay. Rustle up every man in the camp, all the digging equipment you can, pile them into the trucks and get down to that fall as fast as you can. We've got to have that road cleared by to-morrow morning. And there's the driver of the truck. He's buried under it somewhere. I want every man—you understand? No cooks or clerks skulking around, avoiding work. I want every man—the men guarding the hoist—every Goddam man. And don't think I won't know if any are left behind. I'll have a roll call before we're through. Every man, you understand. This is an emergency."

"Where are you speaking from?" His voice sounded doubtful. " I've been trying to ring——"

"For Christ's sake get on with it, damn you. I want the whole lot of you down here in half an hour. I'll be working up with my men from the other——" I pulled off the wires then and wiped the sweat from my forehead. God, I felt tired! Would he bring them all down or would he balls it up. Suppose he decided to recce with just a truckload first? Everything depended on how scared he was of Trevedian. I was banking a lot on Trevedian's reputation for ruthlessness.

Slowly I climbed into the cab. " Okay," I murmured as I sank back into the seat, absorbing gratefully the hot smell of the engine. " Let's go and join the others."

The driver was staring at me. His face looked white and scared in the dashboard lights. He switched on the heads and instantly the snow was a white, drifting wall. *Would they risk it coming down through this?* I wondered. The heavy diesel coughed and roared, the tanker ground forward round the curve of the hill, down the straight run to the swamp ground, across the hard core—and then Garry was there, white like a ghost in the snow, signalling us in, guiding the driver as he backed the tanker alongside the other trucks.

" What was that noise?" Garry asked as the driver cut his engine. The world became suddenly black as the lights were switched off. And then Garry was beside me, gripping my arm. "What have you been up to?" His face, too, looked scared in the faint light from the cab.

"Got a cigarette?" I said.

He handed me one and lit it for me. "Well?" he said.

"There's been a bit of a fall," I said wearily.

"A fall?" Then he saw the dynamiting equipment lying beside me on the seat. "Do you mean you've blown the road, by that overhang?"

"That's about it," I said.

"But Christ, man—that's a criminal offence. They'll have the Mounties up here. . . ."

"We'll see," I said. "It won't be easy to prove."

"I should have insisted on your telling me your plan before——"

"There wasn't time," I said. And then suddenly losing my temper. "Damn it, how did you think we were going to get a rig up there? Ask Trevedian to be kind enough to bring it up for us? Well, I did that. I warned him this was a public highway, built with Government money. He laughed in my face."

Boy had come up beside him. "What do we do next, Bruce?" His voice was steady, quite natural, as though this were the most ordinary thing in the world. I liked Boy for that. He understood. For him a thing that was done was done. He just accepted it.

"I've phoned the camp," I said. "We wait here until they're all down at the fall."

"And then we blow up the camp, I suppose?" Garry said sarcastically.

"No," I replied. "Just a bridge. Better get some rest, both of you," I added. "We've got a long night's work ahead of us."

Boy turned away, but Garry hesitated and then he nodded slowly. "Guess you're right," he said and went back to his truck.

Half an hour later headlights pierced the snow for a moment and a truck rumbled past. There were men in the back of it, white shapes huddled against the blinding snow. Another truck followed a few minutes afterwards and then another. They showed for an instant in the murk and then vanished quite suddenly, swallowed up in the storm. A branch creaked and split, broken off by the weight of snow. It fell across one of the trucks. We waited and watched. There was still two more trucks. Five minutes . . . ten. Nothing came. At length I got out of the cab and walked up the line to Garry's truck. " I think we'll risk it," I said. " Go one mile and then stop. As soon as I've blown the bridge I'll change places with Boy and ride up with you. Okay?"

Garry opened his mouth to say something, but then closed it again. " Okay," he said.

One by one the trucks pulled out and swung on to the road. I followed in the last truck. Our headlights nosed the red tail light of the truck ahead. The hill was short and steep. I saw the truck ahead begin to swing and then we stopped, back wheels spinning. For an awful moment I thought we were going to get stuck. To fit chains would take half an hour. But then the wheels suddenly gripped as they dug down through the snow to the surface of the road. We nosed forward, touched the truck ahead and again stuck with wheel spin. But a moment later both of us were grinding forward, lipping the top of the hill and running down to the torrent. The logs of the bridge were heavy with snow. There was no hollow sound of wheels on wood as we crossed, only a slight change in the noise of the engine.

A hundred yards further on I had my driver stop and ran back to fix my battery wires. The explosion was much sharper this time. It was like the sound of a gun and the echoes vanished abruptly, masked by the falling snow. When I went forward to look at the bridge it was a tumbled mass of logs. The drop to the torrent bed was only a few feet. Nobody would get hurt if a truck failed to pull up in time.

I got back into the cab and half a mile further on we caught up with the tail light of the truck ahead. They had pulled up, engines panting softly in the darkness. I ran up to the leading truck and sent Boy back to bring up the rear. Garry looked at me once out of the corners of his eyes as I settled down beside him, but he said nothing and we started forward up the long drag to the camp.

It was twelve-forty when we saw the lights of a hut. More lights appeared as we slowly followed the road across the camp area. From somewhere in the darkness came the faint hum of a diesel electric plant. " Do you reckon they've all gone down in those trucks?" Garry asked. It was the first time he had spoken.

" I don't know," I said. " I hope so."

We were almost clear of the camp when a man suddenly ran out into the middle of the road, flagging us down with his arm. " What do we do now?" the driver asked. " Ignore him?"

But I knew we couldn't ignore him. " You'll have to pull up," I said. I could feel myself trembling and my feet and hands felt deathly cold. Something had gone wrong. Another man appeared beside the first ; another and another—a whole bunch of them. As we pulled up they crowded round us. " Switch the dashboard light off," I said to the driver. And then leaning out of the darkness of the cab I flashed the beam of my torch on them, blinding them. " What the hell are you boys doing up here?" I rasped. " Didn't you get Trevedian's orders? Every man is wanted down the trail. There's been a bad fall. One of our trucks is buried."

A man stepped forward, a big gangling fellow with a battered nose. " We only got here yesterday. We heard some sort of a commotion going on and then the trucks pulled out. They must have forgotten about us, I guess. We didn't know what in hell was going on. We'd just about decided to take one of the trucks and go down and find out. We thought mebbe they were scared of another slide."

I said, " Well, you'd better get down there as fast as you can. It's an emergency call. Trevedian wants everybody down there."

" Then why didn't you boys stay there?"

" We had to clear the road," I said quickly. " Besides he wasn't risking this stuff. It's got to be up the top and ready to start operating to-morrow. Anybody on the hoist?"

" I don't know," the big fellow answered. " We're new here."

" Well, if you're new here you'd better look lively and get down the road. Trevedian's a bad man to fall out with."

" Tough, eh? Well, nobody ain't going to get tough with me." His voice was drowned in a babble of talk. Then the men began to drift away to their hut. I signalled the driver to go on and we rumbled into the trees and down the slope to the edge of the slide. A glow pierced the darkness ahead, resolved itself into an arc light hanging from a tall pine pole. There were others, a whole circle of lights blazing on the dazzling white of the snow, lighting up the concrete box of the cable housing. A figure appeared, armed with a rifle. "Hell!" I breathed. That damned fool Butler had failed to collect the guard.

I clambered down from the cab and started to explain. But as soon as I told him we'd got to get our trucks up the hoist he began asking for my pass. "Don't be a Goddam fool, man," I shouted. "Trevedian's down at the fall trying to clear it. How in hell would he issue passes. Can you work the motor?"

He shook his head uncertainly.

"Well, probably one of my men can handle it," I said.

But he said, "Nobody's allowed to touch the engine except the hoist men."

"Oh, for God's sake," I yelled at him. "This isn't routine. This in an emergency. Don't you know what's happened?" He shook his head. I leaned closer. "Better keep this under your hat. Nobody's supposed to know. There's a bad crack developed in the foundations of the dam. They think the cliff face may be moving. We've got to drill and find out what the strata underneath is formed of. And we've got to do it damned quick." I caught hold of his arm. "Christ, man, what do you think we're doing up here when one of our own trucks is buried under a fall? We wanted to stay and help dig him out. But Trevedian wouldn't let us. He said it was more important to get our trucks up on schedule."

The man hesitated, conviction struggling against caution. "You wait here," he said and hurried back to the housing. Garry joined me. Through the slit I could see him winding and winding at the telephone. "What's going to happen?" Garry asked.

"It'll work out," I said.

"Well, no rough stuff," he growled. "We've done about $10,000 worth of damage already to-night."

"They'd have a job to prove we did it," I said.

"Mebbe. But if you try pulling a gun on this guy ..."

"I haven't got a gun on me," I snapped irritably. "And anyway I'm not that much of a fool."

The guard came out of the housing. "I can't get any reply." His voice was hesitant. He was unsure of himself.

"What did you expect?" I snarled at him. "There's a million tons of rock down on the road and the line's under it. In any case, Trevedian's at the fall, not in his office." I turned as figures emerged into the glare of the lights led by the man with the battered nose. "What's the trouble?" I said.

"No keys in the trucks," he said. "What do we do now?" They were muffled in fur jackets and windbreakers. Some carried picks and shovels. "If we could have one of your trucks," he said.

I hesitated. But the snow was falling thick. Much as I wanted to get rid of them I didn't dare risk one of the trucks. "Are you just labourers or have any of you been taken on as engineers on the draw works of the hoist here?"

It was a shot in the dark, a hundred to one chance, but it came off. One of them stepped forward. "Please. I am engaged to replace an engineer who is seek." Dark eyes flashed in a sallow face. "I am shown how eet works yesterday." He smiled ingratiatingly.

"Good," I said. "Get in there and get the engine started." And as the little Italian hurried over to the housing I turned to the guard. "There. Does that satisfy you? Goddam it," I added. "You think that piece of machinery was something new in atomic weapons the way you fuss about it."

"But my orders——"

"Damn your orders!" I screamed, catching hold of him by his coat and shaking him. "It's just a diesel engine. Like any other damned diesel engine. And this stuff has got to be up there first thing. And because of your blasted Trevedian and this bloody dam we're up here instead of helping to dig out one of our pals. I wish to God we'd never been given the job. But it's a thousand bucks a day this outfit costs and there'll be hell to pay if we're not up there on schedule, snow or no snow." I swung round on the silent, gaping crowd of men. "All right. You stay here and give us a hand loading the trucks. Garry!" He didn't answer. He stood there, staring at me and for the first time that night I saw a gleam of excitement in his eyes, a hint of laughter. "Get your first truck on to the staging. These men will help you load and secure. Boy! You ride up with the first vehicle and supervise the off-loading at the top. And see that you don't waste any time." I turned to the bunch of men, standing there like sheep. "Any of you cook?" It was the inevitable Chinaman who came forward. "All right," I said. "You get up to the cookhouse. I want hot chow for all of us in two hours' time. Okay?"

"Okay, mister. I can do. Velly good cook."

"See it's hot," I shouted at him. "That's all I care about."

I turned then and went into the housing. The pilot motor was already running. The little Italian engineer grinned at me. The guard hovered uncertainly. The cable wheel trembled and the cage bumped as the rig truck was driven on to the staging. The guard touched my arm. His face was pale and he was still uncertain. He opened his mouth to say something and then the big diesel started with a roar that drowned all other sound. I saw a look of helplessness come into his eyes and he turned away.

I knew then that we were through the worst. He couldn't hold the whole gang of us up with his rifle. Besides it must have seemed all right. I'd more than twenty men from the camp working with me. I had come in quite openly. All that made him doubtful, I imagine, was that his instructions had been dinned into him very thoroughly and forcefully.

Five minutes later the draw works began to turn and the first and heaviest truck went floating off into the whirling, driving white of the night. It was there for a second, white under its canopy of snow, looking strangely unreal suspended from the cable, and then it reached the limits of the lights and vanished abruptly. It was like a scene from a pantomime where some object takes to the air and is lost as it moves from the circle of the spotlight.

I stayed inside the engine housing. I was safe there. Nobody could talk to me against the roar of the engine. One or two tried, but gave it up. I had warned Garry to see that all his men knew the story and stuck to it if they got into conversation with any of the men from the camp or if the guard started asking questions. Shortly after two-thirty the Chinaman brought down big themos flasks full of thick soup, piping hot, and a great pile of meat sandwiches. Three trucks were up by then. A fourth was just leaving. We sent one flask up with it. The snow was still falling. " It sure must be hell up top," one of the drivers said. His face was a white circle in the fur of his hood. " Have you been up on this thing, Mr. Wetheral?"

"Yes," I said. And suddenly I realised he was scared. "It's

all right," I said. " You won't see anything. It'll just be cold as hell."

He nodded and swallowed awkwardly. "I'm scared of heights, I guess."

Somebody shouted to him. His mouth worked convulsively. " I must go now. That's my truck."

" Switch your cab lights on," I called after him as he climbed on the staging. " It'll just be like a road then."

He nodded. And a moment later he was on his way, a white bloodless face staring at the wheel he was gripping as the diesel roared and the cables swung him up and out into the night.

By four o'clock the sixth truck was being loaded. Every few minutes now I found myself glancing at my watch. Eight minutes past four and the hoist was running again. Only one more truck. "What's worrying you?" Garry shouted above the din of the engine.

" Nothing," I said.

He didn't say anything, but I noticed that his eyes kept straying now to the point where the roadway up to the camp plunged into darkness. Suppose Butler and his gang had smelt a rat. Or maybe he'd send a truck up for more equipment. They'd find the bridge down. It wouldn't take them long to repair it. Any moment they might drive in, asking what the hell was going on. My hands gripped each other, my eyes alternating between the road and the big iron cable wheel. At last the wheel stopped and we waited for the phone call that would tell us they had unloaded. " They're taking their time," Garry growled. His face looked tired and strained. I had started to tremble again. I tried to pretend it was the cold, but I knew it was nervous strain. At last the bell rang, the indicator fell and the engineer started the cage down. That ten minutes seemed like hours. And then at last the cage bumped into the housing, the diesel slowed to a gentle rumble and we could hear the engine of the last tanker roaring as it drove on to the cage. We went out into the driving snow then and watched the securing ropes being made fast.

It was ten to five and the faintest greyness was creeping into the darkness of the night as Garry and I climbed up beside the driver. I raised my hand, there was a shout, the cable ahead of us jerked tight and then we, too, were being slung out into the void.

I don't remember much about that trip up. I know I clutched at the seat, fighting back the overwhelming fear of last minute failure. I remember Garry voicing my thoughts: "I hope they don't catch us now," he said. "We'd look pretty foolish swinging up here in space till morning."

"Shut up," I barked at him, my voice unrecognisable in its tenseness.

He looked at me and then suddenly he grinned and his big hand squeezed my arm. "They don't breed many of your type around this part of the world."

The minutes ticked slowly by. A shadow slipped past my window. The pylon at the top. We were over the lip. Two minutes later our progress slowed. There was a slight bump and then we were in the housing. Figures appeared. The lashings were unhitched, the engine roared and with our headlights blazing on to a wall of snow we crawled off the staging and floundered through a drift to stop above the dam.

As we climbed out the cage lifted from the housing and disappeared abruptly. The ground seemed to move under my feet. I heard Boy's voice say, "Well, that's the lot, I guess. You're in the Kingdom now, Garry—rig and all." Then my knees were giving under me and I blacked out.

I came to in the firm belief that I was on board a ship. There was a reek of hot engine oil and the cabin swayed and dipped. And then I opened my eyes and found myself staring at the luminous dial of an oil gauge. Raising my eyes I saw a faint glimmering of grey through a windscreen. "You okay, Bruce?" It was Boy's voice. He was propping me up in the seat of a cab and we were grinding slowly through thick snow. "You'll be all right soon. There's hot food waiting for us at the ranch-house. We had to stop to fix chains. The snow is pretty deep in places."

I remember vaguely being spoon fed hot soup and men moving about, talking excitedly, laughing, pumping my hand. And then I was lying in a bed. But this time it was different. It wasn't because I was ill. It was only because I was physically and nervously exhausted. And I was back in the Kingdom. The rig was here at last. We were going to drill now. And with that thought I went to sleep and stayed asleep for twelve hours.

And when I woke up Boy was there beside me and he was grinning and saying that the rig would be up before nightfall. When I went down to the drilling site next morning I found the rig erected and the draw works being tightened down on to the steel plates of the platform. The travelling block was already suspended from the crown and the kelly was in its rat housing. They had already begun to dig a mud sump and there were several lengths of pipe in the rack.

I stood there with Boy and Garry and stared across to the dam less than a mile away. The sun was shining and already the snow was beginning to melt. I was thinking it was time Trevedian came storming into our camp. But nobody seemed to be taking any notice of us. The hoist moved regularly in and out of the housing, the loads of cement were stacked under their tarpaulins, the mixers chattered noisily and every now and then there was the heavy roar of blasting and more stone was run down in the tip wagons or slung on the cable across to the centre of the dam. "We'll have to mount a guard," I said.

Boy wiped the sweat from his face. "I'm sleeping down here," he said. "And I've got that pistol of yours. There are four rifles on the site as well."

I nodded, still looking across the dam. "The next move is with them," I murmured half to myself.

Garry chuckled. "Mebbe he's had enough. You sure fooled them."

I turned away. I didn't like it. The natural thing would have been for Trevedian to come and raise hell. It wasn't in the nature of the man to take it lying down. But he didn't come that day, or the next, or the next. I didn't feel up to heavy work so I took over the cooking again.

On the morning of Tuesday, June 9th, just a week after the rig had rolled into Thunder Valley, Garry spudded in. I stood on the platform and watched the block come down and the bit lowered into the hole. The bushing was dropped into the table, gripping the grief stem, and then at a signal from Garry the platform trembled under my feet, the big diesel of the draw works roared and the table began to turn. We had started to drill Campbell Number Two.

I walked slowly back to the ranch-house to the music of the

drill, the noise of it drowning the irritating chatter of the mixers at the dam. Strangely I felt no elation. It was as though I had sailed out of a calm and felt the threatening presence of the approaching storm. I went into the kitchen and began peeling the potatoes for the evening meal.

Half an hour later I heard the patter of feet, the door was pushed open and a big brown collie fell upon me, barking and licking my hand and jumping up to get at my face. It was Moses. He was spattered with mud and his coat was as wet as if he'd just swam the Jordan. I went out into the grey murk of the morning and there, coming up beside the barn, was Jean riding a small pinto. She pulled up as she saw me and sat there, looking at me. Her hair was plastered down with the rain so that it clung to her scalp showing the shape of her head like a boy. Her face looked strained and almost sad. The pony drooped its head. She sat motionless. Only her eyes seemed alive. "Mac said you needed a cook?" Her voice was toneless.

"Yes," I said. And I just stared at her. I couldn't think of anything to say. And yet there was a singing in my blood as though the sun were shining and the violets just opening.

"Well, I hope I'll do." She climbed stiffly down from the saddle, undid her pack and walked slowly towards me. She stopped when she reached the doorway. She had to, I suppose, because I was blocking it. We looked at each other for a moment.

"Why did you come?" I asked at length. My voice sounded hoarse.

She lowered her gaze. "I don't know," she said slowly. "I just had to, I guess. I brought you this." She handed me a bulky envelope. "Now I'd like to change please."

I stood aside and she went through into the bedroom. I turned the envelope over. It was postmarked London. Inside was a whole sheaf of typewritten pages, the newspaper report of my grandfather's trial which I had asked a friend to copy for me. I stabled the pinto and then I sat down and read through the report. Stuart Campbell had himself gone into the witness box. His evidence was the story of his discovery of the seep, of the abortive drilling in 1913, of his sincere conviction that there was oil in the Kingdom. Most of it I now knew, but one section of it hit me like a blow between the eyes. It occurred during cross-examinataion by his own counsel:

Counsel: This well you were drilling in 1913—why did you suddenly abandon it?

Witness: We couldn't go on.

Counsel: Why not?

Witness: We struck a sill of igneous rock. We were operating a cable-tool drill and it was too light for the job.

Counsel: At what depth was this?

Witness: About five thousand six hundred feet. We had to have a heavier drill and that meant more capital.

Counsel: And so you came to England?

Witness: Not at once. I tried to raise money in Canada. Then the war came. . . .

I leaned back and closed my eyes. Five thousand six hundred! And our geophysical survey showed an anticline at five thousand five hundred. The anticline was nothing but the sill of igneous rock that my grandfather had struck in 1913. God, what a fool I'd been not to get hold of the account of this case before starting to drill. Why hadn't my grandfather mentioned it in his progress report? Afraid of discouraging me, I suppose. I got to my feet and went over to the window and stood there staring across the alfalfa to the rig, wondering what the hell I was going to do. But there wasn't anything I could do. It hadn't stopped my grandfather from trying to drill another well.

"I wish somebody from back home would write me nice long letters like that."

I swung round to find Jean standing beside me. "It's just a business letter," I said quickly. I folded it up and put it back in the envelope. I couldn't tell her that what she had brought me was the full account of Stuart Campbell's trial.

That night the stars shone and it was almost warm. The second shift was working and we strolled down to the rig where it blazed like a Christmas tree with lights rigged up as far as the derrick man's platform. We were talking trivialities, carefully avoiding anything that could be regarded as personal. And then in a pause I said, "Didn't you like it in Vancouver?"

"Yes, I was having fun—dancing and sailing. But——"

She hesitated and then sighed. "Somehow it wasn't real. I think. I've lost the capacity to enjoy myself."

"So you came back to Come Lucky?" She nodded. "To escape again?"

"To escape?" She looked up at me and there was a tired set to her mouth. "No. Because it was the only place I could call home. And then——" She walked on in silence for a bit. Finally she said, "Did you have to slap Peter Trevedian in the face like that?"

"I had to get the rig up here. It was the only way."

She didn't say anything for a moment. Then she sighed. "Yes. I suppose so."

We came to the rig and climbed on to the platform and stood there watching the table turning and the block slowly inching down as the drill bit into the rock two hundred feet below us. Beneath us the screen shook and the rock chips sifted out of the mud as it returned to the sump. Bill was standing beside the driller. "What are you making now?" I shouted to him.

"About eight feet an hour."

Eight feet an hour. I did a quick calculation. Roughly two hundred a day. "Then twenty-five days—say a month—should see us down to the anticline?"

He nodded. "If we can keep this rate of drilling up."

We stayed until they shut down at midnight. We were working two teams of four on ten-hour shifts and closing down from midnight to 4 a.m. It was the most the men could do and keep it up day after day. Boy and I were taking it in turns to stand guard on the rig. Moses acting as watch dog.

We were soon settled into a regular routine. One day followed another and each was the same, the monotony broken only by the variable nature of the weather. June dragged into July and each day two more lengths of pipe had been added to the length of the drill. The heat at midday became intense when the sun shone and the nights were less cold. Snow storms became less frequent, but whenever the sun shone throughout the morning thunder heads would build up over the mountains around midday and then there'd be rain and the thunder would rumble round the peaks and they would be assailed by jabbing streaks of lightning. And

C.K.   G all the time the alfalfa grew and the Kingdom was carpeted with lupins and tiger lilies and a host of other flowers.

And in all that time Trevedian had not once come near us. The work at the dam was going on night and day now. Once we rode over at night to have a look at it and where Campbell land stopped and Trevedian land began, the boundary was marked by a heavy barbed wire fence. There was a guard on the hoist and on the dam itself and they carried guns and had guard dogs.

The sense of being cut off gradually overlaid all our other feelings. The drill might probe lower and lower, boring steadily nearer to the dome of the anticline, but in all our minds was that sense of being trapped, of not being able to get out. We were completely isolated in a world of our own, the radio our only contact with the outside world. And when that broke down the Kingdom closed in on us.

I wouldn't have minded for myself. If I'd been up there on my own I should have been happy. But my mood reacted inevitably to the mood of the others and all the time I had the uncanny feeling that we were all waiting for something to happen. Our isolation wasn't natural. Fergus couldn't ignore us indefinitely. He didn't dare let us bring in a well. And there was Trevedian. That phrase of Jean's—about slapping Trevedian in the face—stuck in my mind. The man was biding his time. I felt it. And so did Jean. Sometimes I'd find her standing, alone and solitary, her work forgotten, staring towards the dam.

And then the blow fell. It was on July 4th. Boy had left that morning taking core samples down to Winnick in Calgary. The weather was bad and when I came on watch at midnight it was blowing half a gale with the wind driving a murk of rain before it that was sometimes sleet, sometimes hail and occasionally snow. I was wearing practically everything I could muster for the wind was from the east and it was bitterly cold. As usual I had Moses with me and the Luger was strapped to my belt.

The team on duty closed down the draw works and the drill clattered to a standstill. The rig stopped shaking and all was suddenly silent except for a queer howling sound made by the wind in the steel struts of the rig. As the big diesel of the draw works stopped the lights snapped off and blackness closed in. Torches flickered and then the boys called out

Goodnight and followed along the line of markers that led back to the ranch-house, four hunched figures against the flickering light of their torches. Then a curtain of sleet blotted them out and the dog and I were alone on the empty platform of the rig.

The switch from noisy activity to utter blackness was, I remember, very sudden that night. The lights of the dam were completely blotted out and there was not even the ugly rattle of the mixers to keep me company since they were down-wind. I was alone in the solitude of the mountains.

I made the usual round of the trucks which were drawn up at various points in the vicinity of the rig. It was a routine inspection and my torch did not probe very inquisitively. It was too cold. The dog, I remember, was restless, but whether because he smelt smoking or had a premonition or just because he didn't like the weather I cannot say. I finished the round as quickly as possible and then climbed to the platform. For a time I paced up and down and at length I sought the comparative warmth of the little crew shelter, a wooden hut at the back of the platform fitted with a bench. I smoked cigarettes, occasionally opening the door and peering out.

Time passed slowly that night. The dog kept moving about. I tried to make him settle, but every time he got himself curled up something made him get to his feet again.

It was about two-thirty and I had just peered out to see it snowing hard. As I closed the door, Moses suddenly cocked his head on one side and gave a low growl. The next moment he leapt for the door. I opened it and he shot through. And at the same instant there was a great roar of flame, a whoof of hot air that seemed to fling back the snow and seared my eyeballs with the hot blast of it. It was followed almost instantly by two more explosions in close succession that shook the rig and sent great gobs of flaming fuel high into the night.

In the lurid glare of one of these liquid torches I saw a figure running, a shapeless unrecognisable bundle of clothing heading for the dam. And behind him came Moses in great bounds. The figure checked turned and as Moses leapt I saw the quick stab of a gun, though the sound of it was lost in the holocaust of flame that surrounded me. The dog checked in mid leap, twisted and fell.

I had my gun out now and I began firing, emptying the magazine at the fleeing figure. Then suddenly the pool of flame that had illuminated him died out and he vanished into the red curtain of the driving snow.

As suddenly as they had started the flames died down. For a moment I saw the skeletons of the two tankers, black and twisted against the lurid background. And then quite abruptly everything was dark again, except for a few bits of metal that showed a lingering tendency to remain red hot. I hurried down from the platform of the rig and at the bottom I met Moses, dragging himself painfully on three legs. In the light of the torch I saw a bullet had furrowed his shoulder. He was bleeding badly and his right front leg would support no weight. I tried to feel whether the blade of the shoulder had been broken, but he wouldn't let me touch it.

I made a quick round of the remaining vehicles to check that there was nothing smouldering. Wisps of smoke still came from the burnt-out tankers, but there was no danger of any more fire. They were already sizzling gently and steaming as the snow settled on their twisted metal frames. Then I hurried to the ranch-house with Moses following as best he could.

Every moment I expected to meet the others running to the rig to find out what had happened. It seemed incredible to me that they couldn't have seen the glare of that blaze. And yet when I reached the house it was in darkness. There was no sound. They were all fast asleep and blissfully ignorant of the disaster. For disaster it was; I knew that by the time I'd covered half the distance to the house. The attack had been made on the one thing that could stop us dead. Without fuel we could not drill. And like my blowing up of the road it would be a hard thing to prove in a court of law.

The first person I woke was Jean and I gave Moses into her care, avoiding meeting her gaze as I told her briefly what had happened. I was scared of the reproach I knew must be in her eyes. She loved that dog. After that I woke Garry.

I think that was one of the hardest things I ever had to do, to tell Garry that two of his trucks were gone and all his fuel. I knew what he'd think—that I had started the rough stuff, that I had invited this raid. He didn't say anything when I had finished, but put on his clothes and strode out into the storm. I followed him.

When he'd looked at the damage he said, "Well, I hope the insurance company pay up, that's all." We went into the hut then. "Cigarette?" He thrust the packet towards me. As we lit up he said, "It might have been worse, I guess. The whole rig could have gone." He leaned back and closed his eyes, drawing on his cigarette. "We're down just over four thousand two hundred. Fortunately the rig tank was filled up yesterday. There's probably two hundred gallons or so in it. That'll get us down to about four thousand five hundred. With luck we'll only need another seven hundred gallons—say a thousand." He had been talking to himself, but now he opened his eyes and looked across at me. "Any idea how we'll get a thousand gallons of fuel up here?"

"We'll have to bring it in by the pony trail," I said.

"Hmmm. Twenty gallons to a pony; that means fifty ponies. Know where you can get fifty ponies? It'll make the cost about a dollar a gallon. That's a thousand bucks and I'm broke. Can you raise a thousand bucks?"

There was nothing I could say. His big frame looked crumpled and tired. An hour later the morning shift came on. They stood and stared at the gutted trucks, talking in low, excited whispers. "Well, what are you waiting for?" Garry shouted at them. "Get the rig going."

He remained with them and I walked slowly back to the ranch-house, hearing the clatter of the drill behind me, very conscious that they could go on drilling for just over a week and then we'd have to close down.

Jean was still up as I staggered wearily in. "How's Moses?" I asked as I pulled off my wet clothes.

"He'll be all right," she said and went through into the kitchen. She came back with a mug of tea. "Drink that," she said.

"What about Moses?" I said, taking the mug. "Is his shoulder all right?"

"The bone's not broken, if that's what you mean. It's just a flesh wound. He'll be all right."

I drank the tea and flung myself into a chair. She brought in logs and built the fire up into a blaze. "Hungry?"

I nodded. And then I fell asleep and she had to wake me when she brought in a plate of bacon and fried potatoes. She sat down opposite me, watching me as I began to eat. Moses came in, moving stiffly, and sat himself beside me, licking my hand much as to say, "Sorry I didn't get that bastard for you." I stared down, fondling his head. And then I gave him the plate of food. Suddenly I didn't feel like eating. Instead I lit a cigarette and watched the dog as he cleared the plate.

There was a dry sob and I looked across the table to see Jean staring at me, tears in her eyes. She turned quickly as our eyes met and went out into the kitchen. I got to my feet and went over to the window. The snow had stopped now. Dawn had broken and the wisps of ragged cloud were lifting and breaking up. Even as I watched, the clouds drew apart from the face of Solomon's Judgment. I went out to the barn where I slept, got my things together and took them across to the stables. As I was saddling up Jean came in. "What are you going to do?" she asked.

"Get on to Johnnie," I said. "See if he'll pack the fuel up for me."

"You're going alone?"

"Yes."

She hesitated and then went back to the house. Before I'd finished saddling, however, she returned, dressed for the trail. "What's the idea?" I said. "There's no point in your coming with me."

She didn't say anything, but got out her pinto and flung the saddle on it. I tried to dissuade her, but all she said was, "You're in no state to go down on your own."

"What about Moses?"

"Moses will be all right. And the boys can cook for themselves for a day or so."

Something in the set of her face warned me not to argue with her. I had an uneasy feeling that her coming with me was inevitable, a necessary part of the future. I scribbled a note for Garry, left it on the table in the living-room and then we rode up the mountainside. It was quiet in the timber, a quiet that was full of an aching, damp cold. And when we emerged the mist had clamped down again. We rode in silence, forcing the reluctant horses forward. At times we had to lead them, particularly near the top where the mist was freezing and coating the rocks with a thin layer of ice. Then suddenly there was a breath of wind on our faces and the white miasma of the mist began to swirl in an agitated manner. A rent appeared, a glimpse of the Kingdom and of the rig with the two burnt-out trucks, and then as though a screen had been lifted bodily the whole mountainside was suddenly visible and there was the Saddle and beyond it the nearer peak of Solomon's Judgment.

It was fortunate for us that the mist did clear for the trail over the Saddle was not an easy one and in places it was difficult to follow. It was dangerous, too, for a slight deviation at the top brought one out on to the edge of a sheer drop of several hundred feet. It is possible that the fact that I have described several trips made over this trail will give the impression that it was straightforward. In good weather conditions this would certainly be true. But these are the Rocky Mountains, and though not particularly high, the great mass of mountains together with the wide variations in climatic conditions, particularly of humidity, between the coast and the prairies to the east, makes them very uncertain as regards weather and subject to great extremes of conditions. At this altitude, for instance, there is not a month in the year when it does not snow and storms can come upon the traveller with astonishing rapidity if he is not high enough up to get an unobstructed view of the sky.

Having started so early we were down into the timber again before ten. Jean insisted on a rest here and we sat on a deadfall and ate the biscuits and cheese which she had very thoughtfully included in her pack. I was very tired after my sleepless night and extremely depressed. We had not yet drilled deep enough for me to feel any of the excitement that is inherent in drilling when the bit is approaching the probable area of oil. Without fuel success was as remote as ever and I cursed myself for not having foreseen the most probable means by which Trevedian would get back at us.

"What do you plan to do when we get down into the valley?" Jean asked suddenly.

I looked at her in surprise. "Phone Johnnie," I said. "I can always get him through Jeff."

"Where are you going to phone from?"

"The Golden Calf, of course. Mac will——" I stopped then for she was laughing at me. It wasn't a natural laugh. It was half bitter, half contemptuous. "What's the matter?"

"Don't you understand what you did when you blew the Thunder Valley road? You'd get battered to pulp if you went into Come Lucky now."

"Who by—Trevedian?" I asked.

"Of course not. By the boys you fooled. You actually got some of them to help you load the trucks on to the hoist, didn't you?" I nodded. "Trevedian was pretty sarcastic when he hauled them over the coals for being such mutts. If any of those boys got their hands on you——" She shrugged her shoulders. "That's why I came up to the Kingdom, to stop you walking into a bad beating up."

"Sort of nursemaid, eh?" I felt, suddenly, violently angry. What right had this girl to act as though she were responsible for me? "Pity you weren't around last night. You might have saved me from making a fool of myself, which would have been more to the point."

"You'll have to ride into Keithley and phone from there," she said quietly.

"I'll do no such thing." I got abruptly to my feet and went over to my horse. "The nearest phone is at the Golden Calf and that's where I'm going."

She didn't attempt to argue. She just shrugged her shoulders and swung herself up into the saddle. "I'll pick up the pieces," she said.

The sun was shining as we rode up the hill to Come Lucky. The door of Trevedian's office was open. He must have seen us coming for as we drew level he came to the door and stood there watching us, leaning against the jamb and smoking a cheroot. His skin was the colour of mahogany against the white of his nylon shirt, and he wore scarlet braces. No words were exchanged between us, but out of the corners of my eyes I could see he was smiling. I wondered how long he had sat at his desk with the door open watching for me to come down the trail from the Kingdom.

We met nobody in the sun-drenched street. The place seemed dead as though the whole population were up working on the dam. We tied our horses to the hotel rail and Jean led me in by the back way. Pauline stared at us as we entered and then there was the rasp of a chair and James McClellan stormed towards me, his face scowling with sudden anger. "I've been wanting to have a word with you, Wetheral, for a long time." His fists were clenched. His eyes were cold and there was an ugly set to his jaw.

There was only one thing to do. "Was it you or Trevedian —or both of you—who set fire to our trucks last night?"

He stopped in his tracks. "What's that? Are you trying to swing something on——"

"I'm not swinging anything on you," I said. "I'm just asking you, McClellan—were you in on it?"

"In on what?" He had halted. Pauline had hold of his arm. Her face was white. They were both staring at me.

"There's about two thousand gallons of fuel gone up and two trucks. Shots were fired. You're damn lucky it was only a dog that got hit." I turned towards the office. "Mind if I use the phone?"

"You brought it on yourself," he said. "If you phone the police, then Trevedian will report what happened——"

"I'm not phoning the police," I said over my shoulder. "I'm phoning for more fuel."

The office was empty. I got hold of the phone and put a personal call through to Jeff Hart at Jasper. Then I sat there, waiting, feeling sleep creeping up on me, trying to keep myself awake. I heard voices in the kitchen and then a door slammed and all was quiet. Half an hour later my call came through and I explained to Jeff Hart what had happened. He couldn't get away himself, but he'd talk to Johnnie and ring me back in the evening.

I went out into the kitchen then. It was empty. I sat down in the chair by the stove and went to sleep. It was Pauline who woke me. She had made me some coffee and there was a plate full of bacon and eggs waiting for me. "You shouldn't have bothered," I murmured sleepily.

"It's no trouble."

"Where's Jean?"

The corners of her mouth turned down and she gave a slight shrug—a very Latin gesture. "She is with Miss Garret, I think." She came and sat near me as I ate, watching me with her big, dark eyes. "You look tired."

"I am tired," I said. "I was up all night."

She nodded slowly, understandingly.

"Jean told you what happened?"

"*Oui.* I am very sorry." She smiled, a flash of white teeth. "I am sorry also that you do not stay. But it is dangerous for you."

"I'll have to stay till this evening. I'm waiting for a call."

"No, no. It is dangerous, I tell you."

I looked at her, a mood of frustration and annoyance taking hold of me. "Another nursemaid, eh?"

"Please?"

"It doesn't matter."

Jean came in then. "We must go now, Bruce. There are some men coming up from the bunkhouse. I think Trevedian sent them up."

I explained about the phone call. But all she said was, "Do you want to get beaten up?"

"You think I'm no good in a scrap?"

She hesitated fractionally. "You've been ill," she said. "I don't think you're very strong." She must have guessed what I was thinking for she added, "The way you handled Jimmy won't work with them."

She was right, of course, but it went against the grain to appear a coward. And yet it wouldn't do any good. Reluctantly I got to my feet. Pauline suddenly touched my arm. "I will take your call for you, if you wish."

"That's kind of you, Pauline," Jean said.

I hesitated, feeling caught in the web of a woman's world, feeling like a skunk. "All right," I said and told her what I wanted to say. "If he can come arrange where I can meet him. Okay?"

She nodded, smiling. "Okay. I will leave a message for you with Miss Garret."

I thanked her and we went out the back way and round to the front to get our horses. There were about a dozen men coming up the street, a rough-looking bunch headed by a man I recognised, the man who had been on guard at the hoist the night we ran the rig up to the Kingdom. He was a little fellow with bandy legs and a mean face. He had been cowed when I had seen him before, but now, backed up by the men behind him, he had a cocky air. "That's him," he shouted. "That's the bastard." And he began to run towards us. The others followed at his heels and they were almost on us as we unhitched our ponies and swung into the saddle. I heeled my animal into a canter and side by side we drove through them. But as I passed, the fellow shouted a remark. It wasn't aimed at me. It was aimed at Jean. It was just one word and without thinking I reined up and swung round. I caught a glimpse of the colour flaring in Jean's face as she called to me to ride on.

The whole bunch of them were laughing now and thus emboldened the little bow-legged swine called out. "Why d'yer keep her all to yerselves? Why don't yer let her visit us—alternate nights, say?" He leered at Jean and then let his filthy tongue run riot with further and more detailed abuse.

I don't know what got into me. I hadn't felt this way in years—that sense of being swept up in a red blur of rage. I pushed my horse towards him. "Say that again," I said. All that had happened in the last twelve hours seemed condensed into that one sordid little figure. I saw the trucks blossom into flame, the spurt of the gun as it was emptied at the dog, the look of tired resignation on Garry Keogh's face. The man hesitated, glancing round at his companions and then, with sudden truculence born of the herd, he mouthed that one word again.

I dug my heels into my horse's ribs and drove straight at him. I saw him fall back, momentarily knocked off balance and as the horse reared I flung myself from the saddle, grappling for his throat as my arms closed around him. We hit the dirt of the street and I felt his breath hot on my face as it was forced out of his lungs with a grunt. Then hands reached for me, clutching at my arms, twisting me back and pinning me down against the gravel. Fingers gripped my hair and as my skull was pounded against the hard earth I saw half a dozen faces, panting and sweaty, bending over me.

And then there was the sharp crack of an explosion and something whined out of the dust. The faces fell back and as I sat up I saw Jean sitting close alongside my horse, the Luger that had been in my saddle-bag smoking in her hand. And her face was calm and set. She held the ugly weapon as thought it were a part of her, as though shooting were as natural as walking or riding. The men saw it, too, and they hudded together uncertainly, their faces unnaturally pale, their eyes looking all ways for a place to run. "Are you all right, Bruce?"

"Yes," I said, struggling to my feet.

"Then get on your horse."

She levelled her gun at the bunch standing there in the street. "Now get back to Trevedian. And tell him next time he tries to shoot my dog I'll kill him."

She slipped the automatic back into my saddle-bag and in

silence we turned and rode down the street out of Come Lucky. For a long time I couldn't bring myself to speak. Only when we had reached a clearing above the ford and had dismounted did I manage to thank her. It wasn't pride or anything like that. It was just that I'd caught a glimpse of the other side of Jean, the side she had tried to forget.

She looked at me and then said with a wry smile, " Maybe I should thank you—for rushing in like a school kid just because of a word." The way she put it hurt, particularly as I was confused as to my motives, but there was a softness in her eyes and I let it go. " How did you know the gun was in my saddle-bag?"

" I felt it there when we stopped on the way down. It was partly why I came. I was scared you might——" She hesitated and then turned away. " I don't quite understand you, Bruce. You're not predictable like most people." She swung round and faced me. " Why didn't you give up when you found you were faced with a big company?" And when I didn't answer, she said, " It wasn't ignorance, was it? You knew what you were up against?"

" Yes, I knew," I said, sinking down into the warmth of the grass.

" Then why did you go on?"

" Why did you come back to Come Lucky—to the Kingdom?"

She came and sat beside me, chewing on a blade of grass. There was a long silence and then she said, " Isn't it about time we had things out together?"

" Why were you running away and then suddenly turned and faced life—why I refused to give up a hopeless project? Maybe." But I knew I couldn't tell her the truth. I knew I had to quench this growing intimacy. And yet I said, almost involuntarily, " Why did you leave me that gun?"

" I thought you might need it."

I looked at her, knowing it wasn't the real reason. She knew it, too, for she put out her hand. " Just leave it at that, Bruce. The message is there, in the weapon itself. You know what that message is as well as I do. You know the truth about my father, why I had to come back and see Stuart. You know that, don't you?" I nodded. " Then leave it at that please. Don't let's talk about it, ever again."

" I'm sorry," I said.

" No, there's nothing to be sorry about." Her voice was very quiet, but quite firm—no tremor in it at all, no regrets. " He died as a man should die—fighting for something he believed in. He was half French, you know—and when it came to the pinch he found he loved France more than money, more than life itself."

She got up and walked away then. And I lay back in the grass, closed my eyes and was instantly asleep. It was cold when she woke me and the valley was deep in shadow. We ate the few remaining biscuits and then, as night closed in, we hobbled the horses and cut across the road and along the slope of the hillside. We made a detour and entered Come Lucky from above. The two Miss Garrets welcomed us with a sort of breathless excitement. They had heard what had happened that morning and to them our nocturnal arrival, the sense that they were hiding us from a gang of wicked men was pure Victorian melodrama. Sarah Garret was particularly affected, talking in whispers, a high colour in her cheeks and a sparkle in her eyes. Miss Ruth Garret was more practical, several times looking to the bolting of the door, getting us food and coffee and trying desperately to maintain an aloof, matter-of-fact air. I found it all a little ridiculous, rather like a game—and yet the reality of it was there, in our need of a place to stay the night, in the two burnt-out trucks up in the Kingdom.

Shortly after our meal, when we were sitting having coffee, Pauline arrived. Johnnie would meet me at 150 Mile House to-morrow evening or, if he couldn't make it, the following morning. She had other news, too. A stranger had arrived at the Golden Calf. He wasn't a fisherman and he was busy plying Mac with drinks and pumping him about our activities in the Kingdom. Boy's visit to Calgary and Edmonton was evidently bearing fruit.

That night I slept in the Victorian grandeur of a feather bed. It was Sarah Garret's room. She had moved in with her sister for the night. It was not a large room and it was cluttered with heavy, painted furniture, the marble mantelpiece and the dressing-table littered with china bric-à-brac. The bedstead was a heavy iron affair adorned with brass. For a long time I lay awake looking at the stars, conscious of the smell of the room that took me back to my childhood—it was a compound of lavender and starch and lace. My mind was busy, going over and over the possibilities of packing the necessary fuel up to the Kingdom. And then just as I was dropping off to sleep I heard the door open. A figure came softly into the room and stood beside my bed, looking down at me.

It was Sarah Garret. I could just see the tiny outline of her head against the window. "Are you awake?" she asked. Her voice trembled slightly.

"Yes," I said.

"Then light a candle please."

I got out of bed, wrapping a blanket round me, and found my lighter. As the thin light of the candle illuminated the room I turned to her, wondering why she was here, what had driven her to this nocturnal escapade. She took the candlestick from me, her hand trembling and spilling grease. "I have something to show you," she said.

She crossed over to a big trunk in the corner. It was one of those great leather-covered things with a curved top. There was a jingle of keys and then she had it open and was lifting the lid. It was full of clothes and the smell of lavender and mothballs was very strong. "Will you lift the tray out, please?"

I did as she asked. Underneath were more clothes. Her joints creaked slightly as she bent and began to lift them out. Dresses of satin and silk piled up on the floor, beautiful lace-edged nightgowns, a dressing-gown that was like something out of Madam Butterfly, a parasol, painted ivory fans, necklaces of onyx and amber, a bedspread of the finest needlework.

At last the trunk was empty. With trembling fingers she felt around the edges. There was a click and the bottom moved. She took the candle from me then. "Lift it out, please."

The false bottom of that trunk was of steel and quite heavy. And underneath were neat little tin boxes. She lifted the lid of one. It was filled with gold coins. There were several bars of gold wrapped in tissue paper, and another box contained gold dust. The last one she opened revealed several pieces of jewellery. "I have never shown anybody this," she said.

"Why have you shown me?" I asked.

She looked up at me. She had a brooch in her hand. It was gold studded with amethyst, and the amethysts matched the colour of her eyes and both gleamed as brightly in the candlelight. "This was my favourite."

"Why have you shown me all this?" I asked again.

She sighed and put the brooch back. Then she signalled me to replace the false bottom. She operated the hidden catch fixing it in position and then returned the clothes to the trunk. When the lid was finally down and locked she pulled herself to her feet. She was crying gently and dabbing at her eyes with a lace handkerchief. "That is all I have left of my father," she said, her voice trembling slightly. "He made it in the Come Lucky mine and when he died that was my share. There was more, of course, but we have had to live."

"You mean that was how he left you his money?"

She nodded. "Yes. He did not believe in banks and modern innovations like that. He liked to see what he had made. My sister——" She sighed and blew her nose delicately. "My sister thought she knew better. She was engaged to a man in Vancouver and he invested it for her. She lost it all. The stocks were no good."

"And her fiancé?"

She gave a little shrug. "The man was no good either."

"Why have you told me this? Why have you shown me where you keep your money?"

She stared at me for a moment and then she gave me a beautiful little smile. "Because I like you," she said. "I had a—friend once. He was rather like you. A Scotsman. But he was already married." She got to her feet. "I must go now. I do not want my sister to know that I have done anything so naughty as visiting a man in his bedroom." Her eyes twinkled at me. And then she touched my arm. "I am an old lady now. There has been very little in my life. You remember the parable of the talents? Now that I am old I see that I have made too little use of the money my father gave me. Jean told us what had happened up in the Kingdom. I would like to you to know that you do not have to worry about money. You only have to ask——"

"I couldn't possibly——" I began, but she silenced me.

"Don't be silly. It is no good to me and I would like to help." She hesitated and then smiled. "Stuart Campbell was the friend I spoke about. Now perhaps you understand. Goodnight."

I watched her as she went out and then I sat down on the

bed, staring at the old leather trunk with a strong desire to cry. I still remember every detail of that visit from Sarah Garret and I treasure it as one of the most beautiful memories I have.

A few hours later I left. The house was silent and as I walked down through the shacks of Come Lucky the sky was just beginning to pale over Solomon's Judgment. I walked along the lake-shore and waited for a truck coming down from Slide Camp. It took me as far as Hydraulic and from there I got a timber wagon down to 150 Mile House. Jean was to take my horse back up to the Kingdom and now that I was on my own I found a mood of depression creeping over me.

But when Johnnie arrived everything was different. He came with a couple of Americans. They were on holiday and they regarded the whole thing as a game, part of the fun of being in the Rockies a long way from their offices in Chicago. As soon as they knew the situation they got on the phone to a whole list of farmers along the valley. But we soon discovered that though horses were easy to hire it was difficult to get them complete with packing gear. The farms were widely dispersed and the better part of a week had passed before we had a total of twenty-six animals with gear coralled at a homestead a few miles west of Beaver Dam Lake.

On the 15th July we moved them up to the entrance to Thunder Creek and the following morning, as arranged, we rendezvoused with the vehicle trucking in our containers. It took us over 24 hours to pack that first 500 gallons up to the Kingdom. Every four hours we off-loaded and let the animals rest. It was back-breaking work and the weather was bad with several thunderstorms and thick mist on the slopes of the Saddle. Without Johnnie I should have turned back, but he seemed to be able to smell the trail out through mist and blinding hail. And the men who were hiring him to show them the Rockies were in high spirits, always anticipating worse conditions than we actually experienced, apparently thoroughly happy to combine pleasure with some real outdoor work.

The atmosphere when we came down into the Kingdom was one of tense excitement. The whole bunch came out to meet us. The rig had stopped drilling three days back for lack of fuel and Jean told me afterwards that if I hadn't turned up when I did Garry would have asked Trevedian to hoist the rig down. Time was running out for him. But just before we arrived an Imperial Oil scout had ridden in. This recognition from the outside world had lifted their spirits slightly and with the arrival of the fuel and the starting up of the rig again enthusiasm was suddenly unbounded.

Two days later the four of us brought a second 500 gallons up. We now had enough fuel to drill to nearly six thousand feet at the present rate. At the time they started the rig again they were at four thousand six hundred and making over twelve feet an hour through softish rock. By the time we packed in the second load of fuel they were past the five thousand mark and going strong.

I remember Johnnie standing in front of the rig the day he and his two Americans took the pack animals down. " I'd sure like to stay on up here, Bruce," he said. He, too, had been caught by the mood of excitement. Boy had arrived that morning and with him was a reporter from the *Calgary Tribune*. Five thousand five hundred feet was the level at which they expected to reach the anticline and hanging over me all the time was the knowledge that it wasn't oil we were going to strike there, but the sill of igneous rock that had stopped Campbell Number One. I couldn't tell anybody this. I just had to brace myself to combat the sense of defeat when it came.

" Oil isn't much in your line, is it, Johnnie?" Jean said.

He grinned. " I guess not. But I'll need to know what we're to put on old Campbell's tombstone."

"Just quote him as saying, 'There's oil in the Rocky Mountains,'" Garry said. " That'll be enough.

Everybody laughed. It was a thin, feverish sound against the racket of the drill and I thought of the grave I had found behind the ranch-house and how they were all up here because of him. They were pretty keyed up now, and their optimism had a feverish undercurrent that wasn't healthy.

As the days went by the suspense became almost unbearable. At first there were anxious inquiries as each shift came off duty, but as we approached the end of July the mood changed and we'd just glance at the shift coming off, unwilling to voice our interest, one look at their faces being sufficient to tell us that there were no new developments. The waiting was intolerable and a mood of depression gradually settled on the camp. We were drilling through quartzite and making slower progress than we had hoped. Time was against us. With each day's drilling our fuel reserves were dwindling. And meanwhile the dam was moving steadily towards completion. Sometimes on an evening Jean and I would ride up to the rock buttress and look at the work. Already by the first week in August there was only a small section to be completed and engineers were working on the installation of the sluices and pens. From higher up the mountainside we could see that work on the power station beside the slide had also started. Some of the drilling crew were in touch with men working on the dam from whom they were able to purchase cigarettes at an inflated price, and from them they learned that the completion date was fixed for August 20th. Worse still, the Larsen Company planned to begin flooding immediately in order to build up a sufficient head of water to run a pilot plant during the winter.

At the beginning of August we were approaching five thousand five hundred and Garry was getting restive. So were his crew. They had been up in the Kingdom for almost two months. The cuttings, screened from the mud as it flowed back into the sump pit, showed us still in the metamorphic rock. No jokes were cracked on the site now. Nobody spoke much. Four of the boys had started a poker school. I tried to break it up, but there was nothing else for them to do. They'd no liquor and no women and they were fed up.

The inevitable happened. There was a fight and one of them, a fellow called Weary Dodds, got a finger smashed in the draw works. He was lucky not to have had his arm ripped off for he was flung right against the steel hawser that was lifting the travelling block. Jean patched it up as best she could, but she couldn't patch up the atmosphere of the camp —it was very tense.

Just after nine on the morning of August 5th they pulled pipe for what they all hoped might be the last time. The depth was five thousand four hundred and ninety feet. They were all down on the rig, waiting. They waited there all morning, watching the grief stem inching down through the turntable and I stood there with them feeling sick with apprehension. They pulled pipe again at two-fifteen. Another sixty-foot length of pipe was run on and down went the drill again, section by section. The depth was now five thousand five hundred and fifty feet. Those not on shift drifted back to the ranch-house. We had some food and a tense silence brooded over the meal.

At length I could stand the suspense no longer. I drew Garry on one side. "Suppose we don't strike the anticline exactly where we expect to," I said. "What depth are you willing to drill to?"

"I don't know," he said. "The boys are getting restive."

"Will you give it a margin of two thousand feet?"

"Two thousand!" He stared at me as though I were crazy. "That's nearly a fortnight's drilling. It'd take us right up to the date of completion of the dam. Anyway, we haven't the fuel."

"I can pack some more up."

He looked at me, his eyes narrowed. "There's something on your mind. What is it?"

"I just want to know the margin of error you're willing to give it."

He hesitated and then said, "All right, I'll tell you. I'll drill till we've exhausted the fuel that's already up here. That's four days more. That'll take us over six thousand."

"You've got to give a bigger margin than that," I said.

He caught hold of my arm then. "See here, Bruce. The boys wouldn't stand for it."

"For God's sake," I said. "You've been drilling up here now for two months. Are you going to throw all that effort away for the sake of another fortnight?"

"And risk losing my rig when they flood the place? Good Christ, man, you don't seem to realise that we've all had about as much as we can take. I've lost two trucks; neither the rig nor any of the boys are earning their keep. If we don't bring in a well——"

He stopped then for the door burst open and Clif Lindy, the driller on shift, came in. There was a wild look in his eyes. "What is it, Clif?" Garry asked.

"We're in new country," he said.

"The anticline?"

But I knew it wasn't the anticline. His face, his whole manner told me that this was the moment I had dreaded. They had reached the sill.

"We're down to rock as hard as granite and we've worn a bit out in an hour's drilling." He caught hold of Garry's arm. "For God's sake," he said, "let's get the hell out of here before we're all of us broke."

"How much have you made in the last hour?" Garry asked.

"Two feet. The boys want to know shall we stop drilling?"

Garry didn't say anything. He just stood there, looking at me, waiting to see what I was going to say.

"You're just throwing away good bits and wearing out your rig for nothing," Clif said excitedly.

"What do you say, Bruce?" Garry asked.

"It's the same formation that stopped Campbell's cable-tool rig. If you get through this——"

"At two feet an hour," Clif said with a laugh that trembled slightly. "We could be a month drilling through this." He turned to Garry. "The boys won't stand for it, not any more. Nor will I, Garry. I don't mind risking a couple of months for the chance of making big dough. But we know damn well now that we're not going to bring in a——"

"How do you know?" I cut in.

He laughed. "You go and ask Boy. You ask him what he thinks about it. Only you won't find him, not around camp here. He's away into the mountains to brood over Campbell's folly—and his own. He thought when the country changed we'd be down to the anticline. He didn't expect to get into igneous country this deep." His fingers dug into my flesh as he gripped my arm. "If you want my opinion Boy Bladen doesn't know enough about geophysics to plot a gopher hole. As for Winnick, well damn it, isn't it obvious? His office is right next door to Henry Fergus. He'd put it across you." He looked across at Garry and his tone was suddenly quieter as he said, "The boys want to haul out."

Garry didn't say anything for a moment. He stood there rasping his fingers along the line of his jaw. "I wonder how thick through this sill is," he murmured. "Most of them around here are not more than a hundred, two hundred feet—those that are exposed on the mountain slopes, that is."

"That's four day's drilling," Clif said. "And what's below the sill, when we get through it? I ain't a geologist, but I'm not such a fool as to expect oil bearing country directly below a volcanic intrusion."

Garry nodded slowly. "I guess you're right, Clif." He turned towards the door. "I'll come down and have a look at what's going on. Coming, Bruce?"

I shook my head. I stood there, watching them disappear through the doorway, a mood of anger and bitterness struggling with the wretchedness of failure.

"I'm sorry, Bruce." A hand touched my arm and I turned to find Jean beside me.

"You heard?"

"No, Boy told me. I went down to see to the horses and found him in there, saddling up. I came back to——" She hesitated and then finished on a note of tenderness: "To break it to you."

"Why the hell didn't Boy have the guts to come and tell me himself?" I exploded.

"Boy's sensitive," she murmured.

"Sensitive?" I cried, giving rein to my feelings. "You mean he's a moral coward. Instead of supporting me and trying to lick some enthusiasm into this miserable bunch of defeatists, he immediately concludes his survey is inaccurate and goes crawling off into the mountains like a wounded cur. I suppose that's the Indian in him."

"That's a rotten thing to say." Her cheeks were flushed and her eyes bright with sudden anger.

"If you think so much of the little half-breed," I said, "why don't you go with him to nurse his wounded pride?"

She opened her mouth to speak, and then slowly closed it. "I'll get you some coffee," she said quietly and went through into the kitchen.

I flung myself into the one armchair. Probably Stuart Campbell had flung himself into the self-same chair when he got the news that drilling was no longer possible on Campbell Number One. It wasn't Boy's fault any more than it was Garry's. They'd both of them taken a chance on the property. They couldn't be expected to go on when they'd lost all hope of bringing in a well. The anger and bitterness I had felt had subsided by the time Jean returned with the coffee. "I'm sorry," I said. "I shouldn't have let fly like that."

She put the tray down and came and stood near me. Her hand reached out and touched my hair. Without thinking I took hold of it, grasping it tightly like a drowning man clutching at a straw. The next moment she was in my arms, holding my head down against her breast. The feel of her body comforted me. The promise of happiness whatever happened to the Kingdom filled me with a sudden feeling that life was good. I kissed her lips and her hair, holding her close, not caring any longer about anything but the fact that she was there in my arms. And then very gently I pulled myself clear of her and got to my feet. "I must go down to the rig," I said.

"I'll come with you."

"No. I'd rather go alone. I want to talk to them."

But when I got there I knew by the expression on their faces that this wasn't the moment. They were sitting around in the hut and the rig was silent. They were as angry and bitter as I had been, but with them it was the bitterness of defeat.

The decision to quit was taken the following morning. And as though he'd been given a cue Trevedian arrived whilst we were still sitting around the breakfast table. We all sat and stared at him, wondering what the hell he wanted. I saw Garry's big hand clench into a fist and Clif half rose to his feet. I think Trevedian sensed the violence of the hostility for he kept the door open behind him and he didn't come more than a step into the room. His black eyes took in the bitterness and the anger and then fastened on me. "I've brought a telegram for you, Wetheral. Thought it might be urgent."

I got slowly to my feet wondering why he should have bothered to come all the way up with it. But as soon as I'd read it I knew why. It was from my lawyers. *Henry Fergus instituting proceedings against you in civil courts for fraudulently gaining possession mineral rights Campbell's Kingdom mortgaged to Roger Fergus. Essential you return Calgary soonest. Willing to act for you provided assured you financial position. Please advise us immediately. Grange and Letour, solicitors.*

I looked up at Trevedian. "You know the contents, of course?"

He hesitated, but there was no point in denying it. "Yes," he said. "If you care to let me have your reply I'll see that it's sent off." There was a note of satisfaction in his voice, though he tried to conceal it. I wondered which of the boys kept him informed about what was happening on the rig. The timing was too good for it to be coincidence.

"What is it?" Jean asked.

I handed her the wire. It was passed from hand to hand. And as I watched them reading it I knew that this was the end of any hope I might have had of getting them to drill deeper. With the mineral rights themselves in doubt the ground was cut away from under my feet. And yet . . . I was thinking of Sarah Garret and what she had said there in my room that night.

" So they're starting to work on you," Garry said.

" I've ample proof of what happened," I said.

" Sure, you have—that is till you see what the witnesses themselves are willing to say in the box. I'm sorry, Bruce," he added. " But looks like they're going to put you through the mincer now."

" Fergus told me to give you a message," Trevedian said. " Settle the whole business out of court, sell the Kingdom and he'll give you the $50,000 he originally offered."

I didn't say anything. I was still thinking about Sarah Garret. Had she meant it? But I knew she had. She'd not only meant it, but she wanted to help. I went over to the desk and scribbled a reply.

As I finished it Garry's voice suddenly broke the tense silence of the room: " Two thousand dollars a vehicle! You must be crazy."

I turned and saw that he'd taken Trevedian on one side. Trevedian was smiling. " If you want to get your trucks down, that's what it's going to cost you."

Garry stared at him. The muscles of his arms tightened. " You know damn well I couldn't pay it. I'm broke. We're all of us broke." He took a step towards Trevedian. " Now then, suppose you quote me a proper price for the use of the hoist."

Trevedian was back at the open door now. Through the window I saw he hadn't come alone. Three of his men were waiting for him out there. Garry had seen them too and his voice was under control as he said, " For God's sake be reasonable, Trevedian."

" Reasonable! By God I'm only getting back what it cost us to repair the road after you'd been through."

" I didn't have anything to do with that," Garry said.

" No?" Trevedian laughed. " It was just coincidence that your trucks were in the Kingdom by the time we'd cleared the rubble of that fall. Okay. You didn't use the hoist. You had nothing to do with blocking the road." He leaned slightly forward, his round head sunk between his shoulders, his voice hard. " I suppose you'll tell me you packed the whole damned outfit up the pony trail. Well, pack 'em down the same way if you don't like my terms. See which costs you most in the end." He turned to me. " What will I tell Fergus?" he asked.

I hesitated, glancing round the room. They were all watching me, all except Jean who had turned her face away and Garry who was so angry that I was afraid for the moment that he would rush Trevedian.

" Well?"

I turned to Trevedian. " Tell him," I said, " that I'm going to seek an injunction to restrain him from flooding the Kingdom. And let him know that if he doesn't want to lose any more money he'd better stop work on the dam and the power station until he knows what the courts decide. And you might have this wire sent off for me." I handed him the slip of paper.

He took it automatically. I think he was too astonished to speak. Then he glanced down at the message and read it. " You're crazy," he said. " You haven't the dough to start an action like this."

" I think I have."

" Well, whether you have or not is immaterial," he said harshly. " No Canadian court is going to grant you an injunction against the damming up of a useless bit of territory like this. You don't seem to realise what you're up against. This dam is going to open up a big mining industry, feed a whole new area with——"

" I know quite well what I'm up against," I said, suddenly losing control of myself. " I'm up against a bunch of crooks who don't stop at falsifying surveys, setting fire to fuel tankers, trespassing on other people's property, shooting and attempting to expropriate land that doesn't belong to them. It hadn't occurred to me to start legal proceedings. But if Fergus wants it that way, he can have it. Tell him I'm fighting him every inch of the ground. Tell him that what we've proved already by drilling, together with Winnick's evidence, will be enough to satisfy any Canadian court. And by the time he's got his dam finished I'll have brought in a well up here. Now get out."

Trevedian hesitated, a bewildered expression on his face. " Then why does Keogh want to get his trucks down?"

" Because we're just about through here," I said quickly.

"Now get the hell out of here and tell your boss, Henry Fergus, that the gloves are off."

He stood there, his mouth half open as though he was about to say something further. "You heard what Wetheral said." Garry was moving towards him, his hands low at his side, the fingers crooked, expressive of his urgent desire to throw Trevedian through the doorway. The boys were closing in on him, too. He turned suddenly and ducked through the doorway.

For a moment we all stood there without moving. Then Garry came over and grasped my hand. "By God, I got to hand it to you," he said.

I pushed my hand wearily across my face. "It was all bluff," I said.

He peered down at me. "How do you mean? Aren't you going to fight 'em?"

"Yes, of course I'm going to fight them." I suddenly felt very tired. I think it was the knowledge that I'd got to go back to Calgary.

"Did you really mean you'd got a backer?" Clif asked.

"Yes." I looked across at Jean. "Would you make me up a parcel of food?"

She nodded slowly. "You're going to Calgary?"

"Yes." I turned back to Garry. "You're willing to go on drilling?"

He looked round at his crew. "And why not, eh, boys? We go on drilling till we have to swim for it? That right?" They were suddenly all grinning and shouting agreement. "We're right with you, Bruce." There was a gleam in his eyes and he added, "I'd sure like to get even with that bastard." And then the gleam died away. "There's one or two things though. We've only got fuel for four more days of drilling. We're getting short of food up here, too. There's a whole lot of things we need."

"I know," I said. "Make out a list of your requirements for another month. Get hold of Boy, tell him to hire the pack animals Johnnie and I had before. He's to have them corralled at Wessels Farm the other side of Beaver Dam Lake in three days' time—that's the 8th August. I'll meet him there. Tell him to have all the supplies laid on ready. I'll wire him the money at Keithley."

"I'll do that." His big hand gripped my shoulder. "You

look like you weren't strong enough to hold your own against a puff of wind. But by God you're tougher than I am." He turned towards the door. " C'm on, boys. We'll get the rig started up again." He waved his hand to me. " Good luck!" he said. " And just keep your fingers crossed in case this sill goes deep."

I got my things together and then went out to the stables. I was saddling up when Jean came in with a package of food. "Shall I come with you?" she asked.

"No," I said. "This is something I have to do alone."

She hesitated then said, "You're going to see Sarah, aren't you?" I didn't say anything and she added, "She's your backer, isn't she?"

"How did you know?"

She smiled a trifle sadly. " I lived there for three years, you know." She pushed the food into my pack. " Does she have enough?" I was tightening my cinch. She caught hold of my arm. " It'll cost a lot to fight a legal battle."

"A delaying action, that's all," I said. "If we don't bring in a well . . ." I shrugged my shoulders. " Then I don't care very much."

"We'll bring in a well." She reached up and kissed me. For a second I felt the warmth of her lips on mine and then she was gone.

As I rode up the trail to the Saddle I could hear the draw works of the rig sounding their challenge across the Kingdom. It was like music to hear it working again, to know that the whole crowd were solidly behind me. " Pray God it comes out right," I murmured aloud. But I felt tired and depressed. Calgary scared me and I wasn't sure of myself.

I waited till nightfall before entering Come Lucky, riding in from above it and wending my way through the huddle of shacks. There was a glow of lamplight in the windows of the Garret home. Ruth Garret answered my knock. She stared at me coldly through her lorgnette. " Have you brought Jean back, Mr. Wetheral?"

"Jean? No."

"Oh, dear. What a pity. There's so much talk in the town. It was bad enough when she insisted on living up there with that queer old man. But keeping house for a lot of——" She hesitated. " Roughnecks is what they call them."

"That's only the name for men who work a rig," I said.

"They're a good crowd. May I come in? I want to see your sister."

"My sister? Yes, of course. Come in."

Sarah Garret rose as I entered. She seemed to know what I had come for. "You're in a hurry, I expect," she said.

"I have to go to Calgary."

She nodded. "There's a rumour you're going to get the courts to stop the work on the dam. That's why you've come, isn't it?"

I nodded.

Her eyes were bright and there was a little spot of colour in each of the waxen cheeks. "I'm glad," she said. She took me through into her room, talking all the time, a little breathless, a little excited. She wanted to know all my plans, everything that had happened that morning. And whilst I talked she unlocked the tin trunk and took out the clothes. When I had lifted out the false bottom, she picked out two of the little tin boxes and put them into my hands. "There," she said. "I do hope it will be enough, but I must keep sufficient for my sister and me to live on." One of the boxes contained gold dust, the other two small bars of gold.

"You do realise," I said, "that I may not be able to repay you. We may fail."

She smiled. "You foolish man. It isn't a loan. It's a gift." She let the lid of the trunk fall. "I think my father would have been glad to think that I had saved it for something that was important to someone."

"I don't know how to thank you," I murmured.

"Nonsense. I haven't had so much excitement since——" She looked at me and I swear she blushed. "Well, not for a very long time." Her eyes twinkled up at me. "Will you promise me something? When all this is over, will you take me up to the Kingdom? I haven't been out of Come Lucky for so long and I would like to see it again, and the log houses and the tiger lilies. Are there tiger lilies there still?"

I nodded. For some reason I couldn't trust myself to speak.

"Now you must hurry. If they hear you are in Come Lucky——" She hustled me to the door. "Put the boxes under your coat. Yes, that's right. Ruth mustn't see them. I think she suspects, but——" Her frail fingers squeezed my arm. "It's our secret, eh? She wouldn't understand."

Ruth Garret was waiting for us in the living-room. "What

have you two been up to?" The playfulness of the remark was lost in the sharpness of her eyes.

"We were just talking," her sister said quickly. She put her hand on my arm and led me out. She paused at the front door. "Are you going to marry Jean?"

The suddenness of the question took me by surprise.

"You're an extraordinary person," I said.

"You haven't answered my question."

I looked down at her and then slowly shook my head. "No."

"Why not? She's in love with you." I didn't answer. "Did you know that?"

"Yes."

"And you? Are you in love with her?"

Slowly I nodded my head. "But I can't marry her," I said. And then briefly I told her why. "That's also a secret between us," I said when I had finished.

"Doesn't it occur to you she might want to look after you?"

"She's been hurt once," I said. "She doesn't want to be hurt again. I can't do that to her. I must go now."

"Yes, you must go now." She opened the door for me. As I stepped out into the night I turned. She looked very frail and lonely, standing there in the lamplight. And yet beneath the patina of age I thought I saw the girl who'd known my grandfather. She must have been very lovely. I bent and kissed her. Then I got on my horse and rode quickly out of Come Lucky.

Part Three

THE DAM

I

I FLEW INTO Calgary from Edmonton on the morning of August 7th to be met by *Calgary Tribune* placards announcing: Larsen Company's Dam Nearing Completion. There was a news story on the front page and inside they had devoted a full feature article to it. There was no mention of our drilling operations in the article, only a brief paragraph in the news story. It gave me a sense of impotence at the outset. I felt as though I were batting my head against a brick wall. It was in this mood that I reached the bank. In an English bank the arrival of a man with a box of gold dust and another containing gold bars would have caused a sensation and necessitated the completion of innumerable forms and declarations. In Calgary they just took it in their stride. I arranged for the necessary funds to be mailed to Boy at Wessels Farm and then went on to my lawyers. There I learned that the case I had come to fight had been dropped. I asked Letour whether this was a result of my threat to seek an injunction restraining Fergus from flooding the Kingdom, but he shook his head. No application for an injunction had been made and he explained to me at some length the legal difficulties of making such an application. The Act authorising the construction of the dam had been passed by the Provincial Parliament of British Columbia. It could only be repealed by a further Act. This would be a lengthy process. He advised me that my only hope was to bring in a well before the flooding of the Kingdom. The scale of compensation likely to be granted by the courts would then be so great as to make it impracticable for the Larsen Company to proceed with the project.

I went back to my hotel feeling that my trip to Calgary had been wasted. Not only that, but Fergus was apparently so sure of himself that he hadn't even bothered to proceed with his charges in connection with the mineral rights. It left me with the impression that he didn't consider me worth bothering about. And since Trevedian was undoubtedly keeping a watch on the rig I could well understand this. He must know by now that we were in bad country and drilling only two feet per hour.

I would have pulled out of Calgary the next morning only something happened that evening which radically altered my plans. I hadn't been near the *Calgary Tribune,* feeling it would be a waste of time and that they had now lost interest in our drilling operations. However, I had phoned Winnick and I suppose he must have let them know I was in town for the editor himself rang me up in the afternoon and asked me to have dinner with him. And when I got to his club I found he had a CBC man with him and the whole picture suddenly brightened, for the CBC man wanted me to broadcast. The reason for his interest was in the copy of a big American magazine he had with him which contained an article headed: *OIL VERSUS ELECTRICITY—Will the dream of an old-timer come true? Will his grandson strike oil up in his Rocky Mountain kingdom or will the men building the dam flood the place first? The author went up there and saw the start of this fantastic race.* The author was Steve Strachan, the *Calgary Tribune* reporter who had first visited us.

This sudden interest in what we were doing gave me fresh heart. I stayed on and did the broadcast, for now that I was down in a town and forced to face the situation with realism I found I could not sustain the forced optimism that had been engendered by the tense atmosphere of the Kingdom. I was already subconsciously working towards obtaining the best compensation I could from the courts. Upon what they awarded me depended the extent to which I could repay those who had helped me. I made it clear, therefore, both in the broadcast and in the article I wrote for the *Calgary Tribune,* that we were into the igneous country that had stopped Campbell Number One and that given a few more weeks we should undoubtedly bring in a well.

This false optimism produced immediate dividends for on the morning after the broadcast Acheson came to see me. He looked pale and angry, which was not surprising since Fergus had sent him with an offer of $100,000. I was very tempted to accept. And then Acheson said, "Of course, in view of the publicity you have been getting, we shall require a statement that you are now of the opinion that Campbell was wrong and there is no oil in that area of the Rockies."

"And if I don't make the statement?"

"Then I'm instructed to withdraw the offer."

I went over to the window and stood looking out across the railway tracks. To make that statement meant finally branding my grandfather as a liar and a cheat. It meant reversing all I'd aimed at in the last few months. It would be a final act of cowardice. "Would Fergus agree to free transportation of all vehicles and personnel down by the hoist and over the Thunder Valley road?"

"Yes."

"All right," I said. "I'll think about it."

He glanced at his watch. "You'll have to think fast then. This offer is open till midday."

"What's the hurry?"

"Fergus wants to get shot of the whole business."

He left me then and for an hour I paced up and down the room, trying to balance my unwillingness to accept defeat against the need to repay the men who had helped me. And then the bell-hop came and I knew why they had been in such a hurry to get a decision out of me. It was a telegram from Boy, dispatched from Keithley: *Through sill at fifty-eight hundred. Drilling ten per hour. Everyone optmistic. Second consignment fuel on way. Boy.*

I stared at it, excitement mounting inside me, reviving my hopes, bursting like a flood over my mood of pessimism. I seized hold of the phone and rang Acheson. "I just wanted to let you know that half a million dollars wouldn't buy the Kingdom now," I told him. "We're in the clear and drilling ten feet an hour. You knew that damn well, didn't you? Well, you can tell Fergus it's going to cost him a fortune to flood the Kingdom." I slammed down the receiver without waiting for him to reply. The damned crooks! They'd known we were through the sill. They'd known it by the speed at which the travelling block moved down the rig. That's why they'd increased their offer. I was laughing aloud in my excitement as I picked up the phone and rang the editor of the *Calgary Tribune.* I told him the whole thing, how they'd offered me $100,000 and they'd known all the time we were in the clear. "If they'll only give us long enough," I said, "we'll bring in that well."

"I'll see what I can do," he said. "We'll run this story and I'll write a leader that won't do you any harm. When are you planning to go up there?"

"I'll be leaving first thing in the morning," I said.

"Okay. Well, don't worry about transport. I'll have Steve pick you up in the station wagon around nine. You don't mind him coming up with you?"

"Of course not."

Early the following evening Steve and I arrived in Jasper. There was little snow on the mountains now and it was still warm after the blistering heat of the day. It was only that evening, as I sat drinking beer with Jeff, that I realised I had been over a week in Calgary and hadn't felt ill. "It's our dry, healthy climate, I guess," Jeff said. I nodded, abstractedly, thinking how much had happened since that first time I had come through Jasper. "Don't reckon they gave you much time to be ill, anyway." Jeff took a newspaper from his pocket and passed it across to me. It was the Edmonton paper and it carried a long news story on development in the Kingdom.

The effect was to make me even more impatient to get up to the Kingdom. Somehow I couldn't bear the thought that they might strike oil before I got up there. From a mood of despair I had swung over to wild, unreasoned optimism. For a long time I lay awake that night watching the moon over the peak of Edith Cavell, praying to God that it would be all right, that we'd get deep enough in time. I was sorry Johnnie couldn't come up with me; he was out riding trail with a party of dudes and Jeff was tied up with his garage now the tourist season was in full swing.

The next night we bunked down in the straw of the Wessels hayloft and early the following morning we rode round the north shore of Beaver Dam Lake and when we emerged from the cottonwoods there, suddenly, straight ahead of us, were the peaks of Solomon's Judgment. I reined in my pony and sat there for a moment, staring at them, thinking of the activity going on up there, hearing the clatter of the drill, seeing the travelling block slowly descending. Jean would be there and with luck. . . .

I shook my reins and heeled the pony forward. It didn't bear thinking about. There just had to be oil there. My eyes were dazzled for a moment by the flash of sun on glass. It was a lorry moving on the road up to Thunder Creek.

Another and another followed it; materials for the dam moving up to the hoist. "Seems a lot more traffic on that road now," Steve said.

I nodded and pushed on up the trail. I didn't want to think about that dam. I hoped to God they were behind schedule. Already it was the 15th and their completion date was supposed to be the 20th. Only five more days.

As we wound our way up through the timber I smelt the old, familiar smell of warm resin. It seemed to me as heady as wine. It made the blood sing in my veins and my heart pound. I felt as though this were my country, as though it were a part of me as it had been a part of old Stuart Campbell.

Thunder heads were building up as we reached the timber line. The peaks became cold and grey and streaks of forked lightning stabbed at the mountains to the roll of thunder echoing through the valleys. And then the hail came. The Kingdom was blanketed with it as we crossed the Saddle in a freak shaft of sunlight.

An hour later Moses was barking a welcome to us as we rode up to the ranch-house. Jean came in as we unsaddled. Her eyes were bright in the gloom of the stable and as I gripped her arms and felt the trembling excitement of her body the place seemed like home. "Have we brought in a well?" I asked her.

She shook her head. "The boys are working shifts round the clock now," she said. "They're determined that if its there, they'll get down to it." The tightness of her voice revealed the strain they were working under and when we went out into the sunlight I was shocked to see how tired she looked.

"What are they down to now?" I asked.

"Six thousand four hundred."

"Let's go down to the rig," I said. "I've got some mail for them and a lot of newspapers."

"Sure you're not too tired?" She was looking at me anxiously. "I was afraid——" She turned away and stared towards the rig. "They've nearly finished the dam," she said quickly. "They've been working at it like beavers. A week ago they took on fifty extra men."

"When do they expect to complete it?"

"In two days' time."

C.K. H

Two days! I turned to Steve. "You hear that, Steve? Two days."

He nodded. "It'll be quite a race."

"Better get yourself settled in," I told him, and Jean and I set out for the rig, Moses limping along beside us. We didn't talk. Somehow, now I was here it didn't seem necessary. We just walked in silence and across the deep grass came the clatter of the rig like music on the still air. But something was missing and my eyes slid unconsciously to the cleft between the peaks of Solomon's Judgment. "What's happened to the cement mixers," I asked.

"They stopped yesterday." Her hand came up and gripped my arm. "They've finished concreting."

I began to tell her what had happened in Calgary, but somehow the publicity I had got seemed unimportant. Up here only one thing mattered—if there was oil, would we reach it in time?

The strain I had seen in Jean's face was stamped on the faces of everyone on the rig. They were pulling pipe when we arrived. Garry working the draw works and Boy acting as derrick man. "Where are the others?" I asked Jean.

"Sleeping. I told you, they're working round the clock now."

As soon as they'd changed the bit and were drilling again, they all crowded round me, wanting to hear the news from Calgary, eagerly scanning the papers I had brought and searching the bundle of mail for their own letters. And I stood and watched them, noticing the dark shadows under their eyes, the quick, tense way they spoke. The atmosphere was electric with fatigue and the desperate hope that was driving them.

"Did you see Winnick?" Garry asked me. His voice was hard and tense.

I nodded.

"What did he say?"

"He's been over the seismograms again. He thinks we'll strike it around seven thousand or not at all."

"We'll be at seven thousand the day after to-morrow."

"Have you taken a core sample since you got clear of the sill?"

"Yeh. I don't know much about geology, I guess, but it looked like Devonian all right to me."

"We'll just have to make it," I said.

"Oh, sure. We'll make it." But his voice didn't carry conviction. He looked dead beat.

"Seen anything of Trevedian?"

"No. But he's got somebody posted on top of that buttress, keeping an eye on us through glasses. If that bastard shows his face down here——" He turned and stared towards the dam. His battered face looked crumpled and old in the hard sunlight. "I wish to God we'd got a geologist up here. If we do strike it, as like as not it'll be gas and we'll blow the rig to hell."

"If you do strike it," I said, "you won't need to worry about the rig."

"It's not the rig I'm worrying about," he snapped. "It's the drilling crew." He gave a quick nervous laugh. "I've never drilled a well without knowing what was going on under the surface."

His manner as much as his appearance warned me that nerves were strung taut. It was not surprising for there were only nine of them to keep the rig going the twenty-four hours and it needed four men on each shift. Pretty soon both myself and Steve Strachan were doing our stint. Fortunately it was largely just a matter of standing by, so that our inexperience was not put to the test. Now that we were in softish country it was only necessary to pull pipe every other day and about all that was required of a roughneck on each shift was to add a length of pipe when the travelling block was down to the turntable. I did the shift from eight to twelve and by the time I had been called at four to go on duty again I began to understand the strain they had been working under. I came off duty at eight, had some breakfast and turned in.

I hadn't been asleep more than an hour before I was woken with the news that Trevedian had arrived and wanted to see me. He was in the main room of the ranch-house and he had an officer of the Provincial Police with him. Garry was there, too, and he held a sheet of paper in his hand. "Trevedian's just served us with notice to quit," he said, handing me the paper.

It was a warning that floodings of the Kingdom under the provisions of the Provincial Government Act of 1939 might be expected any time after 18th August. It was written on the Larsen Company's notepaper and signed by Henry Fergus.

I looked across at Trevedian. "The dam's complete, is it?"
I asked.

He nodded. "Just about."

"When are you closing the sluice gates?"

He shrugged his shoulders. "Maybe to-morrow. Maybe
the day after. As soon as we're ready." He turned to the
policeman. "Well, Eddie, you've seen the note delivered.
Anything you want to say?"

The officer shook his head. "You've read the notice, Mr.
Wetheral. I'd just remind you that as from 10.00 hours to-
morrow morning the Larsen Company is entitled to flood
this area and that from that time they cannot be held responsible for any loss of movable equipment."

"Meaning the rig?"

He nodded. "I'm sorry, fellows, but there it is."

One or two of the drilling crew had drifted in. They stared
in silence at Trevedian and the policeman. It wasn't difficult
to imagine what they were thinking. They'd been working
up here now for two and a half months without pay. They'd
gambled on the chance of bringing in a well and they'd lost.
Trevedian shifted his feet nervously. He knew enough about
men to know that it only needed a word to touch off the
violence in the atmosphere. "Well, I guess we'd better get
going," he said.

The policeman nodded. In silence they turned and went out
through the door. Nobody moved. Nobody spoke. At length
Garry said, "Better get some sleep, boys. We're on again in
an hour and a half."

"Any chance of bringing in a well between now and ten
o'clock to-morrow?" Steve Strachan asked.

Garry rounded on him with a snarl. "If I knew that do
you think we'd be standing around looking like a bunch of
steers waiting for the slaughter-house." And he flung out of
the room, back to his bunk.

When I went on shift at midday the drill was down to six
thousand six hundred and twenty-two feet. When we came
off again at four we had added another forty-three feet. It
was blazing hot and the sweat streamed off me, for we had
just had the grief stem out and added another length of pipe.
I stood for a while, staring across to the dam. The silence
there was uncanny. Not a soul moved. I mopped my forehead with a sweat-damp handkerchief. There wasn't a breath

of air. The whole Kingdom seemed silent and watching, as though waiting for something. A glint of sun on glasses showed from the rock buttress. They were still keeping us under observation.

" I don't like it," a voice said at my elbow.

I turned to find Boy standing beside me. "What don't you like?" I asked and already I noticed my voice possessed that same sharpness of strain that the others had.

"Just nerves, I guess," he said. "But it's crook sort of weather this with no thunder heads and the mountains burning up under this sudden wave of heat. It's as though——" He paused there, and then turned away with a shrug of his shoulders.

I should have got some sleep, but somehow I couldn't face lying on a sleeping bag in the suffocating heat of the barns. I was too tensed-up for sleep, and the day was too oppressive. I saddled one of the horses and rode out across the Kingdom, past Campbell Number One and along by the stream towards the dam. The water was running deep and fast, carrying off yesterday's hail and the remnants of the winter's snow melted by the gruelling heat. I reached the barbed wire and rode along it up towards the buttress. There didn't seem to be more than a dozen men working on the dam and they weren't labourers, they were engineers in grease-stained jeans. I sat and watched them for a while. They were working on the sluice gates. The cage of the hoist came up only once whilst I sat there. It brought machinery.

The watcher from the buttress came scrambling down towards me. "Better get moving, Wetheral." It was the man I had tangled with outside the Golden Calf, the guard who had been on the hoist when we'd brought the rig up. He wore a dirty cotton vest and he'd a gun in a leather holster on his hip.

" I'm on my own property," I said. " It's you who are trespassing."

He started bawling me out then, using a lot of filthy names. I felt the blood beating at my temples. I wanted to fling myself at him, to give vent to the violence that was pent up inside me. But instead I turned my horse and rode slowly back to the ranch-house.

That night at dinner a brooding silence reigned over the table. It had the stillness of weather before a storm. It was in tune with the sultry heat of the night. The faces of the men gathered round the table were thin and tired and shiny with sweat. They sat around till eight waiting for the change of shift. Every now and then one of them would go to the door and listen, his head cocked on one side, listening for some change in the rhythm of the rig, waiting for the news, that they'd brought in a well.

But the shift changed and the drilling went steadily on, the bit grinding into the rock, six thousand seven hundred and thirteen feet below the surface at the rate of ten and a half feet per hour. I got some sleep and went on shift again at midnight. Jean was still up, standing by the stable, looking at the moon. She didn't say anything, but her hand found mine and gripped it. Boy passed us, going to the rig. " There's a storm brewing," he said.

There was a ring round the moon and though it was still as sultry as an oven, there was a dampness in the air. " Something must break soon," Jean whispered. " I can't stand this suspense any longer."

" It'll all be over to-morrow when they flood the place," I said.

She sighed and pressed my arm and turned away. I watched her go back into the ranch-house. Then slowly I walked down to the rig. Garry was driller on this shift and Don was acting as derrick man. We sat on the bench beside the draw works, smoking and feeling the drill vibrating along our spines. " Queer how the moon reflects on the ground below the dam," Garry said.

" It's the mist rising," Boy murmured.

" I guess so. Queer. It looks as though it were shining on water." A breath of wind touched our faces. " What's that over there—beyond Solomon's Judgment? Looks like a cloud."

We peered beyond the white outline of the peak. The sky there no longer had the luminosity of moonlight. There were no stars. It looked pitch black and strangely solid. The wind was suddenly chill. " It's the storm that's been brewing," Boy said.

I don't know who noticed it first—the change in the note of the draw works' diesel. It penetrated to my mind as something different, a slowing up, a stickiness that deepened the note of the engine. Boy shouted something and then Garry's voice thundered out: "The mud pump—quick!" His big body was across the platform in a flash. Don and I had jumped to our feet, but we stood there, dazed, not knowing what was happening or what had to be done. "Get the hell off that platform," Garry shouted up to us. "Run, you fools! Run for your lives!"

I heard Boy say, "God! We've struck it!" And then we collided in a mad scramble for the ladder. As I reached it I caught a glimpse of the travelling block out of the tail of my eye. The wire hawsers that held it suspended from the crown block were slack and the grief stem was slowly rising, pushing it upwards. Then I was down the ladder and jumping for the ground, running blindly, not knowing what to expect, following the flying figures of my companions. The ground became boggy. It squelched under my feet. Then water splashed in my face and I stopped, thinking we'd reached the stream. The others had stopped, too. They were standing, staring back at the rig.

The grief stem was lifted right up to the crown block now. It was held there for a moment and then with a rending and tearing of steel it thrust the rig up clear of the ground. Then the stem bent over. The rig toppled and came crashing to the ground. The draw works, suddenly freed of their load, raced madly with a clattering cacophony of sound. And then in brilliant moonlight that gave the whole thing an air of un-reality we watched the pipe seemingly squeezed out of the ground like toothpaste out of a tube.

It was like that for a moment, a great snake of piping, turning and twisting upwards and then with a roar like a hundred express trains it was blown clear. "Garry! Garry!" Boy's voice sounded thin against the roar of the gas flare.

We splashed back towards the rig, searching for him. The light was lurid and uncertain. We stumbled against pieces of machinery, the scrap-heap of the rig. "Garry!"

A shape loomed out of the darkness. A hand gripped mine. "Well, we struck it." It was Garry and his voice trembled slightly.

I'd been too dazed to consider the cause of the disaster. I still couldn't believe it. "You mean we've struck oil?"

"Well, we've struck gas. There'll be oil down there, too, I guess."

"It hasn't done your rig much good," I said. I don't know

why, but couldn't think of anything else to say. It was all too sudden, too unreal.

"Oh, to hell with the rig." He laughed. It was a queer sound, violent and trembling and rather high-pitched against the solid roar of the gas. "We've done what we came up here to do. We've proved there's oil down there. And we've done it in time. Come on. Let's rout the boys out. Steve must see this. He's our independent observer. This is going to shake the Larsen outfit." And that high-pitched laugh sent out its trembling challenge again to the din of the gas jet.

It wasn't until we were clear of the site and away from the noise of the gas that I realised that the moon had vanished, swallowed by the inky blackness that was rolling across the night sky. Halfway to the ranch-house a gust of wind struck us. From the slopes of Solomon's Judgment came a hissing sound that enveloped and obliterated the sound of the well. And then, suddenly, a wall of water fell on us. It was a rainstorm, but as solid as if a cloud had condensed and dropped. It drove the breath back into one's throat and made one claw the air as though reaching for something to grasp to pull one out of the flood. And when I looked back there was no sign of the broken rig, only blackness and the sound of water. A flash of lightning ripped across our heads, momentarily revealing my companions as three half-drowned wraiths. And then the thunder came like a gun and went rolling round the circle of the mountains. Flash after flash of lightning followed, often so close that we could hear the hiss of it, feel the crack as it stabbed the ground, and the thunder was incessant.

Somehow we reached the ranch-house. Nobody was up. The place was as silent as if it had been deserted. We stripped to the buff and built up the fire, huddling our bodies close to it and drinking some rye that Boy had found. There seemed no point in waking the others. There was nothing to see and the storm was so violent that it was quite out of the question to take them down to have a look at the well. We drifted off to our bunks and as my head touched the pillow I remember thinking that everything was going to be all right now. We had proved there was oil in the Kingdom. My grandfather's beliefs were confirmed, my own life justified. And then I was asleep.

It was Jean who woke me. She seemed very excited about

something and I felt desperately tired. She kept on shaking me. "Quick, Bruce. Something's happened."

"I know," I mumbled. "We didn't wake you because there was a storm——" I rolled out of my bunk and pulled a coat on over my pyjamas. I was really rather enjoying myself as she took hold of my hand and pulled me through into the ranch-house and over to the window.

I don't know quite how I had expected it to look by daylight, but when I reached the window and looked out across the Kingdom, drab grey and swept by rain, I stood appalled. There was no sign of the gas jet. There was nothing to show we'd ever drilled there or ever had a rig there. I was looking out across a wide expanse of water. It began just beyond the barns and extended right across to the slopes of the mountains on the farther side. The Kingdom was already half flooded. It was a lake and the wind was driving across it, ploughing it up into waves and flecking it with white. "Oh God!" I said and I dropped my head on my arms.

Steve Strachan did his best to try and visualise the well blowing in as we had seen it, but I knew he wasn't really convinced. It wasn't that he thought we were crooks, making up the story for the sake of proving what we knew wasn't true. It was just that he knew how strung up we all were. I suppose he felt that in these circumstances a man is capable of seeing something that never really happened. He did his best. He made polite noises as we described every detail of it. But every now and then he'd say, "Yes, I know, but I've got to convince my editor." Or in answer to a question: "Sure I believe you, but just show me something concrete that'll prove it really happened."

But what evidence had we? Soaked to the skin, we trudged along the shores of that damned lake looking for a slick of oil, or stood, searching the spot where the rig had been, trying to locate the bubbles that the escaping gas must be making. But little white-caps frisked across the spot and even through glasses we could see no sign of bubbles. The memory of that gas vent flaring high into the night faded until it was difficult for those of us who had actually seen it to believe that it had been real.

I remember Garry standing there cursing whilst the rain streamed down his lined face as though he were crying. We were huddled there in a little bunch by the edge of that sudden lake, our faces grey as the leaden cloud that blanketed the slopes of the mountains opposite with rain, and exhaustion and despair were stamped on our features. We had the grim, hopeless, half-drowned look of a shipwrecked crew.

"If only they'd waited till the time they said," Boy murmured.

"They could see it blow in as well as we could," Garry said. He turned to me. "Remember the water we ran into when we got clear of the rig and the reflection of the moonlight? They were flooding then, flooding up to the rig, just in case. And when they saw the rig go . . ." He shrugged his shoulders. "God dammit. One more day." There was all the bitterness of a gambler who has lost in his voice. "Our only hope is to persuade them to drain the Kingdom. Independent judges could tell at a glance that we'd struck oil bearing country."

"How?" Steve Strachan asked.

"How?" By the way the pipe is bent, you fool. By the way the rig is smashed." His voice was high and taut. "Come on, Bruce. We'd better get over there and have a word with them."

I nodded reluctantly, afraid he might do something stupid when faced with Trevedian. He was at the end of his tether and his big hands twitched as though he wanted to get them round the throat of some adversary. We took two horses and cantered along the shores of the lake, below the buttress and across the rock outcrops to where the wire ran down the mountainside and into the water. They had seen us coming and there was a little group waiting for us like a reception committee. There was Trevedian and the policeman who had come with him the previous day and two of Trevedian's men with rifles slung over their shoulders.

For a moment we sat our horses looking at them and they stood looking at us. I could see anger building up inside Garry's big frame. Trevedian waited, his small eyes alert, watching us curiously. The policeman said nothing. For my part I knew it was useless. Words suddenly burst from Garry's lips with explosive force. "What the hell do you mean by drowning my rig? You gave us till ten this morning."

"My warning referred to the house and buildings." Trevedian glanced at his watch. " It's now nine-twenty. You've forty minutes to get clear of the buildings."

" But what about the rig?" Garry demanded. " What right had you——"

" You could have moved it," Trevedian cut in. " However, since you haven't I've no doubt the courts will include the value of it in their grant of compensation."

Garry turned to the police officer. " Were you up here last night when they began flooding?"

The man shook his head. " No. I came up here this morning in case there was trouble."

" Well, there's going to be plenty of trouble," Garry snapped. " Do you realise you've drowned an oil well? We struck it at aproximately two-fifteen this morning."

Trevedian laughed. " Be damned to that for a tale," he said.

" You know damn well it's true," Garry shouted. " Don't tell me you couldn't see what happened from here."

" I didn't see anything." Trevedian turned to the two guards. " Did you?" They shook their heads dutifully. " They were with me when I gave the order to close the sluices," Trevedian added as he turned to face us, hardly troubling to conceal a slight smile. " We were naturally watching the rig to see that you all got clear of the water. We saw nothing unusual."

" By God," Garry cried, " you dirty, crooked little liar! Don't ever let me get my hands on you or as sure as hell I'll wring your neck."

" It seems I was right in insisting on police protection up here." Trevedian smiled and glanced at his watch again. " Better get your things clear of the ranch buildings now, Wetheral," he said. " I'm going to finish flooding." He turned away, the policeman followed him.

" Just a minute," I called. " What time did you come up here?" They had paused and I was addressing the policeman.

" At eight o'clock this morning," he answered.

" And you weren't up here when the order to flood was given?"

" No."

" Why not?"

" Mr. Trevedian didn't expect any trouble until this morning."

"You mean he was prepared to deal with it himself during the hours of darkness."

The other shrugged his shoulders. "My orders were to be up here at eight this morning."

"Are you here as an official of the Provincial Police or have the company hired you as a watch-dog?"

"Both," he said rather tersely.

"I see," I said. "In other words, you're employed by the company and take your orders from Trevedian. That's all I wanted to know." I turned my horse. "We're wasting our time here," I said to Garry. "This will have to be fought out in the courts."

He nodded slowly and we rode back to the ranch-house in silence. His face looked drawn and haggard. The fire of anger had gone out of him and he slumped in his saddle like a bag of bones and flesh. He didn't say anything all the way back, but I was very conscious of the fact that he'd lost his rig, everything he had made in over fifteen years. It deepened the mood of black despair that had gripped me since I woke up and found the Kingdom had become a lake overnight. It was difficult to remember the elation that had filled us in the early hours when the drenching rain had obliterated the broken rig from our sight.

When we reached the ranch-house we were greeted with the news that the water was rising again. They had thrust a stake in at the edge of the lake and even as we watched the water ran past it and in a moment it was several feet out from the lake's edge. All our energies were concentrated then on salvaging what we could. We loaded Boy's vehicles with all our kit and movable equipment and drove them up to the edge of the timber. Jean and I harnessed the horses to an old wagon we found and in this way I managed to get some of my grandfather's belongings out. And then as the rain slackened and a misty sun shone through we made camp in the shelter of the trees and drank hot tea and watched the water creep slowly up to the ends of the barns and then trickle in clutching fingers round the back of the ranch-house. By midday the place my grandfather had built with his own hands was a quarter of a mile out in the lake and the water was up to the windows. For five miles there was nothing but water flecked with white as the wind whipped across it.

It was the end of the Kingdom.

II

I DON'T know whether it was the reaction after the strain of the last two months or the physical effect of suddenly having nothing to work for any more, but that night my feet and hands were swollen and painful and my heart was thudding against my ribs. I felt exhausted and drained of all energy. They made me a bed in the back of Boy's instrument truck and though I was reasonably comfortable I lay awake half the night, feeling certain that now my time was up and the end had at last come. I slipped off into a sort of coma and when I woke sometimes Jean was there, holding my hand, sometimes I was alone. The moon was bright and by craning my head I could just see out of the back of the truck and get a glimpse of the lake that now filled the Kingdom. The ranch-house had disappeared completely, swallowed by the waters. There was no sign left that my grandfather had ever been in the country.

I felt better in the morning, but very tired. I slept intermittently and once Boy came and sat beside me and told me he had been over to the dam and had phoned Trevedian from the control room. We were to have the trucks at the hoist by midday to-morrow. I lay back realising that this was our final exodus, that we should not be coming back. The rest of the business would be conducted in the stuffy, soul-destroying atmosphere of a court room. I didn't feel that I wanted to live. There would be weeks, maybe months of litigation. I couldn't face that. Jean seemed to understand my mood for she kept assuring me that it would be all right, that the lawyers would look after it all and that we'd get the compensation required to repay everyone. But I didn't really believe her. And then, late in the evening, Johnnie rode in with a couple of American newspaper boys, the same who had been up with him the previous fall when they had found the body of my grandfather.

I remember they came to see me that night. They were a surprisingly quiet, slow-spoken pair and somehow their interest in the whole business as a story put new heart into me. They had listened to Garry's story of the night we'd struck the anticline. They'd got the pictures so vividly in their minds that I could see it all again as they talked. " But who'll believe us?" I said. "Even Steve Strachan, who was up here with us, isn't entirely convinced."

The taller of them laughed. "He's not used to this sort of thing," he said. "We are. We've put the four of you through a detailed cross-examination. And it's okay. The detail is too good to have been fabricated. Soon as we get down I'll send off my story and I'm going to ask my paper to put up the dough for us to get divers down before the weather breaks. If we can drag that pipe up, that'll prove it. In the meantime, I take it you've no objection to Ed taking a few pictures of you." His big, warm-hearted laugh boomed out. "Boy, you certainly provide the final touch to make this one of the most human dramas I've ever been handed. Now if you'd been running around full of health and vigour . . ." He shook his head and grinned. "But here you are, King Campbell's grandson, lying sick with no roof over your head because these bastards. . . ." There was a flash as Ed took the first picture. "Well, don't worry. Fergus will have half the North American continent gunning for him by the time I've finished writing this up. And by a stroke of luck we've got pictures of the Campbell homestead and the whole Kingdom before they flooded it."

Next morning we started out towards the dam. The going was very rough for the water forced us up into the rock-strewn country at the foot of the mountains. In places boulders had to be hefted aside and at one point the timber came right down to the water's edge and it took us an hour to cut a way through for the trucks. I started off in the instrument truck, but pretty soon I got out and walked. It was less tiring than being jolted and flung from side to side.

It was well after midday by the time we turned the base of the buttress and ground to a halt at the barbed wire. There was nobody on the dam or up at the concrete housing of the hoist. The whole place seemed strangely deserted. We hung about for a time, blowing on the horns and shouting to attract attention. But nobody came and in the end we found a join in the wire, rolled it back and drove the vehicles through. I had taken the precaution of hiding all the rifles under a pile of bedding. The Luger I had slipped into my pocket. The drillers, exhausted and despondent, were in an ugly mood. It only wanted a crack or two from some of the men working on the power house at the bottom of the hoist and there would be trouble. I was taking no chances of it coming to shooting.

We took the vehicle and the cart straight up to the cable terminal. There wasn't a soul there. Boy went down to the dam and disappeared down concrete steps into the bowels of it. We stood and stared down at the dam, a little bewildered and I think even then with an odd sense of waiting for something. The silence was uncanny. The dam was a flat-topped battlement of concrete flung across the cleft that divided the peaks of Solomon's Judgment. It was smooth and curved with clean, fresh lines as yet unmarked by weather. On the Thunder Valley side it sloped down like a great wall into the gloom of the cleft. From where we stood we couldn't see the bottom. It gave me the feeling that it went on dropping down indefinitely till it reached the slide two thousand feet below. On the other side of the lake of the Kingdom swept to within a yard or so of the top. The wall of concrete seemed to be leaning into the lake as though straining to hold the weight of the water in check. It was hot in the sunshine as we waited and the air was still, the water lying flat and sultry like a sheet of metal. The noise of water running was the only sound that broke the utter stillness.

Boy came up out of the smooth top of the dam and climbed towards us, a puzzled frown on his sun-tanned face. " Not a soul there," he said. " And all the sluices are fully open."

" Isn't there a phone down in the control room?" Jean asked.

Boy nodded. " I tried it, but I couldn't get any answer. It seemed dead."

We stood there for a moment, talking softly, wondering what to do. At length Garry said, "Well anyway, the cage is here. We'd better start loading the first truck."

As Don moved towards the instrument truck there was a sudden splintering sound and the noise of falling stone. It was followed by a faint shout half-drowned in a roar of water. Then a man came clambering up the sides of the cleft. He was one of the engineers and he was followed by the guards and another engineer. They saw us and came running towards us. Their faces looked white and scared.

" What's happened?" Garry called out.

" The dam," shouted one of the engineers. " There's a crack. . . . It's leaking. . . . The whole thing will go any minute." He was out of breath and his voice was pitched high with fright.

We stared at him, hardly able to comprehend what he was saying—convinced only by the fear on his face.

"Can't you relieve the pressure?" Boy asked.

"The sluice gates are wide open already."

"Have you told them down below?" Steve Strachan asked him.

"No. The phone was cut in that storm the night before last. It's terrible. I don't know what to do. There are nearly a hundred men working down on the slide where they're going to build the power house. What can I do?" He stood there, wringing his hands hopelessly.

"What about the phone in the cable house?" I asked.

"Yes, yes, of course. But I don't think there'll be anyone in the lower housing, not until six this evening."

Everybody was talking at once now and I watched the engineer as he ran stumbling to the cable terminal. If there was nobody at the bottom to get his warning. . . . I looked at the lake. It was six miles or more across and in the centre it would be as deep as the dam was high—over two hundred feet. I thought of the men working down there on the slide, directly in the path of that great sheet of water if the dam collapsed. It would come thundering through the cleft and then fall, millions of tons of it falling two thousand feet; all the water that had fallen on the mountains in twelve hours tumbling over in one great solid sheet. Jean's hand gripped my arm. "What can we do?" Her voice trembled and I saw by her face that she, too, was picturing that effect of a breach. But the dam looked solid enough. The great sweep of it swung smoothly and uninterruptedly across the cleft. It looked as though it could hold an ocean.

The others were already scrambling down to have a look at the damage. I followed. Johnnie came slithering down with me. And from the top of the dam itself we looked down the smooth face of it to a great jet of water fifty feet long and two or three feet across. It was coming from a jagged rent about halfway down the dam face and all around the hole were great splintering cracks through which the water seeped. Down below at the very foot of the dam the sluice gates added their rush of water.

"It's that cement they used on the original dam." Johnnie

had to shout in my ear to make himself heard above the din of the water. "It was old stuff and it's cracking up. The goldarned fools!"

As we turned away from the appalling sight the engineer who had gone to the hoist to try and telephone came slithering down to us. "There's nobody there," he shouted.

"Can't you go down and warn them?" Johnnie asked.

"There's nobody down there, I tell you," he almost screamed. "Nobody hears the telephone. There's nobody to work the engine."

I was looking up towards the hoist, remembering the night Jeff and I had examined the cradle together to see if there was a safety device to get the cage down if the engine packed up. "How long before this dam goes?" I asked the engineer.

"I don't know. It may go any minute. It may last till we have drained the lake."

"It won't do that. Look." Johnnie was peering over the edge, pointing to the great thundering jet of brownish water. It had increased in size appreciably in the last few minutes.

The American newspaper correspondent came along the top of the dam towards us. He had been out in the centre with his photographer who was taking pictures regardless of the danger. "Why don't these guys do something—about the boys down below I mean?"

"What can we do?" the engineer demanded petulantly. "We've no phone, no means of communicating."

I called to Boy and together we climbed the side of the cleft to the hoist. Jean caught up with us just as I was climbing into the cage. "What are you going to do?" I was already looking up at the cradle, seeing what I needed to knock the pins out that secured the driving cable to it. Her hand gripped my arm. "No. For God's sake, darling. You can't. They'll be all right. They'll have seen that flow of water coming down——"

"If they have then I'll stop the cage on the lip of the fault." I gently disengaged her fingers. "Don't worry," I said. "I'll be all right." She stared at me, her face suddenly white. I think she knew as well as I did that the chances of the men working down there having noticed an increase in the flow of water from the dam were remote. "Why you?" she whispered. "Why not one of the men who belong to the dam? It's their responsibility."

I turned away and climbed into the cage. I couldn't explain to her why it was better for me to go. "Hand me that bit of timber, Boy." He passed it up and I knocked the pins out. As the last one fell to the floor I had my hand on the brake lever. The driving cable dropped free on to the rollers and the cage began to move. I hauled down on the lever and brought the bottom braking wheel into action, forcing the suspension cable up between the two travelling wheels.

"Okay, let's go," Boy said.

I turned to find Jean clambering into the cage. "For God's sake," I cried.

"I'm coming with you," Boy said. His face was white under his tan. I didn't know it then but he was scared of heights, other than from the air.

"So am I," Jean said.

I stood there, looking at them, wondering how to get rid of them. It was crazy for more than one to go down. There was a rope on the end of the lever and a pulley in the floor. I slid the rope through the sheaves of the block. Then I called to Boy. "For God's sake," I said, "get Jean out of here. Pick her up and throw her out."

He nodded. I was still holding the rope. "Please go, Jean." I called to her. But she clung to the side and Boy picked her up, fighting her to get her hands clear, and then, leaning far out, he put her over the side. At that moment I let go the rope, caught him by the legs and tipped him over after her. As he fell the cage began to move. I turned quickly and caught up the rope, applying the brake gently, holding the cradle to a steady run along the cable. Looking back I saw the two of them standing there, watching me. And away to the right, below them, was the great sweep of the dam with the wall all starred with cracks and the brown water spouting from the huge rent. I stared at it, wondering what it would be like up here, hanging in space, if the whole thing burst wide open, imagining the lake pouring through, thundering in a roaring mass only a few feet below my feet and then tumbling in a gigantic, fantastic fall over the lip of the fault.

Then the pylon on the top of the fault was coming towards me and I hauled on the rope, slowing the cradle up to walking pace. Thunder Valley opened out in front of me. I crawled up to the pylon and stopped. I could see the steep, timbered slopes of the valley, the glint of Beaver Dam Lake, but the

rocks on the lip of the drop hid the slide. I inched past the
pylon. The cradle tipped. I hauled on the rope. The rocks
slid away below me and suddenly I was hanging in space and
there far below me was the slide with the pylon and beyond
it the concrete housing of the hoist. It was all very minute
and unreal. The only thing that was real was that ghastly,
appalling drop and the fact that the only thing that prevented
me crashing the full length of that snaking cable line was this
crude brake. I felt my knees beginning to shake. I don't
think I ever have been so frightened of anything in my life.
For there below me the slide looked like an ant heap. Everywhere men were moving about, working on the foundations
of the power house. I was committed to go down there and
if the dam should burst. . . . The pylon and the cable housing
stood right in the path of the flood. They would be swept
away and the cable would swing loose. I should be dashed to
pieces against the face of the fault.

It was probably only a few seconds that I hesitated there,
not finding the courage to commit myself irrevocably to that
awful drop; but it seemed an age. Then at last I eased the
tension slightly on the rope and the cage dropped down from
the lip, seeming to plunge sickeningly on the steep drop down
the cliff face. Nervously I strained at the rope till I was
hardly moving. But as I gained confidence in the braking
system I let it move faster so that soon I was past the steepest
point and levelling out in a long glide towards the pylon on
the slide up. Once I looked back, fearful that the dam was
breaking up behind me and the pent-up waters of the lake
thundering over the edge of the fault, but all I saw was a
thin trickle, a slender veil of white wavering and falling,
infinitely slowly, to beat in a white froth against the base of
the cliff.

The pylon slid by and then I was running almost free to the
concrete housing. Below me I saw men pausing in their work
to look up at me, faces gleaming white in the sunlight. The
heat from the rocks came up and hit me. The warm resinous
smell of the pines closed round me. It seemed impossible that
disaster should hang over this peaceful scene. I shouted to
them that the dam was breaking as I swung over their heads
and they stared at me with vacant, uncomprehending ex-
pressions. Either they didn't believe me or they didn't understand what I was saying, for I started no panic; they just

stared at me and then got on with their work. And then I was past them and dropping down to the housing. I slid into it gently and climbed out and started back up the roadway to the site where they were working. I reached a bunch of trucks unloading materials. I yelled to the men around them to get them moving back to the camp where they would be safe. " The dam's breaking up," I shouted at them. I climbed to the cab of the first truck and signalled to the men working on the site with the horn. " Get back to the camp!" I shouted to them at the top of my voice. " The dam's going. Get back to the camp!"

My voice seemed a thin reed in the vastness of the place. It was lost in the clatter of the concrete mixers and the din of metal on stone. But here and there men were stopping to stare at me and then talk to men working near them. One or two dropped their tools and moved towards me. I kept on shouting to them, my throat dry with fear and the sweat running out of every pore. I felt weak with the effort of trying to make them understand. I hadn't realised it would be so difficult to get them started up to the camp, to safety. But here and there men began to move, and in a moment it seemed the word buzzed through the whole site and they began to move away from the slide towards the timber, slowly, like bewildered sheep.

And then Trevedian was there, shouting at them, telling them to get back to work. " What are you?" he roared at them. " A bunch of yellow-bellies to be fooled into hiding away in the woods because this fellow Wetheral is so mad at us for drowning the Kingdom that he comes down here shouting a lot of bloody nonsense about the dam. He's a screw-ball, you know that. Otherwise he wouldn't have been drilling for oil up there. Now get back to work and don't be so damned easily fooled." He turned and came towards me. " You get the hell out of here," he shouted. His face was dark with anger.

The men had stopped, hanging uncertainly where they stood. My eyes lifted involuntarily to the cleft between the peaks. Was it my imagination or was the veil of white that wavered down the face of the fault wider and bigger? My legs felt weak and my throat was dry. I had to suppress a great desire to run. I shouted to them again to get clear whilst they could. " Do you think I'd risk coming down the hoist on the brakes, leaving my friends up there, if the situation wasn't serious. There was a hole a yard wide halfway down the dam when I left. It will be a lot bigger now. Any minute the whole thing may collapse. The original structure was built of dud cement." I glanced up again at the cleft. "Well, if you won't save yourself, I can't help it. I've done my best." I jumped down from the truck and started to run. I thought that would get them moving. Trevedian thought so, too. I saw him glance quickly at the men. Doubt and uncertainty and the beginnings of fear showed in the faces of some of those nearest to me. He swung back towards me, started forward to intercept me and then stopped. "Max!" His voice was sharp, domineering. "Max—stop him!"

I glanced quickly towards the timber. It was about fifty yards away and between me and it stood the huge, bear-like figure of Max Trevedian.

"Get him, Max!" Trevedian turned to his men. "And you —stay where you are. Are you going to let a crazy coot like this scare you? Why, we've only just built the dam. We'll soon see what all this is about. Max! Get hold of him. I want to talk to him."

Max had already started forward, moving towards me at a shambling run, his great arms swinging loose. I stopped. "Don't be a fool, Max. It's Bruce. Remember? Up there in the Kingdom. Stay where you are!"

I tried to talk to him as I would to a child. I tried desperately to get the same authority into my voice as his brother had. But my voice trembled with the urgency of my message and I hadn't the intimacy of childhood memories. My words failed to get through, and he came on, moving surprisingly fast. I heard Trevedian telling his men to stay where they were, telling them he'd soon find out what all this was about, and then my hand touched the gun in my pocket. "Max!" I shouted. "For God's sake stay where you are." And as he came steadily on, my fingers, automatically finding the opening to my pocket slipped in and closed over the butt of the gun. I took it out.

Max was not more than thirty yards from me now. I glanced quickly up towards where the men were standing in a close-packed huddle. They were scared and uncertain. Once Max reached me I knew I'd never get them moving in time. It was Max or them—one man or nearly a hundred. "Max!"

I screamed. "Stay where you are!" And then, as he came on, I raised the weapon slowly, took careful aim at his right leg above the knee and fired.

The report was a thin, sharp sound in the rock-strewn valley. Max's mouth opened, a surprised look on his face. He took two stumbling steps and then pitched forward on to his face and lay there, writhing in pain.

"You swine! You'll pay for this."

I swung round to find Trevedian coming at me. I raised the gun. "Get back," I said. And then as he stopped I knew I had the situation under control for the moment. "Now get out of here, all of you," I ordered. "Any man who's still around in one minute from now will get shot. And for God's sake see you find high ground. Now, get moving." To start them I sent a bullet whistling over their heads. They turned then and made for the timber, bunched close together like a herd of stampeding cattle. Only Trevedian and the man who was with him stood their ground. "Get your brother out of here to safety," I ordered him.

He didn't move. He was staring at me, his eyes wide and unblinking. "You *must* be crazy," he murmured.

"Don't be a fool," I snapped. "Come on. Get your brother out of here."

"That dam was all right. Government engineers inspected it at every stage. We had engineers in to inspect it before we started the work of completing it." He shook his head angrily. "I don't believe it. I won't believe it." He turned to the man beside him. "We'll see if we can get them on the hoist phone. If not I'm going up there. Will you run the engine for me?"

"Don't be a fool," I said. "Every moment you delay——"

"Oh, go to hell," he shouted. "Come on, George." They started at a run for the cable terminal. For a second I considered firing, trying to stop them. But my fractional hesitation had put them out of effective range. Anyway, what the hell. Maybe he'd make it, and if he didn't . . .

I turned away and went over to where Max lay with his body doubled up over a big splinter of rock. His face was bloodless and he was unconscious. His right leg was twisted under him and blood was seeping on to the stones, a crimson splash in the sunlight. I got hold of him by the arms and began to drag him over the rocks. He was incredibly heavy.

Each time I paused I called towards the line of trees, hoping one of the men would have the guts to come back and help me. But the timber seemed silent and empty. If anyone heard me, he didn't come down to help. In shooting Max I had finally convinced them of the urgency of the danger, just as I had convinced Trevedian himself.

Foot by foot I dragged Max's body along the stone-packed road, up the hill to the timber. Every few yards I had to pause. I heard the diesel start up and saw the cage move out of its staging. Trevedian still working on the cradle, tapping home the pins that locked the driving cable to it.

I suppose I was about halfway to the timber when I paused and glanced up once again at the cleft between the two peaks that towered high above us. The cage was halfway up the face of the fault, a small box swaying gently on the spider's silk of the cable. And then my eyes lifted to the pylon at the top and suddenly all my body froze. A solid wave of water and rock burst from the lip of the cliff. The pylon vanished, smothered and swept away by it. And as the water spouted outwards over the cliff edge a distant rumbling reached my ears. It went on and on, sifting down from above, echoing from slope to slope down the face of the cliff. I remember seeing the cage sway violently and watching the brown flood fall with slow deliberation down the fault, frothing and spouting great gouts of white as it thundered against ledges and outcrops, smashing away great sections of the rock face with its force, flinging them outwards and down. And I stood there, rigid, unable to move, fascinated and appalled by the spectacle.

A shattering roar filled the whole valley as that monstrous fall of rock and water hit the base of the fault and came thundering on in a mighty, surging wall down the slide. I saw the pylon at the top of the slide smashed to rubble and I remember how the cable suddenly broke and the cage began to swing slowly in towards the cliff. And then I was suddenly running, climbing desperately towards the timber. I heard the angry thunder of those pent-up waters crash down the valley behind me and then the swirling fringe of it reached out to me, sent a line of trees crashing as though cut by a great scythe, caught at my legs and buried me in a frothing flood of water.

I struck out madly, reaching up towards the surface, gasping for breath. Then I was flung against something and all the breath was knocked out of my body. Pain ran like a knife up my right leg. Something swirled against me and I clutched at it, felt the soft texture of clothing and hung on. Then the water sank, my feet touched ground and as pain shot through me again, almost blacking me out, the branch of a tree curled over me and I clutched at it, holding on with the grip of desperate fear.

I must have passed out, for when I next remember anything I was lying on the sodden earth, still clutching the branch with my right hand, my left hand twined in Max's jacket. He was lying face down beside me, his left ear almost torn off by a jagged cut that had opened to show the white of his jaw bone. And just beyond Max, only a few yards below us, a colossal flood of brown water went ripping and roaring down Thunder Creek. The valley was a cataract a thousand yards across and the face of the slide was a monstrous series of falls and rapids. And in the centre of this violent rush of water great rocks were on the move, grinding slowly down through a welter of foam. And on the fringes the scene was one of mad devastation, timber and earth and brush swept clean down to the bare rock by the first rush of the waters. I stared at it all through a blurr of pain, saw the peaks of Solomon's Judgment and the lake spilling through the cleft, felt the sun blazing down on me and passed out again.

I think it was pain that brought me round. I heard a voice say, "It's his leg all right." The words were remote and faintly unreal. I opened my eyes to see two faces bending over me. And then they began to move me and I was screaming as the pain ran up my right side, splintering like sparks of electricity in my brain. For hours it seemed I alternated between periods of blessed unconsciousness and periods of searing pain. I remember the noise and jolting of a truck, the sound of voices, the feel of a spoon against my teeth and the smell of brandy. I think I must have asked at some time about Max. At any rate, I knew somehow that he was alive. And then there were starched uniforms and the smell of ether and the jab of a needle.

I woke at last to full consciousness in a little room where the blinds were drawn against the sunlight. There was a movement beside me and a hand closed over mine. I turned then and saw Jean bending over me. Her face was pale and drawn, but her eyes smiled at me. " Better?"

I nodded, trying to accustom myself to the surroundings, to her presence. It was so quiet after the roar of the waters. I tried to move mybody, but I seemed weighed down. My right leg was wooden and solid, my chest stiff and painful. It hurt to breathe and I had to force myself to speak. " I'm in hospital, aren't I?" I asked her.

She nodded. "Don't talk. And don't worry. You're all right. You've broken a leg, a collar bone and three ribs. The doctor says you'll be fine in a week or two."

" And Max?"

" Fractured skull and left arm's broken. But he'll be all right. There's a bullet wound in his leg, but it's not serious." Her hand reached out, touched my forehead and then her fingers were sliding through my hair in a caress. " Don't worry, darling. Everything's going to be all right."

I lay back and closed my eyes. I felt very sleepy. Her voice seemed a long way away. My mind was drugged. Her voice got fainter and fainter. She was saying something about the rig, about newspaper men, about them knowing now that we'd struck oil. It didn't seem important any more and her voice faded entirely as I slid into sleep again.

When next I woke the room was dark. I tried to raise myself, but the pain in my chest brought on a cold sweat. I lay there for a long time, my eyes open, seeing nothing in the darkness. Somewhere out in the night a train hooted and I heard the rattle of its wheels on the points. I was thinking what a waste of effort this was, this struggle back to life. Why couldn't I have died there, quickly and easily in the flood of the burst dam? And then I remembered Max and how I had held him against the tearing grasp of the flood and I was glad. God had been good to me. He had given me time to get the men away from the slide, and we'd brought in a well. For some reason I found myself remembering how I had knelt on the floor of my digs in London and prayed for God's guidance and for His help in doing what my grandfather had asked of me. And suddenly words were forming on my lips and I was thanking God that I had been able to achieve so much.

Slowly light filtered into the room and day dawned, grey and thick with cloud mist. Dozing gently I was conscious of the beginning of movement in the hospital and in no time, it seemed, a nurse was bringing breakfast in to me. "Well, how's the great oil man this morning?"

I stared at her and she laughed. "You don't imagine anybody's discussing the international situation with you here in town, do you?" She put the tray down on a bed table and swung it across me. "Now, you stay quiet and eat that egg. It's time you got some food inside you. And I brought you the papers so that you can read all about yourself. There's pictures of Campbell's Kingdom and of the discovery well with the rig all broken and twisted. Dr. Graham said he reckoned the papers were about the best tonic for you he had in the hospital. And here's a letter for you."

I took the envelope and slit it open. Inside was a single sheet of paper, most of which was filled with signatures. The letter was very brief and as I read my eyes blurred.

> *The Golden Calf,*
> *Come Lucky.*
> *B.C.*

Dear Mr. Wetheral

> *This letter, signed by all of us who were working on the site of the power station, is to tell you how grateful we all are to you. If you had not risked your life and come down the hoist to warn us, not one of us would be alive to-day. We sure are sorry that you are in hospital because of this and wish you a speedy recovery. We will do what we can to express our gratitude and in the meantime we would like you to know that you can count on the undersigned at any time to do anything to assist you.*

There followed three columns of signatures spreading over on to the back—names that were of Polish, French, Italian and Chinese origin as well as English. I looked up at the nurse. "What day is it?" I asked her.

"Friday."

And the Kingdom had been flooded on Tuesday. "I've been out a long time," I murmured.

"Not as long as you will be if you don't get some food inside you," she said as she went out.

As I ate my breakfast I read through the papers. They were full of the disaster. But there was the story of the well we had brought in, too—interviews with Garry and Johnnie, and in one of them a long feature article headed—'There's Oil in the Rocky Mountains.' The writer was Steve Strachan and in it he acknowledged the quotation as belonging to Stuart Campbell and made it clear that the old man was now completely vindicated. I put the paper down and lay back, suddenly completely happy.

The doctor came in then. He gave my broken bones only a cursory examination and then started to go over me thoroughly, listening to my breathing, taking my blood pressure, feeling my pulse, listening to my heart beats, and all the time asking me questions. "What's the trouble, Doc?" I asked him.

"Oh, just a routine check-up."

But I knew this wasn't routine for a man with a broken leg and a few broken ribs. And when they wheeled in the X-ray apparatus I knew he was on to the real trouble. "You're wasting your time," I said, and I told him what Maclean-Harvey's verdict had been.

He shrugged his shoulders and I bit my lip as they shifted me to get the screen and X-ray tube in position. "How did you know I'd got cancer?" I asked him.

"Jean Lucas told me," he answered.

"Jean!" I tried to turn, but a hand gripped my shoulder, steadying me. All I could see was the nurse's white uniform. I stared at a bone button, wondering how Jean knew.

They were some time taking the photographs and when they had finished they made me comfortable and trundled the equipment out. The doctor was not in the room, but he returned a few minutes later. "All right, Mr. Wetheral? I hope they didn't cause you too much pain moving you."

"No," I said. "It just seemed pointless, that's all."

He nodded and drew up a chair beside me. "Does it occur to you that for a man who was given two to six months to live way back in the spring you've been remarkably active lately?"

"There seemed no point in conserving energy," I murmured.

"No, no, of course not." He hesitated and then said quietly, "There have been cures, you know."

"Have there?" I looked at him, seeing his broad, rather serious features through a blurr of pain as I shifted my position. "I thought cancer was incurable."

"Aye." He nodded. "It's incurable as far as the medical profession is concerned. But there are such things as spontaneous cures. We don't know the cause of them. I wish we did. Some change in the chemistry of the patient, maybe —or a psychological readjustment. Anyway, once in a while it happens." He leaned forward, his large grey eyes peering down at me from behind the thick-lensed glasses. "Listen, Wetheral. I don't want to raise any false hopes. We'll know soon enough when they've developed those X-ray plates. There's just a chance, that's all." There was a glint of excitement in his eyes now. It showed in his manner, in the way he spoke. "I can't believe a case as desperate as yours must have been when Dr. Maclean-Harvey gave you that verdict could have gone on for five months, living the way you have been, unless the condition had improved. There's no internal hæmorrhage and no trace now of secondary anæmia. You've been eating well and instead of getting weaker, you've got stronger." He suddenly sat back, taking his glasses off and polishing them. "I shouldn't really have spoken to you about it. I should have waited till I had the X-ray results. But——" He hesitated and got to his feet. "It's a most interesting case, you see. I didn't want you to feel that I was just taking the opportunity to examine a cancer growth." He smiled suddenly. "You must be about as obstinate a man as your grandfather, I guess. Anyway, I'll be back as soon as I've got a picture of what's going on inside you."

He left me then and for a while I lay there, thinking over what he had said. I felt suddenly restless. The mood of excitement I had seen reflected in the doctor's eyes had communicated itself to me. For the first time in months there was no immediate problem ahead of me and I was free to consider the future. Almost unconsciously I reached for the papers and began reading Steve's article again. I was still reading it when the nurse showed Jean in. She was followed by Johnnie and Garry.

"We just looked in to say good-bye," Johnnie said. "Garry's off to Edmonton to see about a new rig and I'm going up to the Kingdom." He came and stood over me, his eyes narrowed as though he were looking straight into the sun, a lazy smile on his lined face. "You look pretty damn comfortable lying there, Bruce."

"What are you going up to the Kingdom for?" I asked him.

"Well, that's what I came to see you about, I guess." He rubbed his chin awkwardly. "You see, the boys who were working on the power station have got together and put up some dough. A few of them are coming up to the Kingdom with me and my two Americans to clear up Campbell's place and make it snug for the winter. The rest——" He hesitated. "Well, it's like this, Bruce, they came to me and asked what they could do about it. They're a decent bunch and they felt sort of bad about you lying here in hospital and all of them fit and well. I didn't know quite what to say, but I hinted you were figuring on settling down around this neighbourhood so they've decided to buckle to and build you a house down by the ford at the entrance to Thunder Valley. You know, the place we camped."

"But I couldn't possibly allow them to do that," I said. "They've got their living to——"

"Now, listen, Bruce," he cut in. "They feel bad about this. It's their way of showing they're grateful to you. You just got to accept it. It's a sort of——" He glanced at Jean, and then said, "Well, anyway, they want to do it and nothing'll stop them, I guess." He moved awkwardly to the door. "I must be going now. You coming, Garry?"

The big drilling contractor nodded. "I just wanted to say I'm glad you're okay." He gripped my left hand. "And I'm proud to be associated with you." He coughed in embarrassment and added quickly, "I'll go down to Calgary and see Winnick. Things will begin to hum now. I'll tell him you'll be in to see him as soon as you can. I'll see you then and find out whether you want to sell out to one of the big companies or whether you plan to develop the area yourself."

He turned quickly and went out, leaving me alone with Jean. She hadn't moved all the time they had been talking. I glanced at her face. It was very pale and she seemed nervous. "You look much better," she murmured, her eyes sliding away from mine. "Dr. Graham's very pleased with you."

"What's Boy doing?" I asked, shying away from the direct question that was on my mind.

"He stayed on up in the Kingdom." She hesitated. "I think he'll settle in this area now. He's always loved it here."

An awkward silence fell between us. She moved towards the window. "Did Dr. Graham say anything to you?" She had turned to face me.

I closed my eyes. She looked so cool and fresh and—radiant. "How did you know I had cancer of the stomach?" I asked.

"I don't believe you have." Her voice was sharp as though mere words could kill the parasitical growth. "Nobody could do the things you've done——"

"How did you know I had it?" I interrupted her.

"Sarah Garret told me."

"She shouldn't have. I told her because——" What was the use of talking about it? I felt tired now. "I want to sleep," I murmured. Anything to get her out of the room, to avoid having to look at her and have her eyes and face and body reproaching me for the future that might have been. "Please, Jean," I whispered. "Leave me. Let me go to sleep now."

There was no sound in the room only a tense silence. Then I heard her move. "Not until I've said something," she said gently. I opened my eyes to see her bending over me. A shaft of sunlight touched her hair, rimming her face in gold. Her hand touched my face, smoothing my forehead. "I'm not leaving you, Bruce. Whether you marry me or not doesn't matter, but you'll just have to get used to having me around."

I stared up at her for a moment and then closed my eyes. I think I wanted to hold the memory of her face, that little smile that spread up into the eyes. "The doctor may be wrong," I murmured.

"If you weren't injured I'd slap you for that." Her voice trembled slightly. Then she bent over me and her lips touched mine. "I seem fated to fall in love with men who are under sentence of death." Her fingers touched my temple and then I heard her footsteps cross the room, the door closed and I was alone. I lay there, feeling relaxed and happy. I wasn't afraid of anything now. I wasn't alone. Even the pain seemed dull as I sank into a deep sleep.

*　　*　　*　　*

It is winter now and the mountains lie under a white mantle of snow. I am writing this, sitting at the desk my grandfather made. Johnnie brought it down from the Kingdom with him. Through the window I look across a clearing in the cottonwoods to the ford where the waters of Thunder Creek glide swift and black to the lake. Some day that clearing will be a garden. Already Jean has a library of gardening books sent out from England and is planning the layout. We are full of plans—plans for the house, plans for the development of the Kingdom, plans for a family. It is just wonderful to sit back and plan. To plan something is to have a future. And to have a future is to have the whole of life.

As you've probably guessed already, the miracle did happen. Dr. Graham was right. The x-ray pictures showed no trace of a cancer growth. How it happened nobody seems to know. I can only quote the letter I received from Dr. Maclean-Harvey.

Dear Mr. Wetheral,

Dr. Graham has sent me the full details of your case as at 27th August, together with the X-ray photographs he has had taken. I can only say that I entirely agree with his view that there is now no trace of cancer and that you are completely cured and have no need to worry for the future.

You must be wondering now whether I was correct in my original diagnosis. For your benefit I am sending Dr. Graham copies of the X-rays taken at the London Hospital on 17th April together with a copy of the case notes I made at the time. You might like to frame one of the pictures side-by-side with Graham's X-rays as a reminder that you have confounded the experts! I need hardly add that I am delighted that you have.

Dr. Graham will doubtless have told you that occasionally cases of spontaneous cure do occur in cancer. The causes are not known and the instances are few. In your case I am inclined to the view that it may be largely psychological. You underwent a sudden and complete change of environment, coupled with the acquisition of an intense interest— or, since I understand you have recently got married, I should perhaps say interests. This, together with the fact that you became involved in a struggle outside yourself, may well have given you an overwhelming interest in living which you had not before. All this is not strictly within orthodox medicine, but in a case of this sort it is necessary to look beyond the laboratory and the operating theatre. It is perhaps nearer to the miracle than to medicine.

Finally, may I say how happy I am to be able to record in this instance a complete reversal of my expectations. It is cases like yours that place our medical achievements to date in their proper perspective and give to the profession that desire to go on searching diligently for the cure to a terrible disease. I wish you every success and if ever you come to England I hope you will come and see me.

Yours sincerely,

Douglas Maclean-Harvey.

On the wall behind me is a big frame, a sort of montage of pictures and documents. There are the X-ray photographs, before and after, Maclean-Harvey's letter, a picture of Campbell Number Two before it blew in, a photograph of the dam the original of my grandfather's will and the document signed by Roger Fergus returning to me the mineral rights of Campbell's Kingdom. There in that frame is the whole story of the last six months. Now I have put it down on paper. What the future has in store, I do not know. What does it matter? The great thing is to have a future. We will begin drilling operations up in the Kingdom as soon as the snows melt. Maybe I'll end up a millionaire. But all the money in the world cannot buy what I have now.

THE END